Other books by Alan A. Winter

Savior's Day

Snowflakes in the Sahara

Someone Else's Son

Island Bluffs

by

Alan A. Winter

Copyright 2015

PUBLISHING

Published by
KBPublishing House
333 E 14th Street Suite 3C
New York, NY 10003

Copyright © 2015 by Alan A. Winter

All rights reserved. No part of this book may be reproduced or transmitted in any form or by in any means, electronic or mechanical, including photocopying, recording, or by any information storage and retrieval system, without the written permission of the Publisher, except where permitted by law.

Manufactured in the United States of America, or in the
United Kingdom when distributed elsewhere.

Winter, Alan A.
Island Bluffs
Paperback: 978-1-93750-686-5
eBook: 978-1-93750-687-2

Cover design by: Rohaan Malhotra
Interior design: Chris Banks
Photo credits: Jeff Weiner

www.alanwinter.com

*In memory of my father,
Bernard Winter
who was never afraid to take a risk*

*Dedicated to my nephews
Ariel and Marshall
who benefited from grandpa's artistic genes*

"Darkness cannot drive out darkness; only light can do that. Hate cannot drive out hate; only love can do that."

Martin Luther King, Jr.

"Forgiveness is a virtue of the brave."

Indira Gandhi

Acknowledgements

Many individuals contribute to a writer's final work and others inspire. Some are generous with their time, others with their expertise; some with their editing skills, some with their ability to critique, and some with the good sense to give the writer the time and opportunity to apply his craft. To this end, I want to thank my partner and soul mate, Lori Blitz, who gives me the time and space to write, and then provides the commonsense to right my ship when I drift off course. I want to thank my longtime friend (since grammar school in Newark, N.J.) David Lieberfarb and Margaret Cohen for editing and challenging me to make *Island Bluffs* better. A big thank you to Terri Boekhoff for the final edit and helping shape the structure of this novel, and to my publicist, Karen Strauss and KB Publishing for shepherding this book to completion. A special thanks is given to Verity Frizzell, who is a real-life architect, and was kind enough to let me use her name for one of my characters. I did this for the beauty of her name and her accomplishments as an outstanding architect. Please forgive any of my architectural and building faux pas.

Thanks is also extended to friends and relatives who read the manuscript and offered suggestions that made me work harder to improve the story: Dr. Robin Winter, Nannette Soffen Winter, Pam Drucker, Mark McGivern, Art Greco, Adam Swartz, Daniel Rosen, Dr. Cliff Melnick, and Dr. Noah Chivian. Once again, I extend a heartfelt thanks to Olga Vezeris, who has been a constant source of guidance throughout my writing career. And thank you to Marguerite and Burton Abrams, for sharing their incredible story with me. Without Burt's whimsical comment one day, the story of *Island Bluffs* would never have been told.

And finally, thank you to my family—my children and grandchildren—who have graciously indulged me in my passion for writing.

Prologue

This is anything but an ordinary story. Then again, nothing that occurs in Island Bluffs, one of a score of sleepy towns that make up the famed New Jersey Shore, ever is. Not now. Not long ago. Not ever. Many of the important characters in this story are already dead, yet it remains for the living to find the truths in the secrets buried in Island Bluffs.

For starters, Island Bluffs is not an island. It's a promontory that juts into Barnegat Bay opposite Long Beach Island's famed lighthouse. It wasn't that long ago that the top of the World Trade Center was visible from boats plowing through the nearby waters on sunny days. That was before we lost our innocence . . . and before big storms would inexorably change East Coast landscapes—both types: shoreline and political.

But back to our story.

In Island Bluffs, the cast of characters, the living ones, well, most of them, anyway, are everyday folks. Let's introduce the Berks, Gabe and Carly. Try as they may, they cannot conceive a progeny. Abandoning the laissez-faire approach that fails to do the trick, they calculate when Carly is ovulating, increase the frequency of the sex act, take temperatures, eat oysters, put feet in the air, and drink glasses of wine to relax. Nada. They even have a crack at acupuncture. As hard as they try, pregnancy does not seem to be in their cards.

Having exhausted all channels, they seek the magic of a most special baby guru, the renowned specialist of last resort: Dr. Isadore Teplitsky. He is at a minimum an unconventional practitioner.

Then there's Megan Berk, the lone child from Gabe's first marriage, who still cannot get past her mother's death. After six disconsolate years, Megan has yet to accept her stepmother . . . and for no good reason.

And, of course, there is the quite lovable, rock solid, Yehuda Berkowitz, Gabe's father, who has been a widower himself since the ex-actor/California governor ruled the land, and still does not understand why his son needed to shorten the family name. Marrying a *shiksa* was okay. Changing the family name? That's a bitter pill to swallow.

Oh, there are a few more characters to toss into this cauldron of intrigue, and they will be added to this burlesque of souls when needed.

As we forge ahead, tuck into the creases of your mind that a basket of memories will be uncovered that Island Bluffs' town elders would sooner forget. Truth be told, these patriarchs, cocooned in their own stories, almost forgot the town's secrets that had been entrusted to them for safekeeping years back. They are forgotten no more as Gabe and Carly set the seaside hive buzzing when they buy a certain house that has been off everyone's radar for nigh on two generations. That can happen with an abandoned home hidden from the road by overzealous clumps of shrubs and trees, especially if no one's lived in it since not long after the GIs returned from defeating the Krauts and the Japs.

It is the house that time neglected and people forgot.

Along come the Berks, and secrets buried long ago begin to surface like detritus dredged up by a sudden storm. It's the *what*, *where*, and *when* that alters the outcome, and in Island Bluffs, outcomes matter. The *why* and *how* matter, too—too much, some would say—and it is the *why* and *how* that are part of the town's secrets.

What kind of secrets, you ask? Dark ones. The kind that make for tales told when the moon is full and fires crackle and houses creak. The kind that summon the wind to hiss and leaves to rustle and trees to groan and spooks to come out to play. The kind that makes the hairs on the back of your neck prickle and your heart beat quickity-quick. The kind that once heard, no one forgets . . . except, it seems, the elders in Island Bluffs.

Short-term memory loss, you say?

No, not this time.

Not here.

This is out-and-out denial.

So let's begin this tale of twists and turns, where lines of clarity blur, and little is as it seems.

Then again, whatever is?

Especially in the mysterious town of Island Bluffs, a dot of land on the Jersey coast that isn't even an island.

CHAPTER 1

Thursday, June 26, 2008, 1:50 p.m.
By any other measure, Yehuda Berkowitz, a wizened octogenarian dressed for winter on this unseasonably hot, early summer's day, his gnarled fingers hooked around the handle of a light-weight, black tote bag, standing in front of a police station would've been a man out of place, not to mention someone out of his comfort zone. Not today. Today, Yehuda is a man with a cause. A just cause.

Brisk steps carry him to doors programmed to spring wide at the slightest motion. Yehuda triggers the all-seeing, invisible eye, and enters the one-story, red-bricked building. Streams of cool air bellow from air-conditioning ducts that strain to squelch the unseasonable June heat. A mounted ceiling fan, the plastic blades made to look like oak, whirls overhead. It reminds Yehuda of the time he and Sadie went to Aruba and stayed at that fancy hotel. Marble everywhere. Gold spigots. "Can you imagine, Sadie," he said after the attendant strutted away, "they bring ice cold towels to the beach to cool you down. Ice cold, like they were in a freezer. Now that's something."

"And they don't even charge for the bottled water," added Sadie, "what a place!"

His brief reverie over, Yehuda snaps back to the moment. He knows what he is going to say and why. He does not want their sympathy, only their justice. He glides across the gray slate floor, the carry-on's wheels chirping away, only to get sidetracked by a corkboard affixed to a wall painted glossy white.

Faces stare back at him.

Children's faces.

Yehuda examines. He knows none, but they fascinate for all the wrong reasons.

They are arranged in chronological order from the time they went missing. He studies each one with the acumen of a technician trained to study detail. Something he was in another life. His working life. He fancies himself a keen observer. He takes pride in noting the indent of a missing ring from the fourth finger. A widower? A divorcée? A married man on the prowl? Or he notes a fake eye that doesn't trail movement. The gimp of a prosthetic leg. Bleached teeth. Porcelain laminates.

He speaks fluent Russian, Yiddish, Polish, and German, a byproduct of the old days. Spanish comes later, when he sets up business in the Bronx.

In quiet moments, when alone, Yehuda sees faces from a past that he longs to bury, longs to banish to Siberian recesses of his mind and seal shut like a time capsule, to be opened one hundred years hence. Trouble is that frozen time capsules are not meant for people, at least not the ones who buried them. Certainly not people who lived a life like Yehuda Berkowitz. Try as he may to avoid situations that defrost memories, that when they surface they stab him the way freezer burn inflicts acute pain on the palate, their horror is always as severe as if the events happened a mere day or two ago.

And then there are the times he sees phantom images, other than Sadie, and talks to them, tells them stories. He knows they're not real, but he talks to them anyway. It comforts.

Yehuda's spell is broken by the thwack of a trapped horsefly crashing into the front door. Yehuda leans in slow motion so as not to chase it away; he inspects its multi-faceted compound eyes. They are pea green. He steps toward the daylight to trigger the electronic eye; the door jacks open. The fly averts death. This time.

Yehuda returns to the pictures, drifting from one to another. As he is ready to leave the vestibule and pass through a second set of glass doors, a news clipping beckons his notice. It is pinned above the others, a seraph overlooking the fallen angels.

It is not the typical milk-carton poster. This one is a caramel-colored article from the Asbury Park Press. Brown. Baked by age. Withered by time. Print faded. An ancient font.

It's perched too high up for Yehuda to read. He glances about. He seizes a plastic-contoured chair, the kind found in high-school cafeterias or Department of Motor Vehicles' waiting areas or Medicaid offices. He drags it to the wall and hauls himself up for a closer look.

He reads the article. "It's always the innocent children," Yehuda mutters under his breath. "Why can't they leave the *kinder* alone?"

As Yehuda studies the pictures of the missing children in the Island Bluffs Police Station, across town his son and daughter-in-law, Gabe and Carly Berk, scamper out of their pewter-colored Mercedes SUV into the law offices of Thomas Welsh Finley. They are about to close on a house. Finley is the local attorney who was recommended by the bank that held the foreclosure papers. For reasons of his own that will become clear, Gabe needs to buy this particular house. There are others that are nicer and in better shape, and without a doubt, priced higher. He and Carly can afford better. But price is not the motivator in this instance.

He fought hard for this house; Carly was of a different mind.

When all is said and done, Gabe's will prevails and their bid for the house is accepted. The critical point for both, and this Carly willingly concedes, is that they can now be counted as residents of Island Bluffs, a town situated on the shores of Barnegat Bay.

A town that faces an iconic lighthouse.

A town that is proximate to a certain fertility clinic.

No sooner does the ink dry on their contract than unimaginable problems begin to bubble to the surface like the temperature rising within a caldera.

CHAPTER 2

Thursday, 11:30 a.m.

"What do you mean we can't close on the house?" Gabe asks when Finley calls. He stands in the almost-empty house they are about to vacate for good. He glances through the window latticed with white plastic mullions and views the movers cramming the last pieces of furniture into the long, blue-colored van. No last-minute ambush, not even from their own lawyer, no matter what the issue, will stop them from moving into their new house in Island Bluffs. What does Finley expect them to do? They've already sold this one, and the new folks move in tomorrow morning.

A minute before, Carly informed him that his daughter, her stepdaughter, is nowhere to be found.

He threw his hands up. "Why does she have to disappear now? She knows we're moving."

"We need to find her," said Carly.

As he stepped toward the front door, the cell phone rang. It was Finley. After two seconds, he regrets taking the call.

"This is not going to happen, Tom. I don't care what any inspector thinks. We did our due diligence." He takes a furtive look at the front door willing Megan, his daughter, to saunter through. At this moment, he would gratefully tolerate the ever-constant white buds that dangle from her ears to help her tune out the world.

Gabe ignores his lawyer's miserable message. "Look, Tom, the movers are just about finished. Carly and I will leave in a few minutes. Head straight to your office. Whatever the problem, it will be okay. Nothing to worry about."

He hangs up before his lawyer can protest that he needs to leave for another appointment. Gabe knows Finley's quotidian routine includes heading for afternoon refreshments at the Renaissance Country Club in nearby Lakewood. Sorry, Tom, not today.

Gabe needs to find Megan.

There's only one place she could be.

He should be there, too.

Pangs of guilt spread like an acute allergic reaction.

Thursday, 8:06 a.m.

"This box isn't labeled, lady. Where's it going in the new house?"

Carly is distracted.

"Miss? Miss?" She turns to follow the moving man's needle-like finger. "That one?" She gnaws to smooth a chipped nail, furrows her brow, and glances at the controlled chaos before answering. "It came from my husband's study, right? Books and stuff? There's no room in the new house for those now. Until the addition is finished, anything we don't absolutely need goes right into storage." Carly had made a deal with the moving company to hold excess furniture and boxes in their warehouse for a few months. They agreed. Price wasn't too bad. What appeared frivolous at first is now essential.

"Maybe we can put those boxes in the basement." She muses out loud. "Wait. I'm not even sure the house has one."

"You've been there, lady, haven't you?" The youth's raven-colored skin glistens with sweat. He wants to give a head's up that a man's got to have a place for his personal stuff, and that does not mean relegating them to some cold, damp cellar where they can get moldy and wrapped in spider webs. He wants to mention it, but doesn't. He knows better. He wears his gray Montclair High School gym shirt that's cut and frayed at the armpits to display bulging biceps. At the outset that morning, the youth is quick to let Carly know that this is only a summer job. He needs to bulk up when he plays football for Rutgers this coming season. Right corner. Full ride. In a month, he goes to training camp.

Carly feels the baby kick. Babies. Pleural. As in twins. *Can she tell, from the kick, which one is which?* She asks herself this question all the time. Is it the one kicking up to the left or the one tugging on her urethra as if it's a ripcord to an escape hatch? How many times does she try to cajole Dr. Isadore Teplitsky, her world-renowned fertility expert, into telling her the difference between the two *in utero*? His answer's always the same.

"There is no way to tell them apart without performing amniocentesis. That always carries some small risk. Even if we decide to do it, and we're not, it would only determine which one was which at that moment. They're still able to move around, so hours later, we would not be able to tell them apart."

"But I'd like to know."

"We all would," says the doctor. "When it's their time to come out to see the world, that's when we'll both know. For now, be happy they're healthy, active little fellows."

Fellows, as in both are boys.

Though the doctor has been in this country for more than fifty years, he doesn't shake his German accent, which is an endearing trait to many. His words, unlike most others of Teutonic heritage, are not sharp and staccato-like. They roll off his tongue with a softness that encourages and nurtures; his tone evokes respect. Another one, a trait that is, the one that folks travel far and wide to behold and discover, is the magic he possesses when it comes to making babies.

But it doesn't stop there. Dr. Teplitsky is the sort of person who gives back to the community without being asked.

"Dr. T is always good for a check for a worthy cause. Any cause."

"Free screening for the needy."

"Can't pay the bill?" he says to a patient. "We'll worry about it later."

"New computers for the library."

"And those boys! Stars, every one of them. The youngest, though, is a bit overindulged."

Moving day finds Carly entering the last leg of her pregnancy. The timing is not coincidence. Dr. Teplitsky has strict rules that no client dare violate. She and Gabe sign a contract.

* * *

Monday, November 19, 2007
"You do not have a choice," he says at the first consult.

"What if we have difficulty finding a place?" asks Carly.

"Then you live here. In my house. With me and the other children."

"Don't you think that's stretching it a bit?" asks Gabe. "We'll get here in time."

Dr. Teplitsky glares at Gabe, gives an imperceptible nod to Carly, and stands. He closes Carly's chart. "Having a baby is a serious matter."

"We know that, or we wouldn't be here," says Carly, perched on the edge of her seat. She grabs Gabe's hand.

"It is more serious than you think." His accent thickens; its melliferous edges become beveled. "If you do not agree to my terms, then this visit is over." And what he doesn't say, they all think. *And you have just lost your last chance to have a baby.*

The doctor marches out of the room. When the door closes, Carly lets go of Gabe's hand. "How could you challenge him that way? We knew this was part of the deal before we came here. What did you hope to accomplish?"

"I wanted to see how far I could push him."

"That's not your style. Why do it?"

"I don't like being told what I can and can't do."

"Pick that fight with your mother."

"That's mean." Gabe's mother died years ago, but the point is made. This wasn't about him or who maneuvers for the upper hand; this was about Carly and Gabe having a baby. Maybe this is something she wants more than he does.

* * *

Like all others who found fulfillment in their life's dream, the Berks accepted the doctor's absolute condition: at the start of the third trimester, Carly must be within thirty minutes of Teplitsky's fertility clinic. The clinic is located in an old mansion in Lakewood, New Jersey. Island Bluffs is in the outer rim of the acceptable geographic ring, not that they needed his permission to buy that particular house, but it pleases them to get his blessing.

Leading up to that first meeting with Dr. Teplitsky, Carly focused on the need to conceive and avoid dwelling on their inability to do so to date. She could not wrap her mind around the imperative that she needed to be close to the clinic or the toll fulfilling that mandate would take on her, Gabe, and Megan. After all, it was a small price to pay for having the baby she had wanted for eons. When—not if—the good doctor casts his magic spell on her, she had promised to pack every box herself.

Who wouldn't want to spend a summer at the Jersey Shore? Carly's never taken a long vacation. Neither had her mother, may she rest in peace, who waitressed in a Queens diner for all of her adult years. This is not a sacrifice as far as Carly's concerned. No, sir. Euphoria could not be spelled any sweeter than b-a-b-y.

Three months at the most. Probably less given that twins are always premature. No matter how brief a time, the days could not fly by fast enough for Carly.

For so many reasons.

She and Gabe have been married six years, five-and-a-half of which they tried to conceive a baby. During that same time, Carly expended an equivalent amount of energy to win over the good graces of her stepdaughter, Megan. When they first met, Carly saw the web of loss and longing that had enveloped the motherless eleven-year-old. Megan brooded and kept to her room. Efforts to engage her fell short. Each April since Carly was part of the family, she cajoled, begged, and pleaded for Megan to accompany her to Carly's mid-town Manhattan dental practice during the national Take Your Daughter to Work Week. Try as she may, the girl would not budge, preferring to go to school rather than spend a day with her fake mother, which is how she referred to Carly behind her back to her friends.

While others brought their children to Carly's "other" workplace, which was dark, mysterious, and, at times, downright frightening, Carly dared not expose Megan to the gruesome surroundings. Carly was the chief forensic dentist of New York and split her time between her small practice and the Medical Examiner's Office. The last thing Carly wanted to do was to bring the child to the morgue and reinforce Megan's scarred image of Emily in a white dress . . . in a casket.

Megan was ever the challenge from the day she and Carly first met right up until this moment. Not even a clutch of historical American Girl dolls, not the colonial duo of Felicity and Elizabeth or Kaya, the Nez Perce Indian girl, could capture Megan's fancy. No matter how Carly attempted to narrow the chasm between them, their tectonic plates drifted further and further apart and if, by chance, they reversed course only to draw near each other, they soon erupted into tremors of irreconcilable tension.

Dead mothers are damn hard to replace.

CHAPTER 3

September, 2004

Conceiving a baby was not happening by itself.

"Do I really have to jerk off into a jar?"

After months of failing to fertilize anything but weariness and disappointment, they consulted an expert in the NYU Fertility Center on First Avenue off Thirtieth-Eighth Street. Carly was thirty-seven and didn't need a professional opinion to reveal the obvious: the chances of her conceiving were diminishing with the half-life of a decaying element on the periodic chart, one measured in months and years, not centuries or millennia.

"One of you is the culprit," said the white-haired doctor. "We need to find out which one and fix him," he locked into Gabe, and added, "or her." He shot a quick glance at Carly and then turned his attention back to Gabe.

Carly was certain the problem resided inside her. Old eggs. Irregular cycle. Gabe didn't help matters by peppering her with a dash of guilt. "I had no problem making Megan," he said to the doctor, ignoring Carly's glare. He threw up his hands. "It can't possibly be me."

Typical male. Never their fault.

"That was then," answered the doctor. "Most men assume virile once, virile forever."

Carly wanted to utter *Way to tell him, Doc*, but refrained.

Gabe scratched his head and grimaced, catching his drift. "That isn't the case?"

The doctor chuckled. "It doesn't make you less of a man. Sperm die off for any number of reasons. Infection, for one. Then there's the chance that an increase in body heat would kill them off. No sense speculating. Let's get a sample. Then we'll be able to tell if yours can swim for the gold like Michael Phelps."

* * *

Gabe was not the problem. Carly had suffered from endometriosis in her teens and early twenties more than once. The doctor, back then, was clear, "You are going to have trouble conceiving." As an immortal twenty-something, Carly entombed the doctor's warning in a box of denial, and wrapped it with a ribbon of abjuration.

There's no way that could ever happen. Not to me.

"If there's any shot," said that doctor, "find a mate as soon as possible. The sooner the better." That was fifteen or so years ago. Hard to find an egg-worthy mate until you fall in love . . . and love proved as elusive as winning the Mega Million lottery. In the end, she got a consolation "n" added to her reward. For Carly, her "Mega Million" lottery number turned into a "Megan" that was filled with a million little headaches. Talk about having the winning ticket! Oh well!

Megan is packaged with Gabe, and Gabe *is* a prize. Gabriel Berk sticks out in a crowd the way Carly does.

Carly turns heads. She's six feet tall, blond, and played four years of varsity volleyball at Duke. Made second team All-American. One head she turned was Gabe's, who is three inches taller. This is already strange since his father is five feet, five inches. How many times had Gabe broached the subject that he thought *he* might have been switched at birth?

Gabe has sandy-colored hair, hazel eyes, and played point guard for Princeton's jayvee basketball team for two years before giving it up to concentrate on his studies. He didn't get enough playing time, he tells her. It was more important to get into a good law school, which he did: Columbia. Back in the day, Columbia was ranked higher than NYU . . . not anymore.

Gabe followed a track to guaranteed success: a summer internship and then a job at Skadden Arps. He worked ten hard years constructing mergers and acquisitions for Fortune 500 clients that those in the know refer to as "M&A." Gabe steamrolled down the partnership track even though the firm strived to make that goal as rare as a white snow leopard. Not impossible, but an endangered species. Each young lawyer signed up knowing they would plug away in the tundra of endless eighteen-to-twenty-hour days, going days and weeks without seeing the sun, being perpetually pale, working until their heads fell to their desk top, yet all the while thankful to clients for paying for car service to transport them home at ungodly hours of the night only to be expected to return early the next morning. The path for any of these future masters of the universe was lined with potholes of frustration when it came to their personal lives.

Long before Carly, Gabe meets Emily Shapiro on a Five Borough Bike Tour that takes place the first Sunday of each May. They both complete the forty-two mile trek and return to the starting point at Battery Park aboard the Staten Island Ferry. They stand at the railing, gazing at Lady Liberty.

"First time?" asks Gabe. She nods, sucking down orange Gatorade. "You a survivor?"

She turns toward him for the first time. Emily has auburn hair, a face chiseled from a long, narrow block, and sparkles of coal for eyes, diamonds from where Gabe is standing. Her white teeth dazzle.

"Oh, this?" she says, holding the pink ribbon pinned to her jersey. "For my mom. We lost her last year to breast cancer. I wear it every time I bike in a race or run in a 10K. It's my way of honoring her and bringing awareness."

"That's tough. I'm sorry."

When the ferry lands, they don't part. Instead, unspoken, they drift in the same direction.

Gabe steals a glance.

Emily strolls looking down but smiles, feeling his gaze wash over her. They chitchat. Favorite restaurant. Recent movies. Love of Tuscany. Who will replace Johnny: Leno or Letterman? At Eleventh Street, just off Eighth Avenue, she stops. "This is my block." She extends her hand.

He leans and plants a kiss on her cheek. "I don't know why I did that," he says. "Something came over me. It's just that . . ."

"Don't apologize," she answers, fixed on his hazel eyes, "I was hoping you would."

A year later, they marry. Soon after, Megan is born and they move to New Jersey for suburban riches: spacious houses, good schools, fresh air, and plenty of bike trails to ride on sun-drenched weekends. And then there's the Jersey Shore with its abundant sandy beaches, marinas, good fishing, and restaurants that attempt to rival those on the Manhattan scene. None do, but some get passably close to haute cuisine.

Despite the long hours, life is good for them until Emily gets sick. Ovarian cancer. Had she known to take a recently released test, she would have learned that she had the BRCA1 gene. Maybe her cancer could have been prevented through early intervention. Harvest eggs. Remove the vulnerable organs. Attempt to avoid the big "C." Sounds logical now, but whoever suspects *they* need to be this preemptive when still in their early, fertile years? Had Emily been a few years younger, her story may have had a different ending.

"Gabe, you just can't up and leave," says his law firm's managing partner. "That's what nurses are for."

"Would you just leave your wife at home to fend for herself?" Gabe asks.

"My wife had colon cancer. After the surgery, dropped her off when she had chemo and had someone pick her up when she was through. Didn't miss a beat at work."

Figures, Gabe says to himself. *Always knew he was a cold, heartless bastard.*

"And how is she now?" Gabe asks.

"That was four years ago. She passed last year."

That seals Gabe's decision. He takes a leave of absence to help care for Emily and Megan. Emily fights valiantly. She's a champ. In the end, the disease conquers. When it's time to return to Skadden Arps, Gabe hires a full-time nanny from Utah, Becky, who wants to take time off from college to earn some money. Trouble is that Becky spends too much of her time and money at a local pick-up bar, South City Grill, in Mountain Lakes. She oversleeps most mornings.

"Go wake Becky, honey."

It's 7:15 and Megan needs to be at school in thirty minutes so she can work on a class project. "You know she'll just fall back to sleep. Can't you take me?" says his daughter.

Gabe puts his coffee mug down, glances at his watch, glares in the direction of Becky's room. "Grab your backpack, Megan, but don't expect to find Becky here when you return."

"I know."

A parade of nannies follows. At long last, a buxom Jamaican who raised three grown children of her own, has a driver's license, and is the embodiment of a female Paul Prudhomme, saves the day. As competent as Edesia is, Gabe is reluctant to return to the long hours expected of M&A attorneys. He resigns from Skadden and forms a consulting firm that will cater to companies involved in hostile takeovers. Others come with him, willing to take a chance with Gabe, induced by working for a virtual company that has no walls. Gabe knows clients will follow. If all works out, the hours will be better, the money almost as good, and he will have more time to spend with Megan and his boat. And with Edesia around, Gabe will even have time for that occasional date.

Gabe's father, Yehuda, always said, *"Everything works out for the best."*
"Do you really believe that, Dad?"
"I do, and so should you."

No one catches Gabe's eye until he meets Carly Mason. The reaction is catalytic.

Now, four years, eight tries, and one hundred thirty thousand dollars later, Carly still has not conceived. When more than one doctor suggests taking her eggs and Gabe's sperm, fertilizing them in a test tube, and then implanting them in a surrogate mother to carry their fetus, Carly balks. Gabe is willing to have someone carry the little darling, if that will put an end to their string of disappointments and plug the financial drain. Carly is not. Carly wants the entire baby experience. Pregnancy. *Hyperemesis gravidarum* that most call *morning sickness*. Stretch marks. Pain. Sleepless nights. Even an episiotomy would not dissuade. By now, into her early forties, Carly has no intention of missing the cold jelly for the sonograms on a swollen tummy, the fetal jabs and kickboxing of tiny feet at all hours of the night. She salivates at the prospect of eating binges once she becomes pregnant. Pickles and ice cream. Pizza at three in the morning.

She will have all of it or none of it.

For the longest time, *None of It* is ten lengths ahead of *All of It* in the Kentucky Derby of conceiving babies, with a quarter furlong to go. If it were not for meeting a colleague at a forensic dental meeting who had the same problem, Carly would not be in her current state of bliss.

The woman, who hailed from New Iberia, Louisiana, found Dr. Isadore Teplitsky after an exhaustive search for the best doctor in America who could make babies from nothing, so to speak. Sure the old man is eccentric. Strange. Peculiar. He even insists that you move close to his clinic in the last trimester. So what? The man is a genius at making babies. A regular miracle worker. A fertility alchemist *par excellence*.

That's all Carly has to hear. She and Gabe gallop to the good doctor's door in Lakewood, New Jersey. Lakewood is ten miles from the Jersey Shore. In its heyday, a century earlier, it was a winter resort for New Yorkers. There was plenty of snow back then, and visitors flocked there for the roaring fires, the horse-drawn sleigh rides, the homemade hot apple cider, and thrilled to see the likes of Gentleman Jim Corbett, Kid McCoy, Benny Leonard, and both Max Schmeling and Joe Louis, train for their fights. There was an added benefit: the acres and acres of pine trees that surrounded Lakewood tended to trap heat which kept the town three or four degrees warmer than nearby villages. Back then, it was a gem of a place right out of Currier & Ives.

Pine trees aren't the only things that keep the environs surrounding the good Dr. Teplitsky and his fertility clinic warm and snuggly. The temperature begins to rise in nearby Island Bluffs the day the Berks innocently buy their house on the beach.

Consider the story of Island Bluffs as one of a genie escaping from an ancient lamp . . . and genies trapped for an eternity can be a bit cranky.

CHAPTER 4

Thursday, June 26, 2008, 11:31 a.m.
"Where's Megan?" Carly asks, thinking more out loud than asking anyone in particular. When would her stepdaughter play by the rules? Would she ever make a tacit show of cooperating? Of being responsible? Or would she always push the envelope, and most of all Carly's buttons, to exasperate just for the sake of annoying. Typical stepdaughter or protective daughter? Take your pick.

"Doesn't Megan realize that moving day is stressful for everyone?" says Carly. But Gabe is talking to the lawyer and doesn't hear her. From the look on his face, it's not about some minor problem like a rut in the road to the new house; it's more like a major sinkhole ready to engulf all of them.

Getting not so much as a nod from Gabe, Carly ruminates on her stepdaughter. Maybe part of the reason Megan does not listen to adult authority is because she can't hear it. How could she? Megan's ear buds are so much a part of her, like her belly piercing or the delicate butterfly tattoo that landscapes the small of her back, that it's a wonder she can hear anything at all.

When Gabe first saw the tat, what could he do? Drag her to a dermatologist to laser it off? Tell her that she can never be buried in a Jewish cemetery with her mother? Restrict driving privileges? The last thing Gabe or Carly wanted was to be Megan's chauffeur.

Had they known that most referred to it as a "tramp stamp," they would have taken a different course of action.

Other choices? Gabe could give her a hug and say that he loves it. How do you treat a sixteen-year old—now seventeen—whose mother died when she was prepubescent and whose father lived by the parenting code that coaxed love from overindulgence? The deck was stacked against Carly before she ever entered the picture.

It hasn't been easy for her since. For any of them.

Carly married Gabe knowing it would be an uphill struggle to gain Megan's confidence. Six years and she was no closer to that elusive summit of acceptance. And this move to a new house?

"I can't think of anything worse than moving away for senior year," Megan told them. Screamed at them would be more accurate.

"It will be good for all of us," said Gabe.

"Really?" answered Megan. "About as good as cancer or syphilis."

Carly wanted to tell Megan to stop being dramatic, that she has it better than most kids on the planet, but she bit her lip and said nothing.

They could have moved to China or the next town. Both would have meant the same to Megan: punishment.

"She'll come around," Gabe said.

"Before all of the glaciers melt?" said Carly. The earth might be warming, life is more frenzied, and Megan Berk remains Arctic-cold to Carly and the rest of the world.

If it weren't for the pregnancy, Carly would fight against the move as much as Megan has. It was hard enough for Carly to adjust to moving to New Jersey from Manhattan soon after they got married. She was one of those countless New Yorkers who believes that the sun rises and sets over New York, and there's no better place on earth to live. They never consider themselves "islanders," nor can they process that they don't live on the mainland.

Sorry Toto.

"You're asking a lot of me, Gabe," she had said as their wedding day approached.

"New Jersey grows on you," he said.

"So does fungus. I'm used to walking everywhere. Go a couple of blocks and there's Citarellas for fish, the Fairway Market that has the best produce, Zabar's for delicacies, and H&H for the best bagels in the entire world. I'm supposed to leave all that? That's asking too much."

"But it's called the Garden State for a reason."

She scrunches her face. "That's comforting. But Pine Brook?"

Anytime she was asked, Carly had to repeat the name five times and attempt to explain where it is close to.

"It's in Montville Township."

That helps. Still the third planet from the sun?

In the end, no one gave a hoot. The town's only saving grace is that there's an express bus stop just off Route 46 East that treks into the city once an hour. In the morning, during rush hour, buses have their own access lane into the Lincoln Tunnel, so the commute is almost civilized. *Almost* is the operative word. The buses have narrow seats and sway side-to-side. And heaven forbid if a "plus-size" man or woman is your seatmate. Then the ride turns into a contest of inches, waiting for the enemy to jiggle or shift or inhale, only to pounce on the newly liberated space, no matter how infinitesimal. A small gain is a major victory.

Being the chief forensic dentist in the New York City Medical Examiner's office has its rewards, the main one being reasonable hours. And it was easy to adjust the hours of her small dental practice.

Gabe not only changed the rules of the game, he changed the entire ballpark when he bought the house in Island Bluffs to be near Dr. T's clinic. Knowing she would soon move to the Jersey Shore, Carly sold her little practice. She didn't like clinical dentistry all that much anyway, not when she was also New York's head dental CSI honcho. For her, murder trumped caries.

The pregnancy is a much-welcomed hiatus in her career. Carly arranged for a consulting position with the Ocean County ME to start soon after the baby is born, knowing that her forensic skills will not be in as high demand on the Jersey Shore as in the city. The infrequent homicides, industrial accidents, or possibilities of disaster will be quite different from the hectic pace of working New York's crime scenes. Carly is more than ready to swap out her days of high-profile cases, media announcements, heavy case loads and talking to bereaved families searching for answers, for the highs of raising her baby and an occasional consult or two.

"I know how excited you are," she remembers saying to Gabe when he unloaded his megaton surprise. It was this past April. Gabe keeps his boat at the Waretown Marina in the offseason. Offseason for Gabe doesn't take hold until deep into October or early November. Until then, he shuttles down to the Jersey Shore from Pine Brook to get out onto the water, even as the Canadian winds swoop south. As soon as the crocuses signal the spring thaw, Gabe's boat peels out of hibernation and slices through the still-cold waters of Barnegat Bay for jaunts to nowhere in particular, far beyond the skinny spit of land called Long Beach Island. "LBI" to locals.

* * *

"Want to open the throttle a bit?" the mechanic asks Gabe after making some last-minute adjustments. He has completed the annual maintenance on the boat early, knowing that Gabe will call any day. "I'll lower her into the water."

"Just try and stop me," answers Gabe. That's when he speeds into the sound. The fishing boat, a thirty-foot Grady-White 306 Bimini CC with twin 250 HP Yamahas, responds to his touch. He cruises past the mouth of the Forked River that empties into the bay and is about to open her up when his gaze is drawn to a house sitting on a prominence.

He's seen it before. Countless times, in fact. He is sure it's vacant. Yet this April day, it strikes him differently. It is an enchantress, a Siren. It beckons him to come near. Carly's pregnancy is a prism that changes the way everything looks these days.

He angles for a better view. There are no shades on the windows. No furniture in the yard save two crippled Adirondack chairs, its slats rotted and dangling like broken ribs. The lawn, if it can be called that, is wild and overgrown. The paint is peeling and the roof shingles are missing. Gabe would later learn that this elevated spit of land belongs to Island Bluffs, a small, incorporated town that faces Ol' Barney, the famed lighthouse perched on LBI's northern tip.

Until a few years back when it became part of a national park, Ol' Barney served as a beacon for ocean-bound vessels since the days of General George McClellan of Civil War fame. Few know that General McClellan, an architect in his earlier life, was charged with drawing up plans for a new lighthouse to replace the one the sea had encroached on in 1855. The 165-foot tower was commissioned on January 1, 1859.

Like so many others on the bay side or along one of the numerous estuaries that feed into it, this house has a private dock. Gabe secures the boat and mounts the steps leading to the house. They are splintered, and groan under his weight. He makes a mental note they need to be replaced.

At the top he follows the inch-and-a-half thick slate slabs that define a path from the pier toward the house with the adventure of a paleontologist discovering fossil prints. They are blue and burnt red, some chipped, a couple with jagged cracks slicing through their midsection. Tufts of grass and yellow dandelions sprout between each block.

The slate ends for no particular reason, in the middle of the yard. Gabe tramples through a jungle of weeds. Thistles snag his khakis. The notion of owning this carnage of a property insinuates itself into his senses for reasons he can't explain. It is not a pretty sight but something draws him to it.

He nears the house.

"This baby's going to need a lot of work," he says out loud. He flips a tuft of hair off his forehead. "Might as well start planning my funeral right now."

He chuckles, shrugs away the thought, and then marches up to a back window. Splintered roof shingles dot the uncut grass like buffalo chips. A window or two has fractured, spider-web cracks radiating from a tiny hole. BB pellets. He takes his shirttail, spits on a frame, and rubs mud off a window, cups his hands around his eyes, and notes two chairs and a couch, each covered with white sheets, now turned gray with dust. There's a folding wooden chair. Curls of paint peeling off the walls. No lamps or fixtures, but a small canopy in the center of the ceiling that Gabe knows was used to cap gas spigots that once powered the lights.

He pulls back and struts to another window that is separated by a two-part wooden door. He cleans this window through which he can see the kitchen. The appliances are yellowed and dirty. Patches of paint are peeling. A rustic kitchen table is surrounded by a bunch of chairs.

"Whew!" says Gabe. He pictures Carly's face when he describes this. "What am I thinking?"

Waves slap against his boat.

The ocean purrs. It reassures.

Gabe walks the grounds inspecting turned-over planters, bent railings, and the lone tree, a red oak that casts a giant shadow on the north side of the house. It is a tree worthy of Hitchcock's *The Birds*. Gabe fingers the bark and feels an ancient energy.

He edges to the side of the house. Spins. Ocean to his left, pebbled driveway to his right. The house is located on an isolated promontory. It is minutes from town. Both pluses. What's most important is that the trip to Dr. Teplitsky's clinic in Lakewood would take no more than twenty minutes. And when his business calls for it, he's able to drive north—a hop, skip, and a jump—to Atlantic Highlands and take the ferry to Manhattan to meet clients or hold an in-person staff meeting.

And it has a dock. That's important.

No overthinking this.

Gabe marches to the front of the house, scrambles down the driveway, and eyes a bank foreclosure sign. Not thinking about or knowing how much work the house will need, he wants to buy it. He yanks the sign out of the ground. Regardless of how long this house has been in foreclosure and hasn't sold, no one is going to snatch this beauty out from under him. All he has to do is convince Carly to sell their house in Pine Brook and move to Island Bluffs. How hard could that be? Would he need to throw in that tennis bracelet she's hinted about more than once? A romantic trip to Venice after the baby's born? Diamond studs?

He shakes his head. None of that is Carly. He will take the direct route lobbying for this house. What this means is fairly simple when it comes to his wife: he will have to argue his case as if he were in front of the Supreme Court.

"Good thing I went to law school," he says out loud, with a last glance at the house before easing onto the boat. Then he shakes his head, thinking of how Carly will react. He smiles knowing no argument will persuade better than its proximity to the clinic.

The clinic that creates life.

The clinic that is life-changing.

If only Gabe understood what was truly at stake . . . but then again, Island Bluffs has a way of masking life's truths from all but a few.

CHAPTER 5

April 10, 2008, 4:30 p.m.
"It's a steal."

His words are laced with confidence. False confidence.

Her arms are folded across her chest.

He continues. "The house is in foreclosure. Some company has owned it more than fifty years. Something about merging back then, one was a foreign company. One was American. I don't know. They said that the personnel changed and somewhere along the way, no one in the company remembered that they owned this house. At least that's the story the bank gave me."

"And this affects us how?" asks Carly, her left brow rising.

Gabe expected her to be cool about this, but the room is getting downright freezing. He carries on. "You know what's going on around the country. Toxic debt. Bad mortgages. Banks are trying to get these clunkers off their books as fast as they can write the contracts. We got real lucky on this one. It will be good for us. All of us." He glances at her swollen belly.

Carly waits until he finishes. Her eyes are as cool as blue ice. Frost vapors hover around her.

"I know you're excited, but take a step back. Something doesn't make sense. If the house is that old, how can there be a mortgage? Surely it's been paid off by now?"

"I told you the house was an asset in a merger. They just forgot about this one, and as a result, they stopped paying the mortgage."

"And the bank didn't do anything about it all these decades? Contact them? Send certified letters? I can accept an employee's house being lost in the shuffle of paperwork, especially if they owned a lot of them and it was just after the war, but somewhere along the line, there had to be a red flag. When it's waved high enough and long enough, someone should've seen it. And when they did, any responsible company would've corrected the issue."

"They missed it." Gabe wishes Carly would thaw a degree or two, but that is not about to happen. Not yet.

"Obviously," says Carly. "Does this make any sense to you?"

"We're talking a local bank here. You know how people in these small towns are, all in cahoots with each other. The president of the bank probably played golf with the folks who owned it. They let it slide thinking the land would be worth more than the house one day, so they waited to cash in. This wouldn't be the first time a bank has been sloppy and dropped the ball. Especially if it was protecting one of its own."

She shakes her head. "You're trying to tell me they just discovered they own this property and want to unload it for practically nothing? Is that it?"

"It's all the new TARP regulations. Why look a gift horse in the mouth? Who cares why it's available. It is, and that's all that matters."

"It must be a wreck, neglected all these years."

He drew in a deep breath. "It's not that bad. Needs some work." Then he grew animated. "That's why it is such a good deal."

Carly knew it was worse than he was saying, but she felt his enthusiasm. "Great. A fixer-upper. Need I remind you that you are not exactly the emcee of *This Old House*?"

"I have no delusions of ever lifting a hammer. The key point is that the house is sound and most of the problems are cosmetic."

"And you know this how? Did you knock on the wall or something? Did you even go inside?"

"As a matter of fact I did kick it a few times and from what I could see through the window, it's solid. This one is built like they used to build houses."

"You're dreaming."

"It's a good dream. For all of us. Tell you what. If the inspector nixes it, we'll look for something else. Deal?"

Carly rolled her eyes and didn't answer. Her expression said it all.

Gabe rubbed his palms on his pant legs. "It won't take that much to get it ready for us to move in. And there would be no contingencies like owners needing to stay on for a few weeks. It would be ours as soon as we close."

"Is it big enough?" She rubs her belly. "Remember, there has to be room for your father in case you can finally convince him to live with us."

"It'll be tight now, but we can make it even if he joins us. As for enlarging the house, not a problem. We can blow out the attic and push out the back and sides if we want. The important thing is that we'll be close to the clinic." He opens is eyes wider and cocks his head to the side, to further plead his case. "Change is good. What do you say?"

"Where do you want me to start? Let's not talk about what it means to me to move into a house compared to subletting an apartment for the three months we need to be down there. Have you thought about your daughter in all of this? It's not fair to her. How would you like to miss *your* last year of high school? Not be with your lifelong friends for your senior year and not be invited to the prom?"

He shrugs. "Means nothing to me. I never went to mine."

She throws her hands up. "Figures."

Is that directed at him or a slam against all men? He ignores it. "Just because she's moving doesn't mean Megan will lose her friends. Besides, kids who live in other towns are often invited to local proms. I'm sure she'll be asked back to hers."

"Really? Do I need to remind you that our daughter," Carly stumbles over the *our*, "has not won any popularity contests these last couple of years?"

"That could change."

Carly glares as if he has a third eye in the middle of his forehead. "Sure, anything could change. And if I move my arms real fast, I can fly. Wanna see?"

Gabe shakes his head. "Megan needs you in her corner, Carly. You have to believe in her."

Carly turns wide-eyed. "I do believe in her, that's why I'm fighting for us to stay right here where she belongs."

And me, too.

"C'mon, it won't be that bad."

"You're right. It'll be worse than you can imagine. What Megan needs right now is a father who understands that ripping her away from what few friends she has in her last year of high school is a travesty. She'll never forgive you for it."

"I beg to differ. The change will do her good. Ever since Emily passed, Megan has not been the happy child she used to be."

"Who can blame her?" counters Carly, "She lost her mother. What could you expect? That still doesn't solve anything. You're the one who's always wanted to live down the shore. Not me. For that matter, I seriously doubt that Megan wants to either. You know how much she hates the sun."

"This has always been my dream," his voice tinged with hope. "The boat? Fishing? And now that we need to be close to Dr. Teplitsky, it's a win-win for all of us."

Carly throws up her hands and shakes her head. *Why are men both dense and delusional?* She draws in a deep breath and thinks how best to convince him. "Living here has never stopped you from enjoying those things. Isn't that why we rent a shore house in the summer? And let's not forget how many additional weekends you scoot down to the marina and take your boat out in the off-season." She taps her foot. "Like the way you just found this house."

He needs to steamroll over her objections before she rips the heart out of his rehearsed pitch. "You know you need to be close to Dr. Teplitsky. That's a given. You know you have to take it easy this summer. That's a given. Twins and all. Have you forgotten how Pine Brook turns into a ghost town as soon as the heat's turned up? You've always complained about that. That's why we rent down on LBI every year. Now we can own our house and be there year round." He gives it his best smile. *Stop on an up note.*

LBI is New Jersey's answer to the Hamptons. Long Beach Island is an eighteen-mile-long barrier island discovered by Captain Cornelius Jacobsen Mey in 1614 when he sailed in through the rough waters of the northern inlet, where Ol' Barney stands today. Captain Mey named the waterway "Barendegat," which means "Inlet of the Breakers." Over the years, this appellation evolved into "Barnegat." Naming it Long Beach Island, with its divine beaches stretching out for miles was a no brainer. Once the railroad bridge opened in 1886 and made access to the pristine sands as easy as buying a ticket, the island's population grew. A patchwork of communities developed over the years, each with its own unique qualities and attractions: Barnegat Light, Beach Haven, Harvey

Cedars, Ship Bottom, Surf City, and Long Beach Township, to name the prominent ones.

"Renting works just fine for us."

"This is such a great deal," he countered.

"But my work at the Medical Examiner's? I just can't leave them in the lurch."

"You've already set up a rotation with your team to cover you these last few months. One thing New York's not lacking is a contingency of qualified forensic dentists. I'm still waiting for the TV version of what you do."

"Teeth aren't that glamorous."

"Some of your cases are."

He recalls the time they first dated.

Gabe knew Carly was a dentist, albeit one with a small core of patients. In those days, she rented a chair from a dental school classmate, two days per week. She taught in the restorative clinic at NYU's prestigious dental school located on Twenty-fourth Street and First Avenue. The rest of her time, including most evenings, Carly processed bite marks and other forensic evidence in an attempt to identify the unnamed victims lying in the city morgue by matching the way their jaws and fillings fit together. When they were available, she requested dental records from state and federal agencies, from family dentists, or from walk-in clinics. The more points a filling or a bite mark matched the victim's teeth, the more certain the identification.

One day, Gabe skimmed the paper as he drank his morning coffee. "Well, I'll be . . ." He never finishes the sentence. They already had a date for that night, but now he's bursting to see Carly.

"Who ever thought?" He pointed with a measure of pride to the lead article. Under a bold, thirty-six-point headline, the exposé detailed how Carly's keen know-how solved a grim murder that had terrified Manhattan.

"Anyone could have done it," she answered with a modest hitch of her shoulders later that day.

"Bullshit to that," Gabe says. "*You* did it."

The case had sent a tsunami of worries cascading through the city's single women. Bryn Coughlin, a much-loved riding instructor at the

Claremont stables before they would close, had been found stabbed to death inside her sub-street-level West Side apartment. The building's handyman always lingered under the first-floor steps as he readied stacks of discarded newspapers for recycling. That was his usual time to spy through the black wrought iron bars protecting her easy-to-reach windows, installed to make Bryn feel safe. Instead of catching Bryn's undulating hips wriggling out of her riding breeches, he got more than he bargained for: a pool of congealing blood oozed across the hardwood floor. Bryn lay lifeless, facedown, in the blackening gore.

Willie Robinson, the Chief Medical Examiner, arrived on the scene. In the shake of a few moments, it was apparent that Carly Mason's expertise was needed. There were telltale earmarks of a struggle. A struggle could mean the presence of bite marks. Bite marks required a forensic dentist, ergo, Dr. C. Mason, NYC's finest tooth sleuth.

Carly had just returned from running two loops around the Central Park Reservoir's cinder path when she received Willie Robinson's call. Fresh on the scene, she leaned over the body, oblivious to the lingering eyes of assorted police specialists who gather at grisly events. Carly had not bothered to change. Her sweat-drenched sports bra left little to the imagination. Her skimpy running shorts exaggerated her six-foot frame. Her silky blond hair, gathered in a ponytail, emphasized Carly's smooth skin, her no-nonsense nose, and her determined jaw. Carly was a head-turner, no doubt about it. But something stopped men from approaching her . . . everyone except Gabe. He saw beyond the raw beauty and grace. He saw beyond the high intelligence. He saw that she had heart, and that meant the world to him. She captivated him in spite of the fact that she used power tools to saw jaws in half and was as comfortable wallowing in blood as she was applying makeup.

Carly inspected Bryn's bruised wrists.

"These are defensive wounds."

"I needed to hear you say it," said Willie, the city's ME.

Wrist wounds meant a struggle, and a struggle meant the off-hand chance that the victim had bitten the assailant. Alginate molds capture the bite marks; plaster is vibrated into the grooves and indentations to preserve their shape for future comparison. Should the dental configuration of the victim prove to be a match, the dental evidence goes a long way to nailing the vermin.

In this case, a local delivery boy had brought a package of groceries to the very block of the murdered victim. While the boy took forever to return, other delivery orders backed up at the bodega. His boss wondered what was taking so long. When the youth charged into the market dripping with blood, the storeowner's anger evaporated. The gashes were so deep that he encouraged the boy to go to Roosevelt Hospital's emergency room. But the youth waved him off; the slashes were nothing. Still concerned, the owner sent the boy home and finished the deliveries himself.

The next day's screaming headlines made the boss think twice about the boy's explanation of how he tripped and cut his arm on a broken beer bottle. After all, didn't the kid make a delivery two doors down from the murder victim? When he questioned the boy further, the youngster turned skittish. There was something in the way he answered that compelled the bodega owner to call the local precinct. A newly minted citizen, the man felt it was his civic duty to report the boy. Let the authorities figure out if the juvenile was telling the truth.

Police always pray for this sort of break. Without breaks, many crimes go unsolved. It turned out that Bryn Coughlin *had* bitten the delivery boy. The victim's dental molds fit into the suspect's wound the way a missing jigsaw part completes a puzzle. Seeing the evidence against him, the delivery boy confessed.

Though the former media mogul, now mayor, honored the bodega owner on the steps of City Hall, Carly received her share of kudos. Oh, headlines flatter and it was gratifying to be invited to speak at the monthly gathering of the local forensic society, but both paled compared to the rush of using her special skills to catch an innocent victim's killer.

After the hoopla died down, the thank you note from Bryn's parents meant more than peer approval or public acclaim.

"I will need to get back to Manhattan someday," Carly says.

Gabe sees a quark of hope. "And when you do, we'll figure out how. Maybe take a *pied-à-terre*. Take an early bus in and work Tuesday, Wednesday, and Thursday, then take the bus home. You're only gone two nights that way. I could see that happening. But we're not there, yet." He rubs her belly. "This is what's important now."

Carly knows the battle is over. And there's no way she's ever leaving a baby two nights a week. Not after waiting this long to have one. Gabe has his heart set on getting his house with a dock for his boat. No matter how hard he tries to convince her to agree that it's a good idea, she knows it isn't. Not really. The idea of buying a house close to the clinic never came up before, not once. For this reason, Gabe caught her off guard. Had it been discussed, Carly would have spent time researching houses, neighborhoods and the like. But she hadn't, and now there is no time left to find a suitable alternative.

What is true is that Carly must live near Island Bluffs for the last three months of her pregnancy. Maybe a few weeks after that. But no more. As much as she championed Megan's need to complete her senior year in her high school and how critical it is for the girl to keep her friends, by any measure, the girl is on a slippery slope of being a social pariah. Her clothes are getting dark, and her makeup darker still. Gabe's right. A change of venue would be good for all of the Berks.

The silence is awkward.

He takes her hand and leads her to the living room sofa. They sit, angled toward each other.

"It's been so hard on Megan ever since Emily passed. I thought that when you and I got married, she'd perk up. I didn't expect her to forget her mother, but I was so certain that she would embrace you as a female in the house. Stability. Love. Nurturing. All that good stuff."

"It didn't happen, did it?" she whispers.

"Not that you haven't been great. You've been a saint with her. Couldn't be any better. And I love you for that, and for so much more. But we all need a new start. To get out of this town. What do you say? Are you with me?"

Who could argue that point?

Carly had never admitted this to anyone before, and tried not to dwell on it when she was by herself, but it was always a struggle. Truth be told, it would be quite the relief to leave Emily's house.

In fact, "my house" has a nice ring all its own.

CHAPTER 6

Thursday, 11:19 a.m.
The pregnancy challenges. Carly leans against the wall at the top of the stairs, clutching the handrail, her chest heaving, needing to settle down. She was forewarned that twins made for a tougher pregnancy. No way could she blow out forty-plus candles at this moment. Her skin grows moist. She swipes beads of sweat off her upper lip. When her breathing slows and heart stops thumping as if ready to burst, she pads to Megan's room. She swings open the door expecting Megan's bobbing head weaving to a beat only she could hear. Implanted ear buds, white cords dangling, deaf to the world. But the room's unoccupied. Boxes *are* sealed, drawers *are* empty, and the closet is cleared out . . . miracles to behold. All is in order, yet no sign of Megan.

Carly grows concerned; the men are almost finished loading the truck.

Navigating down the stairs does not pose the same challenge as hiking up; still, she needs to be careful. One misstep and, lickety-split, the babies could be goners. Her days of grace and elegance are but a memory. She hits the worn carpeted landing and scoots from room to room in her inimitable waddle. Carly dodges the men struggling to extract the seven-foot-tall, cerulean blue lacquered French armoire from their bedroom.

She loves this piece and flashes to the day they strolled into the antique store, Best of France, in Lambertville. It was a perfect day. The fall leaves were a riot of colors—reds and oranges and yellows—and they strolled in and out of the small boutiques in the Jersey river town opposite the funky, touristy New Hope on the other side of the Delaware River, in Buck's County, Pennsylvania. When she saw the piece, she had to have it. Somehow, the armoire made it easier to sleep in Emily's bedroom. *Soon she would have her own bedroom.*

Megan is nowhere to be found. Not in the house. Not in the landscaped yard manicured by itinerant Ecuadorians the gardener picks up across from the Dover train station. Not sneaking a smoke on the side of the house. Nor is she back in the woods in the far corner of the property that can be viewed from the red cedar deck.

Carly speed-dials Gabe. He has an emergency that can't be dodged even on moving day. A pharmaceutical company is making a hostile bid to take over a biotech company that's on the verge of a major breakthrough. Goliath wants to slay David. In this scenario, Goliath will win in acquiring the upstart that is using nanotechnology to develop a more effective drug for lung cancer.

Her call goes straight to voicemail; he is still speaking with his client. She's about to curse when she sees him enter the house, phone pressed against his ear. He says, "Good-bye," and waves, surveying the scene.

The moving men navigate the armoire toward the front door. Gabe sidesteps them and gives Carly a peck. "Everything went great this morning. Sorry I needed to leave you alone for so long." He waves his Blackberry. "I saw that you called. Everything on schedule?"

Rather than acknowledge his absence and the fact that nothing could be so important that it couldn't wait a day until after they've moved, Carly turns to the problem at hand.

"I don't know where Megan is. The movers are almost finished and we need to find her."

Before he can say anything, Gabe's phone chirps. Carly is about to tell him not to take the call when Gabe answers. He mouths "Finley" to her, as if this name connotes royalty. Finley is their real estate lawyer and when it comes to closing day, attorneys trump most anything else.

They had given Finley power of attorney, so they expect to hear that the closing went on without a hitch and that they can now move into the house. Instead, Gabe hears that Finley runs into an unforeseen roadblock. It's more like a complete blockade rather than a major hurdle.

"What are you talking about?" Gabe says. His face contorts as if salmonella-infected food is turning his insides into knots of pain and the need to do the Aztec two-step is moments away. Lawyers do make sphincters cramp.

Carly motions, *what's wrong?*

He shoots up an index finger.

Carly shrugs. *How bad could it be? Bad, judging from Gabe's mangled mien.*

She turns to see mirrors exit the house; there is not much else to move. Breakables and paintings are the final objects to be loaded onto the truck. A last-minute walk-through. Pull open drawers and cabinets. Peek into closets. As soon as they leave, an army of Merry Maids will traipse through the house, scouring it spic-and-span clean for the new owners.

Good-bye Pine Brook; hello Island Bluffs . . . once they find the missing Miss Megan.

She turns her interest back to Gabe, who is still yakking away with the lawyer, comforted that nothing in the house has been overlooked.

Gabe disconnects from Finley. "It's a ton of trouble. Finley couldn't close this morning. Something to do with town ordinances. Makes no sense to me."

"How can there be a problem now? Everything was fine a week ago. Besides, the house passed inspection. We got all the permits we needed. What could be wrong?"

He doesn't answer.

She spits out a nagging thought. "This is a bad omen. What's going to happen now? We can't just have them sit around and wait," she snorts, nodding toward the gaggle of men huddled around the moving truck.

"Whatever it is, it's not going to stop us. Besides we need to vacate so the new folks can move in tomorrow. We'll have to tell the movers to wait for a green light before they can unload once they get to the new house. You and I need to get to Finley's *tout de suite*."

"What if it takes a while? With overtime they make more than neurosurgeons. And have you forgotten that we're meeting your father? We can't keep him waiting."

"Simmer down. It's not good for you or the baby."

"Babies," she corrects.

"Gosh. I know you're carrying two, but I only think of the one that's ours. Got it: babies. I won't forget. Getting back to the issue, one thing I've learned: every problem has a solution. Once Finley explains it to us, then we'll know what to do. And regarding my father, he's a survivor. If we're going to be late, we'll call him on his cell phone."

"He never has his turned on, and even if he does, he rarely answers."

"Just the same, he's not our immediate issue now, Finley is."

"And Megan."

"Her, too."

Carly shakes her head. "You are so the optimist. An eleventh-hour roadblock is thrown at us, and you think you can make it better. I don't have a good feeling about this."

"Woman's intuition aside . . ."

"Don't discount us. We're usually right."

"I've learned that your internal radar works just fine. Regardless of how right you might be, we need to let Finley explain it in person, and then we'll solve it. It's as simple as that."

"Nothing's going to be simple if we don't find Megan. We can't leave without her. If you haven't noticed, the house is cleared out right down to the dust balls. We are ready to go."

"I'm not worried. She has a car and the address. She has GPS. She's a big girl."

"Remind me never to expect sympathy from you. Get serious, Gabe. She's your daughter, and we're moving out of here for good. She's plenty upset. You've got to find her."

He touches both of her arms with a gentle squeeze. He reassures. "You're right. It's no time to kid around. I have a hunch where she is. Be back in a couple."

"Don't take too long; the meter's ticking."

The Berk house, replete with a pool on the terraced backyard that slopes toward Hook Road, is perched at the end of a cul-de-sac on Pellington Road. Gabe rounds the curve and trots to the corner. He turns right onto Windsor Drive. A few long strides and he's in front of a black wrought iron fence. He shades his eyes and scans the greens, then slips through the metal gate. He angles away from the street, heading deeper inside the compound, careful where he steps, weaving in and out, getting closer to where Megan could be.

He calls her name. "Megan?"

He sees her. He stops calling. He's unsure if she has heard him.

He does not want to startle her.

He clears his throat.

She does not turn.

He kneels down and hugs her.

She feels his presence and leans into him.

They sit in silence; each feels the other's heartbeat. She squeezes both of his hands in hers. Then Megan drags the back of her hand across her nose. Gabe rummages through his pocket for his white handkerchief.

"How could you leave her?" Megan asks. They sit on a graveled path in front of a gray and black speckled tombstone. It is one of many that dot the scenic grounds that were once a pasture, but have long since become a Jewish cemetery. Sacred ground.

They rock in concert, back and forth. "I know, baby. I feel the same way."

Glazed over eyes, an unseeing stare. She does not turn toward him. There is no anger, only words. "You don't know how I feel. If you did, you wouldn't be moving away from Mom."

He envelops her tighter. "I talked to God and he said Mom would understand. We can't stay here forever."

"Island Bluffs is so far from here. How'm I ever going to see her?"

The cemetery is a block away from their house. Megan passes it every day. She stops in most.

"You have your pictures," he answers. "And besides, you can drive here whenever you want. It's not as far as you think."

"Get real, Dad. Pictures are not the same. And driving here will not be that easy. After the summer, I've got school and all. I want to stay here, close to her."

With a gentle touch, he nudges her deeper into his embrace. They both arch forward, to be nearer to the stone. Father and daughter paying homage to wife and mother. "Honey, your mother's anywhere and everywhere you are. She knows how much you love her and how much you miss her, and she wouldn't want to see you sad like this."

"She doesn't want me to go. She told me so."

Gabe squeezes her tighter. "Don't you think I miss your mother every day of my life? I do. Just like you do. But she would want both of us to go on with our lives, and that's what we're doing. This is something we both need to do."

"Fine for you to say, Dad. You've got Carly and whatever that thing is she's carrying. You'll be part of a big happy family again. Where does that leave me?"

He lifted her chin to face him. "Baby, you're part of this, too. Give it a chance. I never eliminated your mother from my life; it's just that it expanded with Carly in it. And Carly feels the same way about you. I know that for a fact."

He stands, takes a step, looks about, leans down and grabs a brown rock. He rolls it over in his fingers before placing it on the corner of the tombstone engraved with the Berk family name. He plants his lips on top of Emily's name.

Gabe extends his hand to Megan.

She takes it and wobbles to her feet.

He bends and snags another loose rock, and then grabs her hand and closes her fingers around it. He nods toward the polished, granite marker.

"C'mon, baby, it's time to say good-bye."

CHAPTER 7

Thursday, 11:54 a.m.
With Megan in tow, Carly and Gabe perform one last walk-through of the house. There is little the new owners can complain about once the cleaning service gives it a thorough once-over. The hardwood floors are in excellent shape; they still shine and do not need a new coat of polyurethane. The painted walls are unmarred save for picture hooks that dot the walls like flies. Carly leaves them in place because she is sure the new people will use them where they are. A couple of Formica edges are chipped in the kitchen. The bathrooms are surgical-room spotless. Though the tiles are in perfect condition and the grout is clean and white, Carly would understand the bathrooms being redone with more updated colors. Eisenhower-era pink and turquoise, suitable only for a Plymouth, do not cut it with today's decorating tastes.

Before driving away from their house for the last time and heading for Finley's office, Carly turns to Megan. "Want to come to the lawyer's? You could follow us in your car."

She wriggles her nose. "If there's a way to solve this quickly, dad will figure it out. No point in me being there. I'll follow the moving van. Wait for you there."

"Never know. You could be waiting a bit."

"My money's on dad. Maybe I'll drive through town. See what Island Bluffs is all about."

You may be disappointed

"That's a good idea," says Carly, feigning upbeat approval. "We'll call as soon as we're finished at the lawyer's."

Summer sights, sounds, smells, and tastes creep into the consciousness of all who adore the Jersey Shore: beach volleyball, strolls on the aged boardwalks from Cape May to Seaside Heights to Point Pleasant, foot-long hot dogs, salt-water taffy, blue- or rainbow-colored snow cones and pink cotton candy, the Garden State Parkway and Route 35 both clogged each weekend, the pounding surf, the hot, white burning sand, and the shrill, staccato toots from the lifeguards' whistles commanding swimmers not to venture too far from shore.

Midweek traffic? Not so much. That's why they picked a Thursday to move.

An image of her father-in-law pops back in her mind. "Do you think your father's there, yet?" Carly asks as they head to lawyer Finley's office.

"He never keeps anyone waiting. He's probably on the train as we speak."

"I still don't understand why he didn't sleep over last night and come with us today. It would've been so much easier for him. And we wouldn't have had to worry if he made it or not."

"You know how he is. He needs to say good-bye to his neighbors and friends in his own way. Look how long they lived in that apartment."

"Your mother died, what, close to fifteen years ago? He could've moved in with you then."

He turns to her. "It was sixteen years ago. My dad's a proud man. He wasn't ready to live with Emily and me back then. Megan was only one at the time. He needed to remain on his own. Besides he had a business to run. Now that it's getting harder for him to get around and he's been retired awhile, he caved in when I asked him to live with us. It's all about timing. How many more years does he have left anyway?"

She touches his arm. "Many, I hope. It'll be so good for him and Megan to get to spend more time together. That's going to be special." Carly's thoughts linger on how lucky Megan is that she still has a grandparent, and one who is about to live with her. Carly never knew any of her grandparents. One or two might have been alive to see her born, but they must've died soon after because she has no memory of them.

Gabe and Carly make it to Finlay's nondescript office in an hour. Gray carpet everywhere, desks from IKEA, and sea-faring pictures from Home Goods nailed to eggshell-white painted walls. As they walk in, Carly notes the sun damage etched into the secretary's face. Craters and gullies mark her face; crow's feet extend from her eyes in ripples.

"Mr. Finley is expecting you." Her voice is deep and raspy. Cigarettes and post-menopause.

Thursday, 2:45 p.m.

Yehuda Berkowitz stands under a picture that is too high to reach and impossible to read. In spite of his age, he maneuvers himself onto a plastic chair to get closer. Unlike the others—all photos—this is a curled newspaper clipping the color of singed custard cream.

A thirty-something officer approaches Yehuda. Long ago, Yehuda gave up estimating the age of anyone younger than himself. Why bother?

Yehuda talks out loud, aware that the officer is a few feet from him. "This says she's been missing since 1945." Yehuda removes the clear push-pins holding the clipping to the corkboard. "She must be dead by now," he looks at the officer with raised brows.

The policeman clears his throat. "Excuse me, sir. I can't let you stand on that chair. You might fall down and get hurt."

"That's okay, sonny. If I fall, it's my problem. Not yours. I'm not the suing type." He glances over his shoulder to make eye contact with the officer and then wags the clipping in the air. "I'm just reading this newspaper article. It's pretty old, you know."

"Let me help you down. Then you can finish the article." He extends his hand. Yehuda looks at it, measures the distance to the floor, and then reaches to take it. The officer cups his other hand around Yehuda's waist . . . just in case.

The officer explains. "Buck Hopewell was a sports star in our local high school. All-State football and baseball. He's a local hero of sorts. Served in the South Pacific." He points to the blurred picture in Yehuda's hand. "She was his girl. They were supposed to get married after the war."

"They never did get married, did they?"

The policeman shakes his head. "She went missing when her father's tug sank offshore. Everybody 'round here knows the story. The day he pops the question, she has to leave and help her father. Buck's left standing at the dock. They promise to get married as soon as the war's over, but it never happens. Poor Buck never even got a chance to clink glasses and celebrate with her."

"Must've been very hard on him."

"That's an understatement, mister. Broke the poor man's heart. He never got over it. Been single all his life."

"She's gone," says Yehuda. "Why keep the article up here with all the missing children?"

"She was a child herself. Barely seventeen. We leave it pinned up there in case Buck ever pays us a visit. In the early years, when we were in the old station down the road, Buck used to stop by pretty often. Long as he's alive, it'll be there for him to see any time he stops by. We wouldn't want him to see that we took it down. That's the least we can do for old Buck."

"The man sounds like an eternal optimist to me. Does he still expect her to show up one day?"

"'Course not," says the policeman. "Buck's one of the good guys. He's harmless. You'll see him scooting around town. Can fix anything. Still works at his age. For some doctor over in Lakewood. Handyman. Keeps the doc's clinic running real smooth-like."

The officer takes the clipping in one hand and grunts as he plants a leg on the chair. He steadies himself against the wall with his free hand. With the article replaced, he turns to step, sees Yehuda extending his hand, smiles, takes it and eases onto the floor.

Promising himself for the thousandth time to lose some weight, the officer faces Yehuda. "So, what can I do for you today?"

Finley looks up from a contract on his desk. "Gabe. Carly. Great to see you both."

"Maybe under other circumstances, Tom. Run it by me again. What's this all about?" asks Gabe.

Finley motions for them to take a seat. Each settles onto chairs Carly is certain came from Finley's dining room . . . or a flea market. The attorney's inner sanctum is no different from the outer one. White walls. White Levolier blinds. Uninspired mahogany desk with brown blotter bordered in gold leaf. Expensive pen set. Law degree from Fordham.

"Mr. Finley," says Carly, "our moving men will be arriving at the house any minute. How can there be a problem this late in the game? What happened at the closing?"

Finley has a full head of charcoal gray hair that is combed to the side. Overweight, with spider-web veins laced across his nose and cheeks,

Finley's face could be a poster-child for a Mardi Gras mask made to resemble W.C. Fields.

"I owe both of you an apology."

Carly squeezes Gabe's hand. *This is not good.*

Gabe doesn't give the lawyer a chance to explain. "Tom, nothing came up in the title search. We had an engineer's report. We know there are problems with this house and we've agreed to take it as is. So how can there be an issue?"

"The title to the house is clean. No liens or surprises. And the bank's relieved to get the asset off its books. There's no problem on that score, either."

"Then who or what blocked the closing?" asks Carly.

"The town."

"You'd think they'd be happy that someone's moving into that house after all these years of it being empty," she says. "It increases their tax roll."

"Don't misunderstand, they're thrilled that you bought the house."

Gabe leans forward. "Then where's the hiccup, if you can call it that? I'm not hearing any."

"They've rescinded the C of O."

Carly shoots a quizzical look at Gabe. He explains. "The Certificate of Occupancy."

"How can they do that now?" Carly asks. "Everything was checked out weeks ago. Our engineer gave it thumbs up. Even our architect was amazed that everything still worked after all these years."

"Verity Frizzell? I hear she's a good one," says Tom Finley. "Well, seems I was sitting next to the town's sanitation engineer at our monthly Rotary Club luncheon. Know the fellow for years. Straight-arrow type of guy. Never bends or stretches the code. Know what I mean? Takes his job seriously."

"How seriously?" Gabe asks.

Carly clears her throat. "Mr. Finley. Our moving men are waiting."

The lawyer purses his lips. He licks them. He looks away. He can no longer make eye contact.

"Seems I might have mentioned to him that your father's going to live with you."

Thick silence blankets the room.

"And . . ." Gabe prods.

"When he asked how many others, I said that there's Carly, you, and Megan, and that Carly's pregnant. That you'll be giving birth pretty soon. That would make five living in the house. Based on this new information, he felt obligated to revisit the site."

Gabe caught Carly's eye; no need to complicate matters by mentioning that Carly was carrying twins. What purpose would that serve but to stir up an issue that will disappear the moment she gives birth?

"You mean the house we're about to move into?" says Carly.

Finley nods. "When he recalculated, the septic system can't handle a family of four soon to become five. Personally I can't see what the big deal is, but he says you can't move in until it's changed."

"They can't be serious," Carly says.

"There's probably nothing wrong with it. Best that I've been able to ascertain," says Finley, "is that two people lived in it during World War II. Codes have changed since then. It won't take much to fix but, clearly, it can't be fixed in a day."

Gabe slams an open palm on the lawyer's desk.

Carly winces. *So much for Mr. Calm and there's a solution to every problem.*

"That's simply not acceptable, Tom. Every problem has a price. What will this take to go away?"

Again, Finley looks away. He stares through a window that opens onto a Burger King. "You're not getting it, Gabe." He looks to Carly for help, but she offers none. She doesn't understand what Finley expects her to say or do right now.

"What's there to get about buying an old house that hasn't been lived in for years, Tom?" Gabe's anger comes out in the way he articulates his lawyer's name.

"They don't want you here."

The words dangle in midair.

Gabe bolts up from the chair. He takes a step and then spins around, runs a hand through his thick hair.

"You just said they were thrilled to collect taxes on the property," says Carly.

"Is it because I'm a Jew? Is that what this is all about?" asks Gabe.

Finley manages a feeble laugh. It's weak. "That stuff doesn't exist here any more."

Any more.

"Old prejudices are like crab grass, Tom: the roots go deep. No matter how hard you try, you really never get rid of all of it. The Jersey Shore was always a hotbed for anti-Semitism," Gabe says. "I'm glad my father's not present to hear this bunk. It would kill him. He'd be thinking it was Nazi Germany all over again."

Now it's Finley's turn to stand; he's three inches shorter than Gabe. *Not a threat.* "That's uncalled for, Gabe. That was then. This is a nice town now. There's nothing more at stake than safety. *Your* family's safety. Build a bigger septic and you can move into town regardless if you pray to Buddha, Mohammed, or Moses. Who you are and what you believe in doesn't matter in Island Bluffs. As a card-carrying Mick, I can assure you of that."

Gabe backs up. He paces a few steps, and then spins around. "You just said they don't want us here. Now you're saying to fix the septic and everything will be okay. Which is it? Spit it out, Tom. Reality's tucked in there someplace, but I'll be damned if I can figure out what you're trying to say. What message does the town want us to hear?"

Carly sees the twitch in Finley's left eye. It goes rat-a-tat, rat-a-tat, tugging at the truth. She recognizes that he's mishandled this, that he hasn't communicated the real story. She's good at reading people dead . . . or those who are alive. Comes with the territory of being a forensic dentist. A female one, at that.

Carly doesn't wait for Finley to answer. "Tom, this is a high-risk pregnancy. We need to be close to my doctor so I can give birth in his clinic. That's why we're moving here, and that's why we're moving into this house today. No other option exists." She stands and pushes out her belly. "We want to do the right thing, just like everyone does, but the building inspector will have to get over his potty problem. We promise to fix this so-called problem in the coming weeks. Now before we go, are there any other issues we need to know about before we're on our way to let the movers into *our* new house?"

"But we haven't closed."

"We have the keys," says Carly. "You have power of attorney. Give the bank our money and get us the C of O and close this deal. In the meantime, we're moving in."

He starts to answer, but catches himself.

"What?" asks Gabe. "What aren't you telling us?"

Finley runs his manicured fingers through his thinning hair. "Just that there are rumors."

"Rumors about us?" asked Carly, rolling her eyes. *What sort of place is this Island Bluffs?*

"That the house isn't lucky. That's why it's been empty for so long."

"Is that the best you've got? I spend a good part of my life dispelling business rumors that do not intersect reality," Gabe says. "People create rumors. Some have an ulterior motive. Some are jealous. Some are just plain selfish. So if it's a rumor we should be worried about, Tom, I appreciate your concern but we're not worried."

"Have it your way." He extends his hand. "Don't say I didn't warn you."

CHAPTER 8

Thursday, 2:46 p.m.
Yehuda drops into the plastic chair. He folds his hands in his lap and, with lips upturned, engages the policeman, "You ask why I'm here? I'll tell you." In a fluid movement, he extends his hands outward, fists clenched. "I want you to take me into protective custody."

"You want me to 'cuff you?"

"Do I have to read you the manual? Of course I want you to handcuff me. That's how they do it on *Law and Order*."

The policeman nods as if he understands, slides into the seat next to Yehuda and says, "I get it. Some bad guys are after you. The Russian mob from Brooklyn? Maybe loan sharks from Atlantic City?" He scratches his head. "Drug dealers trying to move into your territory?"

Yehuda does not respond. He wiggles his extended arms, wrists facing each other, with impatience.

"Is that it? Did you stiff one of them on a payment?" The policeman turns to glance at the officer behind the desk, who can hear what they're saying, and stifles a smirk. "They can be really dangerous, you know."

"Do they teach you to be crazy when you're in that police academy? I'm serious," Yehuda says, "and you're making jokes."

The officer turns back to Yehuda. "I don't mean any disrespect, but you gotta admit it's kind of strange for a man such as yourself . . ."

"You mean a man as old as me."

"That, too. That you walk into the station asking us to protect you." He checks Yehuda's face and hands. "Don't see any marks. Someone abusing you, sir? Just say the word. We don't tolerate that sort of thing here. Not for a second."

"Focus, son. I'm getting older by the minute. I'm trying to tell you that it's my son and his new wife." Yehuda thinks for a beat. "She's not so new. Maybe six years. She's a *shiksa*. Do you know what that is?"

The policeman shakes his head.

"A gentile," says Yehuda. "Not one of the tribe."

The policeman puzzles over what Yehuda is saying.

"We're Jews; she's not. A *shiksa*. Capiche?"

"Is that bad? If she's the problem, want me to lock her up instead of you?"

A phone rings at the main desk; a distant voice answers it. The policeman turns his attention back to Yehuda, as if he is the most important person in the world.

Yehuda wags his finger. "When I was a young man, much younger than you are right now, soldiers marched into my town and took me away. They took my mother, my father, my brother, my two sisters, and everyone else in my neighborhood. They were all killed in the gas chambers. All except me. I was young. Strong. I finagled a way for those *momzers* to keep me alive. When the American soldiers found me, I was close to the end. What little food we ever got had run out."

He paused, his words transporting him back in time. The officer had the good sense to wait until Yehuda could continue.

"The Americans liberated us in the nick of time. When I got my strength back, I swore to protect the memories of each of my family that was lost, to honor them by never surrendering my dignity or freedom to another human being again. Not even to my son. I've managed to uphold that vow all these years. And now my son wants me to move here against my will."

"Island Bluffs is on the ocean. You'll like it. I'd live here if I could afford one of the houses in town. Too pricey on a cop's salary."

"What do I need an ocean for? I'm an old man. I need a room and a vegetable garden. Simple as that. No fancy, schmancy house by the shore."

"I'm sure they have a reason for having you move in with them. Think of it as a new beginning. You'll make new friends. And you'll be right across the bay from Ol' Barney. And the sea air's good for you."

"I know about your lighthouse. Very nice. I have a flashlight, thank you very much. Friends, you say? I'm an old man. There're not many left my age. And they're set it their ways. Crabby. Who wants to be around old farts?"

Yehuda could see from the policeman's expression that he was not used to an elderly citizen being so blunt. Yehuda enjoyed shocking someone new.

"Most folks have lived in Island Bluffs for generations. It's a tight community. Not like other places where the kids grow up and leave, slowly turning it into a ghost town. In Island Bluffs, when the children grow up, most want to stay or come back here. Not many leave. Makes for a nice little town. Keeps the real estate prices up, too."

Yehuda tilts his head.

There's a subtext in the policeman's words that has a faint ring of a time gone by. Yehuda doesn't explore their meaning. He knows what he meant was harmless, but he cannot ignore the feelings they stir in him.

What Yehuda senses does not bode well for Island Bluffs.

The policeman hands him his card. "How 'bout if I drive you to your new home?"

Yehuda stands. "If they kill me, don't say I didn't warn you."

Thursday, 2:07 p.m.

Leaving the lawyer's office, Carly phones the foreman. She's given him a key to the new house. "Start unloading." She glances from Gabe to the speedometer. She's anxious to get there so she can direct the men; she wills Gabe to drive faster.

She knows Gabe and his penchant for speed and doesn't need to say anything.

His head jerks down to the speedometer. "I know what you're thinking," he says. "Not worth getting a ticket." No sooner does he set the cruise control button to thirty-eight in a thirty-five MPH zone than Gabe glimpses a flickering in the rearview mirror. "Shit. Looks like we're getting an official greeting before we even move into the house."

Carly grabs her belly. *"Could anything else go wrong today?"* she asks herself. She finds an answer. *There is still time for a flat tire.* Only minutes in Island Bluffs, and her gut fears are being proven right: moving here was one big, gigantic mistake.

Gabe rolls to the edge of the narrow road. There are no sidewalks in Island Bluffs. A mix of sand, dirt, and bits of clamshells lines the street between the asphalt and a carpet of thick-bladed grass cultivated to survive in sea air.

The cop ambles to the driver's window without urgency; Gabe has his license, insurance card, and registration in hand. He tops the sandwich of documents with his PBA card. It is dark blue with the image of a police shield superimposed on the American flag. "We Will Never Forget" is printed across twin columns. The Trade Towers.

Gabe tries to see the man's eyes; they are hidden behind wrap-around dark glasses. The Island Bluffs uniform is military khaki. The brim on his hat is black patent leather, and his polished black boots rest high on the calves. Gabe can't help but notice the unclipped black gun case, the officer's right hand resting on the grip, his ample midsection protruding like a cushion, and the way he leans toward the open window, his left hand prepared to deflect a barrel pointed at him.

Gabe, in his best, non-lawyer's voice, says, "Gee, officer, can you tell me what this is about?"

"You were doing thirty-eight in a thirty-five." His voice is matter-of-fact. Jack Webb-like. Just the facts.

Is this some sort of parallel universe?

"I'm sorry for that, officer. It must have gotten away from me. The empty road and all. We *are* in a bit of a hurry. We just left our lawyer's office. Maybe you know him. Tom Finley. We're closing on a house today, and we're anxious to meet the movers."

"Finley? Good man." He studies Gabe's documents. "Wait here," he says, ignoring the Police Benevolent Association card.

Gabe shoots a furtive look at Carly; words are unnecessary. His look speaks volumes. *Not good.*

The officer punches Gabe's driver's license number into the onboard computer, writes up the stop, shuffles through some papers to make them wait longer, glances at the day's newspaper headlines, checks out the previous evening's baseball scores, and finally opens the cruiser's door.

Gabe watches him approach in his side mirror.

The policeman hands Gabe a ticket.

"Because you know Finley, I'm giving you a pass on a court appearance."

Hearing that the officer even contemplated issuing an order for him to appear before the local judge for a minor offense, if it could be even called that, causes Gabe's self-control to expire. "For friggin' three miles over the speed limit on a deserted street? What kind of town is this? And what about my PBA card? Doesn't that mean anything anymore?"

"You can't believe who's able to wrangle these PBA cards these days. Lawyers, dentists, even real estate agents. Not worth the plastic they're printed on."

"Every other cop in the state honors them," Gabe says.

The officer ignores that remark. "Just 'cause you're moving here doesn't mean you're one of us, Mr. Berk." Both Gabe and Carly noted the emphasis on the way the man pronounces Gabe's surname. The officer draws his right index finger to his cap brim. "Now you folks have a nice day and mind the speed limits, please. Next time, I won't be so generous."

Gabe's facial muscles pulse in ripples of anger.

Carly strokes the top of his right hand. "It's only a ticket. C'mon. We've got lots to do. And besides, I want to be there when your father shows up."

Gabe pulls into the driveway of their new house to find that the moving men have emptied the back of the truck of the smaller, more delicate things, and are now moving the bigger pieces into the house.

Carly finds a second wind and springs out of the car at a trot, as best a six-month pregnant woman hauling twins can shuffle about, and barks orders where each piece of furniture should be placed. The house, which sits on a rise that may have lent itself to the town's name, would have been swallowed inside the Pine Brook house with, literally, rooms to spare. Carly's challenge is not to clutter the rooms but leave only the pieces needed for the next few months. The rest will be stored until the addition is completed, which, if all goes according to plan, will be before she gives birth.

Birth.

Dream as she might, she never thought the day would come when she would ever conceive a baby. Too many problems said the doctors, discouraging her through the years, plus not the right fellas with which to even try. And now she was carrying two! Granted, the manner in which she arrived at this blessed state would make most uncomfortable, but Carly—and, in turn Gabe—was desperate, having exhausted every other reasonable option until meeting Dr. Teplitsky and agreeing to his unorthodox methods. For the most part, Carly was happy she had agreed to his conditions. For the most part.

For now, the movers get her full attention.

Carly tracks up the porch steps and enters the house, the green-painted screen door slamming behind her. The entranceway foyer is dark. She looks up. There is a capped off gas outlet in the ceiling. Not even an electrical box. She shakes her head. The house needs to be knocked down, not remodeled. What was Gabe thinking? Worse, yet, what was she thinking when she agreed to move here? Why did she leave Emily's house? It was a nice house. A sweet house. Haunted with someone else's memories, but nonetheless, a nice house. It was fine for the last six years, wasn't it? Given the choice right now, she'd welcome the ghost of Emily with open arms.

A fair-sized room sits to the right. It serves as the living room/den. Beyond it, a dark hallway leads to two bedrooms; the one on the left is the master bedroom. It's ample in size, fourteen-by-sixteen feet. It has its own bathroom with black and white square tiles, little ones, the kind found in French brasseries like Pastisse or Orsay in New York City.

The bathtub is the house's point of elegance. White porcelain on sturdy clawfoot legs. Six feet long. Good for soaking. A stainless steel pole erupts vertically from the front and then sprouts wings that encircle the tub, like a halo, five feet from the floor. There's a European nozzle sprouting from the main spigot. All that's missing is a shower curtain. This is good. So are the two windows on the far wall that face the ocean. With the decades of rain splatter and grime removed, the view is spectacular.

The other bedroom to the right is smaller, ten by twelve feet; it will be Megan's. When her bed is installed, there is barely enough room for a dresser. No room for a desk. The closet is too small for all her clothes. There's no bathroom for Megan. Either she shares Carly's and Gabe's or her grandfather's on the other side of the house. Neither is a good choice for a teenage girl who cherishes privacy. This is another reason to extend the house . . . to give Megan her own bathroom and a bigger closet, and to enlarge the master bedroom suite to include a larger bathroom, steam sauna, exercise room, and walk-in closets.

The dining room is to the left of the foyer. Tiny, tiny. She calculates in her head. Her polished brown mahogany table with the inlaid trim will fit in it, so will six of the chairs. Not all eight. Should they host a party, only an anorexic server could squeeze behind someone seated to dish out food. Forget the leaves that extend the table to seat eighteen. No parties in this house until Verity Frizzell does her magic. More about the noted architect later.

At the far side of the house, where the dining room and kitchen meet, a small hallway branches off. To the ocean side is a peach-tiled bathroom, with a tub/shower and a study that will be turned into Yehuda's room. At the end of the hall is a door that exits to the side of the house.

As is most of the house, the kitchen is from a bygone era. The appliances, the gas stove, the pint-sized refrigerator, all once white, are now yellowed from smoke and time. A wooden table sits in a nook. This is surprising. It's made from honey-colored pine and seats twelve. Carly is curious why so big? Supposedly two people lived here. At least that's what Finley was able to learn. Allegedly a married couple with no children. Later, Carly will find this was not the case.

The kitchen sink is deep, deeper than most. It sits under a window that faces the sea. The spigot is dull pewter. The knobs have white enamel centers similar to those found in showers. "Hot" and "Cold" are imprinted on them. Opposite the lone kitchen window with its unfettered view of Barnegat Bay and Ol' Barney in the distance, are two wooden doors on the back wall. One leads to the basement, the other to the attic stairs.

Carly will not explore either now. She knows from Gabe that the attic is a single room, empty, with a lone window facing the front yard and driveway. Not much of a view. Luggage and a box or two will be stored there until the construction begins.

As for the basement, Gabe told her about a few benches stacked against one wall, a row of hooks with some slickers dangling from them, a chest against one wall, and few pine doors that he didn't bother to open. The key for him, he said, was that the basement appeared dry. She can only imagine creepy things lurking down there, things that Stephen King best describes. Carly can root around the guts or brain case of a corpse, but spiders and crawly things give her a case of the heebie jeebies.

Out back, the ocean view grabs Gabe the way the Sirens called out to sailors. He stands on the bluff and draws in a deep breath, filling his lungs with salt air. Clean air. Purifying air. He exhales. Can't let a stupid speeding ticket bother him. He pulls out his new iPhone 2 and taps Safari to find a company that can rectify the septic tank. He never thought to see if there was cell phone service on the point. He assumed there was. There isn't. "Great," he mutters to himself. Maybe Carly was right, he was too impetuous in insisting they buy this house.

Thursday, 3:16 p.m.
A motor ruffles the air; a car rumbles up the driveway. Gravel, mixed with crushed shells, crunches. Gabe turns and heads to the front of the house. He moans when he sees a black-and-white. Why would the cop who gave him the welcome-to-Island-Bluffs ticket be here now?

Gabe freezes mid-step.

Same insignia, different cop.

Yehuda exits the passenger door. The police officer hops out and retrieves the black carry-on luggage. Gabe notes how his father and the cop shake hands. The officer waves to Gabe, Gabe offers a feeble "Hi" in return, and then the officer retreats to his vehicle and reverses out the driveway. Dust and loose gravel fly up as his wheels spin backwards.

Gabe trots to his dad. The men hug and kiss each other on the cheek. "What was that all about?"

"Community relations."

"Dad, I haven't been in this town more than twenty minutes, but I know that's a crock of baloney. Did something happen to you? Did you get lost? Is that it?"

Yehuda waves him off. "Nothing like that. When I got off the train, I was looking for a cab and saw the police station and thought it would be a nice gesture to stop in and introduce myself."

Gabe screws up his face in disbelief. "And there's a bridge in Brooklyn I want to sell you."

"What? You don't believe me?"

"Should I?"

"Truth is I needed to vent."

"About what? At least you're making sense now, though I still can't imagine what the heck you are trying to say."

"I resented being made to come here. To live with you and Megan, and Carly."

"You could've said no."

"I didn't want to hurt your feelings."

"My feelings would not have been hurt. I thought it was best for you. Safer. There are all those muggings in your neighborhood."

"It's not that bad."

"Not if you're a black belt or carry mace. What about all the fresh air? More time with Megan. And here you'll have that garden you always wanted."

"I realized all that the moment I walked into the police station and looked at those faces?"

"The prisoners? How many were there?"

"No. The missing children. That's when I realized I was being completely silly. A chance to live with my family. I am the lucky one . . . and I got to meet that nice, young officer."

"Seems your introduction to this town was way better than ours." Gabe tells Yehuda about the ticket and the problem with the septic.

"Haven't I always taught you to be nice to everyone you meet? That's been my motto and look what happens? I get the royal treatment with a police escort to my new house. That just didn't happen because I'm adorable."

Gabe notes that Yehuda's emphasis on *his new house*. "I know, Dad. Kill 'em with kindness. I get it."

"Then what's the trouble?" asks Yehuda.

"Did I say there was any trouble?"

Gabe didn't have to; one look at the house and Yehuda sensed a passel of aggravation lurking under that weathered wood. Yehuda grabbed the handle of his carry-on. "Are we going to stand out here all day? Show this old man to his room. It's time for my nap," he said with a wink and the widest grin.

Hearing those words gave Gabe comfort.

CHAPTER 9

Monday, 7:45 a.m.
After spending the weekend cleaning cabinets, lining shelves, opening most boxes, and putting clothes away, Carly is anxious for her appointment with Dr. Teplitsky. She arrives late. What is supposed to take twenty minutes from Island Bluffs to Lakewood takes forty-five. The GPS takes her along Central Avenue, where she hits every red light. In time, she will learn which roads to take. For now, she turns off Central onto Lapsley Lane. She turns left on South Lake and pulls into the lot adjacent to the clinic entrance. The clinic is on one side of the lot; the doctor's house is on the other.

Teplitsky owns all the land between Lapsley and Myrtle Lane. The main structures face Lake Carasaljo. Lake Carasaljo is a man-made lake in the center of town created by damming a northern tributary of the Metedeconk River back in 1883. The lake was named after Joseph Wooston Brick's three daughters: Caroline, Sally, and Josephine. Brick, for whom the nearby Brick Township is named, owned the Bergen Iron Works. Pop folklore, verified by E Street Band drummer Vini Lopez, says that Lake Carasaljo was part of the basis for Jersey's local hero, Bruce Springsteen's, song, "Greasy Lake." In the song, Greasy Lake is located a *mile down the dark side of Route 88*, just as Lake Carasaljo is. One more Garden State tale. As a New Yorker, Carly lets Jerseyans have their pride any way they can find it. Even their professional football teams—the Giants and the Jets—don't have the moxie or desire to embrace their state of residence, this after playing for decades in the Meadowlands.

Carly makes her way to the clinic. She notes the wooden umbilicus, a long covered walkway, dotted with a dozen hanging pots overflowing with red begonias that connects the clinic to the main house. It's a grand old Victorian house, replete with a wrap-around porch. The porch, with its wide floorboards that creak with every step, is highlighted by a glistening white railing supported by thick spindles the size of overgrown piano legs. There's a hammock tied to posts at the end of the porch. Flowerpots hooked to the railing bubble over with a riot of impatiens and zinnias— oranges and purples and pinks and lavenders—rimmed by ringlets of asparagus ferns.

Dr. Teplitsky's house, just from the outside, is a display of charm and taste, in stark contrast to the house Carly has just moved into. She cringes at what she will find when she returns home. Then she thinks of Gabe and how happy the house makes him. She remembers meeting the architect and discussing how the addition will address the house's shortcomings. She feels better about their shack by the sea, picturing not how it is now, but how it will turn out in the end. And by then, it will include their new baby.

Carly stops. Strains of music waft out an open window. Mendelssohn's "*Sonate Écossaise*," his Fantasia in F Sharp Minor, Op. 28. She knows the piece because her mother insisted she take piano lessons through her high school graduation from Francis Lewis High School in Fresh Meadows, NY. It was important to her mom, a waitress in a local diner, that Carly take piano lessons. Shirley Mason's daughter would have culture. Carly smiles. Her mom would pronounce it as two words, "Cul tschure," with emphasis on the second. Piano was a constant battle. Her mom wanted her to audition for Juilliard; Carly would have none of it.

"Watch your step, Miss," says a craggy-faced handyman atop an aluminum ladder. She's noticed him before, but never exchanged pleasantries. His name is Buck Hopewell. Afterwards, when Carly tells Yehuda about Buck, his name registers: Buck Hopewell is the one whose girl went missing eons ago.

Buck balances on a ladder. He squirts an aqua-colored cleaning fluid on one of four glass panes to remove bits and pieces of bugs and moths splattered on the former gas lamp now converted into a post light. A new energy-saving bulb rests in the well of the red plastic ledge designed to hold a can of paint. He is swapping out the incandescent bulbs on each of the outdoor fixtures that surround the clinic.

Buck wears faded denim jeans. A red handkerchief, the type ascribed to train engineers, is draped from his back right pocket. Though faded from years of use, Carly notes that it is ironed.

The handyman is particular, with routines that will not vary. Buck lives in Lakewood now, in what was once a barn. Part of it serves as his tool shop. But Buck didn't always live there; he was born in Island Bluffs eighty-two years earlier. He lived in the small village on the shore until the end of his junior year in high school.

* * *

June 23, 1943

"Son, you know the rules. Got to be eighteen to enlist," says the sergeant at the recruiting center in Toms River. "Things not bad enough to send babies to fight the Krauts and the Japs. Least not yet."

"By the time I'm old enough to fight, sir, the war'll be over," answers young Buck. As a teen, Buck, an all-star athlete, is six-feet and one hundred eighty pounds of pure muscle. "I can shoot better than any recruit you ever signed up. And I'm way big enough. You gotta let me join, mister. I told my friends I was going . . . and I got to go now."

The sergeant leaves him standing there for a few minutes and then returns.

"Parents alive?" asks the recruiting officer.

"My mom is. Father split. Hopped a train west. Wanted to be a hobo. Never heard from him again."

"You got a brother or sister?"

"Younger brother."

"Is he planning to enlist, too?"

Buck shifts his weight from one foot to the other. "Shucks, sir, he's only twelve."

"Is he big enough to help your mom?"

An ear-to-ear erupted across Buck's gaunt face. "My brother's near big as me now, sir. Anything happen to me, he'd be able to take care of my mom without a problem."

"You realize what you're saying, son? That if I let you in, there's a chance you won't be coming back."

Buck wins the lottery. True to his word, his shooting skills qualify him as a marksman. While most privates able to shoot the eyelids off a charging bull are sent to the infantry, Buck's ability to fix anything mechanical does not go unrecognized; he is assigned to ordnance. He spends his first year in the army stationed in Hollywood where movie stars are only too happy to do their patriotic duty and pick up hitchhiking soldiers. Joseph Cotton. Dana Winters. Richard Widmark. Buck hitches rides with them and others. And all the while he's stationed in California, he writes to his special girl at home.

Nineteen-forty-five dawns. Each day brings encouraging news. In early January, the U.S. Sixth Army invades Lingayen Gulf on Luzon in the Philippines. A couple of weeks later, the Burma Road is reopened. The following week, early February, the vaunted Sixth Army attacks the Japanese in Manila. Bataan is recaptured. Fighting is furious. Guns break down and need quick repairs. Buck gets his orders: he will ship out to New Caledonia the following week. He is given three days furlough. While he makes his way back east to see his girl, his mother and his brother, the U.S. Marines invade Iwo Jima.

* * *

"You must be real happy that the doc's able to help you, Miss." Carly drifts past the ladder and mounts the first of two limestone steps leading into the clinic. There's a ramp for wheelchair access alongside the white stucco clinic wall.

She turns to Buck and says, "Isn't everyone who walks through these doors a happy camper?"

"Most are. But he isn't able to help all of 'em. You're a lucky girl, that's all I'm saying." Her bulging belly broadcasts a Teplitsky success.

Carly pauses a pulse, cocks her head, thinks, agrees with her own thought, steps back down with care, and angles towards him. "Forgive me for being bold, but I've seen you before and don't know your name."

Buck climbs down the aluminum stepladder and wipes his brow with his ever-present red engineer's bandana-cum-kerchief. He tells her.

"Well, Mr. Buck Hopewell," says Carly, "We're new in town. Over in Island Bluffs."

He interrupts. "Raised there myself. Long time ago. Which house you buy?"

"The old one on the point. Facing the lighthouse. Near Barnegat Beach Drive."

He removes the beige baseball cap that has a jumping blue sailfish stitched onto the emblem above the bill. It's as crisp and spotless as the day he bought it ten years earlier. He scratches his hair, once sandy-brown, now thinning and wavy white.

"The one off High Tide Drive. At the end, to the left?"

"You know it?"

"It's been empty's long as I can remember."

"We got it for a good price."

"Well, if you need any help fixing things, I'm your man."

"We actually do, but for now, I need your help of a different sort."

"Oh?" He takes out a stick of Juicy Fruit gum, unwraps it, and then remembers to offer her a piece. She shakes it off.

"I'd like to introduce you to my father-in-law. You're about the same age. It's tough on him moving to a new place and not knowing anyone. You'd like him. What do you say? Can you come around one day? Have some coffee or a beer?"

Buck's eyes twinkle. Carly has hit a chord. Most people march past Buck as if he doesn't exist. Pay no mind to who he is or what his story might be. All they see is that he's old. They probably think the same about Yehuda, too, and other folks their age.

"Can he play chess?"

"I believe he plays a decent game of chess. Consider yourself warned."

"That's a plus. How 'bout this coming Saturday?"

"I believe his dance card is open that day, Mr. Buck Hopewell. I am sure he will look forward to meeting you."

He tips his head toward her with a slight salute and a toothy smile. For the rest of the day, Buck experiences a bit of lightness to his steps.

CHAPTER 10

Monday, 8:40 a.m.
Inside the clinic, a middle-aged nurse, stocky, and as curt as her starched white uniform, points to the "sign-in" sheet. "Be sure to include your arrival time," she tells Carly. She then adds, "I assume you moved closer to the clinic and may have had a hard time judging the traffic early in the morning. This isn't the hick town it used to be."

"I thought I left plenty of time. I will be better prepared for my next visit."

"That would be appreciated." The nurse reviews Carly's chart and leans forward, speaking in a whisper. "We expected you a few weeks ago. At the beginning of your last trimester. The doctor isn't pleased."

"We had to wait for my stepdaughter to finish her junior year of high school. I am certain the doctor will understand. What's important is that I am here now."

"He likes his patient to do what they are supposed to do."

Carly knows the type: pedagogical. Demanding. Controlling. Likes to chastise others because it makes her feel superior. Carly chooses not to challenge but instead, signs the patient register. There's a lone patient in the reception area, sitting off to the side, wearing flats, legs firmly planted, reading *Parents Magazine*. The chairs are wide and comfortable, upholstered in a teal print stretched over a wooden frame. Danish style. An aquarium mounted into the far wall coos comforting sounds. Carly marches in front of it. For a few moments, Carly is absorbed as the zebra fish dart about, and then blue and yellow fish emerge, followed by a pink angelfish. Bubbles float to the top and burst. This makes her smile. She parks herself to the woman's right, three chairs removed.

"It's very reassuring," says the woman in the corner, referring to the aquarium. Carly doesn't hear her at first. The woman clears her throat. "Is this your first?" she asks.

Carly looks towards her. As a reflex, she puts her right hand on her swollen belly. "Yes." She sees that the woman is earlier in her pregnancy. "And you?"

"Second time. I never thought I would have even one. Now look at me." She had the slightest of baby bumps.

In the beginning, Carly was so happy to be pregnant that she didn't let her rational brain ask questions that deep down inside she knew to ask after getting onboard the Teplitsky baby train. For Carly, bliss trumped logic. Of late, submerged questions she should have asked long ago were now beginning to surface.

"Excuse me, what are you expecting?"

"Another boy."

"Just one?" Carly asks.

"Thank God it's only one." The woman raises a brow that is still limited by the effects of her last series of Botox injections before she found out she was pregnant. "My first is quite the little buster. Gets into everything. You know the type." *I don't now, but I will.* The woman hugs her barely bulging belly. "This one's a bonus, even if he is a boy. Don't know if I'm going to press my luck again. Dr. T's a genius. What about you? What are you having?"

Carly doesn't hear her. She had assumed that Dr. Teplitsky's quirky arrangements were imposed on all of his high-risk patients. When he proposed it to her, she reluctantly agreed.

* * *

"What do you mean an extra baby?" Gabe asks at the consult. "Twins would be fine . . . I guess."

Carly remains silent. *That's not what the doctor means.*

Dr. Teplitsky removes his glasses and lowers his head; his eyes bulge, frog-like, displaying more white.

"Just the way it sounds," says Dr. Teplitsky. "I will help get Carly pregnant and, in return, she will thank me by carrying a second baby."

"I got it," repeats Gabe, "twins."

Carly eases her hand on top of Gabe's. "Not exactly, honey." She faces the doctor. "You want me to be a surrogate for another baby. Isn't that it?"

"Was that so difficult to understand?"

"Why?" she asks the doctor.

Gabe jumps in. "I missed that. Are you saying you want her to carry someone else's baby? No way. We didn't even consider a surrogate for ours. It was offered, you know, but I wouldn't hear of it. Now you are suggesting the only way we can have our own biological child is for Carly to carry someone else's? That's preposterous. I won't do it."

The doctor continues to stare at Carly. "What do *you* want?"

"I want a baby," she says in hushed tones.

"Then it's settled." He slaps his knee. "One for you and one for me."

Gabe stands. Runs his hand through his hair. "Hold on there. It's not settled by a long shot." He turns to Carly. "There are two of us here. Carly, what do you really want?"

"I want a baby, and if this is the price I have to pay, then I am willing to do it. It won't affect you."

"But it will be someone else's," Gabe's voice is higher pitched, exasperated.

She faces him and takes a hand. "What choice do I have?" She lowers her gaze. "We have?"

"Plenty."

"No, Gabe. It's my body and I'm going to agree to this." She turns to the doctor. "When do we start?"

"Not so fast," says Gabe, risking Carly's ire. "If you're not going to ask the question, I have to."

"Which is?" asks the doctor.

"Assuming we go through with this, what will happen to this other baby?"

"Nothing you wouldn't want for your own child."

"I don't know what that means," says Gabe.

"It means that the doctor will take good care of this baby, nurture it, make sure that it has a good life," says Carly.

"Is there a Mrs. Teplitsky?" asks Gabe.

"In a manner of speaking."

"That's not really an answer."

"It will have to do for now."

"And where will this child live?"

"In my house, of course." Gabe starts to ask another question. Teplitsky interrupts. "Let me reassure both of you that nothing nefarious is going on here. Without getting into personal details, I lost my family many years ago. I promised myself that if I ever had the means to have a family again, I would. That is all I am asking of you, to help create my new family."

Carly turns to Gabe. "See. It's for a good cause. Let's not be selfish and help the doctor. After all, think of what he will be doing for us in return. It's only fair."

Teplitsky seizes the moment. "There are papers to sign and then we can get right to it. I need to state the obvious."

"Which is?" says Gabe.

"You will never see the baby you are carrying for me. The moment it is born, it will be taken away." His face softens and the corners of his eyes crease to reflect a countenance of delight. "Of, course, you will be left with your little Berk."

"How will you know which is which?" Gabe's voice is halting. Unsure.

"From their genes. But there will be other obvious characteristics."

"Such as?"

"Hair color."

"Wait a second. You know what they're going to look like already?"

"I do mine."

It takes a moment for both Carly and Gabe to process this. *I do mine.*

"You've done this before?" asks Carly.

He nods.

"How many times?" Gabe wants to know.

"Enough to know what I am doing."

Once outside the clinic, Gabe grabs Carly's elbow, more to display moral support than to get her attention. "The last thing Teplitsky said was that he knows what he is doing. Do you?"

She pulls her arm free. "How can you ask me that question? My back is against the wall." Tears well up in her eyes. She wipes them away with the back of her hand. "It's now or never. Now that he's given us a glimmer of hope, you're having second thoughts. That's not fair."

"Who is talking fair? He just threw us quite the curveball. I didn't sign up for us to have someone else's baby."

Carly gently touches his arm. "What does that change for us? We will still have our baby." She shrugs. "And the other one? I'm okay with doing him that favor."

"Really? You can be that nonchalant about carrying someone else's baby? What troubles me is that we don't actually know what he is going to do with the baby. Or whose it really is. I'm not comfortable with any of this."

"You heard him; the baby will be his."

Gabe starts to say something else.

Carly puts her fingers to her lips. "No more. If this is the price we have to pay to have our baby, then we are doing it. Now, do you have anything else to add?"

Gabe knows her resolve, knows her mind is made up, and knows when to join the team. "I guess not."

* * *

Speaking with this woman, Carly wonders why she is not part of this two-for-one baby deal. What makes Carly so special and not the other woman? For that matter, is being special in Dr. Teplitsky's eyes a good or bad thing? Should she be worried? For all his squawking in the beginning, Gabe has made peace with her "predicament," and now that he's been onboard for half-a-year, he would be the first one to tell her that she is being ridiculous when she second-guesses her decision to help Dr. Teplitsky and carry a second baby for him.

At the moment, tiny regrets seep into the fabric that has cloaked her since she was a small girl, into the tapestry of having a baby. That tapestry of motherhood was fast turning into cheesecloth.

Carly looks down and answers the woman, "Two."

Gabe opens one of the remaining boxes, half-pleased he no longer needs to commute into Manhattan to work. The other half of him wishing he were anywhere else but in a new house opening cartons and trying to figure out where to put things. Helping is one thing; doing woman's work is quite something else. Men bash nails. They squeeze pliers, use wire cutters, and break down cartons with razors. Putting kitchen stuff away? Not his pay grade, but he is willing to try if it makes it easier for his wife.

After the movers leave, he and Carly fill the armoire and dresser with essentials: his underwear, her lingerie, tee shirts, shorts, pajamas, etc. The master bedroom closet is minuscule, about the size of a foyer coat closet.

Gabe leaves it empty for Carly to use. The movers leave clothing boxes, large cardboard rectangles with a metal bar across the top. They will use these for their clothes until the addition is built with the large his-and-hers walk-in closets.

There is adequate room to put away most of the dishes and silverware; it is left to Gabe to wrestle the pots and pans into whatever space he's able to find or create in wall-mounted cabinets made of thick pine with equally thick white paint. He tries to snake a cookie tray alongside a huge stainless pot when he hears a knock on the door. The tray is half in and half out. Wedged. Gabe leaves it that way, positive that sawing a person in half would be easier than stashing away this tray.

He pushes the patched screen door open. "I take it you're not the Welcome Wagon, are you?" says Gabe.

The man standing in front of Gabe is five-seven, weighs about a buck-fifty. He wears faded jeans and a mustard-yellow short-sleeve shirt that has a white plastic pen liner in his breast pocket. His hands are stashed into his pockets. His scuffed cowboy boots—the leather cracked in shades of brown—are inlaid with swirls of a filigree pattern; he rocks on his heels. A cell phone and walkie-talkie are attached like barnacles to his belt that is crowned with a large silver buckle that brandishes crossed pistols.

"No, but you want me to be your friend," says the man in a matter-of-fact tone.

"And you are?" Gabe nods to encourage an answer.

"The town's building inspector."

"And I am Gabe Berk." He extends his hand; the stranger ignores it.

"I know who you are, Mr. Berk. That's why I'm here."

"I'm getting the feeling that's not a good thing."

"Not when you ignore your lawyer. I inspected your house last week and your septic's not up to code. Needed to rescind the C of O 'cause of it. Without a C of O, you can't live here. You folks have to vacate the premises immediately until it's corrected. I trust that won't be too much of an inconvenience?" he says with a straight, narrow face that Gabe would like to rearrange. Flatten his nose. Pin back the ears. Square the chin. Needed cosmetic corrections.

Gabe is stunned. What kind of town is this? He runs his hand through his hair. He does that when he needs to buy time or think through a problem. Of late, he's been doing it more and more.

"Let's start over. I'm Gabe Berk." He extends his hand again. "What's your name?"

Again, he doesn't take it, but answers, "Steve Freiberg."

"That's better," says Gabe. "Tell you what I'm going to do, Steve Freiberg. Since I can't imagine that the system will back up into the house in just a few days, how about if I make you a promise that three weeks from today, we will have a proper-sized septic. In that way, you'll be doing your job and we get to stay here and straighten out the mess. You know, we're getting ready to have a new baby."

Steve grunts. The mention of babies does nothing to warm the cockles of his heart. "Better make it four weeks. Can't start without a permit and that will take some doing. Need engineering plans to get it issued. See what I can do for you. But four weeks. Not a day more." No smile, no flicker of kindness.

Gabe imagines Freiberg would feel the same running over a squirrel in his car: both give him pleasure.

Gabe bites his lower lip. What was he thinking moving into this town? Whatever happened to the concept of welcoming new neighbors? A casualty to the techno-age we live in? Or is this behavior limited to Island Bluffs?

"Why the quick change of heart? First you want us to vacate, and then you give us a month. What gives?"

"I'm not a prick, Berk. I'm a reasonable man as long as you don't try to buy me off or bend the rules. You passed the Freiberg straight-arrow litmus test. Ergo, you get a four-week pass."

"I'll get it done, Steve. I promise. Thank you."

"Promises mean nothing. And don't thank me 'til it's approved, Berk." With that, Steve Freiberg spins on his three-inch heels and returns to his royal blue Ram 1500 truck. Gabe can't help but notice the shotgun mounted to the outside above the plate glass window behind the driver's seat.

It's Monday morning. Carly has left for an early doctor's appointment. Megan's father is talking to some jerk at the front door; she is drinking a can of chocolate Slim Fast for breakfast. She knocks on Yehuda's door and finds him gripping an antique silver picture frame. It's his wedding picture. "Grandpa? Did you hear any strange noises last night?"

Yehuda holds it out. "Do you remember your Grandma? She loved you so much."

"I would like to, but I was like one-year old when she died. Remember, Grandpa?"

He doesn't answer right away; he's caught in a vortex of his own memories. She waits until he is ready to speak. "She used to hold you and sing until you laughed from your belly. Don't you remember that? You laughed so hard that you made us tear up from happiness."

Megan shakes her head. "And mom's parents died before I was born." She hugs him. "You're the only grandparent I've ever known or can remember." She plants a kiss on his cheek.

"It's a shame you didn't have a chance to know your mother's mother. Juliette. She was an art teacher and very talented. She was a good woman. A tough nut to crack, but when you did, there was a heart of gold inside her. She was strong and loving, just like Emily was."

Megan sniffles and dabs the corner of her eyes. "I know," she whispers. "Mom used to talk about Grandma Juliette. She sounded so cool."

"I think there's a little bit of her in you, too." Then he quickly adds, "Besides, of course, your mother and father."

They hold each other, lost in their own thoughts, remembering loved ones when bars of music blare out. They startle. Megan jumps up. She and Yehuda crane their necks; the notes appear to erupt from beyond Yehuda's room. Megan steps into the hall, slips into the kitchen, cocks her head to listen. Nothing is plugged in that could make music. She knows everyone's ringtones, and it wasn't any of them.

Her father is still talking to the man on the porch, nothing melodious coming from that direction.

She returns to Yehuda's room.

"What was that?" Megan asks.

"Did you leave music on in your room?" asks Yehuda.

She yanks her iPod from her jeans and waggles it in front of him. "It's off."

"Then where did it come from?"

She shrugs. "Outside?"

"We're too far from the street to hear music from a car," says Yehuda.

"Maybe a passing boat?"

"It is definitely from inside the house," he says.

Another burst of music, this time louder, fills the room. They stare at each other, wide-eyed. "Should I be scared?" she asks.

Yehuda blows out a stream of stale air and pats the top of her head, his eyes darting furtively about the room. "Not yet."

The musical outburst confirms the energy force Yehuda sensed the moment he climbed out of the policeman's car and stepped toward the house. Electric tentacles pulsed, sending a chill though his body in spite of the day's heat. On that day, he looked about but saw nothing out of the ordinary. He didn't have to see it. He felt it. The fact that no one else seemed aware of—he didn't know what to call it—the same arc of energy, didn't matter. Now, only a few days later, he remains uncertain if what he sensed—and now, what he has heard—is either harmless or something they need to beware of. Not every source of energy is positive. He should know. He's experienced enough negativity in his life.

Maybe that's why this house has been vacant for years.

If his inborn radar were right, it would explain much of what he senses.

He hopes he is wrong.

CHAPTER 11

Monday, 9 a.m.
It's Carly's turn to be examined. She slips into an institutional-colored green paper gown. The nurse, who is from the Philippines, takes her weight, checks her blood pressure, draws enough blood to check for anemia, glucose levels plus analyze a routine panel of other tests, and when done, leaves a plastic jar for a urine sample. Three months earlier, at the beginning of her second trimester, Carly's anxieties peaked when the quad marker screen was performed to test for risk factors for neural tube defects and genetic diseases such as Down syndrome. While not a diagnostic test, the quad marker screen takes the pregnant mother's age, ethnicity and family history into consideration and determines the likelihood that certain problems may be present in the fetus. Carly could hardly breathe until she heard that Dr. Teplitsky had few concerns about anything that could be wrong with either fetus.

Carly lies down on the white paper; it crinkles. Even though it is early summer and mild outside, not humid the way it can be, the air conditioner is on high. The tiny hairs on her arms prickle from the cold. She shivers.

The nurse performs an EKG. Carly searches her eyes for a sign that something might be wrong. Nothing registers. Carly is relieved.

Carly's breaths grow a bit shallow as the nurse reaches for the tube of jelly. She is glad the nurse puts the tube in a machine that warms the goo before oozing it onto her belly. The nurse works the wand this way and that, up and down, then to the sides, until she has all the images Dr. Teplitsky will need.

"One more thing," says the nurse. She motions Carly to put her feet in the stirrups. Carly eyes the nurse extract a long cotton swab from a sterile packet and duck down; she feels her swabbing the vaginal area.

"What's that for?" Carly asks, her fists clenched.

"Making sure there's no group B strep. Doesn't harm the mother but not good for the baby." She corrected herself. "Babies."

"The doctor will be with you shortly." No smile. No words of comfort. The nurse pivots on white rubber souls that squeak and leaves Carly—with her thoughts—staring at the ceiling. She props up on her right elbow and then wriggles to a sitting position.

Not sixty seconds pass and Dr. Teplitsky saunters into the room only to find Carly reading her chart. Saunter is not the correct word. Dragging a lame left leg is more accurate. He speaks with a soft accent. Carly cannot place it. Polish? Yiddish? German? His intonations are similar to Yehuda's, but not quite.

"And how are you, today?" His voice is forced, as if each word is shaped, measured and squeezed through a strainer for uniform texture.

The doctor is short. His curved spine makes him even shorter and appear to round at the waist. His pupils are different colors. *Heterochromia iridum*. The left eye is deep and beautiful, almost violet; the right eye is a pale turquoise. Carly is uncertain if he can see out of that eye.

"Truth be told, I'm exhausted from moving into our new house." The air is sterile, the room cold to an extreme. Arms crossed, she rubs the exposed flesh to create friction. Get her blood circulating. She expects her words to dangle above her and jingle like frozen bell chimes in the wind.

He frowns.

"It's important not to strain yourself at this stage. Think of this as the last leg of the Tour de France. You want to finish in grand style."

"Is there a chance I won't?" Carly's smile turns into a fake grimace.

"Not at all. Your vitals are excellent. No anemia at this stage. Considering you're carrying two, that's remarkable."

She wants to ask him a boatload of questions that nag to be asked, that need answers . . . but waits.

The nurse reappears at the door, more of a witness than assistant.

He studies the sonogram.

Dr. Teplitsky warms the stethoscope in the palm of his hand; she is sitting on the exam table with her feet dangling down. He asks her to take in a deep breath and places the chest piece against her skin. Hold it. Again. He lifts the paper gown, and places the diaphragm on her back. Another deep breath.

He motions for her to lie down.

He places it on all sides of her belly.

He checks for swelling in the ankles.

As if choreographed, with no words or even the slightest nod of a head that she could note, the nurse approaches and guides Carly's legs back into the stirrups.

"Is everything all right?" Carly asks Dr. Teplitsky.

She struggles to hear the doctor's clipped speech; it is crisp and precise, but not easy to discern. "Checking to make certain the cervix is strong. Wouldn't want those little fellas to pay us a visit too early, now would we?"

When he finishes, he asks her to dress and meet him in his office.

The office is light. Pale blue walls. From the window behind his high-backed leather chair, Carly glimpses Carasaljo Lake. There's nothing on his desk. No mementos. No family photos. No books. No files. No papers. Only a Mont Blanc pen and a note pad.

Where are the pictures of his sons? His wife?

The walls display diplomas. Harvard undergrad. Residency in obstetrics at Johns Hopkins. Fellowship in fertility at the University of Berne, Switzerland. Another fellowship at the Roslin Institute in Edinburgh where he trained Keith Campbell and Ian Wilmut, who would later gain fame when they cloned a sheep named Dolly. Another certificate for a third post-doc stint earned at Columbia Presbyterian.

There is a solitary picture.

The picture is of a serious man in a white lab coat. His eyes penetrate. He is smiling with teeth that snarl. He sports a shock of black hair. Carly thinks she has seen a picture of this man before. Not here. Elsewhere. In a magazine. A long time ago. It's a face she feels she should know but cannot place. In time, she will come to know who it is and why it hangs on the wall. If she could identify this man now, it would trigger an avalanche of questions that could only point to a singular conclusion: Teplitsky is not the man she thought he was. But she does not know to ask.

For now, Teplitsky is that man—the man who helped her conceive.

Dr. Teplitsky begins. "You are progressing beautifully." He places an amber-tinted jar in front of her. "These are multi-vitamins with a formula I have patented for my special patients." The doctor owns other patents. "Please take two per day. From here on in, those little fellows will be zapping more of your strength."

"They're already zapping me. Can I still exercise?"

"No jogging."

"Yoga? I feel better when I do it," says Carly.

"Not that Bikram stuff. The heat will raise your blood pressure too high. Stress the babies."

There's a knock on the door. A young boy enters, chart in hand. He's fourteen or fifteen. Carly can't be certain. His cheeks have a rose flush. Baby fat, yet a hint of muscles in his arms. Weight lifting. He has dirty blond hair that is surrendering to brown and a genuine smile when Dr. Teplitsky introduces him to her. "Here's the chart you requested, Father."

"Thank you Iario." The boy looks Carly in the eye and does not hesitate. "Pleased to meet you, Mrs. Berk."

How refreshing. A young gentleman.

The youth retreats. "When we first met, you were vague about your children. How many do you have?" Carly asks. She notes the age difference between father and son. At least sixty years. Maybe sixty-five. It could be more.

Carly studies Dr. Teplitsky. His skin is pale. Chalky. No sun for him. Liver spots colonize his face with scattered actinic keratoses on his cheeks and forehead. His eyes are a bit close together, his nose somewhat prominent and his hairline retreating, hidden by a slight comb-over. The more she looks, the more she is convinced he is similar in age to Yehuda. And to Buck.

"Ten."

This startles her. "What?" Her mind drifts from the question she asked about his children back to her concerns about carrying the extra baby. Her pulse grows rapid. Now is not the time to take her vitals.

He senses her surprise. "You asked how many children I have. I have ten. I love them all, but Iario is the most special."

She strains to focus. "Is he the oldest?"

"They're all between nine and fifteen, except Iario. He's sixteen."

Iario is short for his age, but she refrains from saying the obvious. "Same mother?" She knows the answer but has to ask.

"Different mothers. All like you." He engages her as he says this; he measures her reaction. She does not flinch. She should be shocked but is not, at least that is what she wants him to sense, or to be more accurate, not sense.

"How many are girls?"

He shakes his head.

"That defies the odds," she says.

"I control that."

"Then why all boys?"

"I have my reasons."

Maintaining an understated facade, Carly's gut just took an incoming missile that blasted through the ring of rationalization she had carefully constructed to be a surrogate for him. Hearing he has ten sons disturbs.

She asks with care, so as not to alarm, "What are their names?"

"You really want to know?"

"I do."

"Besides Iario, there's Macario, Amedeo, Arsenio, Alberto, Felice, Savio, Jacopo, Leonzio, and Jovanni. He's the baby."

She cocks her head. "All Italian names?"

"On some levels, the most innovative, cultured, and artistic of peoples in all history. Despite some of their obvious shortcomings, the advancement of civilization stopped with the end of the Roman Empire. They were, of course, the first Italians."

Carly is not sure what he means by all of that. If he's referring to aqueducts and mosaic baths, she understands. She visited Pompeii in college. She challenges him. "Besides Michelangelo and Leonardo, name some others."

Teplitsky blinks; he collects his thoughts. He thrusts his right palm forward and extends one finger for each name. "Dante, Machiavielli, Bernini, Galileo, Marconi . . . should I continue?" She nods for no greater reason than amusement. He thrusts his left hand out, palm up. Finger by finger he ticks off. "Pavarotti, Mario Lanza, and Bocelli, then there's Sinatra, let's add Yogi Berra and DiMaggio . . . that's six," sticking out the thumb on his right hand, "and I'll throw Bruce Springsteen in for good measure."

There are so many more, she muses. Back to her concerns, for his sons' actual names do not matter. "The closer I'm getting to giving birth the more I realize I never asked you what happens the moment you take your new son."

"I told you there's not a worry in the world. He will be taken care of like a prince."

"Doctor, we've all heard promises made and then they don't quite work out that way, even with the best of intentions."

"You just met Iario. Need I point out the obvious? Respectful. Well-groomed. Bright. Intelligent. Each boy is a gem of a child." *Jovanni, the youngest, well, he is a work in progress.*

Carly could not argue with that; she was pleased to see the way Iario interacted with his father and her, as a patient. "I heard Mendelssohn through an open window when I came in. Is that sort of culture typical for the boys?"

Even more than you can imagine. "Plus science, painting, and literature. I want to give them every opportunity to realize their full potential."

"I am guessing there is no Mrs. Teplitsky."

"Correct."

"Has there ever been?"

He doesn't answer.

"Are you going for an even dozen?"

"How many I have, or will have, is not important. How they turn out, how they love one another, is."

She considers the beauty of the house, the size of the clinic, the artwork on the walls, and the obvious fact that money is not an issue. "Surely, you've had your opportunities."

He turns quizzical. "Excuse me?"

"I'm curious. Were you ever close?" she asks.

He is still baffled.

"To get married," she says.

"Marriage was never on my agenda."

She ruminates on this. "But raising a passel of children was? Wouldn't you say that's a bit peculiar?"

"Not in the least. I want and love children the way I'm sure you do." *No fertility doctor could ever have helped me father a child, but Carly does not have to know this.* "As for a wife? I never felt I needed one. After ten sons, I still don't."

He pushes away from his desk; the consult is over. "I'm certain you have more questions, but I need to see the next patient." Her thin lips turn down enough for him to gather her disappointment at being cut off. He sees this and attempts to reassure. "I promise you that by the time you're ready to give birth, you will have a better understanding of what I'm doing here and what this is all about."

She starts to answer.

"It will all make sense." He reassures.

It doesn't now, she thinks to herself. Uncertainty hangs over her. *He has a long way to go to convince me that it is safe to give up the "other" baby.*

He stands to leave; Carly remains seated. She turns to him. "Why me? Why not the woman you're about to examine? The one I was talking to in the reception room. She's having a single birth. Not twins." *Carly leaves the obvious unasked, "Is it that she didn't make the deal?" Am I the fool?*

Dr. Teplitsky stops at the side of his desk and rests his hands on her chart. Palms down. She notices for the first time how long his fingers are.

"Are you having doubts?"

She doesn't reply right away. He grabs the moment to explain, knowing "all" of them had their doubts. "Because you are very special."

"And she's not?"

"Not in the way that serves my purposes."

Ever the forensic investigator, she asks, "What's your game, Dr. Teplitsky?"

He turns his palms upward. "The stakes couldn't be higher, Carly. Rest assured there are no games being played here. Giving life, creating life is a very serious matter. One that is as precious to me as it is for you. Much more than you realize."

She never wanted to admit this to herself, and certainly does not discuss this with Gabe but it is clear, now, that Dr. Teplitsky is more concerned about the baby she will give birth to for him rather than helping her conceive her own child. She knows she should feel used, and might at some other time, but for now she is still grateful.

"Then I need to ask you, again, why me?"

"You're intelligent. A professional."

"How does that matter? I'm nothing more than an oven to cook a baby for you. A surrogate. I and, apparently, ten other women you made the same deal with. We're nothing more than vessels to have your babies.

Now I discover that they are all boys. This worries me. Don't you find that having only boys is strange? It certainly has the earmarks of being extremely peculiar."

"I couldn't very well give birth to them myself now, could I? That's why I enlisted you and the others. That's why I need your help now, to help me complete my goals. As for why they are all boys, that's my business."

"Your goals, whatever they are, give me the creeps. Seeing your son, Iario, as nice as he appears, brought it home for me. What's going to happen to the child I give you? What will you call him?"

"He's not the child you need to worry about, and as I said earlier, this child will have every advantage possible. More than the others, because he will have ten older brothers to help nurture and guide him."

"I'm having a lot of trouble wrapping my arms around this whole concept."

"Well, it's a bit late for second thoughts. The thing you need to remember is that you're carrying your baby, conceived from your egg and Gabe's sperm. Mine comes from another source. Every precaution has been taken to insure your safety and your baby's safety. Every variable has been checked and rechecked. Neither of you are at risk. That is all you need to know."

"Risk isn't the issue; I assume I'm safe or I wouldn't be sitting here. What I want to know is where does *your* baby come from? Who is its mother? Where is she now?"

He moves to leave. "Carly. We made a deal. Two for one. Your questions will be answered in due time. For now, all you need to know is that I've kept my end of the bargain, and I expect you to keep yours."

Carly does not budge. "You still haven't answered my question. Why me and not the woman out in the reception area?"

The doctor steps toward the door without answering.

Carly calls out again.

"Why me?"

CHAPTER 12

Monday, 9:35 a.m.

He glances at the door, not wanting to keep the next patient waiting. He turns and steps closer. He sizes Carly up. Though she is seated and he is standing, they are eye to eye. He pauses, weighs what he will say, and returns to his chair before answering.

She stares at his teeth, crooked and yellow, waiting for the words to trip over the edges, hoping they will not be shredded by the jagged points.

"Why you? Because you were more desperate," says Teplitsky.

"Why should that matter?"

"Desperate women do desperate things in order to have a baby."

The words hurt. She wants to refute him, to tell him how wrong he is. That he has no clue about her, but fails to say anything because his words sting from the truth. Why else would she agree to carry his baby and then hand it over nine months later? That was then. Now, she's not sure of anything. He may think he is putting her questions to rest and easing her concerns, but from her point of view he is not, not by a long shot.

Teplitsky opens his desk drawer and extracts a white envelope. Her name is printed across the front in thick, black, block letters. The back flap is glued down and sealed with a blob of red wax. There is an imprint in the paraffin that, when she sees it, will think it is an eagle. It is, but not the bald variety.

"Here is an answer to your other question."

"What's this?"

"I wasn't ready to give this to you just yet, but in light of all your questions, I think this is as good a time as any."

"I don't understand." She feels the envelope's edges and runs her index finger over the wax signet.

"You wanted to know the other baby's name. The one you're carrying for me." He points to the envelope. "There it is."

She slips a nail under the flap.

He springs out of his chair. "Stop. You can only open it if I die before you give birth."

She drops the envelope on the desktop as if it were a hot potato.

"You have to promise me that you will give him the name I've chosen."

The eleventh son.

She stares at the envelope. She is not prepared for this. This transcends being a surrogate.

"Do you promise?"

Carly doesn't want to adhere to his wishes but whispers, "I do." She wonders why she agrees to this. She does not like taking orders from anyone, even the doctor who's giving her the chance to fulfill her greatest wish. All she knows is that Dr. Teplitsky had better live long enough to deliver her child.

"What about the other mothers?"

"What about them? Each has the same arrangement as you."

"Haven't any tried to see your sons? It seems only natural that they would."

"It's in the contract that they can't."

"Contracts are broken all the time. We're talking about mothers and sons."

Teplitsky takes short, deep breaths. This troubles him. "I have all the patience in the world to answer your questions, to quell your fears, but this is where I draw the line. The contract is clear: you give up all rights to the baby including ever trying to see him. The others signed this, too, and I have not allowed any to breach it."

She absorbs the impact of his words, the fervor behind them. She presses her lips together as hard as she can, holding back on lashing out at him. *What would it serve?*

"Do we have a problem?"

She shakes her head.

Monday, 10:05 a.m.

Carly leaves the clinic more troubled than when she entered. She plunges into the sun. The light is white hot. Blinding. She fishes in her pocketbook for her sunglass case. CC imitations. As she does, movement across the street catches her eye. She slips the Polarized glasses on, and then peers ahead, catching a flicker again.

A woman leans against a tree. Her clothes are drab. Lifeless. She wears a cream-colored, short-sleeved blouse with a brown skirt to the knee. Brown penny loafers left over from parochial school days. No earrings but a plain gold wedding band. Jowls of fatigue droop down both sides of her face. Hunched, sallow complexion, hair stringy, gray roots an inch long, she could be a cleaning lady.

She casts a long look up and down the street to see if anyone is watching, and then motions Carly closer. She stays in the shadows of an old maple tree.

Carly tilts her head. "Can I help you?" she calls without taking a step. "Is something wrong?"

The woman snaps her finger to her lips to quiet Carly. She gestures to her, again, and then murmurs, casting furtive glances left and right again, "Over here."

Carly slides her right foot half off the curb and hesitates. Every fiber of Carly's body strains to pull herself back, to make herself backpedal away so she can turn and head for her car and drive to safety. For whatever reason, she doesn't. Carly moves an inch closer, as if another inch would give her radiation burns . . . but she is intrigued.

Why? Maybe because Carly is outside Teplitsky's clinic and still has unanswered questions. And a sealed envelope in her purse.

The woman waves Carly to come still closer.

Carly edges to the middle of the street; she pauses. No cars coming.

Carly studies her. No lipstick or makeup. Nothing in either hand. No weapon that Carly can see. Not even a handbag. Carly checks; the woman is not wild-eyed. Carly halves the distance between them. She calculates how close she can get and still turn to move away if she feels threatened.

"Are you one of them?" the woman asks without introducing herself.

"Excuse me?" Carly tilts her head, uncertain what the question can mean.

"Did the doctor do it to you, too?"

The woman wrings one hand in the other, yanking and bending her fingers without stop, twisting and cracking them to Carly's discomfort. Her face is as knotted as her contorted digits. She is a woman in pain.

"Do you need a doctor? Are you ill?" Carly reaches for her cell phone.

"Only in my head. I see a shrink for that, but it doesn't help much. I don't sleep. I used to, but not anymore."

"I'm sorry," says Carly. "You asked if I was one of them?"

"You know," she points to Carly's abdomen. "A *twofer*."

"You mean twins?"

She nods.

Carly smiles and rubs her belly. "I *am* having twins."

The corner of mouth turns up. "*His* kind of twins. He did that to me, too."

"Did what?" *Are we talking* Rosemary's Baby *here?*

"Made me agree to give one back."

Now she has Carly's attention. "Did he force you?"

"Oh, I went along with it the way I'm sure you're doing now. The way all the others did. I wasn't the first, you know."

The doctor's words echo in Carly's mind. "He told me I was desperate," says Carly.

The woman nods. No need to confirm the obvious.

"What's your name?" asks Carly.

"Olivia."

Carly steps onto the sidewalk. They are a yard apart. Thirty-six inches. Carly tastes fear, fear of the unknown, and squelches it down. She removes her sunglasses. As best Carly can determine, there is only a mental threat, not a physical one. "What happened, Olivia? After you had the babies?"

"They were both healthy. Giving birth was the happiest day in my life. Both for me and my husband." There is longing in her eyes, of a past remembrance. "Back then, I didn't think about the other baby very much. I was so busy raising little Robbie."

Carly makes a deliberate show of checking her watch. She does not know how long this will take, and she wants to cue the woman that she will soon need to leave.

"You know he won't let you visit them," Olivia continues.

Echoes of words spoken a few minutes ago. "That was in the contract. Part of the deal. I signed it, too. Why is that so important? It *is* his baby."

"That's not the point," Olivia says.

Carly struggles to remain nonchalant, but Olivia is putting words to her own fears. Carly spins the logic card. "If you signed the same papers I did, then you knew that once you gave birth, you agreed to give up all rights to the other baby. So why now? Why are you standing out here across from the clinic?"

"Hoping to see him."

"Who? The other boy?"

"He's still my son."

"Not according to Dr. Teplitsky, he isn't."

"That's malarkey. Carry a baby and it will always be yours."

"But the other one, Teplitsky's, isn't biologically related to you. There's no part of you or your husband in that child," says Carly.

"You'd like to think that, but it doesn't work that way. You feel that bond forever. I know I do." She pauses and then lowers her voice. "And so do the others."

"Do you know which of his sons is yours?"

She shakes her head. "He's eleven. I don't even know what he looks like. I've been out here many times. There are so many of them. They're all around the same age and size. I can't tell one from the other."

"Most boys look alike from a distance. That's why, sometimes, parents can't tell which kid is theirs on the soccer field."

Then Olivia blurts out. "My Robbie died." A bead of sadness puddles and then floats down her cheek. Then another.

"I'm so sorry," says Carly. Sisters now, she asks Olivia, "What happened?" Carly is certain that it wasn't anything congenital. Dr. Teplitsky screens for every genetic entity under the sun.

"He developed asthma."

"It happens."

"He passed out taking a shower. He was nine. He drowned in two inches of water."

Two years ago.

Carly wants so very much to reach out and hug her. Embrace her. Give her comfort. She does not know how the woman will react.

Carly remains still, hoping stillness will comfort.

"I cannot imagine how you feel."

"That's why I want to see my other son. To hold him. Tell him about his brother. But I don't even know his name." Carly runs through as many of the boys' names as she can remember, but has no clue which might be Olivia's "other" son.

"Have you tried the direct approach? Ring the doorbell and explain why this is so important to you?"

"More than once. He won't let me meet him. Says he is not my son. The doctor, he . . ." she brushes away the wetness with the back of her hand, "doesn't understand."

If the tables were reversed, Carly would feel the same. But she needs to calm her. "You did sign those papers."

Olivia steps back. Her face gains color. "Those papers mean nothing. I don't know how it will happen, but I will get my boy back one day. That man can't live forever."

Hearing Olivia, Carly clutches her purse tighter, as if cradling the envelope closer to her body will insure she would not suffer Olivia's sense of loss by not meeting the *other* son. She flashes on what's inside the envelope, what the boy's name will be. What other post-mortem gem might be in store for her and Gabe?

Carly turns to walk away. Nothing she can say will give comfort. "I hope you get your wish, Olivia."

"And I hope you won't be tortured like me."

CHAPTER 13

Monday, 11:15 a.m.

Carly returns to Island Bluffs in a trance. She rehashes over and over what the doctor revealed about his house of boys and tries to project what it means to her and the baby she's carrying for him. This unlocks greater concerns and second thoughts about giving up the child. Perplexed when she should be lighthearted and delighted that giving birth was less than a dozen weeks away, having encountered Olivia challenged Carly anew. Ever the skeptic and always an investigator, a whirlwind of questions pinball from point to point in her brain.

Will the doctor's house be safe for the baby she's carrying for him?

For that matter, is Teplitsky safe? Benign? Harmless? Or is he playing out a dastardly plot to which she, Olivia, and at least nine other women have fallen prey?

How will this baby respond to a house filled with so many other boys? To the doctor's exposure to cultural enrichments? Teplitsky reassured her that there are ample staff and resources to care for the boys, but the child will still lack a mother to nurture him. Carly knows that can never be good. And then there's the fact that Carly's contribution to the Teplitsky clan will be so much younger than the others. Why is that? Why the gap in time when all the other boys are closer in age? Is that something else to worry about?

Carly drives on autopilot, her thoughts jumbled, her concerns growing. Every child needs a mother. *Why didn't she think of that before? There is so much she didn't consider that first time when she and Gabe met Dr. Teplitsky.*

What about Olivia? Is she psychotic? Schizophrenic? A paranoid schizophrenic? She did appear to have her wits . . . did appear lucid . . . and did make cogent points. She did not exhibit anger, but still . . .

Robbie died.

Do innate maternal feelings trump DNA? Could Olivia ever be a mother to the "other" son?

Will Carly become attached to Dr. T's baby knowing it's not hers for the keeping? Will she want to take a gander at this boy from time to time? Will Teplitsky let her? Will Carly become an Olivia? Would Carly stand across the street from the Teplitsky house in hopes of seeing this baby?

Given the chance, would Carly introduce the boys—the twins—so they could get to know one another? Would *they* want to meet? Should she even tell her son when he is old enough to understand that he has a brother? Will Teplitsky's son, the one Carly is carrying, even be considered her son's brother? After all, they aren't biologically related. Different genes and such. But still.

What have the other mothers, the *twofers*, tried to do to answer these questions? Is Olivia the only one with regrets? She made no mention of having another child.

Is dealing with Teplitsky one gigantic mistake?

Before she can dissect these thoughts, Carly is home.

"How'd it go at Teplitsky's today?" Gabe asks as Carly bounces into the kitchen, the screen door slamming behind her. Gabe makes a mental note to get it fixed assuming he can't do it himself.

"I found a friend for your father," she says, not ready to share all that did happen both inside and outside of Teplitsky's office.

"Just like that? Where?" asks Gabe.

"Where what?" Carly lapses into her thoughts on the return drive. She searches for any answer that will give shape to the distorted pictures she cannot help conjuring.

"You were saying that . . ."

Carly regroups. "The handyman at the doctor's office. He was changing a light bulb when I walked into the clinic. We chatted. He's a sweet old man; he seems lonely. Eager to have a friend. So I suggested your father."

Carly wears a flowery sundress, greens and blues and yellows. Shoulders are covered with a short white sweater with pearl buttons. Fingers slip into her pocket. They touch Olivia's card. It's a business card from Olivia's shop. Antiques. She rents a stall in one of the communal places on Front Street in Red Bank, which is a local mecca for vintage goods.

Without removing the card, Carly runs her finger over the raised ink, edging about, feeling for the phone number, as if touching it is supposed to summon a way out of this maze of conflicted feelings.

Gabe slices open one of the last sealed cartons with a retractable razor. "You spoke to this so-called kindly old man for just a few moments and were certain he wasn't a serial killer? I have no intention of putting my father in harm's way."

Carly loses the thread of conversation, again. "Serial killer? A few moments?" Her imagination tracks toward a light of understanding. An epiphany of sorts. Olivia is the maternal variant of buyer's remorse; Carly isn't like her. There is nothing to be concerned about. Nothing at all. Nothing.

"Well?"

"Well what?" she asks, replaying how it ended with Olivia.

"Is, or is this guy not, safe to be around?"

"Call me any time," Olivia said, thrusting a business card into Carly's hand. Carly mumbled a thank you. Said she might reach out.

"You will," said Olivia over her shoulder when Carly turned to leave. "You will."

Gabe drags her back to the moment. "Is this guy a serial killer or not?"

His voice shatters her trance; she jabs his arm. "Get serious. He's a nice man. His name is Buck Hopewell. Been here forever. He's not the issue."

"Then what is?"

"Bringing your father to this house is. It's so isolated. It's wonderful he's with us and all, but he doesn't drive, and town is too far for him to walk. What's he going to do all day? He can only garden so much."

Carly waits for Gabe to run his fingers through his hair. He does. "I assumed there would be a 'Y,' or some place like that. Doesn't every town have a center for seniors?"

"We're talking about Island Bluffs here," she says with a heavy layer of sarcasm. "No senior center, no synagogue where he'd be among his own, no nothing for him."

The silence between them is palpable; Gabe dares not speak.

Carly snaps her fingers. "I know. Your father can fill his days lunching with the Elks, the Lions, or good ol' boys at the Rotary Club. He just needs a personal chauffeur. Any volunteers?"

Gabe clamps his lips tight before answering. "I never considered he'd be stuck in the house most days. He managed to keep himself busy where he used to live. This is my entire fault. What're we going to do?"

Carly's made her point. "Gabe, you're talking about your own father. Island Bluffs is not the elephant burial grounds. He came here because you worried about him. His neighborhood was no longer safe. The last few years, he's admitted as much. And you did it because you love him. He may not show it now, but he's happy he is here. He will find things to do and I know that he adores the chance to bond more with Megan. But he does need a friend."

"I didn't even ask him if he wanted to live us, I told him he had to. It was selfish of me."

"He was languishing in that apartment." She takes Gabe's hand. "It is special for me to have him around, too."

"He loves you."

"And I love him. But you understand why I want him to make a friend."

Gabe pecks her on the cheek. "I'm glad you invited Mr. B. Hopeful . . ."

"Buck Hopewell."

"Yes, him, to meet dad. That's why I married you, always thinking about others."

"I thought you married me for the sex?"

"I was turned on by you working in a morgue. Nothing is sexier than a women with blood up to her elbows." He grabs his car keys.

"You are so full of it."

"And you love me for it."

"I do love you. Where are you off to now?"

"I got a call from the architect when you were at the doctor's. She wants to go over the plans with me."

"Can't the addition wait until we settle in a bit? Get used to the house? See what works and what doesn't?"

"We both know we need an addition. We talked about it. The idea is to get it built before the baby shows up. Now that I'm getting a sense of how this town works, there's not a day to waste. I need to make a few business calls and then I will drive up there." Up there is to Point Pleasant and the office of Verity Frizzell.

"While you're at the architect's, I am going to get some groceries. I passed a Whole Foods. They will have everything we need."

"Why don't you ask Megan to give you a hand?"

"I think it's better if she hangs out with Yehuda. Sort of keep an eye on him so he won't feel too lonely. It will be good for both of them."

CHAPTER 14

Megan has stayed with her grandfather all morning. When Gabe returns inside after speaking with that strange man, Yehuda makes no mention of the music that seemingly erupted out of nowhere. For the time being, Megan and Yehuda decide to keep this a secret between them.

They have spent the time since moving in, arranging Yehuda's room, putting his clothes in bureau drawers—one drawer just for bow-ties—and attack his closet: shirts on the right, pants on the left, and shoes on the wood-planked floor under the pants. Yehuda installs a white latex-coated rack onto the back of the closet door after which Megan slips on his few belts. Above it, there's a hook for his blue terry-cloth bathrobe.

Yehuda plops into the Shaker-style rocking chair he made Gabe bring from his apartment. The chair is made of maple wood with a classic ladder-back, and is finished in semi-gloss coating. It was too comfortable to leave behind. Yehuda takes a sip of water. He grunts the grunt of a tired man. Megan disregards this and grabs his hand. "C'mon, Grandpa, let's check out the basement."

Neither has heard any more music since the first episode earlier that morning, nor did either feel the need to discuss it further.

"Aren't you tired?" he asks.

"You have all night to sleep, Grandpa. This will be an adventure." She tugs on his hand.

Yehuda looks up to see Megan's shining face. He wants to make her happy. He knows, soon enough, she will find friends and have little time for him. So he pushes off from the arms of the rocker, careful not to tip the chair or lose his balance.

"What if we hear the music again?" he asks.

"Don't be silly, Grandpa. Whatever it was, it's gone now. Maybe it was the wind blowing through the eaves. That used to happen in our old house."

"Just the same, let's be on the lookout for strange things."

She pauses, thinks about what he says, and then hugs him. "You're such a kidder, Grandpa." Megan leads the way, but his words linger, giving shape to the aura she's been sensing since the moment she set foot in the house.

Access to the basement is through the kitchen. It's dark. She swallows hard before edging off the first step. Megan continues to the bottom, holding onto the wood railing with her right hand, her left hand extended outward, swatting the air in case there's an obstruction like a support beam.

"Do you think Dad checked this out before he bought the house?" she calls out.

"He didn't mention anything to me," answers Yehuda. "He made up his mind so fast that I wouldn't be surprised if he skipped over the basement."

Megan gropes the wall, patting up and down, then expanding her search, but does not find a switch. "Dad's usually pretty thorough."

"Find a switch yet?" Yehuda wasn't eager to change the subject. He knows that Gabe has always been what some refer to as a "driver," one who plunges headfirst into a project without thinking about all the ramifications. Not typical lawyer think, but it has served Gabe well. It would not shock anyone that he bought this house having never opened every door and inspected every cranny. As far as Gabe was concerned, he would count on the engineer's report to highlight major issues regarding whether or not the house should be bought.

"Nothing, Grandpa."

"If there's no switch then reach out with your hand. There must be a string from a fixture. When you feel one, pull it."

Megan hesitates. There is a last step before edging onto the floor. She leans from where she is, secure that she is next to the wall, and swings her left hand from side to side. Nothing. She slips the toe of her running shoe onto what feels like a concrete floor and takes a baby step into the darkness. She stretches, willing her arm to grow longer to avoid venturing deeper into the black vortex in front of her. She waves wildly until she hits a dangling cord. She grabs for it and tugs. A twenty-two watt circular fluorescent bulb buzzes to life. There are black rings on either side of the ceramic socket that plugs into the fixture. The bulb is old, emitting crackling sounds before it settles into a low-throated hum, casting a greenish-white, eerie hue over the dank basement.

After a cursory scan, Megan finds the shadows intimidating. The tiny hairs on Megan's arms prickle. She rubs them with brisk strokes to gain assurance all is safe.

She glances up towards Yehuda. "It's okay now, Grandpa."

They stand side-by-side; rapid eye blinks to adjust. Two walls are cinderblock; they are covered with a thick, gray, waterproof paint. The floor has also been waterproofed. The third and fourth walls are made of thin, pine paneling. There are two doors carved out of the paneled wall in front of them. The doors, attached by wrought iron hinges once black and now colored with a gray-green patina, are warped and flimsy.

"I wonder what's behind them?" Megan points at the doors. She marches over and presses down on the metal latch of the door to the right. It creaks inward. Dampness and mildew make her nose twitch.

Knowing that Yehuda is right behind her, Megan slinks into the room and gropes for a dangling string. She knocks it, and needs to wait for it to arc back to her. It grazes her fingers and she grabs it, yanks, and a light shimmers on to illuminate the room.

Yehuda steps into the room and surveys it.

He points to the far wall. "That is an old coal bin. See the chute up there? They would deliver coal through that opening from the outside to fill the bin. The owner would shovel what he needed to keep the boiler going. They did it that way until houses were converted to oil heat."

These facts hold no interest for her. The room is empty.

"Nothing here, Grandpa." She clasps his hand and flicks off the light. "Let's check out the other room." Before Yehuda can answer, Megan spins and returns to the main basement room; she pushes in the second door.

When the light blinks on, Megan blurts out, "Wow! Look at all that stuff."

Thirty yellow rain slickers dangle from thirty tarnished and pitted brass hooks. An equal number of pairs of black rubber boots stand at attention under each hooded coat. There are stacks of Sterno cans, oil lanterns, dust-covered cases of Spam, and bins of clothing that consist of black turtleneck sweaters, dark jeans, cobalt-blue long johns, white sailors' hats, gray wool scarves, heavy duty gloves, thick socks, and dozens of pairs of men's underwear from a bygone era.

"What do you make of all this junk, Grandpa? It's like an Army-Navy store."

Megan unfolds one of the sweaters and drapes it across her chest to see if it fits. It might. "Think my parents would let me keep this?"

"See if there are any moth holes in that one." The reference to Carly as one of her "parents" does not go unnoticed.

Yehuda processes what he sees.

Why so many slickers and boots? Why the rations? Is this a bomb shelter? Why so many pairs of clothes and hats . . . all the same style? All adult sizes; none for women or children. Definitely not a bomb shelter. He steps closer. Inspects the clothes. The labels are cut out. He picks a boot. Blows. Dust flies. He shakes off the rest. It's black. The leather is stiff, but of good quality. Leather laces. He pulls back the tongue. Size 44.5. Equivalent to a man's size ten in the US. The sole and heel are new. No scuff marks. Never worn.

Yehuda replaces the boot onto its dust imprint. Why is all this here? He has an idea why. It's not a pretty thought. For now, he keeps it to himself. "I've seen enough," he says, and yanks on the string to turn the light off.

Back in the larger room, the one with the stairs, Yehuda notes a pile of benches against the far wall that he had missed before. The benches are stacked to the ceiling. Nails and hooks poke out from wood trim that stretches across the wall, ready to hold coats, overalls, or hats.

"I bet they held meetings of some sort down here," Megan offers. Her eyes widen, "Do you think it was the Ku Klux Klan, Grandpa? That would be so dope."

Yehuda knows her slang. "That's a good guess, Megan, but I don't think the Klan was active in these parts," and then adds, "and it would not be 'dope' as you call it. It would be horrific."

"I guess." She snaps her fingers. "I know. This could've been a church of some sort." Her eyes blaze. "What about satanic worship? Or a coven of witches?"

"The clothes were for men, so witches are probably out." He attempts to humor her. "As for satanic worship, do you think they sacrificed babies here to please the Devil?"

"For sure something weird went on down here," she says.

"Megan, I don't know where you get your imagination, but it is not from me."

She cuddles him. "You are the coolest Grandpa ever."

He squeezes her, looking over her head at the surroundings.

She steps back, surveys the room, studies his face, latches onto his concern, and says, "That's not what they did down here, was it, Grandpa?"

His head shakes, ever so slightly, side to side.

Yehuda has mentioned a number of times to her that he has a sixth sense, that he can feel energies that are not aligned. This could be one of those moments. She waits for him to speak.

He does.

"What's clear to me is that people did gather down here. Only men. The question is, 'Who were they?'" Then he adds, "Why here?"

"How can we find out? I want to know. Don't you, Grandpa?"

He does not answer.

His skin crawls.

Something gnaws at him; his body tells him to leave this place. He grabs her hand and turns toward the stairs. "There's nothing else down here for us." He turns and lifts his foot onto the first step.

Megan holds the pull chain, waiting from him to get to the top before she extinguishes the light. Yehuda is on the third step when she calls out. "Wait a second."

She points. "There's something else."

"What is it?"

"A chest."

Yehuda drags himself back down the stairs. He sidles next to her. The chest is made of pine and is propped so as to blockade shut another door. Yehuda notes scuff marks in the cement floor. "This chest used to be over there." Megan follows where he is pointing.

"I wonder what's in the chest, Grandpa. What do you think is behind that door? It could be really neat."

"Let's see what's in the chest first, honey."

Megan yanks on a drawer. It's filled with tools. A hammer, nails, pliers, wrenches, screwdrivers, and assorted nuts and bolts. She opens another. There's a spool of antenna wire. Lamp cord. Plugs. Spatulas. Bars of soap. Cans of car grease. Hinges. Crystal door handles. Junk found in a flea market, the kinds of stuff folks pass by week after week without a second look.

Opening the last drawer raises smiles. She snatches a loose comic book. "Look, it's a *Superman*. I bet this is worth a lot of money." She rummages through the others: *Mary Marvel, Flash, Captain Marvel, Captain America, Super Boy,* and more. Then she breaks out into a big smile. "Look at this." She fans a deck of playing cards with nude women; their privates are covered with feathers. "Ooh la la," coos Megan.

Unfazed, Yehuda says, "Let's leave everything the way we found it and close the drawers."

"Grandpa, let's see if we can push it to the side and see what's behind it." Her eyes are hopeful.

"Not today, Megan. Your Grandpa's run out of gas."

"What if there's a treasure behind the door? Or a secret diary?" She read the *Diary of Ann Frank* in English class that year. "Knowing someone went out of their way to block the door, don't you want to find out what's in there?"

Yehuda eases his foot onto the first step and clasps the warped wooden railing. It shakes as he pulls himself up. Without turning around, he says, "Whatever is in there, pumpkin, will keep another day."

"Okay, Grandpa. Promise me you won't forget."

"You know I'm good for it."

She flicks off the light and trails him up the steps. "I love you, Grandpa." He stops at the top and turns to kiss her cheek. He smiles. Words are not necessary.

In the kitchen, she says, "I'm going to take a walk on the beach. Will you be all right?"

"My room needs a little more organizing," he answers. "Don't get too close to the edge of the property."

"Give me more credit than that, Grandpa."

"Just making sure."

Yehuda steps into his room; a single sealed box remains unpacked. A few personal items, that's all.

"Might as well," he mutters out loud. "Then nap time."

He peels back the tape and pushes the flap out of the way. He scoops up the top item. A frame. With the delicacy of a surgeon, he teases open the bubble wrap protecting the silver edges. The border has gone dark. Oxidized. He studies the face; the face stares back.

"Sadie," he says out loud to his wife who has long since passed, "soon, we will be together. For the meantime," he glances about his room, "you know I didn't really want to come here, but . . ." he hesitates, then nods as if she took part in the decision, "it's not so bad. Shhh. But don't tell Gabe. A little guilt is good for him."

He clops over to the maple-stained wooden dresser and rests the picture to one side. Next he bends to grab a book from the box and feels a darting pain shoot through his left arm. He stumbles back and reaches for the rocking chair, grabs the green vial nestled on the end table, plops a pill under his tongue, and ticks off the seconds in his mind until it works its magic. In moments, the pain dissipates.

He rocks back and forth in the chair.

His eyes flutter and then remained closed. He spirals into heavy breathing; his head drops into his chest.

A noise awakens Yehuda. His neck is stiff. He rubs his eyes and listens. He is still alone. A door closes. He wonders if Megan has returned from her walk. Didn't Carly do an errand? He calls out; no one answers. He grabs both arms of the rocker and musters the strength to push up. The chair fights back and wobbles; he slips down on the seat. This weakness alarms him.

"What a damn shame." He hates thinking age is getting the better of him. He tries again; this time he conquers gravity and stands.

Again, he hears a noise. He can't make it out. Unsure of what it is.

He steps into the kitchen and calls out. "Anyone there?"

He hears a scraping noise. It comes from above. He opens the door to the attic. He doesn't move, holds his breath, cocks his head—his hearing is still good—and listens. He debates if it is wise to climb the stairs given the stab of pain he just experienced. His doctor calls it angina; Yehuda calls it "inconvenient."

Now he hears faint music. He casts about. He crooks his head into the kitchen, takes a step toward Megan's room, opens the basement door and listens, and then leans into the attic stairwell. He catches drifting notes from above, but can't make out the tune. He has narrowed it down to the attic.

He grabs the brown railing; it is crooked and sags. After five steps he needs to rest. He wipes his brow on his shirtsleeve. Always the long-sleeved white shirt. He makes it to the top of the stairs, a triumph in itself. Of late, days have turned into tiny skirmishes that require extra effort and persistence. They tire. They challenge. They frustrate. Today, the top stair is his Mt. Everest. No Sherpas to help him!

Yehuda waits for the pounding in his chest to lessen. He stands in the middle of the room. By now, he knows what to expect. He finds the dangling string, tugs, and a lone bulb bursts to life. Yellow light bathes the room; the corners remain dark. A couple of scattered boxes from the move. Nothing else. There is no closet in the room. No place to hide.

He cups his ear to pick up the sounds again. Unless something in one of the boxes is battery-operated and turned itself on, there is nothing apparent that could make music.

The house has its own sounds. All do. Wood contracting. Expanding. Wind blowing through cracks and vents. Furnaces kicking on, air conditioner condensers humming. Air circulating. Clocks ticking. Sounds that comfort.

These are not what he hears. Yehuda is sure that sounds have occurred. He is also sure they are not ordinary. He turns to leave and freezes; there they are again: faint music.

To his left is a small window. He peers out to see if someone's below. A car radio blaring. A teen with a boom box.

There is no one.

He turns to the opposite wall that faces the ocean. Only there's no window to look out. He cups his ear and presses against the wood. The sound is faint; he strains to hear it. *What is it?* A radio? Someone singing? Maybe it's from the next house. That's not right. There is no house next door. Is it possible to hear sounds from a boat here?

He taps the wall. He hears a faint tap back. An echo? He calls out. There's no answer. He waits twenty seconds. Thirty. A minute is an eternity when nothing is happening. Nothing happens. This disturbs. Not the fact that he hears something and can't find out where it is coming from. No, what worries Yehuda is that there is nothing to hear and that he is imagining it. Is this how it begins? Dementia? Worse yet, Alzheimer's? Is this what Ronnie-boy felt soon after his presidency ended?

Yehuda leans onto the railing and hobbles down the stairs. To be certain, he stops in Megan's room. It's a mess. He steps in. No music coming from here.

He plods out the front door and looks left and then right just to be certain: he cannot see a house to his left. To his right is the lone tree. Beyond it is a grass-filled expanse that ends in a wooded area, dense with trees and low-lying scrub at the edges. Beyond that an estuary. He paces to the back of the house. He has not yet been there. Nothing there either. He still needs to scope out a place for his vegetable patch, but not now. Now he needs to deal with the mysterious music. With the tapping. With the sense that something "otherworldly" has surfaced.

Or has it?

Should he worry?

With his back to Barnegat Bay, Yehuda studies the rear of the house. His eye travels to the peak and back down. No window. Wires run up the side of the house and duck into the attic. The hole is small where the wires enter, too small for a sparrow or squirrel to enter. Is that true? Squirrels can get into the tiniest spaces. And New Jersey is loaded with the flying variety.

He stops. There is a louver built into the outer wall. It's close to four feet square. A vent to let air circulate through the attic? Yehuda knows houses can't be airtight. They need to breathe, like people. He is pleased that Gabe and Megan and Carly are breathing life into this old house. And maybe it's true what he hears from others, that he will feel reborn living near the ocean. For now, there's no answer to the musical question except that the wind is playing tricks on him.

He turns and faces Barnegat Bay. Their house is perched on a baby cliff. A small hill. What the hoity-toity call a *bluff*. Island Bluffs. Makes sense. He shades his eyes. There's a figure churning through the waters. Across the bay. Swimming toward the lighthouse. Yehuda wonders why anyone would swim out there alone? How long has this person been insane?

Beyond the swimmer—how far, Yehuda is unsure—he sees a ship. The way it moves captures his attention. Riveting. The ship plods left through the water and then makes a sharp right turn. Goes a bit and then reverses with a sharp left. Yehuda observes, entranced.

Zigzagging.

Covering a grid.

Searching for something. Yehuda wonders what?

In time, he will learn that the boat is a scavenger ship aptly christened the *Searcher*. What it searches for will surprise. After all, treasures come in all sizes and shapes. In another context, in another place, one man's garbage is another man's treasure. In this instance, the boat is not searching for anyone's garbage. When it does discover what it's looking for, and it will, few will know what to make of it.

Few will know what to call it.

Few will understand its import.

What it will reveal brings pain to some, and relief to others.

CHAPTER 15

Monday, 5:30 p.m.
Dr. Teplitsky dismisses his last patient. She is a twenty-three year old who is two months post uterine cancer surgery.

"You are as good as new," Dr. T reassures.

"What if the cancer comes back when I'm pregnant?"

"It won't."

"But it could happen."

"Anything could happen."

"Well?"

"Well what?" he asks.

"Can I keep the baby if it does come back when I'm pregnant?"

The doctor chuckles. Pats her on the head. "You needn't worry about such things. When the time is right, you will become pregnant and you will have a healthy baby. And you will live to see your grandchildren and your great-grandchildren."

Thankful tears form; she lets them dribble down her cheeks. She takes his hand and kisses it. "You've answered my prayers, Dr. Teplitsky. The doctors in New York told me I would never be able to have children. You've given me so much hope today. Thank you."

Before leaving the office for the evening, Dr. Teplitsky double checks Carly's lab results, her blood pressure, weight, and sonogram.

Taking no chances on this one.

He is satisfied both babies are healthy.

He cups his hands behind his head, leans back, and takes time to reflect. Everything is on schedule, a schedule years in the planning and taking just as long to implement. In a short while, after Carly Mason delivers her babies, Phase Two will be completed which will trigger Phase Three. And when this happens, it will initiate his crowning achievement.

A lifetime in the planning, years in the making, close to finishing.

He thinks back on the day Carly and Gabe came to the office. Her frame was narrow, not a good choice to carry twins. But there was an air about her and a healthy dose of self-assurance laced with desperation.

Carly survived his challenges. How long have you wanted children? Why didn't you have them as a single parent? What have you and Gabe tried in order to conceive? *In vitro?* How many times? Are you willing to carry two babies? Would you be willing to carry your own biological child and be a surrogate at the same time? Are you willing to move nearer to the clinic?

Carly gave all the right answers. She was older than the others, but strong-willed and athletic, and he needed to complete Phase Two.

Dr. Teplitsky agreed to her and was certain of something else: Carly would be the last. No need for others. *Phase Two over, Phase Three next.*

The doctor shuts the light in his office, says good-bye to lingering staff members and drags his damaged leg through the passageway that connects the clinic to his house. He has lived here for more than twenty years. In many ways, he and the boys live in secret behind closed doors, though his house and medical facility are anything but hidden from the curious. Mail is delivered to the dome-shaped, black mailbox mounted on a metal pole close to the curb. FedEx and UPS make daily stops. Other regulars to the house? The Poland Springs truck. The postman. That's about it. Visible yet invisible at the same time. Only in America.

He exits the white, wainscoted walkway that connects the clinic to the house. The causeway is adorned with six pairs of windows on both sides, each window bracketed by green louvered shutters, which fill the space with ample light even on the most overcast days. He enters the kitchen. It is a kitchen fit for a reality show searching for the next great chef. It has two Sub-Zero Pro-48 dual refrigerators, a separate Sub-Zero freezer and wine cooler, and a G60SS-10 Vulcan-Hart stove with ten burners and three standard ovens, plus three 7859 professional Miele dishwashers. The kitchen sparkles.

"Staff" is a word that applies to the doctor's house. Many are needed to care for the dozen or so people who inhabit the mansion. In addition to Buck Hopewell, the ubiquitous handyman, there are two full-time gardeners, and three housekeepers headed by Brigitte O'Leary, who runs the staff. Brigitte is also an RN who covers at the clinic when one of Dr. T's nurses is ill. The coup de grace is the mononymous, full-time French chef, who has a single appellation as do the likes of Cher, Pelé, Madonna, Usher, and Beyoncé, to name a few. In this case, culinary delights are the imaginative creations of Gaston. Arsenio dubbed him such because he looks like the annoying little chef in the animated *Ratatouille*. Gaston fits the part: he is short, with a long, hound-dog face that sports a thick black moustache. He has large ears and is never without his tall chef's hat or a white apron tied around his ample belly. When Gaston gets excited he curses in French to the delight of the children.

Dr. Teplitsky loves this part of the day more than any other because he gets to spend time with all his sons. The boys are home-schooled. They are too bright and too talented to wallow with the mediocre. Surely they will need to mix with everyday sorts in the future. But not now.

All have much to do and much to accomplish. In addition to the expected courses of math, English, history, science, and more, each boy is instructed in Latin, Greek, French, and Italian. Each plays a musical instrument to a high degree of proficiency. Each has been exposed to painting and sculpting, but three display an unusual talent: Macario, Aurelio, and Felice. Writing? Arsenio has more than a fleeting potential. Stardom is his destiny. Leonzio is not far behind, though he has already excelled as a debater. The nascent scientists appear to be Savio, Jacopo, and Alberto. By age eleven, Alberto has mastered both quantum and experimental physics. He loves astronomy and can hold science tutors in rapt attention discussing the crazy paths that stars, dubbed ultra cool subdwarfs, take as they orbit around the Milky Way.

Whatever their individual talents, Dr. T makes certain these are identified and nurtured, each to their fullest. No aspect of their education is overlooked or trivialized. They all balked at penmanship lessons when they were youngsters, but the doctor explained that civilized man should be able to express himself in all forms of communication, even in the arcane. To wit, all except Alberto are accomplished calligraphers.

* * *

"Each is unusual," explains Dr. Teplitsky to Carly at an earlier meeting.

"And the one I'm carrying?"

"The same."

"The same as which one? They all sound special, but not necessarily the same."

A smile erupts. "Carly, I can reassure you these children are special, and I will do everything in my power to make certain they make their mark on society. But I can't be expected to know exactly how they will turn out. No one does."

"Even with the special way you're raising them?"

"How I bring them up can only go so far."

"Hearing this, you're describing quite the upbringing. How can it fail to create fabulous children?"

"That's my goal," answers the doctor.

"But there's no guarantee how they turn out?"

He shakes his head.

She wriggles in her chair. "I guess I have a lot to learn."

"We all do."

"What if one doesn't meet your expectations? Doesn't turn out the way you want?"

"That's not an option."

"But you just said you can't control every aspect of their development."

"Let me worry about that. I'm not being totally open with you. It's too early for that."

"Don't you think I should know everything?" She exaggerates how she pronounces *everything*.

"I don't know *everything* about you, now, do I?"

"You know quite a bit. Those questionnaires I had to fill out were quite extensive."

"Still, there are parts of your life that I know nothing about," he says.

She studies him. His eyelids droop a bit; his mouth softens. She sees an old and gentle soul. "I guess," she says.

"From everything I've told you and from everything you've seen, I can assure you that you have nothing to worry about when I deliver your son."

* * *

As the doctor enters the house, he is confident that Carly, who, in the end, is no different than any of the other women he's enlisted, will come around. They all did, except that one. And she was good with everything in the beginning, too. How could he know her son would die? Accidents happen. The price to pay for his gift is high; the emotional toll is insurmountable for some. But all knew going in: no refunds, no second chances.

Life is not a dress rehearsal. When coupled with Teplitsky's fertility know-how, it is a single performance of a one-act play that cannot be restaged. No second chances.

He sighs recalling her constant phone calls, the unannounced visits, the threats that escalated into holding placards for patients to stay away from the clinic, the flyers posted on street signs and telephone poles warning women not to use the doctor, and the last straw was the website (www.badbabydoctor.com) that venomously castigated the doctor without explaining their *special* arrangement. For whatever reason, Olivia did not reveal *that* secret.

She left him no choice. He had done nothing wrong. A restraining order demanded that she stay at least two hundred feet from both the clinic and house. When that didn't work, the judge threatened Olivia with a civil suit and jail time.

That registered. She followed the court order and abstained from causing further trouble . . . for a time.

To his knowledge, Olivia has obeyed the restraining order, though every once in a while he sensed her presence, as if she were lurking nearby. Probably nothing.

The ironclad contracts, the lawyers, the restraining order were all necessary to protect everything he's worked for oh these many years. Phase One was needed to create Phase Two. With Carly Mason in the fold, Phase Two will be completed. Virtually nothing can derail him now from accomplishing his long sought after goals.

Dr. Teplitsky reaches the top of the stairs and heads for Alberto's room. The door is open. He stands and watches his son absorbed in his book. Dr. T raps on the doorframe. Alberto looks up.

"Enjoying it?" he asks.

Alberto holds the book up, citing the title from memory. "*The Meaning of Relativity: Including the Relativistic Theory of the Non-Symmetric Field.* I'm almost finished."

"What's next?"

"I want to review Neils Bohrs's papers; I don't think they will be *that* difficult." He closes the book. "Papa?" His eyes are brown and wide with excitement. Dr. Teplitsky nods with encouragement to continue. "After I finish at M.I.T., I want to get my Ph.D. at Princeton. Is that a good idea, Papa?"

He ruffles the boy's foppish hair. "Alberto, you'll be fifteen when you finish M.I.T. You have time to decide where you'll go after that."

"But their theoretical physics department is amazing."

"There are other schools equally as good."

"Not like Princeton. Besides, I would be close to you and my brothers."

"Now *that* is a good thing, Alberto." Dr. T chuckles. "You haven't even started M.I.T. and you are already plotting your next move."

"But you taught us that life is one big chess game."

"Ah, you may have learned that lesson too well. We'll see about Princeton. Finish what you're doing; dinner will be ready in thirty minutes. You know how Gaston likes everyone to be on time."

"And you don't?" says Alberto with a sheepish grin.

Teplitsky moves to the next room. "How's your concerto coming?"

Without answering, Felice spins away from his MacBook Pro and tickles the keys of his P600HS Yamaha upright. It's made of Tuscan ash with fluted legs and a sunburst music stand. When he performs his pieces for the family, he plays on the Henry Z. Steinway limited edition grand piano in the conservatory off the living room. The Steinway's notes are warm, their tone rich, and its long sustain transforms the listener's experience to a magical place.

Felice stops after a few bars, and looks up for approval.

Teplitsky claps with deliberate strokes. "Bravissimo. Bravissimo. It's your best work yet." The boy is rail thin, with dark hair, hollow eyes, and gaunt features. At eleven, Felice is a child prodigy. The look on his father's face causes Felice to erupt into a picture of happiness.

"You really think so, Father? I had some doubts."

He shrugs. "I'm prejudiced. Wait until they hear your work performed in Carnegie Hall. When that happens and the *New York Times* music critic writes his review, then you'll understand what you've accomplished at such a tender age."

Felice is the birth brother of Olivia's biological son, the one who died. *If that woman only knew about the gem she carried, she'd probably want to get him back. To make up for her loss.* Teplitsky shakes off this awful image.

"Do you truly believe they will play my works at Carnegie Hall, Father?"

He flashes on the talk he had with Carly Mason, about the effects of nurturing his sons to develop their talents, but not knowing for certain how they would turn out.

"Felice, there are few things I am certain about in this life. Having your works played at the world's most famous concert hall is one of them."

Teplitsky, ever-the-proud father, pivots to check on another son when fourteen-year old Arsenio charges down the stairs from the floor above. He's chasing little Jovanni, who scampers, jackrabbit-quick, ahead of him. Jovanni is nine-years old and the youngest Teplitsky son. Jovanni has dark hair and a somewhat square frame that belies his unusual strength. His dark eyes are more mischievous than brooding. His full-blast gaze makes even the most self-assured adults squirm.

"You little devil. When I get my hands on you, I'll wring your neck." Arsenio stops short to find Jovanni hiding behind the doctor.

Teplitsky holds up his hand. "Thundering down the stairs like that . . . is it necessary, Arsenio?"

Arsenio's face is red. Beads of sweat form on his brow. He stutters. "The little bastard ruined my maquette. It was going so well when that b—"

The doctor stops him short.

What makes fourteen-year-old Arsenio's works exceptional are his simple and direct face carvings. They are not soft like the modeled surfaces of Rodin. Rather, they echo a rebirth of modernism that started during the Cubist period and can be described as "post-modernism." In time, his work will mature and catch the eye of critics and patrons alike. For now, he's an angry teen.

"Arsenio," Teplitsky says in a soft voice, "you're the older brother. It's your job to teach Jovanni that he needs to be respectful of your things. Especially your artwork."

Jovanni squirms from his father's leg. Dr. Teplitsky kneels on his good leg so they are eye to eye. He plumbs the boy's face and knows in his heart that Jovanni has no remorse, and that the boy will cause trouble again and again. It's in Jovanni's genes. Nurture versus nature. Jovanni tests every inner resource and strength the doctor can muster. Dr. T welcomed the challenge nine years ago and, though tested by the youngster more than he wanted to be, will not give up now.

Teplitsky knows that the other boys are kind and gentle. That was expected. Planned. They share without squabbling. They respect each other's privacy and personal things that each loves as his own. They ask. They are polite. They rough it up with the best of them, but know when to quit. They understand "No."

Not Jovanni. Jovanni is a project. He hopes Carly's twin will not be like Jovanni.

"Jovanni," Dr. Teplitsky begins, "you know Arsenio works very hard on his clay figures, don't you?"

The boy does not look down. He does not look away. Unlike most youths who have done wrong, he meets Teplitsky's gaze. He listens. Then he looks up at Arsenio and smiles. "Yes, Father. But I work hard on my projects, too."

"We're not talking about you, Jovanni. We're talking about your brother."

Arsenio slaps his sides. The snapping sound startles, and both Dr. T and Jovanni jump. Then Arsenio stamps his feet. "Father, he is incapable of understanding. Everything must be his way or he rages."

Arsenio edges an inch closer to his youngest brother, his fist opening and closing. Jovanni retreats. If Arsenio could, he would pummel the little brat, teach him a lesson so that the fear of pain would keep the little monster out of his studio forever. *How wonderful would that be*, thinks Arsenio.

"Jovanni," the ever-patient father continues, "do you understand that this is wrong?"

The boy glances away, glares at his brother and, displaying the slightest of grins, nods.

Dr. Teplitsky pats his head, and then draws the boy into him. "Now please apologize to your brother. Tell him you won't do it again." The doctor turns to Arsenio, "You still have your drawing, don't you?" He doesn't wait for an answer. "You'll be able to make another maquette."

CHAPTER 16

Monday, 1:45 p.m.

"Where were you?" Megan asks Carly. Megan is in the kitchen reading *People* magazine, listening to Maroon Five's "If I Never See Your Face Again" on her iPod. She sees the reusable grocery bags in Carly's hands and hops up to help. Carly appreciates how Emily, in spite of failing health, raised Megan to be responsible. Gabe must be given credit for his daughter's upbringing, as well.

Carly slaps her packages onto the kitchen table. "There are more in the car. Thanks." Megan dashes past her. "Is your father back from the architect's yet?"

"Haven't seen him." she calls over her shoulder.

Carly starts to unpack the groceries when she hears a conversation coming from Yehuda's room. She tiptoes closer. The door's half closed. Carly strains to catch the drift.

"It's been too long," he says.

A beat.

"I know," he says.

A beat.

"I'm sorry it happened, too," he says.

Who is he talking to? She glances at the cordless kitchen phone; it's in the cradle. Yehuda does not have a cell phone.

"Perhaps you should," says Yehuda.

A beat.

Megan returns with two bags in each hand.

Carly tiptoes toward her, right index finger to her lips, and waves with her left hand for Megan to put down the packages and come closer. Carly whispers. "Who's in there with your grandfather?"

"No one." She points to her ear buds. "I've had these in most of the day. Haven't heard grandpa at all. But no one's walked past me."

"Are you sure? I met a gentleman named Buck, who is supposed to visit, but that isn't until the weekend."

Megan shakes her head. "Far as I know, no one's stopped by. But I thought old people always talked to themselves."

Carly frowns. "Not the ones in their right mind."

Now Megan grows uneasy at the thought that Yehuda may be losing his grip. She perks up. "I know. Maybe he's talking to Grandma. You know how much he misses her. I bet that's it."

"Let's hope so."

Carly raps on the doorjamb. "May we come in, Yehuda?"

"Who's stopping you?" he calls back.

Carly does a quick surveillance; no one is there who doesn't belong there. Yehuda is holding Sadie's picture. Carly and Megan both feel better.

"We need to make a quick stop. It won't take too long."

He waves them off. "Take your time. I've got all the company I need." He looks toward a spot on the wall and winks.

"Sure you'll be okay, Grandpa?" Megan leans and kisses the top of his head.

"Don't you worry about me, sweetheart. I have my angel watching over me."

"I know, Grandpa." Megan, glancing at the picture in his hand, gives a knowing smile to Carly.

In the kitchen, Carly reassures. "See, nothing to be concerned about. He was talking to your grandmother. I bet he'll fall right to sleep. His eyes looked heavy."

"Then he won't miss us."

They put the last of the groceries away.

"Where're we going?" asks Megan. "You just got here."

Carly studies her stepdaughter for a moment, sees the iPod on the table, her iPod Touch for her games, and her iPhone. Her room is a post-apocalyptic disaster. They've lived in Island Bluffs less than a week and the girl is already heading in the wrong direction. Of course, Carly doesn't know about Megan and Yehuda's little expedition to the basement, but that wouldn't count as being constructive in Carly's book.

"You've been holed up in this house since we moved in," answers Carly.

Megan knows where this is going. "Duh, It's only been like four days. Do you expect me to be totally unpacked by now?" She points to an unopened box on the floor. "Even Dad hasn't finished."

"Your father has been working nonstop to get this house ready. He had an important meeting with the architect or he would've finished everything."

Megan tilts her head and takes half a step back, ready to dodge Carly's next move. She has no comeback for being lazy.

Carly continues. "We're going to find something for you to do. You can't loll around all summer doing nothing."

"I could study for my SATs."

"You could, but I'm betting you won't. I've got something better in mind."

"I could deliver 'Meals on Wheels.'"

"That's a great idea. Let's drive there now and sign you up."

Megan scuffs the floor. "I don't really like that idea."

"If that's the best you got," Carly says, "you and I are going for a ride."

Monday, 2:30 p.m.

They park in front of the Island Bluffs library. There are no parking meters in this town. None will be installed until a major storm causes the municipality to rebuild much of its infrastructure and look for every possible revenue source.

Megan balks as she figures out why Carly parks in this spot. "Working in a library is for geeks."

"Volunteering is good for your college applications, which I might add, you need to start thinking about. You've mentioned B.U. in the past. Where else are you considering applying?"

"I haven't thought much about it. I still have time."

"Before you turn around, the summer will be over and you'll have to get them in. I know your guidance counselor gave you a list to consider before we left Pine Brook. Besides, now that they have the common application for college, it's a lot easier to apply to college than either your father or I had it."

"Back in the day."

"That's right, during the dark ages." Carly sneers in a minor triumph of going toe-to-toe with Megan. "Pretty soon, I'll be busy with the baby, and then it will be more difficult to help. No sense waiting 'til the last minute."

"No need to worry about that with you around," Megan says under her breath as she slams the car door shut.

"Care to mutter a little louder?" says Carly. "I didn't quite make that out."

Megan clears her throat. "I said I would get everything done by the end of the summer."

"That's what I thought you said," says Carly, rounding the car and stepping onto the sidewalk. No sense pressing it further.

Megan halts in front of the library. It's a square building. White stucco front, clapboard on the sides. Lots of windows, the shades pulled down to lessen the glare and heat of the summer sun.

"This is so lame. If I have to work, I want to get paid."

"That's encouraging."

Carly steps toward the door. Megan lags behind.

"Do I have to?"

"The Army recruiter is just down the block."

"You have to be eighteen."

"You'd be a valuable weapon against the enemy. I bet they'd make an exception. Now are we going inside or are you going to make a scene out here?"

Constance Merriweather has her back to the front door when Carly and Megan cross the library threshold.

"Excuse me," says Carly, to get the woman's attention.

The librarian is trim. She wears a white blouse and a straight navy skirt. Her gray hair is shoulder length and held in place with a tortoise-shell hairband that matches her glass frames. She wears no rings, no earrings, no watch, and only a bit of red lipstick.

"Is it too cold in here? I'm forever fiddling with the thermostat," she says by way of a greeting while grabbing the dangling sleeves of the sweater to tie them together.

"It's just fine." Carly introduces herself and Megan and proceeds to explain why they're there.

"This must be my lucky day," the librarian claps in glee. "Mrs. Holmes, she's the other librarian, needed to take a personal leave. I've been all alone for two weeks."

Constance Merriweather speaks rapidly; her voice is high pitched. Her cheeks redden as she speaks. Her arms propel through the air, as if stirring an invisible pot of sauce.

"What's wrong?" asks Carly.

"Lung cancer. Smoked for forty years. The poor soul stopped last September. Joined the gym. Says she never felt better. I tell you she lost weight and was looking younger every day, and now this."

The door opens behind them. A blond-haired, green-eyed teen enters. Megan scopes him out. He is tall. He sports a tee shirt with a silkscreened picture of the Dave Matthews Band's from its Indiana University concert, *Rock for Change*—in support of Barak Obama—no sleeves, calculated slashes in the fabric, ripples of muscles exposed. Killer chops. Megan imagines the rest.

"Hello, Jürgen," the librarian says.

He waves. His glance lingers on Megan for an extra pulse; she grows warm.

"Looking for anything special?" the librarian asks.

"I want to get a jump on my college reading." He holds a scroll of papers in his fist. *Go Tell It On the Mountain* or *Grapes of Wrath*. "Which do you recommend?"

"Both. But if you must pick one, read Steinbeck first. Given the economy these days, his book will resonate for you."

Megan wants to blurt out, *I read that this year. If you need any help . . .*

He shoots a "thumbs up" and flashes a smile that contributes to global warming: icebergs beware. For Megan, it's Streisand seeing Redford for the first time in *The Way We Were*. Her tongue swells. For a moment, she can't speak.

The librarian turns back to Carly and Megan. "Where was I?"

Quick recovery. "Miss Merriweather," chirps Megan. She stands straighter, more animated. "I'd be happy to help any way I can."

Ms. Merriweather's eyes widen. "You're a godsend, child. Sent from the angels above. I was fretting so, just a few moments ago. There's too much here for one person to do. When can you start?" Her arms stop propelling. She clasps them in front of her, fingers interdigitating. She is a supplicant in prayer, thankful for this good fortune.

Megan scans the aisles for Jürgen but does not see him. She turns to Carly, bubbling over. "Can you pick me up in a little while? I'd like to get a head start."

Carly follows Megan's eyes. "I think getting an early start is very wise. I have some errands to run. See you in a little while."

Then, for the first time, of her own volition, Megan plants a kiss on Carly's cheek.

CHAPTER 17

Monday, 11:45 a.m.
Knowing that Carly will challenge Megan to find a summer job after he leaves the house, Gabe dashes out to Point Pleasant, anxious to finalize the architectural plans for the house. Under any other circumstance, logic dictates that they should've built the addition while remaining in their Pine Brook house until it was finished. The noise and dust will overwhelm, not to mention the loss of privacy. They would have taken the commonsense approach if there had not been the imperative for Carly to be close to Dr. Teplitsky in her last trimester. Then there was the irrefutable fact that Gabe was drawn to this particular house. Why? What was so special about it? The dock? The way it sat on a bluff? None stood up to an assault by reason.

If any greater logic existed about choosing this house, the Berks would not have ended up in Island Bluffs. Maybe it was the call of the Sirens?

All this for another baby!

Does he really want one? After all, Megan's seventeen. He and Carly were on the verge of becoming empty nesters. Let the fun begin. But no, he has to be understanding. Loving. Bend over backwards so Carly can have that baby she so desperately wants regardless of the sacrifices and inconveniences that accompany, what has turned out to be, a major project. In the grand scheme of things, there is always time for fun. Really? If you buy that, there's an island for sale for twenty-four dollars' worth of beads.

Gabe rolls into the parking lot of Frizzell and Feltz. Verity is the junior partner of Carl Feltz, a grizzled man whose years of sailing are chiseled into his weather-beaten face like a nautical map. Verity, on the other hand, is petite, with brown hair gathered in a short pony tail, straight lines, and penetrating chocolate eyes made vibrant by her choice of tortoise-shell glasses over contacts. A look akin to McCain's running mate. Verity wears a simple cobalt-blue dress with white sailor's buttons and matching navy two-inch platform heels. She's comfortable in her skin, sure of her skills.

Verity unrolls the blueprints and uses six-inch wide conch shells—a mélange of coral, pink, and white—as paperweights to anchor the corners.

"We'll need to do this in stages," she begins.

Gabe interrupts. "Will it be completed by the time the baby comes? That's my concern."

"If you move out, it can be finished early. Otherwise, it's dicey."

"Moving out's not an option."

She's puzzled. "There are plenty of rentals around. You can drive a hard bargain in this market. It would make it easier for everyone, but particularly for Carly, and it would make your builder's life a cakewalk compared to working around you. I've already discussed this with Cole." Cole is Cole Brancusi, a rough-and-tumble, no-nonsense contractor who specializes in rehabbing older houses along the Jersey Shore. He and Verity have worked on many projects together, which was reason enough for Gabe to go with him despite lower bids.

"Carly and I have talked it over *ad nauseam*. We would move out in a heartbeat if it were just the two of us. But my dad's with us now. We don't want to put him through too many changes. Moving here was traumatic enough." No need to mention Megan. The last thing he needs is another woman lecturing him about taking Megan out of her school her senior year.

Verity sits down, takes her glasses off and, without thinking, puts the stem in her mouth. Gabe remains quiet, hoping she will say what he wants to hear. A car honks, and a delivery truck blares, somewhere outside, that annoying beeping when it shifts into reverse. Verity slips her glasses back on and leans a tad forward, poring over the blueprints again, but not really seeing them. "Look, it's doable while all of you live there. The trouble comes when you take off the roof in an old house. Dust and pounding nails aside, adding extensions—both up and out—onto houses like this one is an adventure into uncharted waters."

Gabe knows this will be a crapshoot, and his high expectations are unreasonable. He tries to sound upbeat. "Cole swears he can make it work, otherwise we would've waited."

"As good as Cole is, no one can guarantee that," says Verity. "What if it rains or a summer storm crops up and tears the covering off the frame once the roof is removed? Your furniture and everything else you own will get ruined."

"We'll use plastic."

"Nowhere near foolproof."

"Then that's what insurance is for."

"Carly will never forgive you," says Verity, "and I don't even know her."

Same species.

Gabe is resolute. "Add it to the list of everything else I do that pisses her off."

"You like living on the edge, don't you?" Verity reveals a twisted lateral incisor when she smiles. Her appeal heightens. "This can turn into your worst nightmare."

Not a rise from him.

"Okay, then, let's start," she says, seeing that Gabe will not waiver. "You can always change your mind and move out during the worst part."

"Can Cole work on the master bedroom at the same time as he works on the rest of the house?"

She hunches her thin shoulders. "Why not? Everything else will be a mess. You may want to consider buying Army surplus gas masks. Soot could be an issue for Carly. It'll make it a lot easier to breathe while you're living through this."

"Not only a talented architect, but a comedian to boot. Does that raise your fee?"

She rolls her lips inward in a *you-have-no-clue-what's-in-store-for-you* look. "I'm serious about the air you'll be forced to breathe. Besides Carly, you need to worry about your father. That construction air is hazardous for someone in his eighties."

"Don't think I don't appreciate what you're saying. If it makes you feel any better, I'll leave this up to Cole. If the day comes when he says the air's too bad to breathe, we'll move out until he says we can move back. Are you good with that?"

She nods. "Glad you finally came to your senses."

"I'm a lawyer but not a total jerk."

"You had me going there for a while." They both smile; Verity continues. "You said there was something else you needed help with?"

"I almost forgot. I need to enlarge the septic. The town inspector's given me thirty days to make it larger. Says code has changed over the years. What used to be good for a house this size isn't good anymore. I tried to talk him into grandfathering us in."

"That's baloney. The one you have is fine. I'll give him a call."

"I'd rather make a new one to be safe. Can you recommend someone reliable who knows the ropes, can get the job done, and get the town off my back?"

"You'll be spending money you don't need to spend."

"Just the same, I'd feel better." He wants to add that he's doing it to be a good neighbor, but knows it will sound lame.

She opens her Outlook contacts and prints the information for him. "Luke Walters. Been in the business forty years. Knows the building inspectors in every town. It's as good as done when he's on your side."

He takes the printout. "When can you file the final plans with their zoning board?"

"I will have them to you by the end of the week so you can review them and I can make any last minutes changes before I submit them."

"When does the zoning board meet next?"

"A week from tomorrow, so we have plenty of time."

"Do you expect them to give us any trouble? I really want to get this done in a timely way."

"That's why you're paying me the big bucks. The plans will sail through. You'll be able to start the next day. Once you and your family are established in Island Bluffs, they will consider you one of them."

"Given that I've already met the sheriff, I don't know if I want to be accepted by this community or continue to remain an outsider. The latter does have its appeal."

"Kreiser? He's all bark and no bite. Once you settle in, Island Bluffs is a great town."

"I need to be convinced of that. Kreiser's idea of issuing speeding tickets has already made an indelible impression."

Verity shrugs. "Just his way of saying hello. You'll see. Give the locals a chance."

A chance to do what?

CHAPTER 18

Monday, 3:15 p.m.

Gabe is anxious to get home. He hits the driveway made of crushed seashells mixed with gravel too fast; the wheels spin. The car fishtails. In time, he learns to take the gentle incline slower. He flips the car door closed; he turns to see Carly ease her car behind his. Megan hops out and sprints toward him, almost tipping him over with a huge hug.

"I heard the football team needs a tight end that can tackle like that," he says, struggling to keep his balance.

Megan makes a sour face. "Not funny. I have to tell you that I got the coolest job just now." Gabe catches the glint in Carly's eye.

"Aren't you the same person who swore up and down that there was nothing cool in this godforsaken place? Or something to that effect."

Carly breaks in. "Mr. Cool's name is Jürgen."

Megan puts her hands on her hips and tosses Carly a *right-you-are* smirk. "I wouldn't say he's the *only* reason."

Carly gives it back, raises her brows and asks, "And the second reason is?"

"Uh," Megan buys time, "I like books?"

"Is that a question?" Carly smiles. She is pleased that Megan is so animated.

Gabe focuses on his daughter. "Regardless of the reason, don't fall for the first guy who gives you a wink. You're too good for that."

How I wished he gave me a wink.

She steps back. "Daaaaad. He doesn't even know my name. I caught a glimpse of him in the library. By the time the librarian, Miss Merriweather, stopped blabbing so I could start filing the book returns away, Jürgen was gone. I never got to meet him."

"Just the same, I wouldn't go throwing myself on him when you do," Gabe says. "Guys respect women who create some intrigue. Make it difficult to get close."

"And what makes you an expert?" Carly asks.

"I got you, didn't I? You acted like I barely existed; I knew you were interested."

"Oh, really? I was interested right from the beginning, but I couldn't let on. I had to make you work for it."

"And I am glad you did," he says.

Carly raises her brow in agreement and then turns to Megan. "Your dad's right. If you think you like this guy, play it cool. If you make it too easy, he'll think you're cheap and not worth pursuing."

Carly tilts her head at Gabe, insinuating how easy men are when you play them right; Megan gets it. A sisterhood is emerging between them.

"Now that that's settled," says Gabe, flashing the rolled blueprints, "I need to show you the latest update." He marches inside the house; they follow.

"Are these the final plans?" asks Carly.

"Those will be submitted Monday. Verity needs to tweak a couple of things, but these have all the changes."

The tumult in the kitchen wakes Yehuda from his lengthy snooze. He shuffles to the doorway. The kitchen is the focal point of the house; it gives comfort. The lone window brackets a view of the bay. Lace curtains render a clichéd scene of rows of waves, birds flapping, lazy clouds and Ol' Barney in the distance, reminiscent of a preprinted art board in a Paradise paint-by-the-numbers kit.

"Sleep well, Dad?" Gabe asks.

"Like a baby."

Carly eyes Megan not to betray overhearing his ramblings when they stood outside of his door.

Gabe unrolls the blueprints on the table. "Want to take a look, Dad?"

"Later," answers Yehuda. He touches Megan's shoulder and motions to the front door. She follows him out; Gabe and Carly are too preoccupied to notice.

Yehuda slips into a weathered wicker chair once white, now colorless. Megan sits cross-legged on the wide-planked porch. "Are you going to give me a lecture about the boy I saw at the library?" She braces for the talk. "I know, I know. He's probably German. But he seems so nice."

"What boy?" There's a twinkle in his pale gray eyes.

"Grandpa, even when you're sleeping, you hear everything we say!"

He scrunches into his most contemplative face, tilts his head this way and that, searching for the right words to pluck out of the air. "Oh, that boy!" Earlier, their cars skidding on the gravel did arouse him. He heard Megan mention someone named Jürgen and, without question, he has to be of German descent. "No, this is not about him or anyone else you might have met today."

Megan blows out a stream of relief. "So what is so hush-hush?"

"It's about someone *I* met."

Could this be about the conversation she and Carly overheard earlier? Is it an imaginary friend?

"Who, Grandpa? When did you have time to meet someone? I thought you were home all day." She is expecting him to discuss Grandma Sadie, but Yehuda surprises her.

"You're right. I never left."

Megan scratches her head. "I don't get it."

"Let me explain." Yehuda tells her about the noise he heard in the attic when she took a walk on the beach. It was melodic.

"What kind of music?" she asks, playing along. "Country? Blues? Hip Hop?"

"It was hard to tell. I searched everywhere to find out where it was coming from. I even went into your room thinking maybe you left something on that played music."

"That's one thing I'm careful about," she says.

"I thought I was losing my mind."

She pales at the thought.

"I'm not scaring you, am I?" he asks. "Because I am perfectly sane. I know what I heard." He says it as much to convince Megan as to reassure himself.

He glances through the screen to make certain Gabe and Carly are not eavesdropping. He turns back to Megan. "When I didn't find anything in your room, I turned to leave and heard something again."

"What did it sound like?"

"It was muffled. Like a voice trapped behind the wall."

"Wait a second. Was it a voice or music? Which was it, Grandpa?"

"It was music and words. Don't you remember we heard that blast of music in my room?"

"I humored you. I really thought it was the wind. Are you telling me you really heard music this time?" Megan asks, her eyes widening with every word.

As Yehuda explains, Megan feels a tap on her shoulder. She whips around. The hairs on her arms stand. Her skin crawls. No one is there. It's the middle of the day, her parents are inside the house, a few feet away, she's sitting with her grandfather, and there is no logical reason for her to be spooked. But she is.

Yehuda beckons her to come closer. She leans in. Their conspiracy heightens. She smells the faded Aqua Velva he splashed on that morning.

"I searched everywhere but didn't find a thing. By then I was tired. So I go to my room and lay down. Just for a few minutes. The house is empty; it's a good time to take a nap. I'm doing that more these days."

Yehuda can see that this amuses her. His heart flutters when he sees this child smile, that maybe it's a sign that her broken heart may finally be mending.

He remains serious. "Naps are the best kept secret for longevity."

Megan loves to hear Yehuda talk, even if it's about something silly. After all, how lucky is she to have her grandfather alive and living with them? "And then what, Grandpa? Did you dream about Grandma Sadie when you were lying down? Is that who you were talking to?"

"I have to confess that it was better than dreaming about your Grandma. No sooner had I put my head on my pillow than she came to visit."

"Who did? Grandma? You're losing me," says Megan.

"No. Her name is Polly."

"Who's Polly?"

"That's what I'm trying to tell you. She's the one making all that fuss."

Megan shakes her head. "I was following you up until the nap. The music. The voice in the wall. I'm good with all that. You lost me with this Polly person."

"Polly is the girl who lives here."

Megan's voice ratchets up a notch. "We live here."

Yehuda shushes her; his voice softens. He points upward. "In the attic."

"Grandpa, what're you talking about? Are you trying to tell me that Polly is a ghost? You're scaring me."

"Shhhh. Not so loud. She's not out to hurt anyone. She's friendly."

She bites her lower lip. "You may not remember, but when I was little, Casper the Ghost scared the bejabbers out of me. Clowns totally freak me out." She slumps. Her breaths quicken and turn shallow. Megan's concern for Yehuda mounts.

"I used to tell you ghost stories. Don't you remember? About walks in the black forest and . . ."

Megan covers her ears. "And the horses and the white sheets. You used to scare me with those stories."

"Some of them were real. You need to know that there are certain things in life we can't explain, but that it's okay."

"You always told me that. I guess your Polly is one of those things?"

He concurs. "She is."

Megan looks over her shoulder toward the front door. Still clear. "Grandpa, I don't think you should tell anyone else about this."

"That's why I'm telling *you*. Your father and Carly won't believe me. They'll say that I'm off my rocker. Make me see a shrink. Maybe I'd be lucky and get off only taking pills. Or worse yet, they'll send me to some nursing home or one of those C & C places."

Megan's confused. "Canadian Club? I'm not following."

"I wish they served hard stuff. I'm talking about the *cane and crutches* crowd. And at those places they only serve Coke. If it comes to that, I might as well kill myself and end it while I still have my dignity."

Megan rolls her eyes. "Uh . . . okay." She swallows hard. "So what did this Polly person say?"

"What did she say?" he repeats. "Let me think." He has a blank stare, and then turns animated. Yehuda did not go to his room after searching for the source of the music as he told Megan.

* * *

An apparition morphs out from the house. It hovers above Yehuda. At first it is not well defined, but then it coalesces into the shape of a young woman. The specter approximates Megan's age. She is surrounded by a golden glow; she gazes at Yehuda. Her translucent lips beam.

Yehuda remains asleep.

The ghost floats nearer to Yehuda's ear.

Her lips move.

Yehuda twitches and swats, as if a fly is buzzing about. He shifts his body, opens a sleepy eye, cocks his head, nuzzles toward the phantom undertones, and a crease expands into upturned lips.

The ghost hovers.

They study each other. Before Yehuda utters a welcome, the ghost morphs back through the wall. Yehuda stands and touches the place in the wall where the ghost passed through. His fingers caress the spot.

"It's a pleasure to meet you, too, Polly," he says to the wall.

He knows she hears him.

* * *

"And then what did you do?" Megan asks.

"I was pleased that Polly appeared, but I was still tired, so I laid back down."

"She visited you again, didn't she?"

"How did you know?"

"Carly and I heard you talking to her. We thought you were talking to Grandma Sadie."

"I showed her Grandma Sadie's picture. And then she told me things."

He is so believable that Megan wants to accept Yehuda's story about Polly. "What sort of things?"

"She made me promise that when the time was right, she would let me tell you and the others what happened to her. For now, I can't share it with you."

"Grandpa, you told me all this and you won't tell me Polly's story? That's not fair."

"Give her time to get used to all of us. Remember, she's been living here a long time without any company. We invaded her space."

"But it's our house."

"It is her house, too, for as long as she needs to stay here."

* * *

While Yehuda and Megan speak in hushed tones on the porch, Gabe reviews the architectural plans with Carly. Blueprints cover the kitchen table. They huddle over the part that depicts the master bedroom.

"So she's extending the south wall seven feet more than we discussed," he says.

"The room will be too large. Are you expecting an army to live with us?"

"Ye of little faith. I was thinking that if we put our bed here," he points to an inner wall, "we could set up workout equipment facing the ocean. That'd be an awesome view while we're sweating away."

She eases her hand on top of his. "Gabe, it would be more awesome if you considered having the bed face the ocean so when we wake up, we will have the most beautiful sight in the world. And I can promise you that there are other ways to work up a sweat gazing out on the water."

He cracks a smile. Gives her a squeeze. "That's just what I was thinking. We'll put the exercise equipment in this extended space. Besides, I don't want a glare to interfere with me watching a football game while I'm working out."

"Who said men aren't adaptable?"

"When it comes to Jewish husbands, 'adaptable' is our middle name."

It was her turn to sport a sly grin. "Truth be told, that's the reason I married you."

"The only reason?"

Hands on hips, she feigns bewilderment. "Isn't that enough?" What she will never admit to Gabe or anyone else is how her mother told her to find a Jewish man to marry. "They treat their women real good," her mother told Carly more than once. "They're wonderful providers and they respect their women. Seen it time and time again. Their mothers know how to raise them. Not like most others."

While Gabe rolls up the blueprints and slips elastic bands around both ends, Carly flashes back to her encounter with Olivia. She reaches into her pocket and fingers the card with the woman's phone number. Say something? Don't mention it? Part of Carly craves to tell Gabe about Olivia, and part of her asks what it would accomplish.

He would tell her that she has every right to be insecure and have doubts, that Olivia suffered a tragedy that has nothing to do with them, and that Carly is worrying over nothing. This from a man who was originally against them dealing with Dr. Teplitsky. Now that Gabe's embraced the notion of having another baby, no matter the emotional toll it is taking on Carly, he would say most anything to comfort her.

Sometimes, even an understanding man may not be able to console someone on so touchy a problem. This was one of those times.

Monday evening

It's twilight. Dr. Teplitsky is in his study. No expense is spared. Philippine mahogany, known as Luan paneling, lines the walls. Its rich caramel patina radiates warmth and safety, virtues Teplitsky imbues in everything. Hand-hewn beams carved with a broadaxe and adze form the coffered ceiling. These are support beams, not designer decorations. The beams have been rescued from the barn on a neighboring farmhouse torn down years back. The wood is at least seventy years old. Probably older.

He opens the humidor and fills his favorite meerschaum pipe, stained yellow and brown from years of use, with a custom blend of cube-cut burley tobacco; it is mild with a natural sweetness. The wafts of smoke remind him of his father, of a time long ago, when the world was less complex. An innocent time. A happy time. A safe time. A time that no longer exists but which he has tried hard to recreate for his sons. By his reckoning, he is succeeding.

He savors the aroma. He takes a long draw, tobacco shards crackle and glow. He holds it and then exhales, the plume curling toward the ceiling. There is a rap on the door. He grabs a metal tool and scrapes off the burning embers. The flame goes out.

"Iario, how were the boys today?"

"Except for Jovanni breaking Aurelio's maquette, it was a good day."

Teplitsky muses out loud. "He seems to be doing more of that sort of stuff lately. How do the other boys get along with him?"

Iario hesitates. He is sixteen, emerging out of the chrysalis of teen awkwardness. Light brown hair. Wavy. Not that tall. Average build. He struggles to create definition by lifting weights and dropping to the floor, at a moment's notice, to do pushups or stomach crunches. He cannot pass a mirror without self-inspection in the hopes that his efforts to transform his body show results. Of late, they do.

Iario likes science. He answers his father. "I don't think you want to know."

"I wouldn't have asked."

Teplitsky gestures for his eldest to sit down.

"It makes me uncomfortable."

"What does? To tell the truth? Try. You will feel better."

"I'm not so sure of that, Father."

Teplitsky motions with the pipe. "Go ahead. I insist. Don't hold anything back."

Iario steels himself, as if he was about to receive a blow. "No one likes Jovanni."

"Not even Leonzio? He's the easiest to get along with."

Iario shakes his head. "Not even Leonzio. Father, Jovanni has a mean streak in him. He's not like the rest of us. He hides our things. Breaks them. Never listens. Doesn't do his chores. Somehow he's different."

Teplitsky wonders how much he should say. The boy is old enough to learn more about his youngest brother, but could he digest it? The doctor struggles, unsure of how much to explain.

"He *is* different, Iario. I've known that from the beginning, yet, in the end, it shouldn't matter. He's in a house filled with love and understanding. We have the finest of everything here: food, music, teachers, and an abundance of art. Plus we have a large family that loves him." *They will. They must.* "Like all of you, he wants for nothing. He may be too young to appreciate these things now, but he will when he gets older. I can assure you of that."

Iario starts to speak and then stops.

Teplitsky raises a brow. He glances at the pipe; he wishes it were still lit. He reaches for the bowl to feel its comforting warmth.

"You don't agree?" Teplitsky asks, waving the pipe.

"It's not that I don't agree, Father, but you're assuming that these surroundings and the love you give us will overcome what makes Jovanni act that way."

He measures the words. "It has served all of you well."

"And we're grateful to you for everything you've done for us. But Jovanni? I don't think he understands or appreciates. And you said yourself, he's different."

"Give him more time. No two of you are alike. Each of you responds differently to your surroundings regardless of how carefully I've planned things or what I may think is right or wrong. You'll see. Jovanni will come around. Everyone else has. Jovanni needs more time."

"And if he doesn't?" asks Iario.

"That's something I cannot contemplate."

Iario stands to leave. "Is there anything else, Father?"

"You may not remember, but Arsenio had a difficult streak in him. He's better now. The same will happen to Jovanni."

The boy turns to leave and stops. "The way you're talking about him, describing what will happen, I can't help but sense that Jovanni is some sort of experiment. Is that what this is about? Because, if he is, we have a right to know."

Teplitsky draws in a sharp breath. He always knew there would be a day this question would be asked. On one hand, he is surprised it has not been asked sooner. Even so, he's not prepared to answer it. Not yet.

Instead, he answers this way. "As much as you and your brothers are."

That seems to satisfy Iario.

Teplitsky has bought time.

He knows time is fleeting.

He cherishes the time he has left.

He hopes there is enough to finish the last part, the part integrally being played out by Carly Berk.

He hopes when he is gone that they understand. That they will accept. That they will forgive him. Approve of what he has done.

At this moment, his hopes are high. How ironic that the turns of life—his life—have brought him a mere step away from his penultimate goal: Phase Three.

CHAPTER 19

Saturday, 9:00 a.m.
During the week the last few boxes are opened except for a couple that are superfluous and are stored in the attic. Gabe and Carly keep track of items they discover they need on a list attached to the refrigerator with a yellow Sponge Bob magnet. Thirteen-gallon kitchen bags. Energy-efficient light bulbs. Aluminum foil. Double-A batteries. The list grows.

Like a transforming chrysalis, each day stirs life into the Berk house in Island Bluffs until it blossoms into a vibrant home. Yehuda is chastised each time he offers to help arrange this or fix that, and for the first time, he does not mind being told what to do by his son and daughter-in-law. Maybe this is the definition of old age: when you can no longer tell your children what to do and it is their turn to tell you what to do . . . and you listen to them. Being free of any duties and responsibilities, Yehuda turns his attention to his small garden patch. Earlier in the week, Gabe took Yehuda to a local nursery where he bought an assortment of plants: Jersey beefsteak tomatoes, green and red peppers, Italian eggplant, cucumbers, radishes, and carrots. Each day since, Yehuda has planted his treasures, waters them, and scrupulously weeds the patch. At day's end, he would sit in his rocker on the porch until he dozed off.

Yehuda welcomes the weekend. He sits on the veranda reading the Saturday Asbury Park Press and parts of the Sunday New York Times that are delivered a day early when the roar of an engine shatters the morning calm. It is a sight to behold: a vintage World War II motorcycle painted in faded military green, with a torpedo-shaped empty sidecar hooked to its side. The driver wears a helmet with side flaps and goggles. Think Snoopy versus the Red Baron. The driver fishtails to a stop in a cloud of calcium chalk that erupts from the crushed seashells with the flair of Jackie Robinson sliding under a tag at home.

As the dust settles, Buck Hopewell peels off his goggles and helmet. Rings of brown give him an owlish appearance. He is a hoot. Buck is slightly bowlegged and sashays up the steps; Carly opens the door to greet him. Yehuda is amused.

"Dad, this is the gentleman I was telling you about. Buck works over at the clinic. I thought it would be nice if the two of you met." She turns to Buck and embraces his hand. She winks as she says, "I really appreciate you coming over today, Buck."

"It's the neighborly thing to do, Miss Carly. Besides, you probably saved my life. Thought about doing a little skydiving today. Driving here's a lot safer."

She eyes his mode of transportation. "I'm not so sure."

Yehuda stands next to her. "Don't listen to her, Buck. What do these kids know about having fun?"

He reaches out to Yehuda. "I like you already," says Buck. Buck's leathery face is sunbaked. He's muscular and lean. He wears a denim shirt with faded jeans and well-worn leather boots. In another time, he would have been plucked from central casting for a Marlboro ad. The archetype macho man.

"I was warned that Island Bluffs is not the friendliest town." Yehuda implies that Buck breaks the mold. "However, I did meet a nice young policeman over at the station last week."

"If you did, he's still green. Give him a little seasoning and he'll be like the others," says Buck. "Folks 'round here stay pretty much to themselves. Prefer to mind their own beeswax, if you know what I mean. Strangers, well, they need to find their own way. Time has a way of sorting most things out."

"Where do you fit into this story?" Carly asks.

"I'm too old for the nonsense that goes on 'round here. Thing about me is that I can fix near anything you have, and I'm only a holler up the road in the next town."

"Would you like some iced tea? It's hot out here," she says.

"Beer'd be better." Buck points to Yehuda's covered arms. "Why're you wearing long sleeves? No need to be wearing a bow tie and dressed like that when it's ninety degrees. You going to work or somethin'?"

"It's my uniform."

"Ice cream truck?"

"Dental technician in my past life."

"No fooling."

"He makes a mean set of dentures, if you ever need them," Carly adds.

Buck wiggles his front teeth. "Choppers still working fine, but I'll keep that in mind."

The octogenarians talk for a bit. Where are you from? Did you serve in the war?

Buck talks about being assigned to ordnance in Hollywood before being transferred to the infantry in the South Pacific. He missed Iwo Jima but was in the thick of things when our forces retook Manila. Buck did see action in the battle of Okinawa.

Yehuda is vague. Says the Germans captured him. Worked in the camps. One of the lucky ones to survive. He talks about Sadie.

Buck mentions a would-be bride lost at sea.

Then Yehuda snaps his fingers. "You're the one!"

"The one what?"

"In that newspaper article pinned to the wall in the police station."

"You saw that?"

"My condolences. That's a hard loss to get over."

Buck starts to answer, then stops. He clears his throat. "Never been able to," he manages to say. "All these years later, and I still think about her most every day."

"Same as I miss my bride," says Yehuda, pining for days gone by when Sadie was alive.

Carly puts a crimp in the moment. "Sorry to interfere, fellas, but I need to call a locksmith to change the locks on the outside doors. No telling who has keys to this house."

"No need, Miss Carly. I have one errand to run down at the marina and then I'll be back in a jiff. Those locksmiths can put quite the dent in your wallet." He points to his sidecar. "Always have tools with me. I'll take care of it soon's I get back."

"Buck, I invited you here so you could meet Yehuda, not to do any work."

He taps Yehuda's shoulder. "It's not work when you are helping friends. Don't you fret none."

Carly doesn't challenge Buck any further. They discuss types of locks, she hands him money, and then she leaves right behind Buck to tackle the list of missing items she needs to buy.

Buck zips over to the marina. Thoughts of a quick return to change the locks at the Berk house are put on hold when the captain of the *Searcher* asks him to fix a broken water pump.

"How bad is it?" Buck asks the captain. "Need to get back and help some new folks in town change their locks."

"Anyone else would take half a day. You'll fix it in a shake," says the captain. "Besides, look what we found out there yesterday."

He opens his palm and flashes a silver spoon at Buck. "This is for you." If Buck had any thoughts of blowing off the captain, the spoon helps make up his mind.

"Where?" Buck asking "where" means he expects to hear the exact coordinates where the *Searcher* discovered the piece.

The captain points to a spot on the map. He circles it with a pen.

Buck nods, branding the coordinates into his memory bank. He drops the spoon in his back jeans pocket and turns to the broken pump. He retrieves his tool kit from the sidecar and lays a velvet cloth on the ground. Each tool is placed in a specific order with a surgeon's care. Through grease and oil, Buck is the kind of guy who will remain neat and clean. Spotless. Minutes later, problem solved. The pump pumps, as it should.

Finished, tools stowed back in the sidecar, Buck shades his eyes and searches the blue waters. In the distance, he notes the lone swimmer plowing through the surf, plodding toward the Barnegat Lighthouse. How many years has that man plied these waters? Always alone. Like everyone else, Buck wonders who he is and why he swims the channel each day.

The swimmer is one of the many unsolved mysteries of Island Bluffs. For whatever the reason, no one has ever challenged the man. How easy could it have been to ply the waters alongside him and gain his attention or, better yet, plop in front of him, make him stop and ask, "Who are you?"

Buck has his suspicions, but has never bothered to play out his hunch. There was never a compelling reason to do so. When that changes, when it might be a good thing to know the swimmer's identity, Buck promises himself that he will find out just who he is.

It's Saturday morning; the library will close at one o'clock. Megan parks around back. She skips/walks to the front door and greets Miss Merriweather with a grin and a wave. After a few days of working at the library, Megan has settled into a routine. She grabs the trolley parked under the chute designed to collect books returned when the library is closed, arranges them in order, and then pushes the rolling cart down each aisle, careful to return every book to its rightful place. In most instances, a space greets her; most often it is obvious where the missing books belong. In a rare instance, there is no space. Then Megan questions if she's searching the right spot or if the book had been misfiled in the first place.

Two books remain to be filed. Megan stops to admire a picture of the Barnegat Lighthouse that she has ignored each time she shuffled by it. She steps closer. Two men stand at the base, their arms linked. The caption reads:

Sheriff Kreiser and Larry Hanson
Island Bluffs, May 15, 1948

Megan wonders who Larry Hanson is. She's not the only one. Everyone else viewing the picture in the library has wondered the same thing for all these years.

Sheriff Rudi Kreiser motions Hank Gerhardt to come over to the patrol car. Hank owns the soda fountain/confectionary store in downtown Island Bluffs. Ever since the Woolworth's 5&10 closed back in '97, Hank has carried sundries, sewing supplies, swimming tubes, snorkels, fins, beach towels, and the like. Downtown Island Bluffs is a prototypical Main Street, USA. Kinkos took over the local Post Office in a sweetheart deal that gave it a ninety-nine year lease for peanuts. There's also a beauty salon, a dry cleaner, a bodega open 24/7 run by Guatemalans who are asked to prove their immigrant status more times than necessary, and an L-shaped municipal building. The municipal building contains the Town Hall with a warren of offices that include the tax collector, the building inspector who doubles as the fire inspector, the courtroom, and four jail cells that are used more for storage than to house scalawags. The main drag is called—no surprise here—Main Street.

Given that it is the July Fourth weekend, there are fewer passersby at this time of day than usual: a woman with a baby stroller, a bicyclist who would lose a race to a tortoise, two senior citizens sitting on a bench donated by the Rotary Club eating vanilla ice cream in cups, and a Verizon lineman running FiOS fiber optic cable through the center of town in anticipation of a new marketing campaign to challenge Comcast. The street lamps are converted gas lamps reminiscent of candlepower from Olde London Towne.

Hank Gerhardt kneels down. Sheriff Kreiser's face is hidden behind reflective sunglasses under the black patent leather bill of his cap. His dark blue shirt is trimmed with shiny gold buttons. Epaulets dangle off his broad shoulders. Cold air blasts from the patrol car's open window; the windshield fogs from the heat and humidity.

The sheriff appears ageless and formidable, even though he is out of shape.

He is a soldier of good.

A warrior for Island Bluffs.

A champion for Island Bluffs.

A keeper of secrets.

"Weekend's supposed to be clear and sunny. No rain. Season's gonna finally pick up," says Kreiser.

"Means more business for the both of us," answers Hank. "Already got some from that new family that moved in over at the point. Needed sunscreen. Mother's cute even if she is pregnant. Too tall for my taste."

Each looks away, eyeing the street in case a car rolls past or a pedestrian comes within earshot.

Sheriff Kreiser pushes his dark glasses down his nose; his eyes are street-tough, bloodshot. A blitz of lines radiate from his eyes like shattered plate glass that doesn't crumble. Kreiser turns dead serious. "Talk about a huge fuck-up."

Hank shakes his head. "It was so long ago. When they find out, what do you think they'll do?"

Sheriff Kreiser snorts. "The company? What can they do? They're the ones that messed up."

"I mean the Berks."

Kreiser smiled. "Them?" he said jamming his sunglasses back on, enunciating each word with precision. "That is never going to happen."

"But what if? Humor me."

The sheriff growls. "Not on my watch. They'll be gone before you know it." Then Kreiser points in the direction of Ol' Barney. "Until everything is settled, make certain *he* stays out of town."

"He doesn't come here anymore," Hank says.

"That's what they said about that house *never* selling. Seems every time I turn my back, something that's not supposed to happen in this town has a way of happening."

"That house was a fluke."

"Just the same, let's not have any more fuck ups."

Kreiser makes a U-turn across the solid yellow centerline and drives away as Buck screeches to a hard stop in front of Hank's place. Kreiser adjusts his rearview mirror in time to see Buck stride through the soda shop's door.

The sheriff misses little.

"Heard they finally found something." Hank refers to the scavenger ship, the *Searcher*.

"Just came from fixing their water pump. Worked me up an appetite." Buck fishes in his pocket. "If you call finding a silver spoon 'something,' then they did. They shoved off a few minutes ago for another try."

"Waste of time and a ton of money, if you ask me," says Hank. He nods. "That most likely dropped off someone's boat. Those scavenger people probably think it's an antique or something."

"Maybe it is." Buck has other thoughts about the spoon.

"You want the usual, Buck?"

Buck shrugs.

Hank pumps chocolate syrup into a large glass, adds milk, then fills it with seltzer from the tap, making a foamy egg cream. He places the frothy drink in front of Buck.

"Toasted bagel, too?" Hank asks.

Buck takes a sip, smacks his lips in sheer pleasure, and blots the excess with his sleeve in preparation for the game they play most every day. "How many years I been coming here, Hank?"

Hank wipes a wet spot off the counter. "Since right after WWII, Buck. When my father owned the store."

"And how often do I change my order, Hank?"

"Not since Eisenhower was in office."

Hank fiddles with the toaster.

"Is this going to take all day? I got me a job to do at them new folk's house. You know, the ones who bought the house up on the bluff. The one that's been empty all these years."

Hearing this, Hank takes deliberate steps to stand in front of Buck. "The sheriff's not going to be happy when he hears that, Buck."

"Hears about what? That I'm givin' those folks a hand? Shoot. If they need help, if anyone needs help, that's what I do. Everybody 'round these parts knows that."

He sniffs to the right. "That my bagel burning?"

He stands and grabs a Twinkie.

"Can't wait for you to get it right, Hank. Gotta go. Add it to my bill."

Hank gawks to see Buck hop onto his motorcycle and don his helmet and goggles, turns away when he hears the engine roar to life, leans over the stainless steel sink and scrapes off the burnt edges, slathers cream cheese on top, takes a bite, chews thoughtfully, and then edges his fingers onto the phone to buzz the sheriff.

He hesitates.

Hank takes another bite and munches over his options: call the sheriff or don't call the sheriff. Hank tries to reason it out. Buck's always been a straight shooter. Never caused anyone trouble. Probably won't now. Still, the sheriff ought to know that Buck is crossing boundaries he knows shouldn't be crossed. Not in this town.

"Sorry, Buck," he whispers. Hank knows that he needs to toe an invisible line if he and his store are to survive in Island Bluffs.

Hank lifts the receiver; this time he lets the call go through.

* * *

Carly stops in the local pharmacy. It is small, not like one of those snazzy chain store drug outlets that overwhelm. She idles in front of the dental products. Her gums have become swollen as her pregnancy progresses; as a dentist, she knows this happens. Extra flossing hasn't helped. Heap on the day-to-day stress of moving, and it's a recipe for short-term bleeding. She reads the ingredients on one of the OTC remedies, knowing full well that rinsing with hydrogen peroxide and paying more attention when she brushes her pearlies will do the trick, when she senses someone next to her.

It's Olivia.

For whatever reason, Carly is not startled to see her. "Do you live in Island Bluffs?" asks Carly.

Olivia does not answer Carly's question. Instead, she says, "I was hoping we could speak again."

"I've been meaning to call you, but I didn't know what to say."

Olivia does not mince words. "Do you want to meet the others?"

Carly needs a moment to understand what Olivia's asking. Carly glances down at her belly, her thoughts slip from a grateful pregnancy to the heartbroken mother in front of her to body snatchers. She flashes on the movie *The Omen*. Is Carly reprising that role? Is this baby, Teplitsky's baby, going to control her life until it can be purged from her body?

Olivia repeats the question, but Carly does not hear her. She is too absorbed in horrible thoughts.

Olivia tugs gently on Carly's arm.

Carly refocuses.

"You mean the other mothers who gave up their surrogate child?"

Olivia squeezes her lips together until they blanch. They crack. A droplet of blood appears on her lower lip. In the center. "They want to meet you. To hear about their *other* sons. Teplitsky's sons. You're their only hope."

"We went through this already. Can't they just ask the doctor? I can't imagine that he would be that unreasonable. And besides, I've only met one. The oldest. His name's Iario. I don't know what I could tell them."

Olivia stays on message. "After I met you, I went back and compared with the others: we all signed the same contract." She touches Carly's belly. "You will never see *his* baby come out of you."

Carly waves her hand in the air. *No. No. You've got that all wrong, sister.* "That will not happen with me. At the very least, I am going to see his baby. I specifically requested natural childbirth."

"You can request what you want. Don't you think every one of us wanted to be awake when we gave birth? We all did. But it won't happen."

"Gabe's going to be there with me. He'll make certain nothing happens."

Olivia's face relaxes. "It doesn't work that way."

Carly expected that answer. "It will with me. What about you? The others? Weren't all your husbands there when you gave birth?"

For the first time, she permitted herself the tiniest of smiles. "I get it. You somehow think you're different than us, being a doctor and all?"

"That's not what I mean. I want everything to be perfect when I have my baby. I need to have Gabe with me, to experience it." *And maybe to make certain nothing strange happens.*

Color rises in Olivia's cheeks. "We were all desperate to have that same experience. Natural delivery. Husbands in the room. A camera for pictures. Maybe even a movie. And he let's you believe it will happen that way, too."

"Who does?"

"Teplitsky, of course. He let every husband in the delivery room until *it* happened."

"What happened? Did something go wrong?"

Carly's concerns grow.

"We all heard it. He might have rigged the fetal monitor or the blood pressure machine, but whatever it was, bells blared and we were made to believe the babies were in distress. The doctor barked orders at the nurses, and what started out as a routine, normal delivery for every one of us turned into something else. An anesthesiologist appeared, as if on cue. And in a few seconds, the husbands were escorted out and we were under."

"They put you out?" asked Carly.

"Every one of us. Something they injected into the IV drip. Lights out. When we came to, we had our baby and he had his."

"And you never saw the other baby?"

"None of us did." Her face softened. "But that's the magic of the moment. He counts on it. Plans for it. Every other thought is cast aside when that baby that each of us wanted so desperately is placed in our arms. Nothing is sweeter or more glorious . . . and that's when each of us stopped thinking about the other baby." She takes Carly's hands in hers. "We're sisters. All alike."

"Let me get this straight," says Carly, "none of your husbands were in the room with you?"

She shakes her head, "No."

"He can't just toss Gabe out."

"Regardless of what he tells you or how the delivery is progressing, it will happen at the last moment. I guarantee it."

"I'll pay attention to his every move. I won't let him get away with it."

"Honey, you'll be in the worst pain of your life. You'll cast caution to the wind. You will be in his clinic, in his delivery suite, screaming your pretty head off, and Teplitsky will end up doing what he always does. He'll snatch that baby from you and you'll never get a chance to see it. Forget about bonding with it, it's never going to happen. You will never get to hold that little one. That baby will be gone forever."

As sad as Olivia is about losing her son and not being able to see the "other" twin, she remains dry-eyed.

"And then what?" Carly asks.

"And then nothing. You go home with your baby in a day or two, have a few post-op visits, and then never see Teplitsky again. You won't be any different than any of us."

"What if I want another child and need his help again?"

"What of it?"

"Didn't any of you want another baby?"

"Most of us did."

"That's when you and the other mothers could see their other son. I feel weird calling these surrogate children their *sons*. But you'd be in the clinic and have a good shot at it."

Olivia shakes her head. "The *twofers* never get to see Teplitsky again. He won't take us back as patients."

"How is that possible? He's a fertility specialist. He worked magic for me. For all of us." The *us* did not sound strange now. Without thought, Carly accepted her inclusion into their sisterhood.

"Teplitsky *is* a genius, Carly. When no one else could help us, he did. But it starts and stops there. He doesn't want us snooping around. He knows that regardless of how desperate we were to have our babies, there will also be a maternal bond with the child we carried for him. Even if we never get a chance to see or hold or smell it, that bond is so great that, one day, he knows we will want to meet them. And, for whatever reason, he won't let that happen. That's why you are our only hope."

Could anything be more outlandish to Carly at this moment? When she first met Olivia, she felt sorry for her, for her loss. Now that she's reaching out, again, and speaking for the other *twofer* mothers, Carly's second thoughts are taking a recognizable shape.

She studies Olivia's pleading eyes. They say that the eyes are windows into a person's soul. In Olivia's case her soul is wounded, damaged. Should Olivia's wellbeing and the wellbeing of the other Teplitsky mothers matter to Carly? Carly is going to have the baby she's wanted forever. Does she need to overthink this? Join a cause? So what if she's an incubator for Teplitsky's kid? Who cares?

"So will you?" Olivia asks again.

"Will I what?"

"Meet the others?"

Carly looks away. "This is a lot to digest. I need to think about it." She leaves the pharmacy in a daze, forgetting to buy anything on her list.

CHAPTER 20

Saturday, 2:30 p.m.
Yehuda dozes in the chair in his room waiting fro Buck to return from the marina. The floor creaks and Yehuda bolts up.

"Polly, is that you?"

"It's me, Dad. I'm sorry if I startled you," says Carly. She is upset about meeting Olivia and does not ask who Polly is. "I wanted to make sure you were all right."

A grin of relief spreads across Yehuda's face. She kisses him on the cheek.

"Been puttering around my little garden. The sun got to me," he says.

"We're all moving a little slower since we got here."

"It takes a lot out of you fixing up a new place. Especially this one."

They both share in the conspiracy that buying this house would prove to be a mistake, a mistake they would make the best of. "Let Gabe help you with the garden."

"He's got enough to do."

"Just the same, when was the last time the two of you did something together?"

"When you put it that way, it's been way too long." Yehuda tried to remember a time when he and Gabe assembled something together. All he could think of was a model airplane when Gabe was ten or eleven.

"Dad?"

"Huh?"

"You might be doing Gabe a favor if he asks to lend you a hand."

"Aren't you the smart one?"

"Just trying to help," she answers. She glances at her watch. "Buck should be here any second to fix those locks. He might need your help."

"Don't see how he can do it without me," he answers with a twinkle.

"I don't doubt it." She squeezes his shoulder. "I have some things to tidy up in my room and then I will make lemonade for the two of you."

She leaves.

Yehuda places both hands on his knees, calculates the energy needed to stand, pushes up and, knees cracking, grabs onto the dresser. He waits a second before taking a step. Yehuda no longer takes getting to a standing position for granted, and is careful not to overshoot or wobble, collapse to the floor, and risk breaking a hip or wrist. Yehuda knows that twenty-five percent of all folks his age with broken hips never make it home from the hospital.

He stands in front of the mirror and adjusts his bow tie. As he does, he sees a form on the wall behind him. Yehuda spins to see what it is; it flashes away. He shrugs. He's still groggy from the nap. He returns to straighten his bow tie and sees it again. This time, it is more formed. He leans into the mirror so as not to chase it away. He squints. He peers through the top of his glasses. Could it be Polly? He did tell Megan about her and believed that what he was telling her was real, but at the same time he could just have easily dreamed up the story. Not now. Yehuda is standing in his room and can see her. He's experienced such horror in his life and has seen so many inexplicable things that a ghost is both believable and not a threat. In fact, this amuses.

Polly remains there long enough for Yehuda to see her, to know she is real, as real as any ghost can be, and then she dissolves through the wall.

He shrugs. What's another apparition in the scheme of things?

Yehuda strolls into the kitchen as Carly charges out of her bedroom. Her face is crinkled into puzzle parts. "Was anyone in my room today?" She waves an empty bottle at him. "This was my favorite perfume. Gabe gave it to me for Valentine's Day. I use it sparingly because it costs so much. I dabbed a drop on this morning, like I always do, and I know I replaced the stopper." She tugs on the glass cork. "Still tight. It was two-thirds full, now it's empty. It could not have evaporated since this morning and there is no sign it spilled. How is that possible? It makes no sense."

Yehuda has a notion of what might have happened, but he is not prepared to explain it in case he's wrong. "No one has been here but me." He wants to add that it is not his scent, but knows she will not find humor in it.

Carly stands there and stares at the bottle.

The awkward moment passes when Buck roars up the driveway.

Buck plucks a bag from the sidecar with the new locks, greets Yehuda, sets to work without any chitchat, and as he did in the marina, opens his tool chest and spreads out the velvet cloth. With nimble fingers, he unscrews a corroded brass plate and navigates the intricacies of removing the cylinder when the telltale crunch of a car sailing up the driveway causes them to jerk their heads around.

It's Sheriff Kreiser.

Carly hears the vehicle from the kitchen and slinks behind the screen door. Out of view. Curious.

Buck recognizes the sheriff's car and resumes working on the lock.

Kreiser approaches with a stiff bearing. He knows Buck forever but does not acknowledge him. It's apparent the two do not share warm feelings for each other.

"It's Mr. Berk, isn't it," he states, rather than asks Yehuda. Yehuda has faced men in uniforms who hide behind dark glasses before. He steps forward, reaching out for the railing. His back stiffens.

"I'm Berkowitz. My son is Berk." He flicks the back of his free hand in the air . . . a practiced move. "He says it's for business reasons; I personally think he is trying to hide from his heritage, to blend in. Assimilate. It never works." *They always find us.* "No matter," Yehuda continues, "he's a good boy. Now that you know, which of us do you want? Berk or Berkowitz?"

Sheriff Kreiser tips his cap.

"Welcome to Island Bluffs, Mr. Berkowitz. You've already met one of my officers. Gave you a ride back here the other day. So you know we're a quiet, friendly little town. Been that way close to three hundred years. But when summer comes, we need to remind folks to watch themselves."

Buck rocks on his knees and semi-turns towards the sheriff. "No call for you to say that, Rudi. This is their new home, not some beach cottage they are renting like vacationers do. They are not going to have any wild parties or orgies here."

Kreiser eyes Yehuda before continuing. "You don't need to tell me that, Buck. But seeing's how this house's been vacant so long, it caught us by surprise. That shouldn't be too hard to understand."

"That has more to do with sloppy bookkeeping down at Town Hall, don't it, Rudi?" Buck expects this will get a rise out of the sheriff. "It still isn't reason enough to give these folks a hard time. Surprise or not, having them live in this house has got to be better than leaving it empty. Besides, Rudi, what can you do about it, if you know what I mean." He permits himself a grin of satisfaction.

"You trying to tell me something, Buck? 'Cause I *do* know what you mean."

A subtext floats between them, words of familiarity, of acts and actions of years gone by, of unspoken secrets, of being part of Island Bluffs' inner circle.

Buck reaches for a rasp. He has to shave the wood so the lock can slip into the pre-existing opening. "Not trying to tell you anything you don't know, Sheriff." It wasn't lost on any that the long-time acquaintance, Rudi, is now "Sheriff Kreiser" to Buck.

Carly has heard enough. She opens the door. "I'm Carly Berk, Sheriff. Seems we met the other day when we moved in. Speeding three miles over the limit. It's so nice to see you again. And so soon."

"I remember."

"I couldn't help but overhear you. The last thing we want to do is disturb our neighbors." She studies his face; she's good at reading them—dead or alive. What motivates his visit? It can't be routine, no matter how hokey this town appears. "Is this the extent of your friendly visit? To tell us to mind our Ps and Qs, and be good, law-abiding citizens? Or are you here to sell raffle tickets? I'll take twenty dollars' worth."

Sheriff Kreiser takes off his mirrored sunglasses, wipes them with a white handkerchief, glares at Carly with bloodshot eyes that bulge, and then puts them back on. As warm as the midday air is, a chill settles over them.

"Don't know nothing about that whatchamacallit alphabetical stuff of Ps and Qs, but I sure as hell can tell you, lady, that this is not a Welcome Wagon. And, no, I am not here to sell you any raffle tickets, but you can be sure that when we have our fundraising events, you will get first shot at it."

"Thank you for that consideration, Sheriff," says Carly.

The sheriff is unruffled. "Now you and yours mind themselves and there won't be any trouble . . ." he frowns at Yehuda and then at Carly's swollen belly, ". . . for any of you. Step out of line and you'll wish you had picked another place to have your chocolate biscotti and mocha Frappuccino, which, by the way, if no one's informed you, we don't serve in this town. We call them cookies and egg creams here."

Without another word, the sheriff tips his hat, nods to Buck, and leaves. No one speaks until the patrol car is out of sight and the dust starts to settle.

"Is he always this sweet?" asks Carly.

"Caught him on a good day," answers Buck.

"I've seen men like him before," says Yehuda, "men who hide behind their fancy uniforms in the name of justice and what's right. Men like him never stop until they get what they want. They think they're smarter than everyone else. Even above the law. In the end, they always lose, but along the way, they crush many innocents. They see life through a distorted prism and have no conscience. They collect victims the way trash attracts flies."

Buck stands and puts his hand on Yehuda's shoulder. He forces a gentle squeeze. "Island Bluffs is filled with good people, too. Lived either here, or down the road, my whole life. Otherwise, would've left the area long ago. Give this place some time. The sheriff's just blowing smoke your way, trying to show who is boss around here. Fact is no one pays him much mind. Best way to handle him is to ignore him, like I do."

All the while Buck is talking, Yehuda stares down the driveway, as if he expects the sheriff to return with reinforcements.

"Those kind don't go away. They never do," Yehuda says through gritted teeth.

Carly ponders the moment. *On top of Olivia, now the sheriff. What else can happen?* "It is time for lemonade, gentlemen. I'll be back in a jiff."

Buck reaches for the screwdriver he's been using, but now it's missing. He rummages through his tool chest. "My screwdriver was here a second ago." He stands and pats every pocket in his pants and shirt. He checks again but comes up empty.

Yehuda scours the porch; he feels his pockets.

"Maybe it rolled off the porch?"

"Didn't hear it. Don't know where it could've gone to," he said turning this way and that, "but I've got another."

Carly returns with two glasses of lemonade; they drink in gulps.

Buck demonstrates that the new lock works. "I hate to take advantage of your good will, Buck, but do you have time to do the side door?"

He lifts the bag. "Planned on it, Miss Carly. Have the second one right here."

Yehuda guides Buck around the house. Without a sheriff interrupting, it takes no time. Buck finishes changing that lock, and Yehuda accompanies him back to the motorcycle.

"Got some days coming to me. How 'bout stopping by my place sometime next week? It's not far. Heard you play a good game of chess. We could listen to some Artie Shaw. What do you say?"

"I would be honored. Not only are you a gentleman, but a person of impeccable taste."

Buck grins and places his toolbox into the sidecar. He swings onto his seat and yelps.

"What's wrong? You okay?"

Buck reaches under his tush and flashes the missing screwdriver. He shrugs, as if strange things don't need to be explained.

Yehuda glances about. He can accept strange things, too, but senses he knows how the screwdriver made its way onto the motorcycle seat.

"You've got spunk, girl," Yehuda mutters under his breath to Polly.

CHAPTER 21

Saturday, 2:45 p.m.
By any standard, weekends in the Teplitsky home are grand. If his sons want to play sports, athletes from Princeton, Rutgers, Rider, or Monmouth colleges are hired as much to coach as to supervise so none get hurt. Camp Teplitsky. There are concerts provided by string quartets from Juilliard, field trips to the Barnes Museum outside of Philadelphia or the Metropolitan or MOMA museums in New York City. Geography does not impede. Other trips include the Kennedy Center, the Hirshhorn Museum, and the Smithsonian . . . all in Washington, D.C. Camden Yards in Baltimore. Yankee Stadium. Carnegie Hall. There are deep-sea fishing trips and beach volleyball played on imported sand in the backyard. And of course there is the Olympic-sized pool for both sport and recreation.

Teplitsky's sons want for nothing. They are best friends with one another, and have no need to mix with local teens . . . but the doctor knows that will not last much longer. He sees how the older boys react to female staff members. No amount of culture or reining in the boys can keep hormones in check.

On this particular Saturday, Macario remains in his studio painting and Arsenio polishes the play he's writing. The other boys—Aurelio, Alberto, Felice, Leonzio, Jacopo and Iario—play three-on-three volleyball. Isadore Teplitsky is planted on the balcony overlooking the backyard, bursting with pride. By any measure, his sons are evolving and maturing, and attaining the potential he planned for and hoped they would achieve. Painting, writing, sculpting, theoretical physics, music composition, science, and scholarship . . . their strengths are his dreams come true.

But where's Jovanni? Though he's the youngest and smallest, he is by turns the toughest and the most athletic. Teplitsky whirls around and hobbles from room to room. Jovanni is not in any of the bedrooms. Drat! Why did this house have to be so big? Then Teplitsky recalls once finding

Jovanni in the clinic, trying to decipher patient charts. Sonograms. EKGs. Blood workups. Only nine, he already exhibits an interest in medicine. Could he be in the clinic while the others play?

The doctor scampers down the stairs as best he can. He reminds himself it is time to find an architect to draw up plans to install an elevator. He will ask for a recommendation. Didn't Carly Berk hire one? To enlarge their house? Verity Frizzell? Her reputation grows.

Teplitsky scurries through the kitchen, dragging his bad leg. He enters the passageway to the clinic when he stops. A noise drifts from one of the studio rooms. He tiptoes to the doorway, which for him, means controlling how his gimpy left leg slams into the floor. He peers in to find Jovanni busy at work constructing a model rocket. The boy has somehow managed to take the kit down from the top shelf which is seven feet off the floor, spread the parts out, read the instructions, and start to construct the elaborate missile. It is a model of a World War II German rocket: thirty inches long and an inch-and-a-half wide. Should Jovanni get a chance to launch it, the built-in parachute is designed to preserve the rocket as it floats down without crashing into the ground. In theory, it is a reusable toy, like the space shuttle ships NASA deploys.

The doctor holds onto the doorjamb, barely breathing for fear of disturbing the boy. He relishes Jovanni's intensity, noting that nothing distracts the boy, that he is meticulous, and that he moves with grace.

Could a father be more proud?

CHAPTER 22

Saturday, July 12, 10:30 a.m.
"Megan," coos Miss Merriweather, "I'll be back in a jiff. I'm going to the Post Office before it closes."

"But Kinkos closes late," says Megan.

"It does, but the Post Office portion has the same hours as all the others across the country. It won't take but a minute."

With a bit of good-natured sass, Megan answers, "No hurry. Given that hardly anyone walks in here, I'm pretty sure I can handle a rush."

Megan settles in front of a computer and answers email queries from library members when the whoosh of the automatic door signals a patron-with-a-pulse entering the hallowed halls of book lending, computer research, and—of late—job searches. Megan pushes the "Send" button on the last query. She lifts her head to follow the footsteps trailing down the wall dedicated to historical fiction. It's a small wall. She wonders who it might be. She prays who it might be. And then she knows.

Jürgen hands her the book without saying hello. Her pulse races, her skin radiates heat. She dares to look up. Their eyes lock in a do-si-do. She feels a jolt. She prays that her face does not betray her, that it will not become obvious and turn crimson. Megan turns away. If there is a hole in the floor, it is time to dive in headfirst.

"You changed your hair," he says. "It's shorter. And a little lighter." She nods, unable to get her tongue or lips to work in concert. "I like it," he adds.

She finds her voice. "It's easier to keep for the summer. And mostly the sun caused it to turn colors."

"However it happened, it flatters you." He searches for a nameplate or an ID card dangling on a chain from around her neck. Neither exists.

"You're new here. I saw you the other day. What's your name?"

"Megan. Megan Berk. You walked in and out so fast, how could you notice?"

He extends his hand. She takes it. She's on fire. "I'm Jürgen Hauptmann." There's an awkward pause. "I did notice." He raises the book. "Summer reading. I'm starting Lehigh this fall. Going there to wrestle. Where do you go to college?"

Mouth dry, she licks her lips. "I wish. I'm starting my senior year. I need to get my applications out."

"Have an idea where?"

She would name a college in Pennsylvania close to Lehigh if she knew of one. In time she will learn of Lafayette, Moravian, Muhlenberg, Franklin & Marshall, Cedar Crest, and others. For now she mumbles UMass and Maryland.

"Both good choices."

"But I'm considering other schools a little closer." *Translation: in Pennsylvania.*

She processes the book. He holds it for a lingering second before taking it from her. "Maybe I'll see you around."

"Maybe," is all she manages to say.

He continues to stand there.

He's gorgeous.

"I've got to do something with my dad 'til 'round five today. Would you want to meet me over at Hank's Soda Fountain? Know where it is?"

She nods.

"Then you'll meet me there later?"

She nods again.

At that moment, a motorcycle roars past the library with cries of familiar laughter piercing the silence.

Buck hops off the cracked leather seat and extends a hand to Yehuda.

"I may be old, but I'm not feeble. I can climb out of this tin can by myself."

"I promised your daughter that I'd watch out for you."

"First of all, she's not my daughter, she's my daughter-in-law. And second of all, you've kept your promise: you're watching me . . . and I'm watching you."

Buck blesses Carly; Yehuda reminds Buck of himself. Buck drapes his arm around his new friend's shoulders as they march to the front door.

Buck lives in a spotless Cape Cod-style house. Nautical mementos are everywhere. There's a mounted fish on the wall, WWII memorabilia including a Japanese pith helmet and Imperial flag, and a U.S. Army-issued vintage rifle with the barrel soldered closed.

Buck takes cold beers from the refrigerator. He gives Yehuda a glass, and then takes a swig from the bottle. When Yehuda sees him drink from the bottle, he pushes the glass aside and imitates Buck.

Yehuda plops down on a sofa. It's soft. Much of it is covered in dark brown leather that is dotted with colorless patches from years of wear. There's a coffee table made from gray driftwood topped with a thick, green beveled glass. Yehuda sorts through a pyramid of picture books: one is *The Wall*, the Maya Lin sculpture that embodies the angst and ravages of the Vietnam War. Another is a pictorial essay from *A Day in the Life of America* series. There are books on fishing. Boats. At the bottom is a pebbled, black-green yearbook from the year Buck graduated Lakewood High School. Island Bluffs was too small to have its own secondary school. Yehuda pulls the yearbook out from under the pile.

Buck takes another swig and wipes his mouth with his sleeve. "You know, you're only the second person I've ever invited here?"

Yehuda was about to take another drink and stops. "How can that be? You've been here how long?"

"More 'n fifty years. Closer to sixty."

All kinds of thoughts race through Yehuda's head. Buck's got more than a toe in the waters of being a hermit. A recluse. Maybe he has already submerged himself in being forever alone. But he's so gregarious. Accepting.

"Who was the other one?" asks Yehuda.

"I'd make you guess if you'd have lived here longer."

"The only name that comes to mind is someone I know you wouldn't want to invite here: Sheriff Kreiser."

Buck tips the bottle towards his. They clink. "We're out of his jurisdiction here, but even so, you can bet the bank I'd never invite him."

"Then who?"

"The doc—Dr. T. Your daughter-in-law's obstetrician. The guy I work for. Came here one day, wanted to see the place. Poked into every nook and cranny, like he was looking for something."

"Was he?"

"Nah. Just a curious little bugger. Likes to know everything about the folks who hang around his children. Make sure they're safe and all. Don't blame him a bit."

Yehuda places the bottle on a coaster from the 1964 World's Fair, opens the yearbook on his lap, and flips the pages. There is a sequence of pictures that highlight Buck weaving through defensive players to score a touchdown. Another sequence demonstrates Buck stabbing a ground ball at deep shortstop, and another hitting a line drive off the right field wall. And still another making a winning layup as time runs out on the State Championship, Division III title game. Buck Hopewell was a three-sport letterman.

Yehuda flips through the pages. He is surprised at the caption under Buck's picture. He expects to see "Best Athlete" or "Most Likely To Succeed." Yehuda checks again to make certain he is reading it correctly. "Most Romantic."

Yehuda studies Buck in silence. He chooses not to ask about his sports exploits; the man would downplay them. Instead, Yehuda closes the yearbook and eases it onto the glass tabletop without commenting.

Buck motions to the yearbook. "Never did get to finish my senior year. Enlisted early but they were fool enough to include me in all the graduation stuff. Even got my diploma, but never did formally finish."

"They honored you for your bravery," said Yehuda. "It was the right thing to do."

"Not sure about that. It don't matter now."

Yehuda stands and edges toward the bookshelf. He picks up a framed picture of Buck in an Army uniform holding a rifle. It's probably the same rifle as the one mounted on the wall. "Marksman" medals are embedded in the tan matting in another frame. There are a dozen. Best this, best that. There are no pictures of anyone else in the room.

Yehuda recalls the missing girl in the police station. "Have you always lived alone?"

Buck looks away. He stiffens, uncomfortable with the question.

"You never did get to fight in the war, did you?" Buck asks Yehuda, knowing that Yehuda was in the camps. He asks anyway.

Yehuda considers his answer. "Never got the chance."

"Well, it was no picnic. I made sharpshooter. Could always shoot straighter than most. The geniuses put me in ordnance."

Yehuda has a quizzical look.

"Fixing guns. I was stationed in Hollywood. Can you believe that? For a year, I repaired rifles during the day and rubbed shoulders with movie stars at night. One time Joseph Cotten picked me up hitchhiking. Nicest guy in the world."

"That wasn't enough for you, was it?" asked Yehuda.

"I couldn't stand by while everyone was doing the fighting for me, so I made them ship me out. From New Caledonia, I got to the Philippines and Okinawa. That was the real McCoy."

Buck lifts his shirt. There's a scar across his belly. "Took a bayonet fighting hand-to-hand." Then he stretches his arms out and makes "claws" with his hands. "Strangled the bastard."

A screech of static interrupts them from the next room. Buck motions for Yehuda to follow.

A shortwave radio on a table squawks like a parrot.

Buck snatches a pair of Baldwin Mica Diaphragm radio headphones—the kind used during the war—slips them over his ears, and adjusts the knobs. The screeching fades, the voice more audible.

". . . Not certain . . . (background chatter) . . . about 200 feet."

Buck covers the microphone and whispers, "It's Captain Crenshaw of the scavenger ship working off shore." Buck uncovers the microphone. Presses a button. "Come in, *Searcher*, come in. This is Motorcycle Maven. Come in. Repeat, this is Motorcycle Maven. What did you find? Repeat. What did you find?"

Yehuda drifts to the shelves while Buck tries to raise the ship. It is not lost on Yehuda that tucked behind an antique spyglass is a frame containing two Purple Hearts and a letter from President Truman.

Buck Hopewell, star athlete, three-letter man, most romantic senior at Lakewood High School, is a bona fide war hero.

CHAPTER 23

Saturday, 5:15 p.m.
Megan left the library when it closed, drove home, showered, changed her outfit three times before settling on a straight-fit, midi cranberry skirt and white oxford shirt, with the sleeves rolled up and is now standing in front of Hank's Soda Fountain, shifting from foot to foot on her three-inch platform shoes. She strains to see if Jürgen's inside waiting, but the glare off the window blinds her. She's uncertain what to do. Walk in? Continue to wait on the sidewalk? If he's inside, he could look out and see her. At that moment, a streak of green is reflected in the plate glass, she wheels to hear the clatter of gears shifting and a squeal from applying the emergency brake. The driver's door flings open.

"Hi," says Jürgen, "I wasn't positive you'd show."

Are you kidding?

Her insides are twisted pipes; she prays her voice will not crack or accidentally spit when she speaks. She focuses on a stray lock of hair dangling over a blue eye. She manages to utter a sentence without her voice cracking. "Have you lived here long? We just moved into town."

He reaches behind her to yank open the door; she is aware that he avoids inadvertent contact.

He is not a goon like most others.

"Everyone knows you're new in town."

She slips by him.

"Hank's place is an institution 'round here."

They sit on chrome swivel stools covered in red plastic. Megan remembers that Jürgen met with his father earlier. "How did your afternoon go?"

Pain clouds his eyes. He hesitates to answer.

* * *

Hours earlier, Jürgen shuffles toward a log cabin deep in the pine forest, wishing he could be anywhere else but there . . . wishing he could be talking to that new girl, Megan, from the library.

Hoots and howls fill the air.

Jürgen ambles next to his father, who rests his sinewy hand on the boy's shoulder. His father is aglow. A family tradition is in the making, one Jürgen's father wishes he had had with his father . . . but never had the chance.

"Right on time," says his father.

Jürgen says nothing.

"Ready to do it?" asks Jürgen's father.

"I guess."

"Then let's get going." With his hand still on Jürgen's back, his father nudges him toward the open cabin door. If he could, Jürgen would take baby steps to delay the inevitable. If he could, he'd turn and sprint in the opposite direction.

The slatted pine door is open. Both an American and Confederate flag are pinned to the back wall. Men of different ages enter and exit the cabin. Most wear faded and ripped jean overalls. All sport a baseball cap of every denomination: auto repair, Phillies, Eagles, Cheeca Lodge fly fishing, Penske Trucking, N.Y. Giants, and the like. Each holds a Bud. Moustaches and beards are filled with gnarls and froth. Each shoulders a rifle. All pack a second weapon and a hunting knife. Some are in camouflage outfits.

Jürgen's father holds him back like a school-crossing guard. He wants Jürgen to pause and absorb the moment. Breathe in the testosterone dripping from every sleeve and cap, oozing from every man and each son they brought with them. Jürgen is expected to like it. To desire it. To suck this scene and what is about to occur into his DNA, and pass the genes down to his future offspring.

Wood chips cover the parking lot that, on one side, is filled with pickup trucks, each with a gun rack mounted above the rear cabin windows. Vans of different shapes, colors, and sizes, decorated with business logos and names and addresses of electricians, bricklayers, gutter repairmen, heating and air conditioning, and even a chimney sweep, toe an imaginary line with the precision of a Swiss clock maker. Across the way, there's a clearing that nuzzles a dozen spotless Harleys lined in a perfect row.

Behind these are the fancy cars owned by the club's share of accountants, lawyers, and physicians, not to mention political officials from many local municipalities. Years back, there would never be anything but America-made vehicles, but not so these days. BMWs and Mercedes have replaced the long-finned Cadillacs, the boxy Mercury Marquises, and the ever-decadent Lincoln Town cars.

A salvo of shots is heard from behind the cabin. Then another round. And another. Whoops and hollering. Then more shots.

Jürgen's father tosses him a rifle and tells him to "Wait a sec." He retrieves two beers and hands one to his son. Jürgen holds it out as his father pulls open the tab; foam bubbles onto the ground. Jürgen takes a sip, feigns enjoyment, and offers up a deliberate nod of appreciation, man-to-man.

His father reciprocates with a grunt that is supposed to demonstrate that Jürgen's been elevated to the exalted level of being one of the "boys" at the gun club.

The last thing Jürgen wants to do is shoot a gun or rub shoulders with all who are here.

Cocked and loaded for fun, father and son tramp behind the cabin. Otto Hauptmann does not see Jürgen spill most of his beer behind him as they trudge towards the shooting range.

They find men clad in Army fatigues. Sheriff Kreiser is among them. So is Island Bluff's mayor. Many are with sons, others are alone.

Jürgen prays for the day when he does not have to return to this place. He prays that day will be soon.

Jürgen squirms on the stool. He is angry with himself for letting thoughts overtake him to the extent that they affect the way he breathes. He wants to concentrate on Megan. Though in her presence mere minutes, he can tell she is different than other local girls. Real. Down to earth. No sense of entitlement. No phony airs. She doesn't even know how to flirt, which endears.

"Are you all right?" Megan asks.

He doesn't answer right away. Arranging to meet Megan right after the club shoot . . . what was he thinking?

He spins away; his back is towards her. He stares out the storefront window but sees nothing. He glances up and focuses on the ceiling, which is the original hammered tin, with its ridged, fleurs-de-lis pattern now an oxidized patina. His body stiffens. His face contorts. He bites his lip.

She edges her fingertips on top of his hand. He doesn't pull away . . . but doesn't turn back to her, either.

"Was it that bad?"

With a jerk of his hand, Jürgen springs off the stool, slaps ten dollars on the countertop and calls out to Hank. "Please introduce Megan to your famous egg cream." He struggles to focus on her. "Forgive me, Megan. I thought I'd be all right, but I'm not." He balls his fists. "I hated this afternoon with all my might. I've got to go. I'm no fun to be around."

Let me be the judge of that.

Before she can tell him she would enjoy his company no matter what, he bounds through the door, leaving Megan to try Hank's famous drink.

She takes a slurp. It is tasty but leaves her unsatisfied.

"Do you know him well?" asks Hank, cognizant that she can't.

"I just met him over at the library." She wants to ask if he's always that way, with moods that change like the blowing winds, but waits.

"He's one of the good ones in town. Studious and all that. Not like most others."

"He seems nice."

"He is better than nice," says Hank. "Must've gone to the cabin with his father. It gets him all riled up when he's thrown in with the local rednecks. He'll be okay, Miss."

"What goes on there?"

"Better ask him." Hank dismisses her by clearing away the empty glass and wiping the countertop with a wet rag.

Saturday, 5:32 p.m.

Megan drives back to the house, filled with questions. Is Jürgen an only child? Why is his father making Jürgen do something he dislikes so much? How could it affect him so much that he couldn't sit at a counter and chat for a few minutes? Get to know her better?

More to the point, will he call her again?

Megan rolls up the driveway in time to see Yehuda dismount from Buck's motorcycle. Buck is in the sidecar. She sprints to them.

Buck removes his earflaps, jerking his thumb in Yehuda's direction. "The old geezer drives a mean 'cycle."

Yehuda sports a Cheshire cat grin. Helmet in hand, he asks, "Do you want to take a spin, Megan?"

Buck chimes in. "Your Grandpa is something else. He's okay to give you a ride. Taught him myself. Might be the highlight of your life."

Not mine, she thinks, *and certainly not now.*

Megan feigns disappointment and turns to Buck. "There's nothing I'd rather do more than that, but Grandpa promised to help finish exploring the basement so I could find a spot to set up a darkroom. I'm going to hold him to that promise."

Buck kicks a rock. "Got to admit, little girl, that would be a ton safer."

"See, I told you she's a smart girl," says Yehuda.

Buck and Yehuda agree to see each other soon.

CHAPTER 24

"I like your friend," Megan says as they inch down the dark stairs. At the foot of the stairs, Megan gropes for the pull string to snap on the lone circular fluorescent bulb. Yehuda waits until he can see where he is going. He can drive a motorcycle without a second thought, but falling down the stairs and breaking his hip gives him pause.

"Carly put the two of us together, you know. Buck's got quite a story to tell."

She waits as he nears the bottom step. She rubs her hands together. "I love a juicy story. Can you tell me?"

"I don't know about juicy, but he's a lonely man. I'll leave it for Buck to tell you about it one day. Once he gets to know you, I think he will."

With Yehuda down safely, Megan turns. "Remember, we didn't see a washroom last time we were down here, Grandpa, so how're we going to set up a darkroom without water?"

He doesn't answer but scours the basement for a spigot or something else they might have missed. He glimpses a pipe that disappears through a wall and then notices the top of a door blocked by the Shaker-style chest. Knotty pine. The color of honey maple. The one they chose not to try to move the first time they were down there.

Megan follows his eye. "I forgot about that."

Yehuda leans his shoulder into the side. He grunts. Nothing happens. "Help me move this."

"I wish Buck was still here. Better wait for Dad. It's too heavy for us."

Yehuda taps his chest. "This ticker has a few more beats left in it. We don't need anyone else's help. First, let's empty the drawers." Once done, Yehuda instructs Megan to push from the bottom; he leans above her. The wood creaks and then slides a speck. Encouraged, they renew their effort. Yehuda leans lower for a better angle. He understands leverage, how to move objects with minimal force. He counts to three. They push in unison, and this time the chest scrapes against the cement floor. They don't need to move it very much before changing the point of leverage to cause the chest to pivot on one corner, forcing it to swing away and expose the partially hidden door.

Yehuda leans against the chest to catch his breath. To his surprise, he feels fine, but takes no chances. He reaches into his shirt pocket, plucks a little white pill, and tosses it under his tongue. No sense letting his heart race away from him. He's getting to like living in Island Bluffs. Might've been a good move after all.

"Are you okay, Grandpa?"

Breathless, he nods he is.

She glances at the wrought-iron door handle.

He looks on. "Well," he says, "it won't open by itself."

Megan tries. "It won't budge."

Yehuda searches the doorframe; there's an empty nail where a key might have been kept. "Let the old man give it a try."

Megan moves aside.

Yehuda has thick, powerful fingers. He squeezes and leans down at the same time, and the catch "pops." The hinge shrieks; the door has not been opened in nearly six decades. It swings inward.

Megan steps in front of him.

The room is pitch black.

"I'll get a flashlight," says Yehuda.

"Don't bother. There must be a string connected to a light, like there is in the rest of the basement."

Even though this replicates her past experience in this basement, Megan plunges her hand into the darkness the way a child fears reaching into a drainage sewer for an errant baseball. Stephen King's *It* comes to mind. She yelps touching a cord; it feels like a thick spider's web. She brushes her hand against her jeans in case it *is* a thick spider's web. Emboldened, she reaches out again. This time, when she touches the string, she does not react.

She pulls.

Wood planks line the walls that were once painted sea foam green but are now layered with grime. Dense cobwebs frame the corners. There is a watermark; the basement must have been flooded at least once. How long ago is anyone's guess. There was no mention of it in the engineer's report. The once white porcelain sink is blotched with dead bugs.

Megan pushes the door against the wall and steps inside. A picture of Charles Lindbergh hangs beyond the door. A brown-streaked water tank, perched on the wall close to the ceiling, hovers above the stained porcelain bowl. A rope dangles from the tank that is punctuated with a handmade dowel in the shape of a topless mermaid that needs to be pulled to flush the toilet.

Megan dips her sandal-clad toe farther into the room, testing the waters of uncertainty. She turns to him. "Grandpa, it's disgusting in here now but when it's cleaned up, it'll make a perfect darkroom." She takes another step deeper into the room and inspects the corner recesses.

Yehuda is about to tell her that it won't take much to transform it into a suitable darkroom when her head dips down and then jolts back toward him. Her hand smothers her mouth, her brows arch in terror, and she lunges into him.

He feels her quake.

He holds her as tight as he dares, not knowing what to make of it.

He strokes her hair. He "shushes" to calm her. "What is it?"

Megan opens her mouth but nothing comes out.

Her heart races against his chest. He feels its rapid-fire thumping ease up, her breathing stretches towards normal. She remains still. He continues to squeeze her tight, to comfort, trying to peer over her shoulder. He sees a raggedy, dark-stained towel covering something on the floor that's obscured from his view. Yehuda unfolds his fingers and floats around her; Megan sidesteps to get out of the way.

Yehuda hesitates. A telltale bone lies on the floor, foretelling what's to be discovered. He lifts the towel and uncovers a pile of bones, heaped together like discarded Pick-Up Sticks.

A skull crowns the stack.

It's human.

"We heard a scream. Is everyone all right?" Carly plods down the stairs. Gabe is a step behind.

Megan points. She does not speak.

Yehuda remains stoic. Bones on the floor remind him of the camps.

Carly edges past her.

"They're real," says Yehuda.

Carly remains cool, slips into her forensic dentist's mode, and eases down on one knee. She does not touch the evidence, but twists and contorts to get varied views. "Looks like a male. I can't be a hundred percent until I get a better look at the pelvis, but I'm pretty certain."

Gabe surveys the scene, draws in a breath thinking of the traffic stop that first day they moved in and the sheriff's recent visit, but says anyway, "We should call the police."

What did we get ourselves into? What did I get everyone into?

The last person Yehuda wants to tangle with is Sheriff Kreiser now that he has had the pleasure of the man's acquaintance. It awakens memories; Carly sees this in his face. She grabs Yehuda's hand and gives a reassuring squeeze.

Lightning-fast synapses, her form of muscle memory, trigger her next thought: is Sheriff Kreiser capable of handling this? Carly is certain this is a potential crime scene. Then she flashes on Olivia and the gaggle of *twofers*. As if reading Gabe's mind, she has similar thoughts. *What has she gotten herself into?*

"This has to be processed," she says. "If we move anything, it might cause them to miss a clue."

Not understanding her concerns, Gabe asks, "How can it be a crime scene after all these years?"

"There's no statute of limitations on murder. With the newer technologies, even a microliter of evidence can exonerate or inculpate twenty or even thirty years after the fact."

Megan, still freaked, points and manages to say, "Look. There's the missing key." The steel gray turnkey dangles from a nail next to the inside door jamb. "How did the key get inside if the door only locks from the outside?"

"Maybe it could be locked from the inside, too," says Megan.

Maybe it can't.

From Yehuda's perspective, all sorts of questions arise after living in this house a couple of days. Finding the answers for him continues to point to a single source: Polly.

He wonders how long Polly has been in this house.

He wonders why she is still here, unable to move on.

And if she is trapped in some altered universe, some third-dimensional treadmill that imprisons, what will it take to set her free?

Yehuda studies the crumpled skeleton.

Could Polly have had a hand in this person's death?

Bones, mysteries, and secrets aside, a warmth spreads inside Yehuda knowing he is meant to be in *this* house at *this* time in his life. All things have a purpose; sometimes time is needed to define what that is.

Yehuda is formulating an idea of what his purpose in meeting Polly could be.

It's a challenge he welcomes.

One that Polly not only welcomes, too but has been looking forward to for many years.

CHAPTER 25

Saturday, 7:15 p.m.
Thirty minutes later, Sheriff Kreiser kneels over the bones. He slips on latex gloves, holds a Maglite in his chipped teeth and, to Carly's horror, sifts through the bones with the tip of a retractable pen.

She starts to say something about destroying potential evidence. Gabe touches her arm and shakes his head, "No."

Carly recalls a case Willie Robinson, the Chief Medical Examiner for New York and her former mentor, described to her one day.

"Always create a grid around the body of any forensic scene you investigate. Comb every square millimeter. There's no detail too small to be overlooked: a crumb of food, a single hair follicle, a bit of clay that may have fallen from the perp's shoe. Even a dead fly."

"A fly?" asks Carly. "How can that help in an investigation?" This was early in her career.

"A few years back, an elderly woman was brutally murdered up in Washington Heights. A burglary gone wrong. No way the lady was giving up her food and rent money to anyone. Clues were far and few between. Not a fingerprint. Nada. I scoured her flat a second time, again nothing. Then I did it a third time, and that's when I found the little critter."

"What are you talking about?"

"A mosquito. We were able to extract human DNA from its blood. It didn't match the victim's, so we reasoned it could have come from the perp."

"It might've come from someone else on the scene," Carly says in triumph.

"Not in this case. Everyone wore Hazmat suits. Turns out the mosquito helped solve the case. We extracted the human blood, obtained the DNA, scoured VICAP . . ."

"The Violent Criminal Apprehension Program," she states.

"Exactly. Looked for a match, but came up zeroes."

Her brow wrinkles as she mulls this over. "You caught him later, right? Criminals never figure on the long arm of computers and the data they store."

"Smart girl," Willie says. "This case was heinous. We never gave up searching for the murderer. Every so often, we'd run the DNA found in the mosquito through the system. This one time, it came back positive. The punk was already in Riker's, awaiting trial for another B & E. He was looking at thirty months for that. When we caught him, he sung like a castrati. Punched his ticket into life without parole."

Kreiser's voice brings Carly back to the present. "Probably a vagrant who was living here for a while. This house was empty for quite some time."

"A couple were cracked but there were no broken windows that first day I saw the house. I checked. And all of the doors were locked," says Gabe.

"That means nothing," answers the sheriff. "Whoever lived here could have come and gone as they pleased. Could've been two, maybe more living here at the same time. The roomie may have seen the man die and left for good, locking the door behind him."

Gabe glances at Carly, who gives an imperceptible tilt of her head. When Gabe entered the house for the first time, the place was broom swept. No moldy dishes. No clothes left behind. No newspapers or cans of food strewn about.

Gabe thinks *I should've inspected the basement more carefully instead of just poking my head around at the bottom of the stairs.*

No one buys Kreiser's reasoning.

"How do you explain the fact that this bathroom door was locked from the outside, but we found the key inside the room?" asks Gabe.

"Obviously there was another key," says the sheriff, "or it locked both ways."

Gabe steps into the room and studies the doorknob from the inside. "No keyhole, so locking it from the inside wasn't possible."

Carly picks up Gabe's thread. "How do you explain the huge chest blocking the door? Would you care to speculate how this victim, whoever he was, arranged all of that from inside, Sheriff? Even Houdini could not have pulled off that trick." She struggles to keep from judging the sheriff for his unprofessional conduct and refrains from informing him about how NYC investigations are conducted.

"He must have been hiding from someone," says Megan. Then it dawns on her. Yehuda's invisible friend. Why not? Ghosts are not angels. Girl or not, Yehuda's friend could have a mean edge to her. Megan plumbs Yehuda's face. Is he thinking the same thing?

Yehuda is on the same wavelength. He surprises by saying, "Maybe it was a *something*, not a someone."

"That's right, Grandpa. You said you heard music the first day we moved in . . . and there are no radios in the house."

Sheriff Kreiser grabs the sink and pulls himself up, left knee first, then the right. "You folks certainly do have vivid imaginations." He manages to chortle; Megan knows it's a fake laugh. The sheriff continues. "No one's been reported missing in Island Bluffs since I've been here."

"It's pretty clear this house's been virtually empty since the end of World War II," says Carly. "This must have preceded you, Sheriff."

"Got to give you that one."

"How far do cold cases go back in Island Bluffs?" Carly asks.

"This isn't New York City, Dr. Berk." He revels in her surprise. "Oh, I took time to Google you. Surprised me to find out that we've got ourselves a genuine forensic dentist living right here in town. Explains how you know so much about not disturbing the evidence."

"But I didn't say anything."

"I could smell what you were thinking. That, and the eyes in back of my head."

No argument there, thinks Megan.

Carly knows not to pull the "experience" trump card on him. No need to spray gas on the flames of this man's ego-fueled fires. She doesn't rise to the bait.

"Sheriff," says Gabe, punching his right fist into his left palm, "this is not rocket science. It's a case of foul play. Plain and simple. How can there be no record of someone missing, no matter how long ago?"

The sheriff shakes his head. "Turns out I have resources that go back a ways. You probably don't know—how could you—but my daddy was the sheriff before me. He would've told me 'bout any open cases when I took over from him. Sorry to disappoint you folks. The way I see it, this is just a pile of bones the little lady came across. No crime committed here."

"Sheriff," Carly finally chimes in, "what if a tox report finds something? How can you dismiss that?"

"Like what?"

"Say arsenic. A few years back, they exhumed President Zachary Taylor's body because some historian theorized that he died of arsenic poisoning. They actually got an order to dig up his bones."

"And what'd they find?"

"It wasn't arsenic."

"He died of a stomach problem, didn't he?" says Megan. "Eating cherries with cold milk, or something like that." She beams. "We learned that in history class this year."

"That's right," says Carly.

"Same thing's gonna happen here. No foul play; natural causes. Case closed. No need to look for anything else, *Dr.* Berk. If you get my drift?"

Carly remains undaunted. "Even in the face of compelling evidence? There are procedures to follow." She cannot contain herself. "In New York, the forensic team would make this a full-blown crime scene."

He removes his sunglasses with a deliberate motion, ignoring the fact that Carly is taller than him. "You're in my town now, and what I say goes."

Carly's met this kind before, the kind that defies reason when it flies in the face of their authority, the kind that defies the very laws they're sworn to uphold. "So what *are* you going to do, Sheriff?"

"What any good officer is supposed to do." He turns to Megan. "Little lady, would you be good enough to get me a large trash bag?"

Gabe nods that it's okay and Megan bounces off.

As the sheriff places the last bone in the bag, Megan starts to say something. Carly moves her head from side-to-side to stop her.

"What was that, little girl?"

Megan stumbles through the words. "I'm wondering what you are going to do with the bones."

The sheriff stands and ties a knot in the bag. "Bury them in the Gravelly Cemetery." Then he winks at Megan. "Maybe I should give them to Hank Gerhardt down at the soda shop. Rumor has it he makes a mean *bone* soup."

The sheriff laughs so hard he grabs his belly; everyone else remains stone-faced.

Sheriff Kreiser flips the bag over his shoulder à la Santa Claus. There's spring in his step. "You folks happen to find any more bodies, don't hesitate to call me. Y'hear?" He tips the brim of his cap. "Now you all have a good evening."

They retreat to the kitchen. At first, no one speaks. The air is different. Prickly. Metallic. Polluted by Kreiser.

All are on edge and stand. Even Carly.

Megan speaks first. "Why didn't you let me tell him about the bone under the tank? Now *we* have to get rid of it."

"Honey," says Gabe, "give Carly credit."

Megan wrinkles her brow, not understanding.

"I was hoping he'd miss it," Carly explains. "He tried too hard to make us think these were just a pile of bones. He's deliberately trying to whitewash this, and I want to know why that is."

Yehuda uses few words. "Sometimes it's better not to know."

She manages a knowing smile. She knows why he says this. She knows what he's seen in the past. What he wants to forget.

"You're right, Yehuda, but this is not one of those times."

Megan rocks on her heels. She hunches her shoulders, holds her arms tight across her chest. "At least now I know why I've been feeling so creepy. Those bones. It gave this house a haunted feeling." She glances at Yehuda when she says this. She knows he believes Polly is real. Maybe Polly isn't as real as Yehuda claims she is. Maybe he had a sixth sense that something *was* spooky in this house, and for lack of anything better, gave it the name "Polly." Now that the bones are gone, Yehuda's Polly may very well disappear, too, thinks Megan.

But that is not the case.

As Megan speaks, she sees Yehuda nodding, as if he was engaged in speaking with someone. Or something. Megan searches the room: nothing out of the ordinary. Megan continues to study Yehuda.

"To tell you the truth, I'm flabbergasted that all of your conversations border on ho-hum," says Gabe to the three of them. "It's not every day that people find bones in their houses. What are we going to do about it?"

"You mean like we should sell the house and move?" asks Megan. "I'm beginning to like it here."

All knew why she said that.

"Even after this?" Gabe asks again. He doesn't wait for an answer. "No one loves this house as much as I do, but having someone killed in this house is where I draw the line."

"First of all, that still needs to be proved," says Carly.

"You doubt that his was a murder?" Gabe asks.

"We have no real basis to think so," she explains. "I mean it looks fishy, but it is all circumstantial. No weapon. No motive. No suspect. We shouldn't be too hasty drawing conclusions."

"Even if it's not and by some miracle, we find out the person died from natural causes . . ."

"That doesn't make sense, Dad," says Megan.

"I agree. But let's say that it was harmless. Nothing foul. Do you still want to live here?"

"I see it differently," says Carly, "think of all the older houses around here. In the seventeen and eighteen hundreds, people most often died in their houses. There were no hospitals in those days and even when some came into being, they were far from here."

"So what's your point?" asks Gabe.

"For hundreds of years, houses were bought and sold, and the people who bought them never thought twice about what happened before they owned it. It's the same with this house. Those bones have probably been here for sixty years, or close to it. Would you feel the same way if someone had died of natural causes in their bed, and then was removed and buried?"

"Grandpa, what do you think?" Megan asks.

He turns to Gabe. "Are you forgetting your mother died at home, in our bed?"

"She was sick. She wanted to die at home. Dad, that's different."

"How?" Yehuda asks. "Dead is dead. I continued to live in that apartment without a problem."

"But you were connected to it. You made lots of good memories there," Gabe explains.

"That's not true for the people who just moved in after I left. They don't know from anything. Was I supposed to tell them that my Sadie died there?" He lets the words sink in and then shrugs. "I'll answer that for you. There was no need to tell them. And for the same reason, we really shouldn't think too much about those bones in the basement. They have no bearing on us."

"I feel the same way as Yehuda," says Carly. "Megan, what about you?"

"It's beyond creepy."

"Then do you want us to sell the house?" asks Gabe.

Megan studies Yehuda, who gives a reassuring smile. "No," she says, "if Grandpa's okay with staying here, I'm good with it, too."

Carly looks at Gabe.

"Me?" he points to himself.

"What's it going to be?" Carly asks.

"Daddy, please."

Gabe lets out a long draft of air. "If all of you are good with this, I'm not going to be the spoilsport. We stay."

Megan hugs him.

"Now that that is settled, I'm going to drive up to Freehold as soon as I get a chance," says Carly. "I interned with the Monmouth County Medical Examiner when we were both at the Albert Einstein Medical Center."

Gabe holds up his hand. "Why not the Ocean County ME? That office is closer."

"Too close, as far as I'm concerned," answers Carly. "Kreiser has a lot of clout around here, and he's been ensconced in his job for a long time. Before him, it was his father. I don't want to take a chance that Kreiser and the local ME are buddies from way back."

Megan is wide-eyed. "So what do you hope your guy will find?"

"If my friend can extract some DNA from the bone, at least we'll have a reference to compare to, should something else unexpected turn up in this house."

"What's the chance of that happening?" Gabe asks.

"Given the time we've lived in Island Bluffs, I'd say anything's possible."

Yehuda has no doubts this is true.

CHAPTER 26

Saturday nights, Hank Gerhardt plays cards with a group of men in the back room of the Town Hall. It's a white clapboard, one-story structure, with a cupola. The clapper in the bell was made from a melted Civil War cannon. The mayor is there, too.

Sheriff Kreiser storms into the room carrying the bag of bones. He tosses it onto the table with a crash. Red and blue chips scatter.

The men glare at him wondering what this is all about. Hank has a good hand and is about to raise his bid.

"I want those people out of that house," Kreiser hisses.

The mayor lays down his cards, face down. "This is getting to be old news, Rudi. Granted, it slipped past all of us. We're all to blame. But once the proverbial horse is let out of the barn, it's pretty tough getting it back in there again."

Kreiser pads to the over-stocked mahogany bar that was rescued from a local turn-of-the-century hotel torn down to make way for a golf course years back. He pours two fingers of eighteen-year-old McCallum's. Neat. He tips his head back and feels the golden liquid slide down and ignite a fire in this throat. The searing pain makes him feel alive. He pours another.

"What about the septic?" Hank asks.

Kreiser discards the idea with a wave of the hand holding the glass. A few drops spill to the carpeted floor. Burberry pattern. Gray tones. "That was bullshit from the beginning. There's nothing wrong with their septic."

Hank looks puzzled.

"Wanted to see if they would fold even though they were holding a full house, so to speak." He chuckles at his play on words linking the house in question to poker. He pauses a stitch, waiting for, "That was really clever." "Good one." But nothing is forthcoming. A tinge of disappointment washes over him. What the heck! No one ever accused him of being funny.

"Now what?" the mayor asks.

Hank persists. "You still going to let them dig up a new septic for no reason?"

Kreiser shrugs. "Absolutely."

The sheriff downs the second glass. He turns to the mayor. "They apply for a building permit, make sure it's denied. Condemn the friggin' house. Bad wiring. I don't care how you do it, but get it done. If you don't, my way ain't going to be pretty."

"Give it up, Rudi. After all these years, who's left to care?"

The sheriff studies everyone's face seated around the table. He raises one finger. "Me, for starters. From where I stand, you don't need anyone else. Do you?" He glowers at each of them before continuing. "Are you going to forsake our past? What our parents stood for? The things we still believe in? There's history here in Island Bluffs that we need to protect."

They shift in their seats, clear their throats, and avert each other's gazes.

The sheriff takes a step, wobbles, then draws himself up tall and makes his way behind the mayor.

He slaps his hands on the mayor's shoulders with the force of a thunderclap.

No one stirs; the mayor winces.

Each wonders. *What's the sheriff going to do?* In spite of being friends with the man since most were boys, all feel Kreiser to be a loose cannon. Unpredictable.

The sheriff locks gazes with them, one-by-one; no one speaks. The mayor is frozen in place. Someone wheezes. Another clears his throat.

"I guess this means you all agree with me." He squeezes the mayor's shoulders harder; the mayor sags into the chair but does not yelp. "I'm glad that you've all come to your senses."

Before he sits down, he reaches into the bag of bones. He extracts a rib. He takes a seat, puts the bone in front of him. Rubs it.

"Brought my own special wishbone tonight." He laughs again at his brand of humor. He opens his wallet. Throws two Ben Franklins on the table. "I feel damn lucky tonight, gentlemen. Damn lucky. Whose deal is it?"

Saturday, 5:15 p.m.

For Jürgen, it has been an emotionally charged day of highs and lows. After leaving Megan at the soda fountain, he drives around until he is certain of what to say. He seeks out his father, who is working in his basement workshop. He builds things. Small things.

"I can't go back there," he says to his father.

"What're you talking about? It's in your blood. That's what fathers and sons do when they get together. There is no better place than the lodge for us to bond."

Jürgen is a cauldron of bubbling feelings. He loves his parents. His mother teaches kindergarten. She survives by keeping her opinions to herself. She hides behind the simplicity of what she does. Of what she loves to do. Of the adoration and gratitude she gets from her students and their parents . . . which is great, yet never seems to be enough. Never replaces what is lacking at home. What she craves the most.

"Teaching kindergarten suits you," Otto, Jürgen's father, says to her all the time. His manner makes no effort to mask contempt. It conveys the essence of what she does, of who she is. It implies that her abilities are in tandem with her career; it implies from the words he chooses, and the way he says them, that she is limited when it comes to neuron power.

It is a form of spousal abuse.

Otto needs to denigrate in order to elevate his self-importance, to mask over his own inadequacies.

It works with others, not with his college-bound son.

"Fathers also play hoops with their sons. Tennis. Go sailing. How come we've never done any of those things . . . especially sailing? We live near the water and I've never been on a sailboat."

"I'm not interested in sissy things."

"And guns make you a man?" Jürgen says. "Not in my book."

His father looks up from his workbench. He peers over magnifying glasses. "Are you saying that you'd rather fight someone with a book? Won't get you very far."

This stings. Not so much for what it implies about Jürgen, but it's the same way his father denigrates his mother. Jürgen steps closer, stands straighter. "Seems all you care about is firing a gun. You never acknowledged my grades or how well I did in the 'States' in wrestling. It was never about me being good enough; you never even cared about what I did."

Otto rises. He is shorter than his son, but not by much. "Is that how I raised you? To be disrespectful?"

He wants to point out that his father's logic has more holes than a sieve.

"I'm sorry, it's just that I hate going there. I have nothing in common with any of them."

"In time you will."

CHAPTER 27

Monday, 9:30 a.m.
Morning ushers in a new week for the Berks living in Island Bluffs.

They've already experienced a season's worth of drama since moving into town. Today, the drama escalates. Gabe will work from the house, Carly will drive to Freehold to bring the bone found in the basement to her friend at the Medical Examiner's Office for analysis, and Megan will scurry to the library in hopes of Jürgen appearing. Buck, who has the day off, will invite Yehuda to meet the captain of the *Searcher* at the marina.

Gabe pores over a proposal of behemoth proportions: Microsoft is considering a hostile takeover of Google. Who would have thought Microsoft would be the little guy? When Gabe, one of five consultants used, finishes analyzing the deal, he will recommend that Microsoft nix the idea. He immerses himself in a mountain of paper and is partway through the stack when the phone rings. It's Verity Frizzell.

"Sorry I couldn't get these to you sooner. I know you wanted them last week, but there was one more thing I needed to check before we submit them to the planning board."

"I thought we had all the major elements covered."

"We did. At least I thought I did. I completed all the calculations and then I got to wondering about the height requirements."

"There are rules for that? Can't I build my house as high as I want?"

"Not when it comes to altering views and vistas, or having houses poke above the tree line. Every town has their own rules about this. Remember, your house is on a bluff, which will challenge the regulations."

"I can't see how that would be an issue. We're isolated and overlook the bay. There's not a house nearby. How could that matter? For that matter, who would care?"

"Consider the view from across the bay. If the house is considered too high, it can change the esthetics of the landscape *they* presently enjoy."

"It's our house. How can anyone regulate that?"

"Because they can and they do. And towns are not forgiving if you violate a scintilla of their rules."

Especially this town.

"I'm beginning to learn that," says Gabe, turning a page of the Microsoft document. He focuses on a spreadsheet of numbers. "So is there a problem?" he asks, preoccupied with the five-year projections he's perusing.

"Depends."

He lifts his head. "Depends on what?"

"If they pay attention to the rules."

"You're confusing me. Aren't we talking about height requirements?"

"We are, but Island Bluffs ties a house's height to the amount of property it sits on. You have more than four acres."

"Why should that matter?"

"That's why I need to check. A single-family house on four acres in most of the shore towns is limited to three-and-a-half stories not to exceed fifty feet in height. If you had less land, the height requirement would be lower. They try to make the houses proportionate to the acreage."

"How does that complicate matters?"

"If we measure the house from the back, it's barely over forty feet. But from the front, it's more than fifty. That's because of the bluff. The house sits higher than most so that the back of the first floor, which is on the bluff, is not underground. That's why you have extra steps to climb up to reach the front porch."

"Do you think they are really going to measure this?"

"Gabe, do you think they won't?"

Gabe grows silent.

"Are you still there?" she asks.

He snaps his finger. "Can't we lower the ceilings a bit? Make it conform?"

"If I did, the proportions would be all wrong."

"Let's submit plans that will not agitate the hornet's nest running this town."

"Then I expect you to adhere to these changes. Don't do anything foolish, Gabe, like telling Cole to build it to the original specs. My license is on the line."

"I have no such intention."

Verity was savvy enough to hear the tone that betrayed his thoughts, thoughts she needed to disperse. "This isn't horseshoes where a near miss gets you points. Island Bluffs is the toughest town around these parts when it comes to a building code. They don't look the other way when a violation occurs; don't expect them to *grandfather in* a mistake. Especially a new mistake. If we're off by six inches, they could make us take it down. They've done it before."

"Then bring in truckloads of dirt and level the land in front of the house until it conforms. Let's not take any chances."

"Then you're messing with violating EPA rules."

"You're telling me there's no way around this?"

"That's why I need to check with the town. Maybe there's a zoning exception for your situation, for houses sitting on bluffs. Let me do my homework and I'll get back to you as soon as I can."

"Don't take too long. We need to start the construction yesterday."

"I am well aware of the time constraints. But I can't get the plans approved until the zoning board meets and that won't be for another week."

Gabe grimaces. "They don't meet weekly?"

"Nope. Every other week. This is an off week."

"I underestimated this town. I knew they weren't progressive and I was all right with that. But they are downright antediluvian."

Gabe hangs up and spends the rest of the day assuming Microsoft will proceed against his advice, the same way he would like to ignore Verity's. Both scenarios court trouble. Microsoft can afford to be on the losing side of a takeover; he's not sure he can weather the heavy arm of so-called justice that the powers could mete out running Island Bluffs.

Yehuda hears the phone ring and Gabe talk to someone. He catches a word here and there. If it has anything to do with the town, thinks Yehuda, then Gabe should keep a steady course and not rock the proverbial boat. But that's not Gabe; he will do what he wants to do. That trait comforts Yehuda. No more turning the cheek for his family, the price is too mighty.

The octogenarian readies himself. Buck will arrive any minute. It's been years since he's made a new friend. Come to think of it, it's been years since he has had a friend at all. Yehuda never had the spare time. Working as a dental lab technician got him through the long days. Waxing crowns, casting bridges, and fabricating dentures fulfilled his need for human contact, no matter how indirect. In his day, he learned the intricacies of milling zirconium, how to use CadCam software programs, and how to compensate for titanium implant-supported prostheses. And Sadie. As long as Sadie was alive, Yehuda had the best company in the entire world. Once she passed, loneliness turned into a tumor that grew as the months and years melted away.

And now? He's glad to know Buck.

Yehuda stands in front of the mirror and brushes his hair. It is the color of gray steel, and just as wiry. He feels Polly in the room. Watching. He turns and scours the walls and floor for her. He even opens the closet. He doesn't see but senses her presence. He runs the brush through his hair one last time. A light flickers behind him. Not a lamp bulb, but a vapor.

He calls out softly, so as not to be heard by anyone. "Is that you, Polly? I know you're here. Don't be afraid."

Polly does not react.

He calls out to her again. Nothing.

"Okay, be that way. When you're ready, you and I should have a little talk." And with that, he hears the roar of Buck's motorcycle scream up the driveway.

Make it two friends: one real, the other . . . just as real.

At the marina, Buck introduces Yehuda to Lance Crenshaw, captain of the *Searcher*.

"I've seen your ship out in the water from my house."

Captain Crenshaw bares crooked teeth; his central incisors overlap like fingers making a wish. He's in his late forties, compact, with thick muscles and sun-bleached hair. His skin is landscaped with brown sunspots. There's a crusty patch above his eye, probably a basal cell that needs to be removed. A cream-colored bandana surrounds his neck to protect from thyroid cancer. He and his men are at risk, daily, from the sun's rays that are reflected off, and magnified, by the water. The captain's hands are like Yehuda's: wrinkled and leathery. Crenshaw's eyes are friendly and inviting; they give comfort. Yehuda likes him.

"What do you hope to find?" Yehuda asks.

Crenshaw cracks a yellow-toothed smile. "We're looking for a boat that was sunk offshore during the war." He nods toward Buck. "Means a lot to folks who live 'round here. Buck show you the spoon? Don't know what that's from, but it's not from the rig we're looking for." He looks at his hands and rubs his palms together. "My itch barometer is telling me we could hit pay dirt any day now."

Yehuda has more than a fleeting idea where the spoon comes from, but he's not prepared to discuss it with them. Not until he's sure.

"The ocean's a big place," says Yehuda. "How do you know where to look?"

"We have an idea where the ship went down. Trouble is, sixty-plus years of ocean currents and storms can pretty much camouflage anything down there. Sort of like searching for parts of an airplane crash that're scattered across a large area. Where water's concerned, ship pieces can be pretty far apart. It's not easy."

"What if you find the ship? Then what?" Yehuda asks.

Buck touches Yehuda's arm and answers. "For starters, we'd want to find out what caused her to go down. By all rights, it never should've happened; it was a clear, sunny day. Official line is that the vapors ignited and caused an explosion, but that never made much sense to me. The captain was meticulous; followed every safety rule. Treated that boat almost as good as his own daughter."

"What else could have happened?" Yehuda asked.

"Given it was during the war, lots of things could've happened to her," Buck answered.

Crenshaw shoots a look first at Buck and then at Yehuda. He opens his mouth to say something, and then thinks better of it. Buck encourages the captain to say what's on his mind.

Crenshaw eyes the *Searcher* and then says, "I was thinking that we're not going out for too long today. A short run. Got another job later. How about the two of you join us. See how a scavenger ship works from the deck."

The old men look at each other.

"What're we waiting for?" says Buck. Before Captain Crenshaw changes his mind, the two plant their feet, grab onto the steel railing, and waddle up the metal plank. They are taking no chances that Captain Crenshaw might change his mind.

Carly finds Nick James hunched over a microscope.

"Anything interesting, Nick?"

Nick James is six-five and played hoops for Colgate. He was all-conference small forward, but never good enough to turn pro. A good student, he got his medical degree from Boston University and did his pathology residency at Albert Einstein Hospital in the Bronx, where Carly did her dental residency.

After hugs and hellos, he asks, "Show me what you have."

She fetches a plastic bag from her purse.

He holds the bag up to the light before opening it. "It's a rib." He frowns. "Nothing else?"

"Afraid that's all there is."

He slips on latex gloves and turns the bone over a couple of times. Rubs his fingers along its length. "Best I can do for you is estimate the age, give or take seven years or so."

"I was hoping for a smaller window on the age rather than fifteen years."

"I need more bones for that. Can you get any?"

She plops onto a gunmetal gray lab stool. "I know where the rest of the bones are, or at least who carried them away, but I'll never be able to get my hands on them. That's for sure."

"Even with a court order?"

"You don't understand. The local sheriff has them. Island Bluffs is one of those towns with its own set of rules. They follow their own brand of law and order. Routine police work doesn't exist there. Prying around this town is like the *X Files'* Dana Scully poking around Roswell."

He fondles the bone for a few more beats. "Third or fourth rib. Probably middle-aged. Can't tell the gender, but you say it's a male."

"I saw the pelvis."

He studies the end of the bone. "The sternum side is pitted. This dude's between thirty-five to forty-five."

"With your plus or minus of seven to eight years, the victim could be in his late twenties to his early fifties. Not a very narrow range now, is it?"

"It's the best I can do," says Nick James. "I'd need the tibia to determine height. Get me a few more bones and I'll be able to give you a better description."

"What about getting a DNA sample from the medullary bone in this sample?"

"That I can do. You know the routine. I need to cut the bone into pieces and soak them in a special solution. Give me a few days and I'll have some mitochondrial DNA available to compare against anything else–or any suspect–you come across."

"Like finding a certain rock in the middle of the ocean."

He waves the bone. "Odds are better with this."

Carly spins around and takes in the ME's equipment, the smells, the humming overhead lights. "It's only a couple of months but I miss being connected."

Nick understands. "Big-time forensic dentist like you? There's a spot here for you just for the asking. All you have to do is give me a holler."

She waves as she leaves. "Remember you said it." She rubs her belly. "Expect that call in a few months."

"I hope that's not an idle threat," says Nick James. "In the meantime, I'll process the bone and it will be ready if you ever find a sample to match against it."

Buck joins them for dinner: grilled salmon, Jersey beefsteak tomatoes layered with sweet onions that are drizzled with first-press Italian olive oil, and fresh white corn from a local farm. Buck shaves the kernels off the cob with a knife.

Dinner is a success.

Buck smacks his lips in satisfaction, excuses himself and empties his bladder.

Megan and Yehuda clear the dinner dishes, Gabe washes, and Carly dries.

Carly counts the days until the kitchen is remodeled and a dishwasher is installed.

Yehuda thanks Carly for inviting Buck.

"He's welcome any time."

The toilet flushes. Buck returns to the kitchen.

"I can't remember the last time I had a home-cooked meal, at least one I didn't cook. Appreciate it, folks, 'cause mine doesn't taste nearly as good as yours does."

A thank you and good-byes are exchanged. Yehuda walks Buck to the door. They arrange to meet again.

Buck's steps are lighter since meeting Yehuda and his family, and he can't help feeling that they've brought him good luck. Well, not exactly him but the *Searcher*. In his heart of hearts, Buck feels they are closer than ever to unraveling the mysteries of a certain sunken ship.

As Buck motors away, a spanking new metallic Capri blue Mercedes-Benz SLK 55 AMG growls up the driveway. The driver, hidden by tinted windows, mumbles under his breath about the dust the motorcycle kicks up that blemishes his pristine vehicle.

Yehuda stands on the porch and watches Buck drive away. He is jolted by the car sailing over the crushed shells.

The car conjures a myriad of images for Yehuda.

None good.

A knot forms in his belly.

Yehuda slips through the screen door to get Gabe.

Uninvited cars cruising up their driveway is getting to be a tired event at the Berk house.

CHAPTER 28

Monday, 7:15 p.m.

The driver is dressed in an Armani blue pinstripe suit, open-collared white Brioni shirt, gold cufflinks sporting a sunburst with a diamond in each center, and two-tone tan shoes made from pebbled ostrich leather. He sports a gold pinky ring with a blue sapphire heavy enough to weigh down his hand. He's in his late fifties, trim, and country-club tan. He plays cards with the sheriff and mayor. His teeth are capped top and bottom, back to the wisdom teeth. When the time comes, he will get a facelift and hair plugs.

"May I help you?" asks Gabe.

The man extends his hand. Gabe hesitates to take it. "I assume you're Mr. Berk." He does not wait for Gabe to answer. The man takes a half step back. "My name is Trevor Reichmann. I don't believe in wasting words, Berk; let me get right to the point."

"Which is?"

"I know you've met Sheriff Kreiser."

Gabe stiffens. What *isn't* everyone's business in this town?

"Are you part of the Welcome Wagon committee, too?"

Reichmann ignores the comment; he has an agenda. "You folks impressed him, and that's not easy to do. In his job, he needs to know what side a man is on, in a hair trigger of a second. His life, and the lives of his men, could be on the line if he judges wrong."

Gabe will have none of it. "You're here for a reason and it has little to do with our precious sheriff. Care to tell me what that is? We're in the middle of dinner and there's no need for chitchat."

Reichmann glances toward the driveway. Buck's gone a couple of minutes by now. "Do your guests usually leave in the middle of dinner?"

"Get to the point, Reichmann."

Reichmann's pulse is steady, his breathing slow. He's in his environment, which is almost always the case. He knows to control his emotions and use words that achieve his goal, which is any goal he sets his mind to. "Truth be told, Mr. Berk, you bought this house right from under our noses."

"I saw the same sign everyone else did, Reichmann. Probably up there for years, if not decades. You had your chances. Turns out that I'm the one who bought it, so it's too bad for you. I'm sure you're aware that there are lots of other houses around town for sale. I can recommend a good realtor for you."

Now it is Reichmann's turn to stiffen; his jaw muscles pulsate. "This house was never supposed to be for sale."

"Then someone on your end dropped the ball, Reichmann. One man's tragedy, if you can call losing a house that was in foreclosure a tragedy, is another man's gain. Sorry that displeases you and your cronies back at town hall, like your wonderful sheriff or your kindly mayor. Last time I checked, this was still a free country. That's how things usually work around here. Even in New Jersey."

Gabe knows Reichmann's type does not fold, nor will he leave without putting up more of a fuss. The next move is Reichmann's. The man takes it. What he says is unexpected.

"I'm here to buy the house from you, Berk." He extracts an envelope from his breast pocket and hands it to Gabe. Gabe takes the envelope, his hand drops to his side; he holds Reichmann's gaze and then stretches taller, posturing for control.

Trevor Reichmann gestures at the envelope. "Aren't you going to open it? I promise, you'll be pleased. There's a tidy profit in there for you, and then some."

Gabe glares at his fist, and then crinkles the envelope into a ball, but doesn't throw it away. He says nothing at first. "How do I get the message across to your people? Your attempts to intimidate us are not working. We are here to stay, and let me be clear: this house is not for sale."

"I didn't expect you to take it, Berk, but I want you to think about it. This is a funny town. People don't care much for strangers."

"Tell me something I don't know already."

Reichmann points to the blueprints in Gabe's hand. Gabe had been showing Megan and Yehuda the latest version before Reichmann appeared. He looked down; he forgot he was holding them.

"And they don't like houses being changed here, either."

Gabe brandishes the plans like a sword. "You're still off message, Reichmann. This is my house. I'll make all the changes I like. Now if you've said everything you've come to say, it's time to . . ."

Reichmann rocks from foot to foot. He licks his lips. "Look, Berk, you made a dumb mistake buying this house, only you didn't know it. My offer's good 'til Friday. Don't come running to me if circumstances 'round here change, 'cause things can happen quick, and all of a sudden you will want to take me up on my offer. Then it'll be too late. Way too late. You'll be the loser if you miss our deadline; I bet the missus won't be happy with you."

"So you can sleep better, Reichmann, rest assured you won't be hearing from me anytime soon. Once the zoning board approves our plans, construction starts immediately." As soon as the words *zoning board* fly from his mouth, Gabe has more than a fleeting thought that he shouldn't have been so rough on Reichmann. So absolute. So in-your-face ungracious. The man must be connected to everything that goes on in this town, including what happens at the zoning board meetings.

At that very moment, the house lights flicker behind Gabe. Only Reichmann can see it happen, not Gabe. Reichmann dismisses it as the occasional power outage that lasts fractions of a second. Happens too many times to count each year.

The wind gusts.

The front door creaks and then slams shut.

"Show the check to your wife, Berk. She'll have a different spin about the money, I'm sure of it. Women always do."

Reichmann hands him a business card; Gabe rips it up. Standing his ground, he says, "In a few days, you'll wish you hadn't done that. Good day, Berk."

Reichmann turns his car around, stops at the end of the driveway, gazes back at the house, shrugs his shoulders at Gabe being foolish, and then slips another business card in the mailbox.

Always give a guy a second chance.

* * *

Inside, Gabe drops the balled-up envelope onto the kitchen table. Carly and Megan hear everything, Yehuda joins them. Gabe says nothing. He rips a strip of paper toweling from the wall-mounted dispenser and wipes sweat from his brow. He opens a cabinet door, snatches a clean glass, pours a vodka shot, tosses it down without saying a word, and then pours another.

Carly moves to smooth the crushed envelope. Her eyes widen. "It's two-fifty more than we paid for the house." She waves it in front of him. "Still feel the same?"

He downs the second drink. "This morning you said you liked it here."

"This morning I didn't know we could make a quick profit and buy a bigger house. I'd do anything not to live through a messy renovation. You've driven through town. There are other houses like this one."

"You can't give in to those bastards," Yehuda says. There is no inflection in his voice, no pitch other than his ordinary tone. Yet the strength of his words ricochets off the walls. No one stirs. No one argues.

Yehuda wonders if he should say more. He must. He takes a step forward. He speaks with one hand folded on top of the other, both held close to his chest.

"This is how it began when I was young. In Germany. They knocked on the door. They were polite. Even majestic in their uniforms. Their medals. The insignias. The black shine to the bill on their hats; the polish to their boots. Their eyes were blue. Steel blue. They didn't blink or turn away when they ordered us to leave. They said that we didn't belong in their country. That we soiled it. Ruined it. That we weren't good enough. That rats were better than us."

He looks from one to the other, his gaze lingers on each. His voice grows softer.

"They're doing the same thing here. To us. They want us to leave because we're not one of them." Then his voice grows louder. Stronger. He raises his hand and his right index finger points to the ceiling. "To hell with them and their money. I will not leave this place."

"Dad, this is different. This is America. They can't push us around," Gabe says.

"Haven't you heard a word I've said? The Germans came knocking and we didn't believe them. After all, we were Germans, too. We were educated. Had money. Went to the fancy balls. Rode horses. We were privileged." His voice drops. "Or so we thought." He locks onto Gabe. "You were born here. Had all the benefits. But maybe I forgot to tell you that living in America is no guarantee that those same abuses won't occur here. Gabe, they can and they do. Imagine how many times these bastards have gotten away with this before, bullying people around. Not me." He wags his finger. "Not Yehuda Berkowitz. It stops here."

"But Yehuda," says Carly, "they don't want us here."

"All the more reason to stay. Let them learn to live with us," he answers. "It'll be good for them. They need to see that we don't have horns or that we're not guilty of what the blood libels accuse us of doing."

"What's that?" asks Megan.

Yehuda takes her hand. "Through the ages, Megan, many people believed that Jews killed Christian babies for their blood. To drink it during the holidays."

Megan thinks about the things they found in the basement.

Yehuda's eyes widen; he continues. "There are bigots around who still think the worst about us."

Carly speaks. "You heard what that jerk told Gabe, it's the house, not us. There's something about this place that bothers them so much that they're trying to buy it from us. To my way of thinking, we should push them hard enough so that they throw more money at us. Then, we can buy a better house and have enough leftover to furnish it, too."

"I vote we stay here." All eyes turn to Megan. "Grandpa's right. We can't cave in, just because they say so."

Carly smiles. "We wouldn't be moving to Siberia, you know. You'd still be able to see Jürgen."

Megan turns red.

"Let's not forget that we have less than three months before you're due. We're staying put until then. Everyone agree?" asks Gabe.

They all do.

Without fanfare, Gabe rips up the check.

Megan needs to make an announcement. Trouble is, the last few minutes relegated her nearly invisible. It is about Jürgen.

"When's he supposed to come over?" Carly asks.

"After dinner. We're going to listen to music."

"You just met this Jürgen. It's been a pretty hectic day," says Gabe, having tussled with Microsoft exploring a hostile takeover of Google, and now Island Bluff's emissary with an offer to buy them out. "Can't he come over another time?" Before she answers, "Have you even had a date?"

Megan answers, "Sort of. It started as a date at Hank's Fountain, but he needed to leave early."

"Aren't you rushing this a bit?" Gabe asks.

Carly frowns and is about to tell him to back off. No need. Megan can handle herself.

"Daaaaad. Have you forgotten this is my summer vacation? You dragged me here against my will. You want me to be happy, don't you? You've got to cut me some slack here."

"Before you get totally absorbed in your new friend, you might want to stop in the basement and see if I forgot anything from your list," says Gabe.

She doesn't understand.

It's hard to contain his glee; he explains, "Between everything else that happened today, I managed to get to the store."

Megan frowns, lost in his reference. *What's he talking about?*

"Your photographic developing equipment? Remember? Had the contractor's people come here and set up the tanks and lights while you were at the library."

She gets it. Megan pounces on him with the biggest hug. "You're the best."

Yehuda is stiff, sore, and drained, both physically and emotionally. He boils water to make a cup of decaffeinated chamomile. He steadies his hand, careful not to spill any and carries it to his room.

The last thing he thought he would ever have to do is champion his, Gabe's, Carly's, and Megan's right to live in a house here or anywhere else in this country. Germany? That was a different story. But here?

He pictures Reichmann. The man may have a tough exterior, but he's no different than the others Yehuda has known over the years: filled with hot air and self-importance. Poke a hole in their veneer and they deflate like a punctured Goodyear. Yehuda smiles. Most dandies wrapped in expensive threads cause little concern; Reichmann does not scare.

The sheriff, on the other hand, is a tougher nut.

Yehuda blows on the herbal tea and takes a sip. The angst of the moment lifts as he thinks back to the morning's events after meeting Captain Crenshaw, when he and Buck tagged along for the run out to sea on the *Searcher*.

* * *

"Always wanted to take on ride on this thing," Buck shouts over the wind in their faces.

Yehuda surveys the boat, the crew busy at their stations, and then he studies Buck, the way Buck is sucking in the salt air and becomes more buoyant with each breath, the way Buck continues to hunt for answers that have eluded him for decades, the way Buck is the poster child for a positive outlook.

"This is all good," Yehuda says, his words swallowed by the thunderous waves.

As they hone in to where they expect to explore that day, Captain Crenshaw explains how they troll the ocean bottom.

The captain demonstrates the sonar equipment. "This gives us the ability to discover what's on the seabed for long distances. The side scan sonar and sub-bottom profiling give us detail that was never available before this came along. It's so specific that we can find sunken ships that were previously undetectable."

"How small an object can it find?" Buck asks.

"Small."

This fascinates. "How exactly does it work?" asks Yehuda.

Crenshaw nods to Buck. "'Bout time you had a friend with some intelligence. Basically the sonar sends a signal out. When it hits something, it bounces back and is processed by the hydrophone. Its relative strength creates an image we can see on a screen. If we think it's something important, we go after it."

Buck crosses his fingers behind his back, praying for pay dirt.

The *Searcher* runs a grid back and forth over a prescribed area near where they found the engraved spoon. The sonar pings. It strikes metal.

They are two hundred and fifty feet above the seabed. The boat springs to action.

"How do you get down there?" Yehuda asks. "That's too deep to dive, isn't it?"

"No need to dive." Captain Crenshaw points to a globe-shaped orb dangling from a winch. "We use an ROV."

Buck explains. "That stands for a *remotely operated vehicle*. It's connected to a huge cable, the kind the telecommunications companies use. Once it's down on the seabed, the technician maneuvers it to the object."

"Then what?"

Crenshaw slaps Yehuda on the back. "C'mon fellas, I'll show you."

They scramble down narrow metal stairs. Yehuda holds onto both railings, slithering down with an ease that surprises.

"Sorry, but it's a bit tight," says the Captain, bending so as not to hit his head. Buck needs to bend over, too, but not Yehuda; he stands tall.

"This here is Cameron. He's our computer whiz." He turns to the pimple-faced youth. "Say hello, Cammy." Cameron waves without taking his eyes off the screen. He sits in front of a bevy of controls that are a cross between a video game and a sound engineer's instrument board.

Cameron turns knobs that control the manipulator arms to pick up an object with its claw-like fingers. It reminds of the Seaside Heights boardwalk. *Put a quarter in, manipulate the crane and scoop a prize.*

Crenshaw explains. "There's a powerful fiber optic light attached to the camera on the arm. Makes it possible to see even though no light can penetrate that deep from above. Cammy has gotten so good at this he can pick a dime up with those mechanical fingers."

"They made a buck-twenty-five one time," says Buck to Yehuda, recalling the coins they *did* find one day. "Won't even buy a cup of coffee at Starbucks these days."

The beeping grows louder and faster. The claw closes in on the metal object. The image is sharp: it's shaped like a fork. Cameron performs his wizardry and grasps it in the mechanical fingers. He locks it in, recoils the umbilicus and, once secured, pilots the ROV to the surface.

Buck, Yehuda, and Captain Crenshaw scramble deck side to examine the booty.

The fork matches the spoon.

"Soon," offers the captain, "we'll have a complete set of silverware."

Yehuda recalls what the spoon looked like. Now with the fork, there is no doubt what it is: *German silverware*. He chooses not to say anything to the others, most of all to Buck. This is not the time.

Buck needs to discover the truths represented by these finds for himself. When Buck does, much will make sense, though it is too late to find lasting, inner peace. He needs a miracle for that to happen.

And miracles do happen . . . even in make believe.

Noises fill the house. Gabe and Carly are in the kitchen. Megan talking. In minutes, Megan's young man will drop by. Yehuda will meet the boy another time. For now, even though the sun has not yet set, Yehuda lies on his bed and closes his eyes.

He recalls the day.

The *Searcher*.

The fork.

Reichmann, the man with the check.

As he dozes, the cream-colored lace curtains flutter, making a *shushing* sound.

Yehuda opens his eyes and leans on his elbow.

He smiles the way grandfathers do.

"Sorry I forgot to say 'Hello,' Polly. Forgive a tired, old man. I hope you had a nice time while I was gone."

The curtains flutter an answer, but Yehuda is fast asleep.

CHAPTER 29

Monday, 7:35 p.m.
As Yehuda sleeps, Megan arranges her makeshift darkroom knowing Jürgen will be there any moment. Ordinarily she would be champing at the bit, listening for a sound that heralds the moment of his arrival. But for the first time all day, her thoughts focus on something other than the hunk with the toothy smile.

She busies herself by slipping clips onto the wire Gabe connected to metal eyelets screwed into the wall. She straightens the bottles of developing solution, labels aligned to the front. What Gabe didn't say earlier was that the processing tanks were already filled, the red light developing light was installed, and a supply of both Superia X-TRA 800 ISO film and developing paper were planted on a shelf installed below the high-perched toilet tank.

Megan turns the incandescent bulb off and flips on the special red light. She's anxious. There is unfinished film in her Nikon, but enough exposed for her to process. She depresses the rewind button and cycles the film off the spooler. With any luck, she will have time to develop the film before lover boy—doesn't she ever wish—makes his appearance.

Monday, 7:50 p.m.
Jürgen parks in front of Megan's house. He cannot recollect the drive there. Must have obeyed the speed limits. Avoided the local gendarmes.

"You must be Jürgen," Carly says, extending her hand. "I'll tell Megan you're here. She's in the basement, checking out her new darkroom."

He stands in the dark foyer. Given they've only lived there a few days, it's more orderly than his house. This causes a pang. He knows the Berks will remodel and expand. When they do, neatness will evaporate like the morning fog. The result? It will be worth it.

* * *

The doorbell rings. Megan hears it, but pays it no mind. She's in the middle of a process that can't be stopped.

Footsteps above.

Carly calls down. "Jürgen's here."

"In a minute," she says as loud and ladylike as possible. Megan, bathed in red light, picks up the developing picture with tongs, rinses it off in water, and pins it to a wire stretched across the wall. Satisfied, she flips on the light, primps herself, and dashes up the steps.

Moments later, Megan, Jürgen, Carly, and Gabe drink lemonade.

"Megan tells me you'll be going to Lehigh," says Carly.

Jürgen meets her gaze. He's self-assured, yet respectful. As he speaks, he hears a clump. Then a series of clumps. It is Megan sprinting up the stairs two at a time.

"Megan tells me you'll be going to Lehigh," Carly attempts to distract him from Megan's unladylike stampede.

"I'm going to wrestle there."

"Always been a good school for that." Gabe extends his hand. "I'm Megan's father, Gabe Berk."

They shake. Gabe sizes up Jürgen. The boy is broad across the chest, muscles defined in his arms. Thick neck. "I assume you're on scholarship."

Jürgen nods. "It's not enough. Even if my parents could help, they wouldn't. My dad doesn't believe in handouts. Says he never got anything from his father and he's not about to start with me. That's why I'm working construction this summer." He pauses, thinking whether he should utter the next words. He does. "That's not quite true. My father was born after his father passed. So there really is no history in our family. He just thinks college shouldn't be on his dime."

Enter Megan. She pats down her hair. Runs a finger over her right eyebrow. Her lips are full. She sings out to Carly and her father. "Jürgen's going to work on our house."

Carly reacts. "So you're working for Cole Brancusi?" She glances at Megan. The girl has stars in her eyes. "How convenient," says Carly.

"This will be my third summer." Jürgen beams.

Carly knows she should leave them alone, but she needs to hear more. "Megan tells me your family has lived around Island Bluffs a long time."

"We're still considered immigrants here. I have friends whose ancestors fought in the Revolution. One of my friends, Scotty McKibben, his family goes back something like eight generations here. His great-great-whatever was a Scottish Highlander brought from the old country to fight alongside the British in the French and Indian War. That was before the Revolution."

"So I've heard," says Carly with a glimmer.

He either doesn't hear or chooses to ignore her comment. "After they signed the treaty in 1763, he decided to stay here. He was able to buy a chunk of land in town and his family's been here ever since. They own the local hardware store."

"And your family?"

"The story, at least the way I remember it, is that my grandfather came here as a little boy soon after World War I. He was born in Munich. He worked for a local company here all his life. My grandmother was pregnant with my father when my grandfather died. And she died giving birth to my dad. That's all I know about them."

"That made your father an orphan since birth," says Gabe.

"He never felt that way," answers Jürgen. "He was lucky. He always says that a great family raised him. They brought him up as their own flesh and blood. My father didn't know any different."

Megan looks at Yehuda's closed door. "I'm so lucky I know my grandfather. Some of my friends don't have any grandparents left."

Carly, ever the New Yorker, ever curious, prods. "What does your father do?"

"He works for American Fertilizer, just like my grandfather did."

A thought nags. Then she remembers. "Isn't that the same company that Trevor Reichmann works for?"

The boy shoves his hands in his pockets, not knowing how his answer will measure. "He's my father's boss."

Gabe looks at Carly; Carly looks at him.

While it may have been random that Megan met Jürgen at the library, it is obvious to the adults in the room that there are no coincidences. Jürgen is here to serve a purpose. They're just not sure what that purpose is.

Megan tugs on Jürgen's arm. "C'mon. I want to take some pictures before I lose the light."

A dash to the basement for her Nikon, she grabs Jürgen's hand and they bound behind the house. The camera is cradled in her free hand. She moves to the grass edge—it's slippery—steadies herself, focuses, and then clicks. Pictures of crashing waves. Billowing clouds. A jumping fish.

Jürgen points. "Look. Out there. Someone's swimming."

Megan focuses through the camera lens. Too far for a meaningful picture. "Wish I had my telephoto." She lowers the camera. "We've seen him a few times before. Buck says he is always out there. Swimming the channel for years."

"I've heard about him, but this is the first time I got to see him for myself."

They twist away and walk; they talk. The constant thrum of the ocean calms. Soothes. She aches to turn the lens on Jürgen. In time, she will.

Jürgen gets into the moment, forgets his father and turns playful. He snatches the camera and snaps Megan's picture. Then another. He asks her to pose. Innocence and electricity abound. Peels of laughter ring out.

Carly watches Megan and Jürgen through the window.

Gabe pours a glass of Santa Margarita; Carly drinks Perrier. She adds a wedge of lime; licks her finger. "I have no reason to say this but I sense there's something deep inside that boy that's bubbling to the surface for the first time. Megan tells me he has issues with his father."

"Who doesn't have issues with their father?"

"I might have, had I known mine," she answers, her voice a whisper.

"Are you serious? The fact that your father left you when you were ten, at such an impressionable age, means to me that you must have had issues with him. No one would blame you."

"His leaving broke my mother's heart. And mine, too."

"You have to resent him for that. For Chrissakes, you were just a kid."

She turns to Gabe. "I hated him for the longest time. I mean it's one thing for your parents to get a divorce. That's bad enough. But when my father disappeared and we never heard from him again, that was horrible. I went around thinking everyone was staring at me because I was the little girl whose father abandoned her. It was like having a third eye in the middle of my forehead. Wherever I went, I could hear whispering behind my back."

Gabe slides over and hugs her. He kisses the top of her head. "I can't even imagine how you felt." He edges back a step. "But look how you turned out: a professional, married to a great guy, and a soon-to-be mother."

Her eyes narrow. "Things my mother never got to see. At least you still have your father."

"Don't think I haven't had my issues with him. I have."

"Could've fooled me. I don't sense any tension between you."

"Not now. But there were times that no matter what I did, it wasn't good enough. My grades could've been better. I could've worked harder. It didn't matter to him that I made law review. It didn't matter that I started at Skadden, which is at the top of the legal food chain. In his eyes, I could always have done more."

"Was your mother as tough on you?"

"No, she was a gentle soul. Whatever I did, was okay with her. She would've loved you."

"I wish we had met." Carly pauses, lost in her thoughts. She turns back to Gabe. "At least your father was there for you. He watched you go to college and law school. He got to know Emily. And you see how he and Megan get along. I don't see what you're talking about now. Yehuda doesn't appear so judgmental."

"Age has a way of mellowing even the hardest of critics," Gabe answers.

At that moment, Carly and Gabe are a cyclone of emotions. Both are numb, but for different reasons. They lose the fact that Megan and Jürgen are no longer in view.

The teenagers approach the large northern red oak next to the house. They are away from probing eyes. They ham it up on the rope swing tied to a huge limb eons ago.

He pushes her, their skin touches. Electric.

They take more pictures.

"Still thinking about your dad?" Gabe asks.

She gazes at the ocean. "Is it that obvious?"

"I've seen it before. Someone says something about his or her father, doesn't matter if it's good, bad, or indifferent, and you react with a hollow look that crops up in your eyes. I know you've drifted back to when you were ten, when your father abandoned you and your mom, when you couldn't figure out why or what you did wrong."

She draws in a deep breath to purge those feelings. "How do you feel about Jürgen?"

"Seems like a good sort."

"That's not what I mean."

"What else is there? I just met him?"

"Try his last name. Hauptmann? Like in Jürgen Hauptmann?"

"So?" he asks.

"Hauptmann is not exactly Epstein, Levine or Mandelbaum. Have you stopped to think about your father's feelings?"

"I married you, didn't I?"

"That's different." She faces him. "I'm cute and adorable." She looks down at her belly. "At any rate, I will be, again, as soon as junior is born."

"As cute as you are, you're no more or less Jewish than Jürgen. Besides, why would you care? After all, what are the odds it will go anywhere? For Megan, this is puppy love . . . if that."

"Have you noticed that her world stops when he's around?"

"How can you say that? He just got here."

"She's crazy about him."

"Then let her be happy."

"Like you?"

"Precisely." He strides over and gives her a lingering kiss. "Does that make it better?"

"Nothing needs to be fixed," she says, "but I like your style."

"*Au contraire.* You were making a judgment on Jürgen, by association. He's a full-blooded American. I know where you're going with this. Even if his roots are German, so what? Mine are too."

She jabs his arm. "Get serious. You know what I'm saying. What if his grandfather was in the German army during the war? What if he was a card-carrying . . . ?"

He holds his hand up. "Stop right there. The war's been over a long time. There's no place for guilt-by-association in this house. How many times have you heard my father say the same thing?"

"All I care about is Megan. I don't want to see her get hurt," says Carly. She wanted to add, *again*, thinking of Megan losing her mother.

"You can't protect children from everything. There are times you have to step back and let something happen to them, even if you see it coming before they do. I don't think this infatuation that you're so sure exists is anything to worry about. She's a big girl. My vote is not to say a word to her. Let this take its own course."

"Can't you see how fragile she is? Moving here, taking her away from friends, she needs to feel good about herself."

"And that's why I am saying to trust her to do the right thing." He runs a finger over her tummy. "You'll see. These little tykes don't come with an instruction manual. It's not easy to know what to do, especially with a firstborn. That's the practice one for all parents. The trial child. The others that follow are way easier to raise. Give this some time; you'll see, I'm right."

Outside, a soft wind ripples through the lone oak.

Sunlight bathes Megan and Jürgen in a golden glow.

They take more pictures, unaware that Polly is sitting on a branch above, shining approval on them.

Megan is living the life Polly almost had. Wanted to have.

Just then, a cool wind stirs. Megan and Jürgen shiver.

They go inside but not before Polly grows more agitated, reflecting on what Megan has . . . and what she, Polly, has lost.

CHAPTER 30

Monday, 8:20 p.m.
"It's getting cold all of a sudden." Megan grabs Jürgen's hand. "Besides, I want you to meet my grandfather. He's in his room."

"He's probably sleeping," says Jürgen.

"We won't know unless we check. C'mon."

Yehuda hears a soft rap on the door. It takes a moment to get oriented. Where is he? Back in Berlin? In his apartment in the Bronx? Where's Sadie?

"Grandpa?"

"Just a minute." Yehuda fell asleep in his clothes. He snaps on the light switch and rakes his thinning hair with crooked fingers.

He snatches a book, opens it to the middle, and calls for her to come in. The book's upside down.

"We thought you were sleeping, Grandpa."

"I might have dozed for a moment or two." He closes the book and stands. The sleeves on his white shirt are rolled up revealing thin arms dotted with raised, brown keratoses.

"Grandpa," she says, "this is Jürgen."

Jürgen shakes Yehuda's hand and stares a beat too long. "I . . . I'm pleased to meet you, sir."

Yehuda motions for them to sit. Jürgen folds into the club chair; Megan plants herself on the cushioned arm. There's an awkward silence. Jürgen snags another peek at Yehuda's arm.

Yehuda pushes his sleeve up further and thrusts his arm toward them. "Do you know what these numbers mean?"

"141986" is tattooed on his arm.

"We learned about them in history," says Jürgen, his voice muted.

"Three years. I survived in Auschwitz and Bergen Belsen. Do you want to know how?"

Jürgen gulps; Megan holds her breath. This is the first time she hears him speak about this. Why has he kept this from her? Does her father know? He must.

Yehuda gets up and retrieves a tattered hatbox. Metal clanging against metal pierces the air. Yehuda flips open the box, reaches in, removes a nicked and darkened pliers, and wags it in front of them.

Jürgen recognizes it. "Are you a dentist?"

Yehuda shakes his head. "I was a shoemaker before the war. When we crawled off the train, men went to the left, women and children to the right. They asked for a shoemaker. I was scared. Someone raised his hand quicker than me. That saved him. He made fancy boots for the officers and satin shoes for their whores."

"Didn't they need another shoemaker, Grandpa?"

"Pumpkin, you didn't negotiate with the Nazis. What saved me is that they asked for a dentist. When no one raised his hand, I quick became a dentist. As fanatical as the Nazis were for details, they believed me."

"How'd you know how to fix teeth?" she asked.

He scoffs. "Fix? My job was to pull all the teeth filled with gold after the people were gassed. They didn't need a dentist. Anybody could have done that. Even a shoemaker." He clings to the bed's edge, staving off a torrent of cascading memories that threaten to pull him into a vortex he had tried to seal shut so many times before.

Megan clutches Jürgen's arm; he's pale.

Yehuda continues. "After the war, I was filled with guilt for surviving while so many perished. I promised myself that I would work to help others in some small way."

"But being a shoe repairman would've helped people, Grandpa."

"That wouldn't have been enough, not after what I saw, what I lived through. When I got to America, I walked into a dental laboratory; lucky for me the man was Jewish. I rolled up my sleeve, showed him my arm. That's all I needed to do. He hired me on the spot. It was the only job I ever had."

Unseen by Megan and Jürgen, a wisp floats in the mirror.

Polly is saddened by Yehuda's story.

The three talk a bit longer; Yehuda grows weary. The hours exhaust.

Megan kisses Yehuda; admiration is written on Jürgen's face.

* * *

By day's end, the Berk family has the resolve and fortitude to stay in their new house regardless of how hard the town tries to make them leave. Gabe is uncertain whom Reichmann represents. American Fertilizer, which was the company name printed on the business card he found? The sheriff? The mayor? It doesn't matter. They can't bully him and his family, let alone be permitted to open old wounds Yehuda paid so dearly to heal.

"I need to talk to my father," Gabe says to Carly. They're resting on top of a forest-green duvet, one they've taken from the old house. Fully dressed. Carly will toss the old bedding after the addition is completed. For now, it is serviceable.

"Are you worried that bad memories are being stirred?"

"He has to be shaken by that sheriff stopping by; did you catch that military-like uniform? And then Reichmann offers to buy the house. That must've felt like one step removed from the Nazis confiscating the Jewish properties before the war broke out," says Gabe.

"Maybe not. People, movies, magazines . . . images of the Nazis and the death camps surface all the time. Look at *Schindler's List*. I love that you're so sensitive about your father's feelings. That's one of the reasons I love you so much. But now? In Island Bluffs? We're more than sixty years removed from the war, and your father's heard and seen everything relating to those dark days over and over again."

"You can't ever get used to that. No one can. The lucky ones are able to relegate it to a corner of their brain and leave it untouched most of the time. Then, a day like today comes along and unlocks those memories."

"Even so, the man's exhausted. Let him sleep. Besides, there's something we need to talk about."

"Is this something *I've* heard before?" Doubt and regret have already crept into Gabe's rock solid reasons for bringing his family to Island Bluffs. He now realizes how much he inconvenienced each in a different way. Was he that selfish? He can't bring himself to share this with Carly.

No need . . . she can only imagine how Gabe feels.

She takes his hand. "I can guarantee you that it's nothing either of us has heard before." Carly then proceeds to detail her encounters with

Olivia, the first time outside Dr. Teplitsky's clinic and the second earlier that day at the pharmacy. Then she explains how each of the other Teplitsky successes—there are ten others—have the biological equivalent of "buyer's remorse."

"And this Olivia wants you to meet the others? How do you feel about meeting them?" Gabe asks.

"I don't think I want to. I can't imagine why I should subject myself to that stress."

"Think of their stresses, not having seen the other child each carried for nine months. It's been years and years for all of them. What's the harm in meeting them?"

"It's not my job to ease their stresses."

"Turn the tables. What if it were you trying to meet the new sorority sister who's agreed to carry a Teplitsky baby. Would you take 'No' for an answer?"

"Not if I was desperate."

"From what you're telling me, these women are desperate," says Gabe, "especially Olivia. Imagine losing her only child and knowing that she gave birth to another that's so near, yet out of her reach. And the others? At a minimum they're curious. Doubtless they want to know that their other sons are doing fine. I'm sure it's nothing more than that."

"These boys are not their sons," she says.

"They came out of their bellies," he answers.

She huffs. "You and I made that same deal. Should we expect to be able to visit this Teplitsky child anytime we want? Intrude on his life uninvited?"

"Wouldn't you be curious?"

"I would be, but we agreed never to ever see him again. We can't go back on our word like those other women seem to want to do."

Gabe reaches for her hand; she doesn't move to meet his. "He would still be our son."

"How? He's not biologically related to us. I'm merely a surrogate for this baby. A living incubator. Nothing more."

"Are you spouting those words because you feel you must? To show that you're honorable and trustworthy? Because if you are, that's not what I'm talking about." He points to her belly. "I want to know if you feel anything for this other child."

She pauses. "I can't tell them apart, so I don't have a special feeling for Teplitsky's son. As long as ours is healthy, that's what's important. I can live without ever seeing his son again."

Gabe shakes his head. "Which brings us back to Olivia. What would you do if you were in her spot?"

He mines her face for a clue. He has struck a chord. Carly's stalwart demeanor collapses.

She swipes away bullets of tears. She leans into him. "I'm so afraid of what's going to happen. What if my baby, our baby, has something wrong with it? What if he dies like Olivia's? I wish we never met that bastard."

He cuddles her deep inside him. "Slow down there. This isn't my Carly talking. I understand how you can have your doubts. I have them, too. But you didn't have any until you met this Olivia."

She pulls away. "Oh, I had them all right. I just never expressed them to you. Think about how crazy this whole thing is. I'm supposed to carry a baby to full term and hand it over to the doctor as payment for giving us our baby. It's preposterous. It's a deal with the Devil. The insanity of it all."

"Hold on. No one had a problem until Olivia suffered her tragedy."

"We don't know that. But I will tell you this, Gabe, I'm taking back everything I said before. Olivia *is* reason enough to meet the other *twofers*."

"Excuse me?"

"That's what they call themselves: *twofers*."

"Two for one. I get it."

"Gabe, you can't get babies by bartering. These women are flesh and blood like me. Meeting Olivia caused all my latent fears to surface."

"I get it."

"Good, because I want you do to your magic and get us the best lawyer we can find."

The next morning Megan wakes early, skips breakfast, flies down the basement stairs, yanks on the overhead light, locks the door to her modified darkroom, and gropes around in the darkness until she touches a switch. A soft red glow floats over the developing solutions. One-by-one, Megan develops each picture from the day before. Clouds dancing above white-caps, Jürgen flailing in stiff, robotic moves, Megan on the swing, and then . . . in the tree . . .

Megan reaches for a magnifying glass.

Animated, she hangs the photo from a clip to dry. She hurries to finish the remaining pictures. The processing complete, she pulls the chain and turns on the light.

Megan leans closer.

Polly hovers over Jürgen.

Is that a smile or a scowl?

CHAPTER 31

Tuesday, July 8, 7:30 p.m.
A week later, Verity Frizzell's plans are presented to the Island Bluffs Zoning board. There is an animated discussion about including the house into the historic district.

"As an architect, I can tell you that there is nothing historical about this house. What the Berks propose will enhance the value of their property and increase your tax roll. This project is a plus for the town."

A vote was taken; it was five-to-three with one abstention. The Berks got their permit.

Wednesday, July 9, 7:00 a.m.
Sheriff Kreiser pours a cup of coffee. There is an oversized, bulky manila envelope on this desk: "For Your Eyes Only."

It is a request for a building permit for the Berk house from a local builder, Cole Brancusi, plus a copy of the blueprints stamped by an architect who's becoming more popular, Verity Frizzell. He studies the plans, notes the changes, and picks up the phone faster than a prestidigitator can make a rabbit disappear.

The Berks cross a line they do not know exists.

Crossing a line, no matter how slight, is not a good thing to do in Island Bluffs.

Wednesday, July 9, 8:00 a.m.
A cacophony of heavy machinery greets the day with the noise levels of bulls stampeding at Pamplona: flatbeds hauling cases and boxes, open-backed trucks filled with men and tools, vans with custom-made bins and racks, and duel-exhaust cars that spew black smoke form a caravan that

snakes up the Berk driveway. Jürgen hops off the back of a black truck with silver highlights.

Megan runs toward him. His smile melts, then turns into a frown; his hand shoots up intending to freeze. Then a headshake meant for her to stop. She gets it. *Don't come any closer. The men will never let me live it down if you run up to me. Can't let them witness any mushy stuff.*

Jürgen spins away and drops the truck gate. He reaches over and muscles a tool chest to the edge before heaving it to the ground.

Buck scoots past the hodgepodge of men and metal, and slides to a halt twelve inches before redesigning Yehuda's body parts. Yehuda doesn't flinch. He trusts. He hands Buck a mug of coffee. Not a drop spills.

In the far distance, out at sea, in a world of its own, the *Searcher* plods through a new grid, rejuvenated by the recent find of the fork to go along with the silver spoon. The ship is a lesson in stubborn perseverance . . . a trait exhibited by many in Island Bluffs.

Gabe plows through the front door. "Hey, Cole. Looks like you brought an army."

"We've got a deadline to meet," he said, referring to finishing before Carly gives birth. Cole Brancusi is all business. He might flash an easy, even what might be called an I-am-not-a-serious-guy smile during off hours, but when he unrolls blueprints, Cole's focus is laser-sharp.

"The new septic will be here," he points to a dotted square on the plan and then marks it off in the yard. Although Verity recommended a long-time expert to fabricate the septic tank, Cole reassures Gabe that he's dug out hundreds over the years. The necessary machines and manpower are already on site. He charges next to nothing for this.

"It'll be right next to the old one. Take no time to dig out. Soon's it's done, we'll get the building inspector off our backs. We'll extend the footprint on the side of the house for the master bedroom at the same time. Might be a good idea for you folks to spend as much time as possible away from here the next couple of weeks."

Gabe scratches his head. "I know we talked about that, but it could be a problem for my dad. Day-to-day, it shouldn't be that bad. I have a series of business meetings in New York; Carly has lots to keep her out of the house; and Megan's working at the town library. We'll manage."

"It would be a heck of a lot better if you moved out completely, but I understand. Imagine you'd have to rent another house or take three hotel rooms. Gets pretty expensive."

Gabe motions to Yehuda. Buck joins them. "Dad, meet Cole. He's our contractor."

Buck and Cole know each other.

Gabe takes his father's arm. "Is there any chance you could spend some time with Buck today and maybe part of the week? Cole feels it would be better if we tried to stay away during the day until he finishes digging the trenches and working on the foundation."

Buck answers. "No problem at all. Your dad can stay at my house when I'm working. And even come with me to the clinic. He won't be in the way."

"Sure it'll be okay?" asks Gabe.

Cole chimes in. "Don't let anybody fool you. Buck has the run of this town. And Doc Teplitsky loves him. It'll be real smart to go with him, Mr. Berkowitz."

"Yehuda."

"What do you say, Dad?"

"Is anyone hearing me object?" Yehuda says with a smile. His teeth are yellowed and chipped, but he's quick to tell folks they're all his. No missing teeth. Pretty good for anyone his age, let alone a survivor of the camps.

Wednesday, 8:40 a.m.

A siren blares, flashing red and blue lights, and the crunch of tires up the driveway turns the nectar of promise into a recipe for despair.

"Jesus H. Christ," says Buck. "I don't believe these people."

All heads turn to see Sheriff Kreiser racing towards them. The town's building inspector, Steve Freiberg, is in the car, too. Thin and small, Freiberg has a ragged moustache and eyes that are too close. A weasel comes to mind; ferrets are too adorable.

Sheriff Kreiser sashays up to them. "Sorry to interrupt your little party, folks."

Kreiser nods to Freiberg; it's choreographed for him to say something. Freiberg's cucumber-shaped head drops down to avoid eye contact, especially with Buck and Cole; they all know each other. He thrusts an official document into Gabe's hand without saying a word.

Gabe lets it slip through his fingers; it hits the ground.

"My dance calendar is filled, boys. Sorry I can't make the policemen's ball this year."

The sheriff slides his hand onto his revolver handle. "Your smart-ass mouth is not welcomed here, Berk. Cut us some slack. If you would bother to pick that up and read what's in it, you'd find out your house can't support any new construction. The whole shebang's gonna collapse. We're here to protect you, not cause you problems."

"Strange way to rationalize your point of view, Sheriff. I do appreciate the effort. Now if you'll excuse us, we have work to do." He turns to Cole. "Shall we?"

The sheriff puts his arm on Gabe; Gabe wrenches it away.

"Maybe you're not hearing me, Berk."

"Oh, I heard you, sheriff. And what you're saying just doesn't resonate with anything I know to be true. I've had a structural engineer inspect the house plus my architect, Verity Frizzell, who's a math whiz, to make certain the new loads would be tolerated by the existing structure. Passed with flying colors. Now here's a news flash for you: your own zoning board approved our plans last night. So, if you'll excuse us, Sheriff, you're on a fishing expedition . . . and there's nothing here for you to catch. You had better pull up stake and look for someone else to harass."

Brancusi takes a step. He shoves the plans in front of them. "The plans are stamped, Rudi," he points to Freiberg, "by you, Steve. So what gives?"

No one speaks.

Each calculates his next move.

Cole takes the lead. "This house is built with aged timber, not the green wood we're forced to use these days. Ten houses could be stacked on top of this one. That's how strong it is."

Freiberg finally speaks. "Now look who's blowing smoke. I triple-checked the distribution loads, too. Under the right circumstances, the main support beams could give."

Gabe turns away, takes a step toward the house, and then faces the sheriff and building inspector. His voice is softer. He tries to sound reasonable, yet make his words sharp enough to draw blood. "I don't know what your game is. If you're trying to get rid of us, it's not going to work. Like it or not, Sheriff, we're here to stay. The town should be happy that someone's finally living in this house. It's time to end the games, whatever they might be."

Kreiser bends, grunts, and manages to snatch the court order from the ground without falling down. His face bulges red when he stands, his breathing labored.

"I'm through pussyfooting around. This order trumps your lousy bleeding heart," he says with a gush of air. He edges closer to Cole; their eyes lock. He points at Cole's chest. "Tell your men to back off. There's no work here for them today. Got that?"

Cole turns to Gabe. "It's your call. We've got approved permits. We're not breaking any laws. They're just trying to bully you."

Yehuda steps forward, his fists clenched; Buck stops him.

Megan doesn't grasp what's happening, she's ogling Jürgen.

Cole's crew loafs about, waiting for an order to proceed or desist. If it comes to blows, they will support Cole. Short of that, they're indifferent. Regardless of the cause of this particular administrative brushfire, they know that flames get squelched and smoke always clears. It's the order of all things.

In the distance, the *Searcher* drops anchor.

Gabe studies the sheriff and Freiberg, and then takes Cole by the arm so the sheriff can't hear what he says. "Will your men work if you ask them to?"

"Just say the word. They're loyal to me. Do whatever I ask."

Sheriff Kreiser takes out handcuffs and nods toward Buck, speaking right at Gabe. "Don't be a stubborn sonofabitch, Berk. Buck will tell you I don't bluff."

Buck remains stone-faced; the fact that he does not protest speaks volumes.

Gabe freezes. He prides himself on making good choices, of being able to analyze a circumstance or problem and opt to take the right path. He does so with frequent success, successes that yield probable outcomes. Probable outcomes require reasonable people. Reasonable and rational people, by any measure of appraisal, are elements lacking in this particular scenario.

Gabe opens his cell phone. He catches Verity Frizzell out of the office, on site, overseeing a new wing being added to Bay Shore Medical Center. To date, this will be the crowning achievement of her young and already illustrious career.

"Let me talk to Freiberg," she says to Gabe. Gabe hands him the phone. A dozen pairs of eyes scan the building inspector's every nuanced facial expression, the way he pinches his lips together, gazes toward the blue sky, shifts his feet, tugs at his ear, hitches his belt, and switches the phone from hand-to-hand. She must be having quite a go at him because he remains silent for a full two minutes.

Freiberg hangs up without saying anything other than "I understand."

Gabe and Cole expect Freiberg to back off. Instead, Freiberg tugs on the sheriff's sleeve and nods. They step away. The sheriff takes off his black-billed trooper-styled hat and holds it to shield the others from reading their lips the way a pitcher converses with his catcher over a change-of-pace sign. Heads bob; they speak in whispers. After a while, the sheriff drops his hand, buffs the brim of his hat, and replaces it with a deliberateness . . . the manager strutting back to the dugout to buy time.

Sheriff Kreiser takes a furtive glance toward the building inspector. "Steve, here, says your architect, Chastity . . ."

"Verity," Gabe corrects.

"Whatever." Kreiser does not miss a beat. "He says she's a crackerjack. Knows what she's doing."

Cole Brancusi interrupts. "Gabe, no matter what Verity told them, we have the permits we need. This is total bull crap. They're razzing you for no reason." He glances at his men lolling around. "This is costing us money." He wheels and barks orders for them to dismount the heavy machinery in order to start digging the new septic and expanding the foundation.

A drowsy beehive comes to life.

Kreiser's eyes bulge; his bloated face turns dark shades of ripe, heirloom tomatoes. The purple kind.

"I was going to give you a day for your architect to fix what needs fixing, but not if you start your men today."

"Sheriff, we have the permits."

"You've said that before. They are no longer valid, Cole." The sheriff raises his voice. "Now order your men to stop." His hand instinctively edges back to the gun handle.

A backhoe rolls behind them.

Gabe draws in a deep breath. He stands his full measure. Cole and his men can't afford to lose even one day if they are to finish on time.

Gabe dismisses the last few minutes; he still believes reason can prevail.

"Sheriff, I don't know why you have it in for us. We've done nothing wrong. I've made certain that all applications are in order. Triple-checked them, in fact. Your job is to enforce local laws and catch bad guys. Given that no laws are being broken here, and that we're in compliance with all town ordinances, forgive me if I insist that you and Mr. Freiberg leave so Cole's men can get going. Otherwise . . ."

"Otherwise what?"

"Otherwise I'll be forced to call my attorney."

"You can call the governor for all I care." Kreiser whips out handcuffs. "I run the show here and you've crossed the line. You can make this real easy on yourself or play it the hard way, Berk. Doesn't matter a rat's ass to me how I take you in." The sheriff looks from face to face. "I don't think you want your pretty little girl to see her daddy taken away like this."

When Kreiser's gaze falls on Megan, Gabe cringes in disgust. Gabe cannot view Kreiser as anything but an overweight lecher who abuses the public trust.

Megan points her cell phone at the sheriff; she records it all.

That's my daughter!

Kreiser pauses, thinks YouTube, lawsuit, mayor, town hall meetings, and media coverage. His pension is secure, no matter what, but still . . .

The scene crumbles before his eyes.

What no one knows is that Kreiser is not making orders but carrying them out. This is not his doing, yet there is no denying that he gets more than a fleeting pleasure hassling the Berks, especially Gabe. There's something about these interlopers that irks the sheriff more than a sharp rock in his boot. It doesn't matter that they are fellow New Jerseyans; these folks are outsiders. For any number of reasons, the house notwithstanding, he wants Gabe and his family to move out of town.

And for those whom he answers to, that time has come.

* * *

The backhoe belches; a plume of black smoke curls upward.

Gabe motions Cole to start the excavations. Gabe sticks out his hands. "Go ahead Sheriff. Arrest a tax-paying citizen for putting an addition on his house and increasing the tax roll for the town." He turns to Megan. "Call the Asbury Park Press. Tell them to get a reporter here as fast as possible. Then call Fox News. Upload that recording to both of them." Back to the sheriff. "How long do you plan on having your job, Kreiser?"

Diffidence splatters across the sheriff's face. The man wrestles with himself between an urge to snatch the phone from Megan and knowing that, if he does, it will make matters worse. Much worse.

This has not gone the way he and Freiberg rehearsed it. "It doesn't have to play this way, Berk. Remember, you're a lawyer. You don't want to jeopardize your license."

"Thanks for caring, but I don't practice law anymore. Be an asshole, Kreiser. Arrest me."

Kreiser wants to spin around and leave, and drag Freiberg back to the squad car with him, but he knows that those he's answerable to, will come down on him hard.

In a deliberate show of who is in control, the sheriff clamps handcuffs on Gabe's wrists. Gabe barks to Yehuda. "Dad, call Carly on her cell." Yehuda nods. "Then call Tom Finley. Tell him what happened. He'll know what to do."

Kreiser leads Gabe to the patrol car; Freiberg follows, eyes to the ground. They speed away, skidding on the crushed shells.

Yehuda, still planted in the same spot, says to Buck, "They're all the same."

Buck understands why Yehuda says that, but can't wrap his mind around what he has just witnessed. "They've never been this bad before," he says in a whisper of disbelief. "Not even when that black family moved into town years back."

Yehuda places his right hand on Buck's shoulder. "Let me tell you something, my new friend, that I've had to learn the hard way. The line between law and tyranny is thinner than most people think. Sometimes, it can be as wide as the Raritan River right here in New Jersey. Other times, it's razor thin, like the trickle of a creek during a drought. This much I know: something is very wrong in Island Bluffs."

Buck lets the words hang in midair, fearing to acknowledge what he's known for longer than he wants to admit. He tries to remember when Island Bluffs was a congenial place to live, when it was neighborly and everyone looked out for one another. The Fourth of July parade down Main Street, baked pie sales, the 4H fairs, the carnival every June with proceeds going to the Kiwanis, the farmers' market, and so much more. Even during those good times, there was an undercurrent that Island Bluffs was not like other towns.

Sometimes it takes a new situation to cause a buried problem to claw to the surface.

From where Buck was standing, he just witnessed one of those times.

CHAPTER 32

Wednesday, 9:05 a.m.
Yehuda bids good-bye to Buck and heads for the house.

Megan sprints to Jürgen. "What the hell just happened?" Her eyes plumb his, trying to make sense of seeing her father handcuffed for no apparent cause. Her body quakes; her face turns as white as the inside of a turnip.

He eases an arm around her shoulders; she snuggles into him. For a second, she forgets her father, but then focuses. Jürgen's voice is muffled. "I hear plenty of stories about Kreiser and the crap he gets away with. He runs roughshod over this town. Some like it, most turn away from his shenanigans. My dad and most of his cronies consider the sheriff their local John Wayne. But this is the first time I ever saw him in action. I'm really sorry."

Megan looks up at him. Her eyes puddle. "It's not your fault."

"If it happens in my town, it reflects on me."

"There's no way this could've been stopped. That man is evil."

More than you know.

She steps away. He catches her hand and gives a reassuring squeeze. Megan nods. She sniffles and manages to turn the corners of her lips upward. "My Dad will be okay. He always lands on his feet."

"It's amazing how most fathers seem to know what to do," Jürgen says.

Had Megan not been so upset, she would have heard the subtext of disdain and disappointment. Disillusion tinged with despair. Despair directed at his father. Disgust that he's connected to Sheriff Kreiser in ways he wants to forget . . . and can't shake.

Jürgen promises to call later. He wheels and helps the others stack equipment. When they're done, they leave with no work performed on the Berk house.

She waves good-bye. "Got to go, too. My dad wants me to get this to the newspaper and Fox News. I wonder if this is important enough to cover?"

Not if the powers-that-be want it squelched.

Yehuda reaches Tom Finley on the first try. He explains. ". . . Then he handcuffs my son. Can you imagine? For putting an addition onto the house! What's wrong with these people?"

"Mr. Berkowitz. I'm not going to beat around the bush. They want you out of this house. I don't know why, but they do. I told the same thing to both Gabe and Carly on moving day, but they would hear none of it." Finley wants to add that when the Island Bluff town elders want something, they stop at nothing, or for no one, to get it. He could have mentioned the time the Phoenix House bought the old Brick Mansion. Oh, they bought it, all right, but they never got to move in and set up their rehab center. And that family from Pakistan who was selling imported rugs out of their basement . . . they didn't last a week. It was a three-alarmer. Fire trucks from six towns tried but couldn't save the house.

"What are those bastards trying to hide, Mr. Finley? What do they want from us?"

"I don't know, Mr. Berkowitz, but whatever it is, they're determined to succeed. And I am sorry to tell you . . . they most likely will."

Regardless of what Finley says about the town and no matter what might have happened in the past, Yehuda extracts a promise from Mr. Finley to drop what he's doing and hustle over to the Island Bluffs jail.

Next, Yehuda dials Carly. He catches her in Toms River.

Against her wishes, Nick James, her ME friend in the adjoining county, the one processing the bone the sheriff left behind, asks Carly to introduce herself to his counterpart in Ocean County.

"I don't want to work with them," she tells Nick. "Given how tight the officials seem to be around here, he's probably in cahoots with Sheriff Kreiser. That's why I came to you in the first place."

"I thought it was because we trained together."

"Lucky for me you *are* here."

"I get it. You would've brought the bone to a perfect stranger as opposed to going to your local ME."

"But I didn't have to do that, did I?"

"Here's the thing. Not a lot goes on in these shore towns between Newark and Atlantic City. It's not every day we get someone with your credentials to move down here. He's going to find out you came to me instead of him."

"But that's easy to explain."

"Just do me the favor of calling and telling him we'll be working together. That's all I ask. Consider it a professional courtesy. This way, he won't hear it from someone else."

"I don't see why I have to waste the time?"

"We're too small a community not to work together. He needs to know you're a possible resource for him. We don't get that many dental cases."

"And it gets you off the hook as to why I went to you first."

"That, too."

Carly missed all the commotion that occurred at the house that morning. Rather than call, as Nick James wanted her to do, Carly pulls into the Ocean County Health Department parking lot on Sunset Avenue in Toms River. She believes in face-to-face meetings. Only way to judge someone and what they say. Nuance and body language cannot be interpreted through phone calls or texting.

"It must be fate that you walked through the door at this moment," the Ocean County ME says to Carly.

This was not the greeting she expected. "I only wanted to introduce myself," she answers. "I'm . . ."

"Your reputation precedes you, Dr. Berk."

Did Nick James call to say she had moved into the area?

"What do you make of this?"

He flicks on a fluorescent view box that illuminates two sets of dental X-rays. The first set is unremarkable: wisdom teeth missing, all four first premolars missing, and a couple of porcelain fillings. The second set displays no teeth, but what appears to be recent, serial extractions.

"We have an unidentified body whose teeth were removed to thwart identification. Probably drug related. This other set is of a missing person with a known identity. A frantic mother is trying to find her daughter. We're trying to rule out any connection. What's your opinion?"

Carly compares the two sets, looking from one to the other a couple of times. It takes ten seconds.

"Not the same person."

"You're sure?" asks the ME.

"As the nose on my face." She points to an opaque line that squiggles above the maxillary molars on the set with teeth. "See the outline of the maxillary sinus? It is completely different than the other case. And look here," she draws her finger just above the jaw line, "the inferior alveolar nerve has a different shape, and the mental foramen exists in a different spot. Even the trabeculae in the bone have different patterns. You don't need teeth to determine these are not from the same person."

The ME was an instant fan.

Carly left promising to help in future cases.

Carly answers her cell phone. "Yehuda, when I left, everything was okay. Slow down. Tell me what happened?" Yehuda explains that Kreiser and Freiberg drove up soon after Carly was on her way, that he's already called Finley.

"Thanks for taking care of that. I'm about to get in my car. I'll be there in a jiff."

Yehuda hangs the phone up on the kitchen wall. The excitement exhausts him. He fills a glass with water but nearly drops it when a searing pain cuts through his chest. He backs into a chair, reaches into his shirt pocket, and tucks a pill under his tongue.

Without missing a beat, he talks to the empty room. "Polly, what's going on here? This sort of madness was supposed to end a long time ago."

The house lights flicker. The blueprints, perched on the table, roll to the floor. Yehuda picks up the packet. He balances them in the palm of his hand, as if weighing their impact on his family. He looks out to the bay through the kitchen window. He looks down at the rolled prints. The lights flicker a second time.

What are you trying to tell me, Polly?

He slips the green rubber band off the blueprints, unrolls them on the table, and flattens the architectural plans with a firm hand. Yehuda bends closer and examines each detail. If the bones in the basement are an indication that this house holds secrets, there could be others. There must be more to it; otherwise why would they try so hard to get them to move? There is something we are all missing.

Wayne Gay and his house of secrets?

Ariel Castro and three imprisoned women in Cleveland?

Not here. Not in Island Bluffs.

How to explain the rain slickers in the basement? The dozens of rubber boots? The provisions?

The bones? Yes, the bones. What about them?

The locked door from the outside; the key inside. Explain that!

Yehuda repeats the process. Studies every room on the blueprints. Every line and detail. Is there something everyone is missing?

He lifts his head. Looks up, as if the ceiling will reveal the truth.

Yehuda looks down again. Then he sees it. At least he thinks he sees it.

He rolls up the plans and resolves to follow his hunch.

Beyond the house, in the distance, the *Searcher*'s Captain Crenshaw huddles over the sonar radar screen. He rubs his eyes. Day after day he directs his ship in grids that cover acres of ocean floor. Treasure comes in many forms. Spanish doubloons. Silver chalices. Brass bells. Pewter platters. Compasses. Canon. Cannonballs. Personal artifacts from ships sunk long ago.

Captain Crenshaw is most interested in the ones from the Second World War. Many ill-fated ships were sunk and lay off the bottom of the eastern seaboard. Few recall just how many or, for that matter, even know that it happened.

The damage inflicted on America in those days was greater than what happened to the Twin Towers.

It started on January 12, 1942 when the freighter *Cyclops* was sunk off the coast of Nantucket. It didn't stop until mid-June, 1942. The scorecard? Three hundred ninety-seven American ships sunk off the Atlantic seaboard in six months. Five thousand killed; two million tons of shipping lost. This was the greatest naval defeat and the worst direct attack on America in our history . . . and it doesn't even have a name!

Pearl Harbor, you ask? Numbers vary, but roughly twenty-four hundred casualties, including civilians and those killed by friendly fire.

Call this unnamed battle the "Massacre of the Atlantic."

Captain Crenshaw does.

"Bring the ship to full stop," Crenshaw calls out. "Drop anchor. There's a spark of something below."

Carly storms into the police station. An officer, the one Yehuda first met, ushers her to the cell area. Gabe is reading *Guns and Ammo* magazine. His cell door is wide open. They hug. No need for words.

Two divers jump off the *Searcher* into the churning waters. They drop down eighty-five feet. Stripers, flounder, bluefish and Spanish mackerel swim past as they descend deeper and deeper into the black waters.

Carly and Gabe separate. Both hesitate before speaking. They talk at the same time, stop, motion for the other to speak first, and try again. If this were dancing, they'd be crushing each other's toes. They laugh; it cuts the tension.

Carly waits.

"Is Tom coming?" asks Gabe.

It's Carly's turn. "What kind of town locks you up for putting an addition onto your house?"

Before Gabe answers, a distant door creaks open. Footsteps clop toward them.

Trevor Reichmann and another man enter the cell area. Sheriff Kreiser lags behind.

Gabe points. "He's the man who wants to buy our house." Gabe steps in front of Carly. "What're you doing here, Reichmann?"

Reichmann nods at the sheriff, who twists and leaves without protest.

Reichmann speaks without preamble. "This is Horst Von Schroeter. Mr. Von Schroeter is president of our company."

Von Schroeter stands tall. Erect. He's a tad over six feet. His bearing is imperial. He traces his lineage to barons and baronesses, to castles and royal privilege, to wild boar hunts and falconry. To the rule of the Hapsburgs. His voice is low, raspy, as if the words are filtered through a strainer before they become audible. There is a slight accent.

He nods. No handshake. "I'm aware that your move here has been, shall we say, rocky, at best."

Gabe gives Carly a look that says it all. *Is this guy for real?*

Gabe turns back to Von Schroeter. "It's had its moments."

Von Schroeter engages Carly. "I trust this has not been too traumatic for you, Mrs. Berk. I mean, for a woman in your condition."

"If the sheriff and the rest of the goons in this town were concerned about my condition, we wouldn't be standing here talking right now, would we?"

Von Schroeter does not answer.

Reichmann flinches.

Carly continues. "Considering that in spite of us having engineer reports that said the house was fine, and in spite of the fact that we have all the correct permits, and, oh yes, in spite of the town's zoning board that approved our plans, the building inspector has seen fit to give us an ultimatum to move out on the first day, my husband's been arrested for putting an addition onto our house, and . . . the coup de grace . . . there was a pile of human bones in the basement that nearly scared my daughter half to death. I'd say I'm doing quite well. Thank you for asking, Mr. Von Schroeter."

If Carly's sarcasm registers, Von Schroeter remains pokerfaced. "It's unfortunate that this affair has been, shall we saw, a tad uncomfortable."

"I would choose other words to describe it, Mr. Von Schroeter," says Carly.

Von Schroeter continues as if not interrupted. "This was handled improperly from the beginning; I apologize for that. If you'll let me, I'd like to set matters straight." He speaks to Gabe. "Paperwork is being arranged to get you out, as we speak. I'd suggest that your lawyer meet us here. There will be waivers to absolve blame. The usual formalities."

"Isn't it too late for that?" asks Gabe.

Von Schroeter stays on script. "It's never too late to right a wrong, Mr. Berk. As an attorney, of any of us, you should know that."

"That just may not be the case this time," says Gabe. "My daughter captured this debacle on her phone. By now, she has gotten it to the Asbury Park Press and Fox News. Knowing her, it's already posted on YouTube."

"We're here about damage control that affects all of us, including you, Mr. Berk . . . and your family. Channel Five has called to verify the facts, and we reassured them it was all a mistake and that you had already been released from jail. That it was all a misunderstanding. There is no story."

Gabe glares. "Leave it to you. You make a mockery of the whole system. What's one more lie thrown into the mix?"

"It's the truth. You will be released as soon as we finish our housekeeping."

Carly takes Gabe's arm. "Our attorney is on his way," she says. "As for signing anything, we'll see about that after he arrives."

Gabe whispers in her ear. She shakes her head.

"Reichmann is capable of making the same bullshit apology. What's the real reason for *you* being here Von Schroeter?" asks Gabe. "It can't be because a seventeen-year-old caught the whole thing on video. Jersey politicos are used to that sort of thing."

Mr. Von Schroeter glances at Reichmann; neither feels a need to reply. Instead, he extracts an envelope from his jacket's inner pocket. Gabe reaches for it, but Von Schroeter jabs it into Carly's hand. "Trevor told me how much you both love this house. I don't blame you. It has a lot of, shall we say, character."

"A lot," says Carly. "After today, it has more character than ever."

Mr. Von Schroeter nods toward the envelope. "Open it."

Carly passes the sealed envelope to Gabe, disregarding Von Schroeter's intent for her to see what's in it first. He slips his index finger under the flap and rips open the envelope. No surprise, it's a check. He hands it to Carly.

Mr. Von Schroeter points to her belly. "Why bother renovating your house in your condition? Buy yourselves a finished house big enough for your whole family."

"You're wasting your time. Reichmann already tried that. Didn't he tell you we're not interested in selling?" says Gabe.

The man cracks a smile for the first time. "Trevor said *you* weren't interested, Mr. Berk. Nothing was ever said about Mrs. Berk. Dr. Berk, if you will. Frankly, we don't see how you can refuse our offer this time."

"Thank you, Mr. Von Schroeter, but we need to be here," she says. "And for the record, my professional name is Dr. Mason."

"Ah, yes. The forensic dentist. I Googled you. Quite impressive." Carly doesn't respond. Von Schroeter continues. "I'm aware of your fertility issues. But if you're counting on Dr. Teplitsky to be around to deliver you, you might be in for a surprise."

Gabe steps forward. "How low will you people stoop to get what you want? Teplitsky doesn't live here. Your reach can't go that far."

Von Schroeter chuckles. "You can't be serious, Berk." He motions to Carly. "If you want your doctor around, look at the check and do the right thing. It's obvious your husband isn't considering every factor. It's strange how accidents happen when they're least expected."

The import of that last statement is ominous . . . and hard to ignore. Are these goons for real? Do they control more than their little fiefdom? What have Gabe and Carly done to themselves? To Yehuda and Megan?

At last, Carly glances at the check. "It's blank."

Von Schroeter turns gleeful. "Fill in the right number. Just leave a squinch for our office Christmas party. Wouldn't want to see the kiddies disappointed."

Carly looks from Gabe to Von Schroeter.

This will not be an easy decision.

Her gut reaction? Cast principle to the wind. After all, the check is blank. It would certainly make life easier to take the money, buy a new house, avoid the construction, and get on with their lives. Carly senses that if they take this path, their troubles with the powers that run Island Bluffs will be over for good.

CHAPTER 33

Wednesday, 11:30 a.m.
As the drama of Gabe's arrest unfolds, the *Searcher* is in relatively shallow waters. Fourteen fathoms.

A glint of metal pokes out from the ocean floor. Captain Crenshaw dispatches two divers. What they find is the size of an adult leatherback's shell. Six feet across. The whole of it is buried deep in shifting sands.

It is a ship, though not enough is exposed to tell its shape or what kind of ship it is.

Nationality unknown.

Could the fork and spoon have come from this vessel?

"Who are you people? This is growing tired. Don't you ever give up?" says Carly. The latter is not a question. She knows the answer.

Von Schroeter slips his hand from his pocket. He opens his palm. He converts to selling mode. A car salesman comes to mind. "We're plain folks doing our civic duty. That house rightfully belongs to my company. Since before the war."

Gabe and Carly do not buy this concocted story.

"The lawyer in me needs to correct that statement, Von Schroeter. This house does not rightfully belong to you. It belongs to us."

Von Schroeter dismisses this with the wave of his hand. "Posh. Posh. Semantics."

"I'm the first to admit that sentimentality has its price, but not a blank check's worth? Not after what you folks have put us through," says Gabe. "What is it, Von Schroeter? The house isn't worth all that much. We all know that. So what's so valuable? Is it oil? Gas? A deposit of rare earth minerals?"

Trevor Reichmann speaks for the first time. "Call it war reparations. For your father's suffering. Justify it any way you want. Only, and I say this in the nicest way I know how, we'd like to buy back the house and see you out of there as soon as possible. We will provide men to help. You won't have to lift a finger. We can't be any clearer . . . or nicer."

Sheriff Kreiser pokes his head through the open doorway. He tries to catch some of the words. Carly glances at him, then turns to Reichmann and Von Schroeter. "Is this about the bones we found the other day? Because if it's to buy our silence, it's too late."

Sheriff Kreiser creeps into the cell area. His voice echoes off the walls.

"It's not about the bones, little lady." Heads turn towards him. "I told you at the house, they're probably from a drifter. From fifty years back. Maybe more. No way of identifying that poor sonofabitch now without dental records or DNA."

"For the record, Sheriff, I've made many identifications on toothless victims using dental X-rays. As for DNA, we have newer techniques that only need the tiniest bit to make a positive ID."

"There's nothing to sample against, in this case," answers the sheriff.

Don't be too sure.

Von Schroeter hands Carly a pen. "The sheriff's right. This is not about the bones. It's about rectifying a mistake we made. We inconvenienced you and your family, and we're sorry we did. We're prepared to pay for this oversight."

Eyes are riveted on Carly. Carly takes the check from Gabe. She writes on it. As she does, Tom Finley rounds the corner and storms toward them.

"Gabe. Carly," he says, handing the sheriff a court order that he picked up from the municipal judge who's a member of his golf foursome, "you're out of here. I'm sure you have better things to do than bottom fishing."

"In a sec," mutters Carly. She finishes writing and hands the check to Mr. Von Schroeter.

Mr. Von Schroeter gulps, shows it to Reichmann, and is about to agree to the sum when Reichmann takes the check. His eyes grow froglike. "This is extortion. Five million dollars? That's beyond reasonable."

"Nothing's been reasonable to date," mutters Von Schroeter.

"As a director in this company, and as your friend, I have to advise against this."

"I am the majority owner. It's my money."

"Even so, this is irrational."

Before anything else is said, Gabe snatches the check from Reichmann's hand and rips it into tiny pieces. "We finally found something we agree on, Reichmann. It is irrational. I'm certain Carly was testing how far you'd go, right honey?"

She blanches. She's flabbergasted. *Did he just rip up five million dollars?*

Mr. Von Schroeter balls his hands into fists. A vein pulses in his temple. Spittle flies out of his mouth. Carly notices his mandibular incisors are crooked and stained black. This gives her pleasure.

"You've just ruined any chance for your family to have a normal life in this town. That beautiful girl of yours? Your father? How many days left does he have? And a new baby on its way? Did you stop to think about any of them, Berk? Or is this about you being so goddamned righteous? Don't bother answering that. Mark my words, this doesn't end here."

Finley steps forward. "Sorry, Horst, but it *is* the end. Whatever the reason you want the house, it's too late. It's time to move on. You'll see. With the changes they make to their house," *their house* was emphasized so all knew who the owners were, "they'll make Island Bluffs proud."

Buck fiddles with the latch on the back door of the Teplitsky house. It's a Dutch door and the top part does not remain shut. The wood has warped with time. Buck planes the edge and then resets the clasp. He uses wood filler to repair the gap in the frame. He's about to light a cigarette when his cell phone rings.

No greeting.

Buck absorbs the message, digests the words and is then direct. "Shipping vessel or sub?" They talk in a clipped jargon as they do on shortwave.

"Not much of the hull poking up. Snapped some pictures. Best guess: a sub. Damned if I know why there'd be one in these waters."

Buck stands straight, his breathing shallow. Trickles of sweat spill down his face like droplets of condensation on a cold pitcher of lemonade on a scorcher of a day.

"One of ours?"

"Who else's could it be? Ordered special equipment that needs to come from Houston. Be here in a few days. Then we'll have a better idea."

"Roger that."

* * *

Atop Ol' Barney, the swimmer known for his marathon dips between the point and Barnegat Light's lighthouse, peers out from the watchtower. Binoculars are pressed to his face. He focuses on the anchored *Searcher*. He sees the divers surface, their arms wide apart, trying to describe what they saw.

Did they find it?

He picks up the phone.

Gabe and Carly return from the town jail; Yehuda is nowhere to be found. There's a note on the kitchen counter by the sink.

Gone to the library.

"How'd he get there?" Carly asks.

"Maybe Buck took him," Gabe answers.

"I don't think so. He only stopped by to see them break ground. Maybe help Yehuda if he needed anything special. Otherwise, Buck told me he needed to be at work today."

"I hope my father didn't try to walk. It's pretty far," says Gabe.

"Does he even know where the library is?"

"Getting lost is not in my father's vocabulary. Even if he's never been to a place, he somehow figures out where he needs to be. He's got like an internal GPS or something."

"Probably it's the amount of iron in his brain. He inherently knows where the magnetic north is."

"You don't believe that nonsense?" Gabe asks.

"How else would you explain how men are able to find things better than women? It has to do with their chemical imbalance. I'm the first to admit that's one defect that yields a benefit."

"Maybe that explains why old men get rusty and forgetful," he concedes with a cat-that-ate-the-canary grin.

She ignores him and plops onto a kitchen chair. "It still doesn't explain how he managed to get there."

Gabe dials Megan's cell phone. He asks about Yehuda, and then smiles. He bids her good-bye.

Carly drums the tabletop with her red-polished nail. Rat-a-tat . . . rat-a-tat.

He ambles to where she's sitting, leans, and plants a big kiss on her forehead. "Shame on us. We forget that Megan drives. Dad called her and she picked him up. How obvious was that!"

* * *

"How do I find something, Megan?" Yehuda sits in front of a computer. If it's not AOL email, he's lost.

"What are you looking for, Grandpa?" Her hand rests on his shoulder; Yehuda stares at the monitor.

"I wish I knew. I don't know where to start."

"Give me a clue so I know where to start."

He looks up at her. "It's bits and pieces. First of all, there's that ship off the point, the *Searcher*. Buck calls them often; talks to them on his shortwave radio every chance he gets. The captain's his friend. I'd like to figure out what they're looking for out there. What could be worth all this time and money?"

"That's a start," says Megan. "We have a scavenger ship trolling off the Jersey Shore. Okay, what else do you know?"

"So far they've found a spoon and fork. Buck showed them to me."

"What about them?"

"The Captain seems to think that they were casually tossed off a boat. You know, people eating, things slip through their fingers, fall into the water. Probably happens a lot."

Megan tilts her head. "But you don't think that's the case, do you?"

He shakes his head. "I've seen utensils like them before. In the camps."

"Grandpa, forgive me for saying this but you've got Nazis on the brain. How could one of their spoons or forks end up off the Jersey Shore. Really!"

He looks up at her. His lower lip quivers; an ache creases his face. "Megan, they don't know what they have. It's a distinctive pattern. It's faded from years being rubbed by sand. No matter. I'd know it anywhere. You heard me tell you and Jürgen that I became the camp dentist. Well, there's more to it. When an officer had a toothache, they had me drill their teeth. Sometimes I even pulled them, too."

"With a needle?"

He nods his head up and down. "I taught myself how to give an injection. I tried not to give them too much, though." He smiles before continuing. "Just enough so they wouldn't kill me, but not enough so it wouldn't hurt. They told me I had better stick to dead patients. What could I do? I laughed and agreed with them. They fed me extra food when I helped them. I ate with a spoon just like the one the *Searcher* found."

"If it really is a German spoon, what does it mean? How'd it get here?" He looks up at her. "Isn't it obvious?"

While Yehuda is at the library with Megan, Carly and Gabe have much to discuss. Much to digest. Carly pours a glass of Uncle Matt's Organic Pulp Free Orange Juice from Whole Foods.

"I think you should call Von Schroeter. Take his offer," she says.

Gabe glares. "How can you say that after all we've gone through to get here? To stay here?"

She doesn't answer right away. She takes a measured drink. Buys time. Puts the glass down. "Exactly what have we gone through to get here? The way I see it, the trials and tribulations to get here are more imagined than real. What is real is that amount of money. Wouldn't you *want* to take it from them if, for no other reason, than to cause them pain?" She glowed remembering Reichmann's reaction and Von Schroeter's grimace when they saw the amount she had written on the check. "To me, that's poetic justice for all the crap and roadblocks they've thrown at us."

"We're not in the same place on this one. We've gone through plenty to get here," he says.

"How do you figure? We sold the house almost as soon as it was listed. How hard was the move? Really? You were on the phone most of the time. And now we're offered a ton of money after living here a matter of a couple of weeks. Let them have this house, Gabe. There're plenty around town for sale, and in much better condition than this one. For the life of me, I can't figure out why you love this house so much."

"Don't you? It's charming. Quaint."

"It's decrepit and creepy. I'm here because I'm your wife and I love you. No other reason."

He holds up his index finger. "And you need to be close to Teplitsky."

"Close, but not necessarily in this house."

She takes another sip. A battery-operated clock ticks.

Gabe runs his hand through his hair. Although a lawyer, Gabe does not like confrontation. Least of all with his wife. She doesn't use his revealing "tell" to her advantage; she uses it to make him see reason. It usually works.

She waits.

"So you'd be happy if we took the money," he states rather than ask. "I was going down the road of causing them more pain by staying here."

"Gabe, honey, it's a lot of money. Why should we both be in pain? Their money will buy us a new house. Given prices these days, there'd be enough to cover Megan's college expenses, all of the baby's education, and there'd be plenty left over so you could retire sooner, if that's what you wanted. How can you turn that down?"

His knee cracks when he stands; too many years of jogging. He worries he will need a knee replacement one day. With the slightest of limps, he ambles to the window and gazes out to sea. Gabe sees the *Searcher* bobbing in the water. He wheels around.

"This house is everything I've ever wanted." He says it with a force that startles. It is more about convincing himself that he's doing the right thing both for him and his family as opposed to admitting he made a poor choice.

Carly sees hurt on his face. In his eyes. He slouches in defeat. This is the critical moment when decisions are made. When triumph prevails. When acquiescence comes with honor. It is her moment. She knows that if she insists, he will capitulate and take the money. Making her happy has its price tag, one that Von Schroeter is only too happy to pay. But is it worth driving a permanent wedge of doubt into Gabe's dreams?

There's a long beat. The clock ticks. She ratchets herself up, one leg at a time, plants a kiss on his cheek, and then drapes her arms around him. She feels his breath on her hair; she knows he is waiting for her to drop the other shoe. To insist that they take the money.

Carly surprises. She drops a different shoe. A space forms between them.

"Now that I think about it, there's no way we should cave in to those bastards. After all, who are they to try to drive us out of here? What're they trying to hide, anyway? We need to find out."

His breathing turns shallow. He doesn't say anything. He knows better than to interrupt. He needs to wait for her to finish. He wants to say something positive, affirm her thoughts, but doesn't. Shouldn't. This needs to play out her way.

"Screw them," she adds.

He lets out a long breath and squeezes her hands. "That's why I married you. You're the best."

"Find what you're looking for, Grandpa?"

His eyes are wide open. "It's amazing. I get more information in a few keystrokes than I ever learned in all the years I went to school."

"A lot has happened since those days, Grandpa," answers Megan. "Wait a second? Didn't you only go through eighth grade?"

"It was enough. Do you know about Q-ships?"

She shakes her head.

"It says it right here." He points to the monitor. "They were ships commissioned by our Navy during World War II—they had them in the First World War, too—that were fighting vessels disguised as merchant ships. These merchant boats were retrofitted to survive torpedo attacks. Their job was to lure unsuspecting German U-boats close enough to cause damage. And if the subs dove deep, they could drop depth charges on top of them."

"What's so important about them?" she asks.

"Because they operated right here off the Jersey coast. Actually, it was more like the entire eastern seaboard. It was early in 1942. It says the fighting was fierce. Sometime that year, the USS *Atik* was sunk by the German submarine *U-123*. Soon after, the Germans announced they had sent twelve more American ships to the bottom."

"I'm still not getting your point, Grandpa. That happened a long time ago."

"Don't you see, there were other ships," he reads off the monitor, "the USS *Asterion*, the USS *Big Horn*, the USS *Gulf Dawn*, the USS *Irene Forsyte*." He raises his voice. "These ships were built or converted to patrol the waters off the Atlantic coast. From Cape Cod to the Gulf. We lost hundreds of ships in those days. It was a raging battle."

Megan pulls a chair next to him. Frustration is etched across her face. "I still don't know why you want to know about this. Does it have to do with the ship that is out there? Is that what they are looking for? Where does Buck come into this?"

He slaps his knee and smiles at her. "What took you so long? Buck doesn't say much about it, but I know he had a girlfriend during the war.

He wanted to marry her. When he came back after his discharge, she wasn't here."

"Maybe she moved away. Maybe another soldier met her and she fell madly in love." Her eyes turn dreamy. "It happens."

"That's not what happened. She went missing."

"As in a runaway?"

"As in that the boat she was on never returned to the marina. She and her father were on it. I saw the newspaper article in the police station the day I came here."

"Is that why Buck never got married?"

Yehuda pictures Buck as a young man. "He still loves her. Can you imagine?"

"Why not? You still love Grandma Sadie."

"I spent most of my life with her. Of course I love her. It's different for Buck. He only had a short time with her. Days, in fact."

"But enough to love her forever. Could anything be more romantic?"

CHAPTER 34

Thursday, July 12, 8:30 a.m.
The following day, Carly brings Yehuda to the clinic with her. Yehuda holds the door open for Carly to pass through as Buck roars up the driveway at that same moment. The two nod as new friends do. They share impish grins.

Yehuda takes a seat and waits for Carly. After a few moments, he sashays over to the fish tank. He taps the glass; fish dart away. He leans and bends to find fish hiding behind coral and filamentous plants, shimmering this way and that. In time, he tires of this and eases back into his seat.

Inside, the nurse takes vital signs, makes notes in the chart, and asks Carly to step on the scale.

"And the damage is?" Carly asks.

She frowns. "Only one pound since your last visit. At this stage of the pregnancy, Dr. T might want you to gain a bit more. Don't forget: you're eating for two little ones," she says.

No, thinks Carly, *there's no way I could ever forget.* Even if she would for a second, somehow Olivia would track her down and remind Carly that she's a *twofer*.

"I don't care if it's one or two," says Carly. "I don't want to add extra ounces that I have to lose afterwards. At my age, it'll be hard to take them off."

Freckles dance the salsa across the nurse's face as she smiles. "Fitting back into a bathing suit is not as important as providing a proper environment for the babies." She clamps the chart shut and slips it into a Lucite holder affixed to the wall by the door. "I'm sure it's all right. See what the doctor says." And with that she leaves.

The room is cold. She rubs her arms to stay warm, wishing she had brought a sweater. With the excitement of Gabe's arrest, she has not had time to think about Olivia and the other *twofers* . . . until now . . . now that she is in Teplitsky's clinic. Carly wrestles with this issue, the issue plaguing the other mothers, the issue that they want to meet their other sons. Olivia's issue leaps in front of the others, she who lost her only son. Should Carly mention that she met with Olivia? Ask Dr. T to reconsider letting Olivia meet her "other" son.

But whose son is it? His or hers?

Is this really Carly's problem?

In a beat, Dr. Teplitsky hobbles in. He plucks the chart from the plastic holder and flips through the pages of the day's entries. He mumbles. He reads the previous entry and looks up. Thoughts of Olivia vanish; Carly cannot read his face. Is everything all right? Given the stress of moving and the events surrounding their arrival at Island Bluffs, she could understand a higher blood pressure or a marker being slightly off base. By how much? Is it time to worry?

"Are the babies okay?"

Teplitsky closes the chart. He steps on a rung in order to sit on the stool opposite her. "Considering that you are carrying twins," he begins. She waits for the verdict by staring at his moving lips as perspiration forms on her upper lip. "All is on schedule," he says to her relief.

He stands to leave.

"Whew!" she spits out, "you had me going there."

He stops and squares up to her. "I didn't mean to. Sorry."

"As long as everything's all right. Anything I should, or should not, be doing?"

Teplitsky's face reassures. His eyes twinkle. Creases stretch at the corners of his mouth. "Nothing to change. Your babies are perfect."

"In that case, can we switch gears?" She grunts pushing off the chair. She feels obligated to discuss Olivia and the *twofers*. But is this her fight? What if Teplitsky resents her for intruding on a delicate topic? Shouldn't she save it for another time? There will be more visits and more opportunities. Maybe she should wait until she meets the others? If . . . she meets the others.

"I have someone I want you to meet," she says to him, shelving Olivia and the *twofers* for another day.

Teplitsky removes his glasses. He clears his throat. "Is this about the town elders in Island Bluffs? I'm aware of what's been happening with you. Buck's kept me informed. Not easy folks to deal with. That's why I set the clinic up in Lakewood. I couldn't be bothered with them. Petty and pedantic sons-a-bitches."

"You certainly have met them," she says. "But it's not that. It's my father-in-law."

"You know I only deal with fertility issues, Carly. And only women. I can recommend a gerontologist if he needs one."

"Dr. Teplitsky, not every problem in life is about patients or medicine. My father-in-law is close to your age. You have much in common."

"I don't need any friends, Carly. I have my work and my family. That's more than most have. No time for anything or anyone else."

Carly expects no less. She ignores his response.

"It'll only take a minute. What's the harm?"

Dr. Teplitsky trails Carly to the reception area. Yehuda is the lone occupant. He stands yet can't see the doctor who lags behind, eclipsed by the six-foot-tall Carly. Carly glides to a stop and Dr. Teplitsky trudges around her, all the while staring at the carpet.

"Dad," she says, "this is Dr. Isadore Teplitsky. He's the doctor helping us have your new grandson."

She extends her right hand to bridge the gap between the men; she misses seeing Yehuda's wizened face turn to sheer puzzlement.

Yehuda stiffens. "I know you," he says to Dr. Teplitsky, his voice spiked with disbelief. "From the camps."

Dr. Teplitsky looks up for the first time. He takes his time to study Yehuda. He measures his answer. "I don't think so."

"I don't forget a face. Not ever. You were there."

"Which were you in?" asks Teplitsky.

"Bergen Belsen."

"I was in Auschwitz."

"I was there, too."

"I don't remember you. I was just a boy," says Dr. Teplitsky almost in an apology. Or is it guilt for being a survivor? Or for not remembering Yehuda? Whatever the reason, the stakes of this chance meeting have escalated by an unquantifiable factor.

No one speaks. The gurgle of the fish tank roars. Carly looks from one to the other, uncertain of what to do or say.

Yehuda breaks the ice. "You were a twin. They took you away. The Angel of Death was responsible. He took so many."

Dr. Teplitsky draws in a deep breath. He is uncomfortable dredging this up, uncomfortable speaking in front of Carly. Maybe even embarrassed for what happened.

The doctor's voice, by turns, grows softer, almost apologetic. "Mengele killed my brother."

Carly grabs her belly by instinct. Pain is etched across her face. She needs to sit down. The doctor guides her to a chair. Yehuda draws nearer. The men are inches apart, as if standing on opposite sides of an imaginary fence.

Dr. Teplitsky's eyes glaze over. He is back in the camp. He cowers. He is transported to another time. Another world filled with horrors and hate. He talks without seeing; his mind is bombarded by images he needs to bury but can't.

"Some days they let us play. That's when we were the happiest. Can you imagine that? That it was possible to be happy there? But most days we were herded on to buses that would take us to a place that turned our innocence into unspeakable nightmares. That's when I wanted to die a thousand times. That's when I cursed myself for living. Afterwards, I couldn't bear to be a survivor. I begged God to take me, to end the misery. It was a hell on earth."

"Are the things they did to the children all true? Those medical experiments?" Carly asks. "We learned about them in high school."

"Worse," he answers. "Most days they started by drawing blood from us. They drew so many vials of blood from our fingers and arms, we thought there couldn't be any left. There were times when they took blood from both arms at the same time to see how much could be drawn out of us and still survive. The youngest children experienced the most pain because they had small fingers and thin arms. When they couldn't find veins in the arms, the Nazis drew blood from their little necks. I remember the screams, how white they turned. Some fainted. And sometimes, for no reason, they performed transfusions from one twin to another. Back and forth went our blood. Out from one, in to the other."

The more he speaks the more Dr. Teplitsky grows pale.

Yehuda fills a cup of water from the water cooler. Poland Springs. Bubbles burble to the top. He hands it to the doctor. Teplitsky drinks without thinking. His voice becomes flat, robotic. "Each day was unique with Mengele. There was no rhyme or reason for what he was doing to us. He appeared to be performing experiments that just popped into his head."

Carly wants him to stop; she does not want to hear anymore, but realizes he has to regurgitate it all.

"Some days, we would lie down next to each other and every part of our anatomy was examined, measured, and studied in minute detail. To him and those who worked for him, we were lab animals. In their eyes, we were worse than rats." He shudders. "I can still remember how cold it felt lying on those stainless steel tables. Our teeth chattered to the point that our bodies shook."

Carly cannot imagine the strength it took for him to survive. To go on living. Hearing this, she has a different respect for him.

Teplitsky needs to continue. "Tests lasted for hours on end, too long for the younger children to endure. Oh, how they cried. How we all cried." He pulled a monogrammed white handkerchief from his pocket and honked into it.

Carly dares not blink.

Yehuda is aware of the experiments, of the torture, of the way Mengele and his cohorts delighted in the daily experiments. He heard as much from his Nazi dental "patients." Hearing it again, firsthand, all these years later . . . the pain is no less excruciating, no less raw.

Teplitsky continues. "They didn't care." He makes no effort to dab away the tears. "Can you believe that they tried to change our eye color? Oh, it wasn't enough to torture us! They wanted to make our eyes blue, like all good Aryans should have. They put drops in our eyes. In some cases, they injected chemicals into them. The pain was excruciating. Some eyes became infected; some went blind."

The doctor leans toward Carly, wide-eyed. "It worked on me." He had one pale turquoise eye, one violet. Carly had noted this the first time they met.

Carly starts to say something; Yehuda holds up his hand and shakes his head for her not to speak.

Dr. Teplitsky continues. "Then there were the injections into our spines and spinal taps with no anesthesia. They'd infect one twin with typhus or tuberculosis, but not the other. When one died, the other was usually killed to compare the effects of the disease to what was normal.

Twin to twin. Brother to brother. Sister to sister. Families extinguished." Dr. Teplitsky blows his nose again, a horn of pain. A blast of memory he can never completely discharge.

Carly loses it. She plucks a tissue from the ever-present box on the end table in the reception area. Did Yehuda endure the same? As she tries to understand the suffering these men and others like them survived, she appreciates that it is not possible to know. The depth of their pain is too great to comprehend, and this comes from someone who has spent years in the Medical Examiner's Office witnessing the worst things one human can do to another. Three score and some years after the fact, with all that was written, for all the documentaries and analyses presented, nothing in Carly's experiences can help her grasp how the Nazis lost their humanity, became crazed with death, and could torture and murder during the day only to return home as loving husbands and caring fathers. Just a day's work . . . killing Jews, Gypsies and homosexuals plus all others deemed not Aryan enough to live.

Dr. Teplitsky's face is impassive. "They performed surgeries on us without anesthesia. They removed organs to see what damage would occur afterwards. They castrated us. Amputated fingers. Limbs. One day, my twin brother was taken away for special experiments. Dr. Mengele had always been more interested in Issacher than me. I couldn't understand why. After all, we were identical twins, the same as each other, weren't we?"

"No," says Yehuda, "you weren't."

Carly and Dr. Teplitsky turn to him.

Yehuda bears down on the doctor. "He was the older twin."

Carly raises her brow, as if to say, *how did you know that?*

Yehuda gives a knowing shrug.

A secret exposed.

Teplitsky strokes his chin: once, twice, a third time. "That escaped me. They always did pick the firstborn." He pauses, assaulted by memories. "Mengele operated on Issacher many times. One spinal surgery left him paralyzed; he never walked after that. Then they removed his sexual organs. There was a third operation, for what, I don't remember. After the fourth, I never saw Issacher again. How does anyone survive losing their mother and their father? Their older sisters? And worst of all, their twin?" He whispers. "My darling Issacher."

At that moment, Iario enters the clinic from one of the warren of rooms off the corridor. He carries charts for the next day's patients. It is not lost on Carly that Dr. Teplitsky follows the boy's every movement with adoring eyes.

She stops herself. Who is she to read into this? Into Teplitsky's world? She cannot help but wonder about their relationship. Is it father to son, as he would like the outside world to believe? Could it be more than that? That would be troubling. Very troubling. For the first time Carly wonders which woman carried Iario? Which of the *twofers* was his mother? Was Iario's twin healthy? Happy? Was his life as advantaged? And what was Iario told of his surrogate mother? Did *he* wonder about her? And what of his many brothers in the Teplitsky household? Yes, what of them? Did any of them wonder about each other's histories?

When Iario retreats out of view, Carly asks, "How did you ever get past those horrors? Go to medical school? Do research over the years? I find it amazing."

"You're kind. Ask your father-in-law," he answers in a whisper. "You never get past it."

"That's not quite the case." Carly and Dr. Teplitsky both turn to Yehuda. His voice is clear. "You learn to forgive. No one says to forget, but forgive? It's necessary because it liberates." He studies Teplitsky; he waits until the doctor raises his eyes. "It's time to let go."

"You talk about forgiveness? They killed so many of us. How can you pardon the *momzers* who killed everyone you ever loved? Forgive them for the torture and the deprivation? Find solace when they treated their dogs better than us? How can you?"

"Because we have to. Because we are better than them. Even the Germans, today, are doing their best to move past the horrors their parents and grandparents caused. They've built their own Holocaust museum in Berlin so they will never forget what happened," says Yehuda. "But to live in bitterness? To squander a scintilla of unproductive emotions on *them* is a waste of energy. It is not good for me, and it's not good for you. We're both too old." He takes a breath and chuckles. His voice softens. "After all, how much time does either of us have left?"

For the first time since meeting Yehuda, Dr. Teplitsky permits a light crease to cross his face. "You speak as if I am angry and bitter at what they did to me. To my brother."

"Aren't you?" Yehuda asks.

The doctor slips his left arm out of his white lab coat and rolls up his sleeve; Yehuda unbuttons his shirt at the wrist. Matching tattoos.

"No, Mr. Yehuda Berkowitz, number 141986, I have dedicated my life to understanding their evil minds."

"And what have you concluded, *Herr* Doctor? That evil cannot be changed or altered, no matter how hard you try? That nothing good ever comes from it?"

"On the contrary, nurture will trump nature any day of the week, and that good can come out of evil if you give it a chance."

"And you have proof of this?" asks Yehuda. "That you can change what is meant to be?"

"I've already done so," Dr. Teplitsky answers without wavering.

Yehuda scoffs. "Forgive me, Doctor, but the Nazis tried to change us and never succeeded. No one knows that better than you. What have *you* tried to do?"

"Tried to do?" the doctor's pitch rises. "I have already gone further than anyone has dared to dream. Soon the world shall know how evil can be turned into good."

This stuns. Yehuda has no clue what this bold statement refers to; Carly has an inkling.

For if she's right, the good doctor is not the saint she thought he was.

And if the doctor is not as saintly as he appears, she has greater worries than she did moments earlier.

Carly clutches her belly.

Two months to go . . . and the days can't fly by fast enough.

CHAPTER 35

Thursday, 9:15 a.m.

Buck hears the whoosh of the clinic door open. He is tamping sand into gaps between sun-bleached gray pavers to prevent weeds and stray grasses from growing where they don't belong. "Game of chess later?" he glances up and asks Yehuda. "I'm only working half-day."

"That would be appreciated," answers Yehuda.

Buck pulls the silver fork and spoon found by the *Searcher* out from his blue denim shirt pocket. "I need to stop by the library first. See if I can figure anything out about these."

Yehuda fingers each. The fork is warm to the touch; it conjures memories of eating their food after pulling their teeth. He can read most of the letters in the bright light. He knows the language and fills in those missing. "Wilhelm Höernberg." Yehuda looks up. "I think that's the name."

Buck is joyous. "Sounds German to me. Probably was in the navy. I have to find out everything I can about him."

"Not our navy," says Yehuda.

Carly asks, "What're you saying, Dad?"

"Hold on there." Buck grasps Yehuda's innuendo, but can't accept it. The thought is alien to Buck. "We had plenty of German-Americans fighting on our side against the Krauts," Buck says. "Lots from right here."

Yehuda remains unfazed. "That's a German name from a German ship. Of this I am certain."

Buck's jaw drops, he squeezes his lips together until they blanche and then nods that Yehuda could be right. It's nothing he ever thought of, but that would answer a lot of nagging questions.

"If that's the case, what are the chances of finding out who he was?" Carly asks. "It's the proverbial needle in the haystack."

"Hold on, Miss Carly. A name's more than most people have to help solve a mystery. As a forensic dentist, you should know that." Buck waves the fork and spoon in the air, a conductor orchestrating his thoughts. "Maybe your father is on to something."

In the car, Carly turns to Yehuda. "I'm sorry the doctor brought up all those memories. I didn't know it was going to be like that. I just thought the two of you might get along seeing that . . ."

He finishes the sentence for her. "We were both in the camps and both survivors." He pats her hand. "I appreciate what you tried to do, and I will make his acquaintance again. But your doctor is still a bitter man after all these years."

"Can you blame him?"

"I will never forget. Never. But I left it all behind. I married my beautiful Sadie, we had Gabe, and I've had a good life since." He gazes through the windshield. "And now I am here."

"And you don't resent the Germans for what they did to you and your family?"

"What does resentment mean? That was then. This is now. I never wanted to end up like your doctor back there, and to the best of my ability, I haven't."

She leans and kisses his cheek. "No, Yehuda, you haven't. But look at the good Dr. Teplitsky is doing." She rubs her belly. "Without him, I wouldn't have had this chance." She engages his soft blue eyes. "And you wouldn't be getting another grandchild."

"Don't let all the good he's doing fool you. Your doctor is both productive and embittered at the same time. He has yet to learn that bitterness is its own pathology." His face grows slack. "Now Buck, on the other hand, he lost the love of his life. Things haven't turned out so well for him. He has every right to be resentful, but he has a rosy outlook. He's happy every day. That's why it's easy to be his friend."

"I'm glad the two of you are playing chess later. I feel guilty when I run errands and leave you alone."

He waves his hand. "I was alone for the longest time and got by just fine. You don't ever need to babysit me."

"Just the same, I feel more comfortable when I know someone's with you." She doesn't want to share her concerns for the way he holds his chest after mounting a few steps or the increased frequency of taking his meds. "I've got to drive to Freehold. See the Medical Examiner there. It's about the bone I dropped off the other day."

Thursday, 12:18 p.m.
At the library, Megan helps Buck load a microfiche into a machine. Now that he has a name to work with, thanks to Yehuda deciphering the monogrammed utensils, Buck wants to check the lists of published crewmen on German vessels sunk off the coast during the war.

Megan shows him how to scroll through headlines.

Alone in the house, Yehuda takes a worn cigar box from the closet. He pries open the lid that's been connected and reconnected with Scotch tape many times over the years. The tape is yellowed. Brittle. He wiggles the lid. The end tears; new tape will be needed.

The doctor has stirred up memories. Memories not of the camps, but of the days before the camps. Days when life was gay and light, and laughter filled the Berkowitz house on Neuenburger Strasse. He moves his passport aside; he picks up his Rotary Club gold pin and shines it on his shirtsleeve. He moves aside the pen from the 1964 World's Fair and inspects a dark brown cowhide wallet Gabe made for him in summer camp. It has scenes from Davy Crockett on it. The borders are threaded with light brown lanyard material. Yehuda dwells over the stub to game four of the '69 World Series . . . the Mets will win the series.

* * *

It is October 15, almost three months after Neil Armstrong spoke his immortal words about man and mankind. Yehuda stays for every pitch. Tom Seaver shuts down the Orioles until Frank Robinson and Boog Powell hit one-out singles in the top of the ninth. With Frank Robinson on third, Ron Swoboda makes his famous diving shoestring catch of the other Oriole Robinson—Brooks—limiting the Birds to the tying run tagging from third. Seaver lasts long enough for the Mets to score in the bottom of the tenth and get the win.

* * *

At the bottom of his battered treasure box, lying flat under his sacred mementos, Yehuda finds a black-and-white photograph with scalloped borders. He has had it since before . . . since before the world changed forever. He hid it from the Nazis; it is irreplaceable.

It is all he has left of lives that were once filled with laughter and kindness and love.

Yehuda studies their faces. His mother's. His father's. His brother and sisters. The gleam in their eyes. Their crisp white shirts and blouses, their suits, and the shine on their shoes. The polished car in front of their house.

All gone. The house. The car. The people. His relatives. No one left. All vaporized. Atoms of smoke. Ashes.

He brings the pictures to his lips and kisses each face.

Droplets form in the corner of both eyes. They angle down the crevices of a face etched in pain.

The ceiling light flickers.

Yehuda knows she's there but does not see her. He calls out. "Polly?" The light flickers again. "Where are you?"

The attic door creaks open and then slams shut. The house reverberates. It slams a second time, and then a third.

"There you are. I'm coming," he calls out. They've developed a bond. An understanding. He thinks nothing of addressing something he can't see or touch. He knows Polly hears him; he reacts to her.

Yehuda threads his way to the foot of the attic stairs. Grabbing the sagging railing, Yehuda struggles to the top. He pushes open the door, looks about, then stands in the center of the attic room. A couple of remaining sealed boxes populates the middle of the room like unwelcomed toadstools. Light comes from a half-window that faces the front of the house. He steps to the window and peers out. He can see the driveway. He cranes to the left and sees the construction equipment that will spring to life the next day; to the right is the lone northern red oak.

Yehuda swivels and faces the far wall. He paces off the room, from one end to the other. He taps the wall opposite the window with his knuckle; it rings hollow. He taps another spot and then another. He scratches his head, surveys the room, and lopes down the stairs with a new energy. His fingers barely graze the banister. Any faster and he will tumble headfirst.

He snatches the architectural plans from the kitchen counter, snaps off the elastics, and unrolls them. He studies the drawings. He flips from one page to the next, and then back to the previous one. Back and forth.

The renderings of the rear of the house do not match the size of the attic. The attic is smaller than it should be . . . at least according to the plans.

No one noticed? So much for the crackerjack architect.

His first impulse is to hike upstairs and recheck the attic. Realizing what the next step would be if his hunch were correct, he scurries outside and beelines for the construction equipment. He prays his memory is not faulty. He pictures Jürgen unloading things. Stuff. Heavy stuff. He edges over to stacks of construction tools.

He smiles.

He finds what he's looking for.

It is worth its weight in gold.

This time, it's harder to manage the stairs. At the top, he drops the sledgehammer to the floor. It is much heavier than he thought it would be. He plops down on a sealed box, not caring what's in it. If it breaks, it breaks. He reaches into his shirt pocket for his pillbox. He slips a tablet under his tongue. He counts the seconds it takes for the pill to melt and get into his bloodstream.

A fly buzzes frenetically, trying ever so hard to crash through the windowpane; there is no escape for it. At another time, Yehuda would open the window but not now. He ignores it.

He finishes counting the seconds before the pill takes hold. "Time," Yehuda says out loud, pushing off the box. He grabs the handle and tries to heft the sledgehammer to his shoulder. It's too heavy. Instead, he swings it like a golfer teeing off. The motion works. The target? The paneled wall opposite the window. The mallet bounces off the wood without so much as a dent. The fly buzzes louder, slicing through the air, trying to escape.

Rather than waste precious strength—how much he can muster?—Yehuda locates the sweet spot between two studs. This time, he cracks the unsupported wood; the jolt travels up his arms. The power feels good. He strikes it again. The crack widens. He summons strength he thought long lost. He hits it again and again until the wood splinters and collapses inward. Again and again, he coaxes the smashed pieces inward.

The cracks widen. He wedges his foot against the fractured wood. He pushes . . . tests it. It gives and bends, but doesn't cave in.

This is more difficult than he thought possible. It is only wood.

Yehuda rests. He should have brought water. He did think to grab a flashlight. He will snap it on as soon as the hole is big enough to see through.

Music erupts from the other side of the wall. Soft at first, then louder. He cannot make out the tune. There is static. He puts his ear to the crack in the wall.

"This *is* where it comes from." He looks up. "I knew it was you, Polly."

With certainty Yehuda stands back and hits the wall with greater force. More wood splinters. The crack widens. He leans down. Pokes his finger through into a void. The air on the other side is cool. Dark. He tries, but can't see anything.

His heart goes rat-a-tat in his chest. His mandible braces against his maxillary teeth; the buccinator and masseter muscles pulse. He's invigorated. Determined. He stands and smashes the wood again and again. Chunks give way. More wood splinters. A hole opens the size of a coffee cup. Yehuda drops to one knee. He shines the flashlight through the hole but can't lean close enough to see anything without blocking the beam. Frustrated, he stands and pushes in on the wood. Kicks it. It bends but does not give; it springs back.

Yehuda's breathing grows shallow.

He hoists the sledgehammer and summons all his power.

One last smash. The opening widens.

He drops the sledgehammer to the floor with a thud

Yehuda clutches his chest.

He bends down.

He squints to see legs of a table.

He maneuvers for a better view.

There is more to see.

Across town, Megan and Buck stare at a microfiche. They read about a German plan codenamed *Paukenschlag*, which means "Operation Drumbeat." It begins on January 13, 1942, and calls for a full-blown surprise attack on American merchant ships. In the following six months that "Operation Drumbeat" is in effect, close to four hundred U.S. ships are sunk from Cape Hatteras to Long Island.

He preempts her question. "Besides this sea battle, the only other times America was attacked were the World Trade Center and Pearl Harbor."

Megan reads out loud. "It says that, overall, 757 U-boats were lost, more than three-quarters of the entire German fleet of subs. That translates to thirty thousand men either killed or missing. None of the U-boats were lost off the Jersey coast."

Buck tugs on his right ear, he reads on. "Listen to this. It says that sixty-eight U-boats were never accounted for." He gapes at her. "Technically, that means they're still missing. If the *Searcher did* find a German sub, it'd be what they call a *lone wolf*. That's a sub that turns renegade and disobeys orders."

Megan pushes away from the table and looks at Buck. "We need to use the Internet. We know the spoon belonged to Wilhelm Höernberg. There must be a web site that lists the names of every U-boat sailor. How many Höernberg's could there have been in the German navy? It couldn't be like Smith or Jones."

Buck is distracted.

He's lost in long-ago memories.

Megan takes his hand and they log onto the Internet in search of finding answers to their questions.

CHAPTER 36

Thursday, 12:42 p.m.
With a lighter step, Buck leaves the library and heads toward the Berk house.

Megan will hurry to get ready for a date with Jürgen.

Shells and pebbles kick up as Buck skids up the Berk driveway. He knocks on the door. No one answers.

He hears a tap against a glass window; he looks about but can't locate its source.

Then he hears the chalk-on-a-blackboard squeal of a window groaning against warped wood.

Yehuda pokes his head out of the opening. "Up here."

They make eye contact. "Whatchya doing up there?" says Buck.

Yehuda points. "The door's unlocked." He waves for Buck to join him.

Buck finds Yehuda perched on a cardboard box. He's panting. Ashen.

"Do you need a doctor? Should I call the EMS squad? They'd be here in a jiff."

Yehuda shakes his head. He points to the smashed-in wall. "Give me a hand?"

Buck assesses the damage. "Nothing to worry about. I need to go to my place and get a few things. Won't take but a minute to fix up. Be good as new."

Yehuda thrusts the flashlight into his hand. He nods toward the opening. "Look inside. I don't want to fix it. I want to make it bigger. Big enough to step through."

Buck kneels down. He looks into the hole and whistles. Buck eyes the sledgehammer. "I get it."

Yehuda stands.

"Sit down. You've done the hard work. Leave the rest to me," says Buck. Lean and muscled, stronger than men twenty years his junior, Buck hammers open a hole that grows with each swing. When it's big enough, Buck steps inside and then helps Yehuda squiggle through the jagged opening.

The flashlight beam swings about; a cord dangles from a lone light bulb.

Buck yanks the string.

The air is stale. Rodent droppings are scattered across the wooden planks.

Neither speaks.

Words are inadequate.

What they see amazes.

There are seventy-five to one hundred antennae shooting up from the floor like a forest of metal spikes. There's a World War II shortwave radio perched on a wooden table. German manuals. Navigation charts. Boat schedules. Tide charts.

There's a microphone in front of the short-wave radio. A German soldier's uniform hangs from a hook. A helmet emblazoned with a swastika. Crossed swords. The Nazi flag. Hitler's picture. A ship-to-shore lamp used for sending messages in Morse code.

Yehuda is ghost-white. He inches to the table. With trembling fingers opens a dusty ledger.

Buck takes it from Yehuda; Buck's eyes widen. It's written in German but he recognizes the weight of the columns of English names. It's a list of ships. Buck does not need a computer printout to cross-reference the list to know what this means: they are the names of ships sunk during World War II off the coast in local waters. He hefts the book the way one picks up a medieval manuscript or the Bible. A fingertip touches a page edge with only enough friction to turn but not bend or leave a residue. His index finger floats down a column. It stops. His eye trails his fingertip by a nanosecond, absorbing and factoring in all that he sees. The ledger is penned in blue ink. Ink from a fountain pen. It is faded but still legible.

His finger hovers over the last entry.

A date.

The letters and numbers sear.

Buck closes the book and staggers to a chair.

"What is it, Buck? Do you recognize something?"

He nods.

Yehuda takes the book. "These appear to be the names of ships."

"Right on the money. Ships sunk in these waters. Whoever lived here had something to do with it. Guided the Germans to their targets. It's pretty clear from all this stuff," he says with contempt as he points, "the Nazi propaganda and all this paraphernalia . . . that a spy lived here."

"What about the boats?" Yehuda stabs the last entry in the ledger.

It jolts.

"Apollina and her father went down in the waters not far from here. It says here that the target—an oil tanker—was missed." Buck points to the date. "Doesn't say anything 'bout a tug, but that's the day she went down. When she and her father were lost. It's strange there were no more entries after that."

Yehuda recalls the aged clipping in the police station. The missing girl. *Leave it up there should Buck ever visit. It's the least we could do for him.*

"That was the girl you were going to marry?"

Buck stares. "Back then, they told me I should be proud. That even though it was an accident–they never did know what did them in–I should consider her and her father casualties of war." He spits out an ironic laugh. "They were right and didn't know it. The enemy *did* kill her. You know," he looks at Yehuda, his eyes watering, "finding the truth doesn't make it any easier to accept. She was so young. We were going to spend the rest of our lives together."

"Such a waste." Then again, Yehuda's life is filled with memories of wasted lives and lost experiences. War does that . . . to both sides.

"I've carried her memory in my heart ever since. The toughest part is that there's never been closure. Not even when I go to the cemetery and put flowers on her grave." He looks at Yehuda. "She has one, you know. There was no one else to take care of it. I put markers up for Apollina and her father in my family plot, even before my mother passed. And then my brother. Never did see my father again. Don't know where he's buried."

Yehuda puts his hand on Buck's shoulder. "Take comfort that she's been with you all these years. I know she has."

Buck looks up at him. "It doesn't work that way. When you lose them, they're lost forever."

"Not from your memory."

"Maybe not, but it's not like the real thing. Holding her hand. Laughing together. Kissing her. Having a family." He was lost in the moment before continuing. "When did you first meet your Sadie?"

"After the war."

"I've known my gal longer. For me, there's no expiration date on love. To my way of thinking, love never sours. Not the way milk does."

Downstairs, Buck grows more dispirited by the second. He excuses himself.

"That chess game will have to wait," says Buck, when they stand at the front door.

Yehuda sees the pain etched on his friend's mug. "Maybe tomorrow."

"Maybe." Buck passes Carly as she turns into the driveway. She waves; he doesn't.

Yehuda hops down the timeworn porch steps to greet her. Carly is barely out of her car when he says, "There's something I've got to show you."

"Hello to you, too! What's with Buck? Didn't he see me wave?"

"You'll have to excuse him. He's got stuff on his mind."

"Apparently so do you."

Yehuda guides her to the attic steps. He ignores her questions. He explains they will soon be answered. They get to the top. She sees light shining through an opening in the wall.

"What the heck?"

A hidden room?

"Watch your step," he cautions. "The edges are sharp." Yehuda holds her hand. Carly takes care to turn sideways; she stoops lower and then lifts her right foot over the shards of wood. Inside, she straightens tall.

"What is this place?"

"A spy lived here."

Carly spins in a slow circle. "What made you do this? Break through the wall, I mean."

"I was standing behind the house the other day. Something didn't look right." He points to a shutter that can be manually yanked open and closed. "I saw the shutter from the outside, but when I looked for it in the attic, I couldn't find it. Then I tapped the wall and it was hollow. I unrolled the architect's plans; the attic looked smaller than it should have been. Or at least, there should have been a crawl space to another area. But there wasn't any."

He does not describe how Polly egged him to study the plans and made the noise that attracted him to venture up to the attic. Or the music.

"So you made your own opening." She sees the sledgehammer. "With that." She points to it.

"With Buck's help."

"I've seen him lift a large stack of pavers."

At that moment, the front screen door slams shut.

"Gabe," calls Carly. "Up here. You've got to see this."

Gabe gets to the top of the stairs and searches for them. "Where are you?"

"In here," Carly calls, leaning into the opening.

He steps into the hidden room. "What's all this?"

"Apparently, Yehuda thinks a spy lived here."

"It's true," states Yehuda.

Gabe strolls to the desk. He sees the German pamphlets, the swastika, the iconic uniform. He lifts a ledger and opens it.

Yehuda takes the book and waves it in front of him. "This is why they tried to scare us away. They didn't want us to find this place."

"Why would they care?" Carly asks.

Yehuda opens the ledger. "This explains everything. I'll tell you downstairs. My heart can't take all this excitement."

Seated around the kitchen table, Yehuda holds a partially filled glass of water, Gabe takes the ledger, sees most is written in German, notices the long columns of boats with English names, and hands it back.

"What does it say?" Carly asks.

Yehuda takes another swallow and wipes his lips on his sleeve. He adjusts his glasses. He wriggles straighter in the chair. He clears his throat. "There are two parts. The first lists the names of the ships, their cargos and weights, and the dates and times they passed the point out there." He points to the ocean beyond the kitchen window. "The other contains the radio frequencies of a dozen German U-boats that attacked our merchant ships starting in January 1942. Whoever lived in this house used the equipment upstairs to contact the German ships and help direct them to their targets."

"You're implying that an American helped the Germans," said Carly.

"Traitors come in all sorts of packages," says Gabe. "With those antennae, he could reach Europe. Who knows how much damage he actually caused?"

Yehuda answers with authority. He has read through the ledger that compounds Buck's story. "I can tell you how much. Whoever lived here helped sink over forty ships off the Jersey coast. All were merchant ships except for one. The last one. It was a tugboat that was about to hook up to an oil tanker."

Gabe speaks. "Wait a second. I know what I said just a second ago, but now it's first registering: we're living in the home of a German spy. Worse, yet, he was an American who turned traitor."

Carly had her epiphany minutes before.

Gabe snaps his fingers. "The bones in the basement. They could be the spy's."

"I'm ahead of you," she answers. "Let me tell you what I learned in Freehold about the one bone we salvaged."

Before she does, Yehuda wipes a tear from his eye. "This explains why the town wanted to buy the house back. They knew a spy lived here and, most likely, he was on American Fertilizer's payroll."

"Makes sense. Years went by and they forgot about this place."

"Until we came along and bought it," adds Carly.

Yehuda explains. "Buck told me that, in the late thirties, the German Bund was active around these parts. They even had a summer camp to brainwash their children. When the war started, popular opinion turned against them. They supposedly disbanded. At least to the outside world."

"But they didn't go away, did they?" says Carly.

"Could you really expect them to stop hating at the snap of a finger?" says Yehuda. "They lived, breathed, and drank praises to the Fatherland. When war broke out, they did what most extremists do, they went underground." He looked from one to the other. "And took their hate with them."

"I wonder how many Bund members lived in Island Bluffs back then?" Gabe asks.

Yehuda waves the ledger. "What do you mean then? We're surrounded by them."

"C'mon, Yehuda. That was over seventy years ago. The Bund disbanded in the Thirties."

"Don't be naïve. The whole town is involved in this cover-up. The sheriff, the mayor, and a lot of others we don't even know about."

"Reichmann and Von Schroeter," adds Gabe.

Carly asks, "What other secrets is this town hiding?"

There is a palpable silence as each absorbs the significance of this discovery. Each wears the mask of disgust, and slouches under the weight of bigotry and hate.

Gabe taps Yehuda's hand. "Dad, it's pretty clear what we're up against. I'm gonna need your help. Come with me."

"Where are you two going? You're not Gregory Peck and this is not *High Noon*. You can't fight a whole town."

"I'll tell you what I'm *not* going to do: sit here and let them continue to make our lives miserable. How many roadblocks have they erected to spook us out of here? To make us give up?"

"Get real, Gabe. They, whoever *they* are, run everything from the mayor to the sheriff to the puny building inspector. Let it be. In time, they'll see we're not going away. And after that fiasco in the jail, Tom Finley has put them on notice. I say we drop it."

"That's what my parents said about the Germans," says Yehuda. "Each time something bad happened, they figured—we all figured—it couldn't get any worse. But then it did."

"Yehuda, these are different times. You live in America now."

"Carly, I've learned a thing or two over the years. One is that hate crimes don't go away. Tell the blacks that the KKK is their friend, tell the gays that gay-bashing doesn't exist anymore, tell the Ecuadorian man who had his skull cracked open by a band of lunatic white teenagers that America is the land of opportunity for all."

Yehuda is right. Carly is well-acquainted with the horrific case of Jose Sucuzhanay, the thirty-one-year-old immigrant who was beaten with a baseball bat and kicked to death by three men who cruised through a neighborhood until they found the perfect prey: a gay Hispanic.

Then there is the eighteen-year-old transgender woman from Greeley, Colorado, found dead in her apartment. When her assailant discovered that she was biologically a male, he beat her to death with fists and a fire extinguisher.

"I guess what you're saying is right," says Carly. "It's almost one hundred years since Leo Frank was lynched by an angry mob in Marietta, Georgia. He was accused of murdering a thirteen-year-old worker in his factory, and his trial was a farce. That didn't matter to the locals who ripped him out of his jail cell when the governor declared that Frank's trial was a miscarriage of justice. They were after blood and hung the northern Jew for what he did to their local little girl. If what you are saying is true, this deep-seeded hatred of Jews continues to this day."

"And it will continue long into the future," says Yehuda, "after all of us are gone. It seems to be the way of the world to make us their scapegoats." He turns to Gabe. "Are you ready?"

Carly sees there is no deterring them. "Do what you have to do. Just please be careful."

They leave without another word.

Carly follows them to the door and continues to stare out long after the dust settles in the driveway.

If they lived in any other place, and Gabe had an issue with the authorities, she would not be concerned.

But this is Island Bluffs.

CHAPTER 37

Thursday, 5:15 p.m.

Gabe and Yehuda march through the door of the American Fertilizer Company. It is after five now. A dozen cars dot the lot like aberrant sagebrush on a desert floor; most are American made. Neither considers that the place could have been closed.

"May I help you?" asks a hard-looking secretary with black-dyed hair that is more punk than stylish. A Jersey-girl. A Soprano groupie who has moved on to more of a Manhattan look. East rather than West Village. Minuscule diamond on the left side of her nose, pierced eyebrow, other piercings hidden from view. She sports a braided tattoo around her wrist and an out-of-view snake wound around her left ankle with its hissing head inked onto her calf.

Gabe takes a quick breath. He tries to modulate his voice. "We're sorry to barge in here without an appointment, but would you be so kind as to inform Mr. Von Schroeter that Gabe Berk and his father are here to see him. He'll know what this is about."

"I'm sorry, but Mr. Von Schroeter is away on business."

Gabe manages a grin. "That's funny. I met with him just yesterday morning. He didn't say anything about . . ."

She's quick to respond. Too quick. "Oh! He was called away on important business. If you wish, you can leave him a message. I'll be speaking with him tomorrow. He checks in every day."

Gabe leans back and looks about the office to buy time. No muffled voices or phones ringing from behind closed doors. "Okay, then. Is Trevor Reichmann here? Or is he traveling, too?"

The secretary is cool. "I'm afraid he's not here either. Is there something *I* can help you with Mr . . . ?" She's well trained.

"There is." Gabe's manner changes. More the lawyer. "Von Schroeter and Reichmann offered to buy my house yesterday. I want to tell them that I've changed my mind. I'm willing to sell. Can you get that message to them as soon as possible?"

The secretary turns more helpful. "Honestly, they're not here. Would you like to speak to the plant manager? He's in touch with them all the time. Maybe he's aware of your situation." Before they can answer, she pages the manager.

They expect a firewall to the top brass and that this will be a waste of time. Gabe and Yehuda glance at each other. No need for words. *Meet the fellow and bolt.*

To pass the seconds, Yehuda and Gabe stroll through the office. Pictures dot the wall. Black-and-whites of John Deeres scooping loads of fertilizer onto trucks; of men holding beer steins; of ships at sea. One of Ol' Barney.

"Here's one of Sheriff Kreiser with Reichmann and Von Schroeter," says Gabe, pointing to the last one on the wall. "They were much younger then."

At that moment, the plant manager struts into the reception area. His bearing telegraphs that he knows who they are and what they want. He introduces himself, cracks his best church-going-how-you-doing-smile, and wonders, to himself, what-in-the-world *they* are doing here.

"My name is Otto Hauptmann, gentlemen. What can I do for you?" He does not extend his hand.

Gabe tells him their names. *Otto Hauptmann.* The name rings familiar to Gabe, but he cannot place it. He will.

Yehuda engages Otto's gaze for an extra beat. Otto is a couple of inches shorter than Gabe. He is wearing khaki pants, a Ralph Lauren button-down oxford shirt that is bisected by a gray tie dotted with flying orange geese. He tugs on his collar. Beads of perspiration form on his brow. He loosens the top button. His discomfort is manifest.

Otto speaks first. "I'm told you're looking for Mr. Von Schroeter. What's this all about?"

"You tell me," answers Gabe. If the man speaks to his bosses all the time, he should know.

Otto takes his hand out of his pocket and clasps both in front of him. A man in prayer. A man who tries to befriend.

He dodges the bait. "Sorry, fellas, you need to give me a clue as to why you're here."

"Why did Von Schroeter want to buy my house? Everything has turned strange since the day we moved into this town. Even before we moved in. Bottom line is the town tried to shut us down and drive us out. When we didn't capitulate, your boss tried to overwhelm us with a truckload of money. The question we have is, 'Why?'"

Yehuda does not flinch. His respiration slows, his pulse steady. He studies this man.

Otto answers in a practiced voice. "Best of my knowledge is that Mr. Von Schroeter heads the board of trustees of the local historical society. His goal is to create an historical district that includes your house, but zoning hasn't passed it yet. Until that happens, he doesn't want your house to change its façade or alter its footprint."

Canned. Rehearsed.

Twenty-four dollars worth of beads and the island is yours.

Gabe expects no less. He is about to unload a tirade when Yehuda touches Gabe's arm. "Wem hat das hans wahrend des krieges gehört?"

Who owned the house during the war?

"Die gesellschaft, das sollte keine überraschung sein. Die haben viele wohnungen entlang der küste bereits gehabt. Sie haben etliche hauser für ihre spezial arbeiter gekauft."

This company did, which should not be a surprise. It owned scores of houses around here. They were for key workers.

Yehuda continues with emphasis. "Wer hat in unserem haus während des drieges gelebt?"

Who lived in our *house during the War?*

Otto shrugs and answers in English. "Those records were lost in a fire right after the war."

"How convenient," says Gabe.

Otto laughs. Stilted. Forced. "Do you see a plot around every corner, Mr. Berk? This is a small town. We're simple people. Surely you can see we're no match for city folks like you and your wife."

Are they being singled out, thinks Gabe, because they are new in town or because it's the house they bought. He can't imagine every new family suffering through these same tribulations. House values would plummet and the tax base would drop, reducing the town's ability to provide critical services. A downward spiral no one wants, especially in this recent economy.

"Mr. Hauptmann, is it?" says Gabe, "I don't see a conspiracy around every corner. But I do see one in Island Bluffs. Certainly one surrounding my family and the house we bought. And regarding our house being part of an historic district? Do you really think we believe that?"

Otto ignores Gabe's comments. He makes a wide sweep of his hand toward the company name affixed in gleaming brass letters on the wall behind the secretary. "If the records were available, I'd share them with you. As you can well imagine, fires and explosions are not exactly rare when it comes to fertilizer companies." He puckers his lips and blows air out to mimic an explosive sound. "Remember, Timothy McVeigh brought down the Federal Building in Oklahoma with fertilizer."

"That's nothing you should be highlighting, Mr. Hauptmann. An American company supplied the goods that killed 168 innocent men, women, and children."

"Whoever sold it didn't know what McVeigh was going to do with the stuff. Same as if you bought a few bags of fertilizer from us. C'mon, Berk, lighten up. Give it some time. You'll see; we're a friendly bunch."

"I beg to differ. You are more like a gang that wants to run us out of town. This place ought to be renamed Dodge City. One thing's for sure, Kreiser is no Wyatt Earp."

Yehuda ignores both of them. "Kennen sie jemanden der sich noch errinern kann wer in unserem haus gelebt hat?"

Is anyone left who would remember who lived in our house?

"Even if someone were alive who did remember, I doubt they'd talk to strangers," answers Otto. He claps his hands together. "Sorry, but that's all the information I have." He pivots to leave. "If there's nothing else I can do for you, I have reports calling my name. And speaking of names, how's Megan? That is your daughter's name, isn't it?"

Then it dawns on Gabe, that Hauptmann is Jürgen's last name and Otto is his father.

"She's fine, thank you. You've got a nice kid there."

"Told you we're good people. He's a perfect example."

Gabe lets it go. There are no farewells, no adieus. Each turns and takes their last thoughts with them. Gabe and Yehuda are at the door when Otto calls to them. "The message? For Mr. Von Schroeter? What did you want to tell him?"

Gabe stops. For the first time since this episode began, a satisfied smile spreads across his face. "Tell him we found the hidden room. Tell him the game's over. His secret's out."

Hauptmann's eyes widen. His mouth drops. He doesn't say anything. There's no need to. Von Schroeter needs to hear about this A-sap.

Gabe and Yehuda stand outside the American Fertilizer Company. They stare at the gray cinder block building.

"How'd you know he could speak German?"

"From his eyes. It's a look I'll never forget."

Inside the building, Otto huddles with Von Schroeter and Reichmann in the CEO's office where they heard the entire exchange over the intercom the secretary knew to leave open.

"I told you we should have burned the house down the minute we found out it was sold to them," says Reichmann. Otto nods in agreement.

Von Schroeter, ever in control, tries to assuage their concerns. "So they discovered some dusty, antiquated equipment that hasn't been used since the war. Maybe they'll think some ham operator owned it, or it could've been someone who worked for the shipping companies."

"With all due respect," Otto counters, "there must've been ledgers and antennae, and a ship-to-shore radio. Wouldn't be surprised if they found pictures of the Fuhrer. Maybe even a Nazi flag. Look, they're not fools. 'Specially the old man. I vote to burn the house down tonight. Do it before they have time to have the stuff analyzed. Before it comes back to haunt us."

"It's too late for that now," says Von Schroeter. "True, we owned the house before the war and then forgot about it. But we're not responsible for anything that happened there any more than a landlord's got anything to do with renters making babies or getting divorced. You're both too paranoid." His words are directed at Trevor Reichmann. What they imply, stings. "We should have left them alone and not brought attention to the house in the first place."

"Hold on there," says Otto. "When we found out that the house was sold out of foreclosure, you're the one who said we had to cover our asses. That if the news ever got out a spy lived there, it would be bad for the company. We all agreed with you. You can't shift the blame onto Trevor or me or anyone else. We are all equal conspirators in this."

Von Schroeter growls. "Maybe so. Given hindsight, it wasn't such a good idea. How terrible would it have been for them to discover that false room and whatever's in it? It would have been their problem, not ours. It might have appeared weird or strange, but they would've tossed the stuff out and it would've stopped right there. Instead, we drew suspicion to the house by giving them such a hard time and offering to buy it, not once, but two separate times. Not our finest hour."

At that moment, a side door, obscured by wood paneling, opens. Larry Hanson, a sun-weathered, crusty man who is somewhere north of eighty years old and known for swimming from the point to Ol' Barney, enters the room.

"I heard." No extra words for him.

"Bad news travels fast," says Reichmann.

"What are you going to do to make it right?" Hanson asks.

CHAPTER 38

Thursday, 7:30 p.m.

Fire engine sirens pierce the night air. Dr. Teplitsky makes certain all the boys are out of the house even though the fire is fifty feet from it.

The tool shed is ablaze.

A red plastic gas can explodes, sending a fireball into the air. Leaves smolder. Embers, fireflies of danger, float upward, trailed by an army of flickers that glow yellow, blue, and orange, sputter then fade into wisps of gray and disappear into the blackness.

The pumper hurtles up the driveway. A second truck rolls up. Then a third. Two white Chevy Blazers join the truck cluster, their lights spinning blue and red, sirens slicing the night air. Neighbors down the block stand in entranceways, concerned and curious. They huddle at a safe distance.

Walkie-talkies chatter. Orders are barked, hoses uncoiled. The fire is squelched. The once-burning wood now hisses and smolders. Charcoal smells replace the fragrances of blooming hyacinths and the scent of fresh-cut grass.

"Is anyone still in the house?" asks the fire chief.

Teplitsky turns and counts. "Where's Jovanni? Has anyone seen Jovanni?"

"He was right here."

"I saw him run 'round to the back of the house when he heard the sirens."

Teplitsky turns to find him. The fire chief holds out his hand. "Hold on there, Doc. You need to stay right here."

"But I've got to find him."

"I'll go, Father," says Iario.

"No," shouts the doctor a bit too loud. He grabs Iario's arm. "Not you." He scours his other sons. "Not any of you."

The fire chief barks orders into the walkie-talkie clipped to his jacket epaulet to search for Jovanni. A minute or two later, a fireman appears with Jovanni in tow. The boy shuffles toward them, eyes cast at his Black/Red Countdowns with their red outer soles. Oh how he cried for this new Air Jordan release.

See how fast I run with them, Father? And how high I can jump?

Teplitsky hobbles to him. He ignores the other boys' snickering. He touches, bends, and leans to inspect Jovanni. "Are you okay? Are you hurt anywhere?"

The boy sniffles. There are streaks of grime across his cheeks. Snot drips. He wipes his nose on his sleeve.

"Excuse me, Doc, let one of my men check him out, just to be sure."

"I'm a doctor. I can see that there's nothing wrong with him."

The fire chief eases his hand onto the doctor's shoulder. "Just to be sure." He wedges himself between Teplitsky and Jovanni. Teplitsky tries to follow; the chief blocks his path. Teplitsky twists this way and that, to get a better view.

"Father," says Felice, "why are they talking to Jovanni? What did he do?"

Teplitsky doesn't answer. There's a hollow in the pit of Teplitsky's stomach. He banishes stray thoughts from his mind. He chides himself for what he's thinking. He studies the chief's lips, trying to read what he's saying to his youngest.

Jovanni's answers are cryptic. A word or two, no more. The boy stares at the ground. Kicks a pebble. A tear escapes. Then another. After a few minutes, the chief guides him back. He nods. He shakes his head. He nods again.

What are they saying? What is he nodding in agreement about? What is he shaking his head no *about?*

"Doc," says the fire chief, "Little Jo, here, has something to tell you."

"You don't have to say anything," says Teplitsky. He reaches for him. "It's okay."

"Beg to differ, Doc, but everything's not okay. Someone could have been hurt here. A ton of damage. Show him," he says to Jovanni.

"Show me what?"

"Blisters on his fingers. He burned himself."

"That doesn't prove anything," Teplitsky says. But in his heart, he knows.

"Maybe not," answers the chief, "but where I come from, when it smells like smoke and looks like smoke, there's probably a fire close by." He shoves Jovanni with more than a gentle push. "You were lucky this time, kid. Next time, you'll do more damage. Someone will get hurt. Maybe even killed. And when that happens, you'll end up where you can never hurt anyone again. Got that?"

After the last fire truck leaves, the boys return to the house. Bit by bit, laughter and music fill the air.

"Jovanni," the doctor's hand is on the boy's shoulder, "sit with me on the bench over there for a minute."

Jovanni knows better than to say he wants to play with his brothers or work on a project. The doctor guides him to a stone bench on the side of the house that's partly obscured by plantings. The bench sits on a patch of white pebbles. It is a place to meditate. Alongside, there is an aged bronze sundial laced with a filigree of lichen that imbues violet shades to the metal. Flowers compete with the last vestiges of smoke to sweeten the air. Scores of day lilies help the cause.

"I need to know what happened, Jovanni."

He swings his right foot; his special sneaker scuffs the stones. "It's what the fire chief said, Father."

"I heard what he said, but I don't believe him. Did he make you say those things?"

Now both legs swing in unison. Lightly grazed pebbles tumble away until two tracks, like skid marks, are left in their wake.

"Did he?"

The boy turns to him, his cheeks rose-colored. "I didn't mean to. I was trying to light a match. To be like the big boys."

"And for this, you might have been hurt. Did you think about this before you tried it?"

Jovanni shakes his head.

Dr. Teplitsky draws the boy into him. He stares above his head, recalling a time gone by. "When I was your age, I lifted a cigarette from my father's tin. They were imported from Egypt. I remember how the aroma filled the room when he smoked. I thought that if I tried one, I would be more grown up. Like you tried to be today."

"And what happened, Father?"

"It was summertime, just like now. It was particularly dry that year. My father complained to the gardener to make the grass greener. It was a carpet of straw. Yellow and brittle."

Jovanni wipes away the tears. He is more at ease now, snuggling into his papa. "What happened when you smoked the cigarette, Father?"

"I never had a chance to try it because, like you, I wasn't any good at lighting a match. I struck the flint over and over. It sparked. The grass caught fire, and I ran like the devil."

"Did the house burn down?" Jovanni's eyes widened and his voice grew stronger.

Teplitsky couldn't tell if the boy was excited because a common link had just been forged or that Jovanni hoped to learn about the details of how the house burned.

"No, but it could've. Luckily for me, the gardener was walking by at that moment. He stamped it out before any real damage occurred." Teplitsky lifted the boy's chin. "So you see, my dear Jovanni, we're not all perfect. Not even me. We all make mistakes. Some bigger than others. Let this be a lesson to you. Promise to be careful, just like the fire chief said."

"I will, Father."

He rubs the boy's mop of hair. "I know you will, Jovanni. Now go inside the house, wash your face, and play with your brothers."

Jovanni throws his arms around Teplitsky. "I love you, Father."

The doctor hesitates. It is the first time Jovanni utters these words.

"I love you, too, son, more than you know."

CHAPTER 39

Friday, 9 a.m.
The following morning, Buck sifts through the charred shed to see which tools can be salvaged.

Dr. Teplitsky sits in the kitchen, sipping Earl Grey from a glass cup. Two lemons float in the amber liquid. His dishes are all glass, the same as when he was a boy in Berlin. He reads the *International Journal of Cell Cloning*, an article entitled "Factors Affecting Blood Stem Cell Collections Following High-Dose Cyclophosphamide Mobilization in Lymphoma, Myeloma and Solid Tumors," when Alberto, Arsenio, and Felice scamper into the kitchen.

Teplitsky smiles. His pride swells at their shining faces. Their innocence. He starts to ask what they want Gaston to fix for breakfast when Arsenio steps forward. It is clear that Arsenio will speak for the others. The doctor enjoys the process, watching Arsenio swallow, and then smack his lips before speaking. He knows that the boy's voice will squeak, that he will be nervous regardless of what this might entail.

"Please excuse us for interrupting you, Father, but we need to ask you a question."

The doctor nods with a twinkle. "I sense a matter of grave concern."

The boys play it straight.

"It is," says Alberto, his brow etched with anxiety.

Felice is pale. He speaks with a slight stutter. "You have to do something about Jovanni."

"Can you imagine how badly he feels?" says Teplitsky. "You boys should be more understanding. I raised you to look for the good in everyone, not tear them down, especially when they are wounded like Jovanni is. The house could have burned. Him knowing that is punishment enough."

Arsenio, taller than the others, remains bold. "There's nothing good about this, Father. We were lucky to escape this time."

"What do you mean, 'this time'? Are you saying that this was no accident? Has this happened before and I didn't know it?"

"That's not what he's saying." Alberto, shorter than the others, is concise and insightful. Dr. Teplitsky marvels at the boy's logic. "It was an accident, Father."

"Then what's your concern? Accidents happen."

"Jovanni's not like any of us. He's different. We all sense it," answers Arsenio, relieved to have blurted out their real concern.

Teplitsky removes his glasses and cleans them on the napkin before answering. "What's important is that you are all brothers. As for being different, each of you is unique. In that respect, Jovanni's just like all of you and, at the same time, he's different from all of you. And like every one of my sons, Jovanni is receiving the same education and advantages while his God-given talents are nurtured and developed. Neither more nor less."

"But none of us are *that* mean," says Alberto.

"Are you saying Jovanni *is* that mean?"

"You don't know what he does to us."

A torrent of pent-up emotion is let loose. A rising tide of anger. Wave after wave causes the doctor to struggle. To gasp in disbelief. If there were a life preserver, he'd be lunging for it about now.

"He didn't mean to break Jacopo's maquette," Dr. Teplitsky struggles to stay afloat.

"That's the least of it," says Arsenio. "Felice had just finished composing a quartet for piano, violin, viola and cello, and Jovanni took it. He did it for spite."

Teplitsky turns to Felice. "What did you and your brothers do to cause Jovanni to be so angry?"

"Nothing, Father."

Dr. Teplitsky is unable to process their innocence. "You must have done *something*."

Arsenio looks at his brothers. Alberto nods for him to continue. Arsenio hesitates. He knows what he is about to say will upset his father. "Tell him," says Alberto.

"Tell me what?"

Arsenio whispers. "Jovanni asked Felice what makes us Jewish?"

Dr. Teplitsky's jaw drops. "He asked that?"

"And then he said that there was no way we were all Jewish. He said that we all may be part of you, but there's no way our mothers were all the same. Are they?" asks Arsenio.

"He's right. They are all different."

They don't ask the next obvious question.

Are we all from your sperm, Father?

"Then how can we be Jewish?" asks Felice.

"Because genetically you are and because that's how I raised you."

"Jovanni, too?" asks Alberto.

Teplitsky blinks one too many times. "He's special."

Alberto looks from Arsenio to Felice. Alberto, the insightful one: "Is this some sort of experiment, Father?"

A clock ticks.

A toilet flushes somewhere in the cavernous house.

Pipes creak.

Floorboards groan.

Dr. Teplitsky looks for an escape hatch. He glances out the kitchen window and sees Buck toss blackened cardboard boxes onto a converted golf cart reconfigured to hold debris. Minimal damage, thinks the doctor, but other types of embers—ideas and experiences, fears and concerns, fan mental flames.

He turns to his sons. "No," he says with a deliberateness meant to protect, "this is no experiment. You will have to take my word for it. But you still haven't told me why he took your work, Felice."

"Because he called me a Jew bastard. I told him to take it back." Tears cascade onto Felice's cheeks. "You know how Jovanni never backs down. All he did was laugh at me, grab my manuscript, and rip it to shreds before I could stop him."

"Don't you have a copy on your computer?"

"That's not the point, Father," Alberto says. "The fact that Jovanni even thought to destroy Felice's piece means he has no respect for Felice or any of us. He has no understanding of what it means to be our brother. You need to punish him."

Dr. Teplitsky's face flushes crimson. Veins pulse on his scalp. "No son of mine will ever be punished. Not in the way you mean. None of you has ever received a reprimand that wasn't based on logic and kindness and understanding, not to mention love. The same holds true for Jovanni.

Just so you know, I've already spoken to him about his behavior. That he needs to be responsible. More respectful. Boys, rest assured he will change his ways and all of this will be relegated to the past."

"How can you be so sure?" stammers Felice.

For the first time since the boys entered the kitchen, Dr. Teplitsky turns from being concerned to impish. "Because I was like him as a boy. Look at me: everything turned out fine. You'll see, so it will for Jovanni."

Dr. Teplitsky adjusts his glasses and picks up the newspaper. Conversation ended. The doctor is pleased at how he handled this, and with its outcome.

Not so fast.

Felice nudges Alberto. Arsenio wiggles closer. They whisper. Alberto nods and takes a step forward. "He's wired differently than all of us, Father. He thinks differently. Behaves differently. He respects no one and honors nothing." He stands taller, hands at his side. "We don't want him here any longer."

Teplitsky does not see this coming, but does it surprise him? From the moment the boy was born, the doctor knew Jovanni would be a project. A major project. Not like the other boys. But still? Asking him to leave? Tossing him out like unwanted furniture? How could they even think this?

He is my son. He is your brother.

"I'll talk to him, again," he says, his voice shades of defeat.

"It won't help."

"It has to," says Teplitsky, "he has no choice but to listen. To be more like all of you."

"And he if doesn't toe the mark?"

"That's something I cannot contemplate at this time."

"But you should," Alberto, Felice, and Arsenio collectively think to themselves. "You should."

Carly pours Gabe another cup of coffee; she drinks decaffeinated herbal peach tea. Gabe slips his finger through the porcelain grasp and steadies the cup with his thumb. He blows off a cloud of steam to cool the surface before taking a sip. "I'm going to ask Cole to have some of his men clear out that junk from the attic. I don't want that stuff in this house an extra minute if we can help it."

She holds her belly; one of the babies kicks. Now both. "Want to feel?"

He stands and holds his right hand out. "Where? I don't feel anything. Am I in the right spot?"

She moves his hand higher. He feels one baby kick. Her belly moves; it reminds him of Sigourney Weaver impregnated with an alien fetus. The second kicks. "I wonder which is which?" he asks.

"We'll know soon enough."

He pulls back. "So how 'bout it? Getting rid of all that junk?"

"I wouldn't. It must have historical value."

"That's not going to cut it for me. Ordinarily, it might. Living in a house with Nazi paraphernalia is worse than buying a house in which someone was murdered. Until we get rid of that stuff, I won't feel comfortable."

"Gabe, you're talking about books and pamphlets. A few pictures. A flag. A uniform. Why are you getting so bent out of shape?"

"More than anything, the antennae creep me out. They're like evil bat sonar doohickey things."

"What are you saying? That they'll give you rabies or something?"

"I'm serious. They helped direct German subs to sink our ships. They're bad. Are you forgetting the bones in the basement? What about them? You're the one who called it a crime scene." *What else could it be?*

"I can't prove it. Not just yet."

"Crime scene or not, I don't need a lab test to tell me they're German bones. Drop your forensic hat for the moment. Are you forgetting my Dad's a survivor? And what do we do? Unknowingly buy a Nazi spy's house. How can that possibly make him feel?"

"It's not like we did it on purpose. Besides, he hasn't said anything about it. If it bothered him, he would be the first to bring it up. We both know that he is not one to stand on ceremony," says Carly.

"You don't know him the way I do. Dad's not a complainer, but I can see it in his face. This town and this house are resurrecting terrible memories. The sooner we clean that junk out of here, the better he'll feel . . . and so will I."

She starts to say something and then stops. "Hold on. The stuff upstairs? It's your problem. No one else's. Not your Dad's, not Megan's, and certainly not mine."

"Just the same, junk is junk. It goes tomorrow."

"When you ran out last night, I had time to call information and get the name of the manager who runs the local historical society. It was closed, but the greeting gave his home number in case of emergency."

"How can something historical ever be an emergency?"

She pauses; a bit of triumph crosses her lips. Not enough to gloat, but enough to claim victory. "Uh . . . yesterday, my darling husband. Right here in this house, we had an historical crisis."

"You mean an hysterical crisis." He tries to lighten the moment.

"Not funny."

"For the last time," asks Gabe, "it doesn't freak you out to live here?"

"Did it freak me out to work in the city morgue? I thought that was a turn on for you?"

"It was . . . then. This is literally too close to home to make it feel okay."

She takes his hands. "The bones, the German stuff in the attic, these are ghosts from a long time ago that had nothing to do with any of us. We're starting a new phase together. Our family is growing; we are here with your dad and Megan. Make your peace with this."

He pecks her on the cheek. "Who can argue with that?" He changes the subject. "I met Jürgen's father last night when we went to American Fertilizer."

"Why didn't you tell me when you got home?"

"I needed to digest everything. My father spoke to him in German. You could see Otto, that's his name, was trying to keep it together, but we rattled him."

"Still, you should've said something when you came home."

"I couldn't get into it all over again. Not last night. I'm telling you now."

"So what kind of man is he?"

"Like the others we've met here so far. Trevor Reichmann. The sheriff. The building inspector. They are all cut from the same cloth. He gave us some spiel how Von Schroeter doesn't want to change any of the houses in order to preserve them. Turn them into landmarks."

"It was historic that anyone bought this house."

"I'm beginning to agree with you."

Gabe picks up the German ledger from the table. He thumbs through it and then continues.

"Careful. It may bite you," she warns with a smirk.

He scrunches into a frog face; the tempest is over. He wags the book. "I'll tell you this: the moment the stuff is out of here, we can start framing. Once the new roof tiles are nailed down, it'll be quick sailing."

"Nothing's quick sailing when it comes to construction. You should know that. You've lived in the suburbs and watched neighbors extend their houses. Marriages are challenged the moment builders come on the scene. Most recover as soon as the contractor's finished, his men leave and the dust settles."

"Not this time. Cole's terrific. No problem with him or his work, and he'll meet our deadline. It's gonna happen, and for all that we get a house to our liking," he rubs her belly, "for our growing family."

Gabe embraces Carly, plants a feather kiss on her lips, and then adds, "So are we agreed to get rid of the junk upstairs?"

"As much as I'd like to, the right thing to do is wait for the historical society. See if they want it."

Gabe scowls. "Stubborn is your middle name."

"Would you have it any other way?"

He releases her. "I'm not waiting around for someone to take his or her sweet time getting over here. They need to show up today; otherwise, one way or another, the stuff will be gone tomorrow."

She salutes him. "Aye, aye, captain."

CHAPTER 40

Saturday, 9:15 a.m.
Megan drops Yehuda off at Buck's house and hurries to the library. She's late. She looks forward to catching up with Jürgen later. She's never been in love before, and is not even sure what it is. She reads *Teen Vogue* and *People* magazines, imbibes *Entertainment Tonight* on the tube, and has memorized every line from the "Twilight" movies, but love? All she knows is that her heart pings the moment she's near Jürgen. It happens like Swiss clockwork. She can only hope he feels the same.

Buck pours Yehuda a cup of coffee. Black. He adds two sugars and heavy cream to his. He stirs, tastes, and then adds more sucrose to his liking. No artificial stuff for Buck. No telling what it's made of.

Yehuda sips the coffee. They speak as if in the middle of a conversation from another day. Yehuda speaks first. "Giving up and knowing when to quit are two different things. When I came to America, I made a decision to live in the present. I left my past in Europe behind. I take every day as a new gift, a gift I did not expect to have." He pauses, thinks of his mother and father, the angelic faces of his siblings, clears his throat and continues. "I vowed not to waste that gift, to make each day count, as my own way of paying homage to the millions killed by the Germans, including everyone in my family."

He spits *German* out as if it was snake venom, knowing that dwelling on the word would pry open the last vestiges of memories he struggled to keep sealed. Even the letters curling over his teeth and skipping through his lips cause a flutter of panic that decades and a continent later, separated by a huge ocean, have a way of reversing time. How often has it been said, *history repeats itself?* For a moment, Yehuda flashes on Sheriff Kreiser. Then on Reichmann.

There are so many layers to history and the DNA of intolerance.

Buck raises his mug. It has a picture of the American flag flapping over the Twin Towers. "I don't believe in luck or gifts, just fate."

"Then if I was fated to live, I owe my life to those who lost theirs. That is only fair," says Yehuda.

Buck scoops a gold-framed picture from inside a bureau drawer. One he keeps hidden. Out of sight. It's too painful a daily reminder.

It's a picture of a young girl with dark hair, and deep, soulful eyes. She wears a white blouse. The picture is old and faded with sepia tones seeping over the grainy black and white images. He touches the girl's lips and then flashes the frame toward Yehuda. "*She* was fated to die. You got to survive."

Silence wraps both in cocoons of thought.

"We're more alike than you know. I've lived my life remembering her. Honoring her," Buck says.

We all have stories.

"I have to tell you a story."

Yehuda grins. "And I have one to tell you, too."

Buck grabs a faded, timeworn manila envelope. The corners are frayed, with shreds of paper stuck to the surface . . . the lint of memories. He undoes the red cord looped around the circular grommet that is used to hold the flap shut.

Yehuda wonders how many times Buck has unwound and rewound this over the years.

Buck extracts a stack of yellowed newspaper articles. At first, he stares at them without speaking. He shuffles through them, his eyes absorbing the words in sponge-like fashion as if he were reading them for the first time. He struggles to turn away from the clippings and look at Yehuda. Buck grimaces. "I've never talked about her since it happened."

"You'll feel better."

"Maybe."

Yehuda prods Buck to tell him about Apollina. He already knows snippets. When Buck finishes, so much more makes sense to Yehuda.

"I was in love, pure and simple. There was no other way to describe it. Apollina and me were going to be married as soon as the war was over. She was the most beautiful girl I ever laid eyes on. And the nicest and sweetest, too. She had long dark brown hair, almost black with natural deep red highlights. It was silky and shiny, and went halfway down her back. Somehow she had freckles and blue eyes, being Greek and all. And she had the cutest dimples when she smiled. When she saw me, her faced turned still more radiant and more beautiful than ever. She was a beacon of happiness the way Ol' Barney used to light the way out there for the ships."

Buck's reference to the lighthouse is both natural and symbolic: once alive and vivacious as a beacon of safety, not to mention a thing of beauty, it has gone dark and no longer offers peace or comfort.

"You were lucky to have such a pure love," says Yehuda. "Most people don't experience that even once in their lifetimes. It was the same for me and my Sadie."

Buck doesn't hear him; he continues. "That's why I've carried her in my heart all these years. I got my orders to be shipped out to the South Pacific. Everyone knew the war was turning, but there was plenty of fighting to do before it was over. We were bombing the heck out of the Krauts, but the Japs were still putting up a pretty good fight. Anyways, I wrangled a seventy-two-hour pass. Wasn't nearly enough time to get home, see my Apollina, and then get back to my division before we shoved off."

"But you managed," Yehuda says with a knowing smile. Buck's kind of love has no boundaries. Rare, but he has seen it before. Yehuda recalls sneaking out of his barracks in the internment camp after the war to catch a glimpse of Sadie, to hold her hand, to steal a kiss. Yehuda knows that Buck would have walked through fire if it meant seeing Apollina one more time before deploying to the South Pacific.

"I was telling a buddy of mine how badly I wanted to see my girl, but I couldn't get back to the East Coast and then return to my outfit in time. That's when he said that I should hitchhike down to San Diego. 'Get to the naval base,' he says, 'and see if you can fly out on one of the transport planes.' It was a damn good idea, too. Most folks don't know that the government had confiscated virtually every plane in the country. Air travel was limited to carrying troops. People couldn't scoot around the country the way they do these days."

"It was a Navy plane," Yehuda says to get Buck back on track.

"Getting onto the Navy base in an Army uniform wasn't a problem. I went right to the officers' dining room and hung around, telling anybody who'd listen about how I had to get home to see my girl. This one fella picked his head up when I was talking. He hustles over to me. Turns out he's a transport pilot and has to make a run to the Navy Air Station down in Wildwood. That's a lick and jump from here."

"So he takes you on the plane?"

Buck slaps his knee. "Was I ever lucky. Seems his job was to chauffeur dive-bomber and fighter pilots out to the coast from New Jersey after their training was complete so they could hook up with their aircraft carriers. Nowadays, they call it the Cape May County Airport and Industrial Park. Back then it housed hundreds of Navy pilots and instructors. What made it special was the field had lights, so they could do night flying training. Imagine, making dive-bombing runs right over Delaware Bay."

"So he flew you back to Jersey?"

"Yup. I was the only cargo, so to speak. Those planes were always empty heading east. No issue, back then, about wasting fuel."

"Did you make it home and back in time to join your battalion, or whatever you called it?"

"Nope." Buck grins. "That's when my luck ran out. Couldn't get back on a plane 'cause they traveled fully loaded going out west. Had to take the train. Made it back a day-and-a-half late."

"What kind of trouble did you get in?"

"Nothing serious. I was a grunt and not that important. They slapped my wrist, told me never to do it again, that I had responsibilities. The usual."

"That doesn't sound like the Army, especially at war."

"They cut me some slack. I had never caused a problem before, so they looked the other way knowing that a GI who was shoving off had a right to say good-bye to his girl. Too often, it was for the last time." Buck's smile withers. His head drops a notch.

Yehuda knows the outcome. He waits for Buck to pick up the thread.

"Turns out, it was the last time. Only it wasn't me that got killed in the war. It was Apollina."

* * *

Cape May, February 1945

The flight is bumpy. Cold. Except for a packet of saltines and a can of Spam, his stomach cries for food. Hunger and discomfort vanish when they bounce to a stop on the Tarmac outside a cavernous hangar. It is big enough to hold a squadron of planes. Play multiple football games at the same time.

Buck hops down the metal plank, thanks the pilot, whirls around to figure out his next move. He's still more than one hundred miles away. Now what? There's no taxi service. No one he knows owns a car. For that matter no one he knows owns a phone, so there's no one to call. Every second he stands there is another second that he has lost being with his girl, and a second closer to when he needs to return to base or be classified AWOL.

He studies his right hand. Kisses his thumb. Rubs it for good luck. "You've gotten me places before, good buddy. Let's see who's gonna pick up this sad excuse for a soldier who is needing to see his girl!" Buck has hitchhiked in California countless times. Always got a ride, usually pretty soon. It's the uniform. Folks feel obligated to be patriotic. It's the thing to do. National pride and all. The other reason they stop, and Buck has no illusions, is the creep of guilt that crawls inside someone because they are safe at home while the G.I. in uniform is the one looking down the enemy's barrel. No matter. Every time he needs a ride, one would come along.

He needs his luck to continue.

Buck nears the front gate. He's in uniform; the guard does not challenge him. Besides, he's leaving, not trying to enter a secured facility. A distant roar grows until two officers motor past the sentry, offering a meager salute. They ride in a khaki-colored two-seat motorcycle manufactured by Harley Davidson. They're laughing, carefree, acting as though life was one big carnival. They park next to a low-lying building made of sheet metal. The walls are painted olive green. They hop out, leave the key in the ignition, and go inside for a quick one.

The phone in the guardhouse rings. Buck sees the sentry answer. The soldier nods his head up and down, and then leaves the four-by-four foot station and stalks along the perimeter fence. He's been ordered to look for something. A breach? Maybe a deer jumping over? Buck steals a glance back at the motorcycle and in that flash, lopes to it, his tired arms pumping new energy into his flight-stiff body. He pauses, hops onto the seat, snatches a helmet out of the sidecar, turns the key, opens the choke, fiddles with the gears and launches forward. He's still sucking wind from the sprint but feels no pain . . . he's on his way to see his girl.

Buck parks next to a clapboard house surrounded by a picket fence. Once white, everything is now washed-out, a war-weary gray. In some places, the paint has faded and the wood bleeds through. Some of the pickets are chipped, some dangle from cross struts like floppy legs. A dog barks inside.

Buck retrieves a bouquet of multi-colored lettuces punctuated by asparagus spears that he bought on the way from a glass-enclosed, victory garden. The florist sold flowers before the war, but being a pragmatic patriot, he converted his facilities to growing and selling vegetables to help the war effort.

The door flings open. A beautiful girl throws her arms around Buck. Buck pulls her into him, kisses her, and twirls her around and around. They shriek. They laugh. He licks away her tears of happiness. She kisses his.

Buck lifts her into the sidecar the way a groom lifts his bride over the threshold. Unspoken, the gesture is not lost on either. They drive across the bridge and head toward the Barnegat Lighthouse. It stands tall against the celery-crisp early morning sky.

* * *

"Were you going to marry her?" asks Yehuda.

"I couldn't wait to get hitched. The next day we went on a picnic. That's when I popped the question."

Yehuda studies a framed picture of Buck in uniform. "You were handsome back then."

"What do you mean, 'back then?'" The two giggle like schoolyard chums.

"What was her full name?"

Buck reaches for an album. Turns the pages until he stops at a photo. She has dark tresses cascading over a light-colored blouse with a fringed collar. She's smiling the smile of infatuation. The look of love. The blush of rapture.

"Apollina Karras."

There's a picture of Apollina in the sidecar sporting a helmet with earflaps. Her head is thrown back, her hair tossed to the side, her left leg high in the air. A picture of defiance, of impetuousness, of casting caution to the wind, of a young girl adoring the man snapping the shutter. Wartime love.

Eternal love.

Yehuda mindlessly rubs his glasses on this shirtsleeve before leaning closer to inspect the picture. "There's a ring on her finger."

"It was my mother's. We tried it on. To see how it'd fit. Seeing her wear it, I was the happiest guy in the world. Apollina was my dream in every way. The minute the war was over, we were going to get married. Start the all-American family. The kids, the dog, the white picket fence. The whole nine yards."

"What happened?" Yehuda knows. He has already pieced it together but wants Buck to tell the story his way. Purge it out of him after all these years. A catharsis.

Buck's voice cracks. "That last day, we planned to spend every minute together. But when I got to her house . . ."

* * *

A rooster crows as Buck sprints to the Karras house. Buck passes the milkman heading back to his truck; the empties jingle against each other. The man salutes. Buck gives a meek return, grunts a good morning and gives a hurried rap with his knuckles on the front door with its curls of paint peeling off. No one answers. Then he sees the note wedged into the doorjamb, by the wrought-iron handle, once black, now pitted with rust:

> Meet me at the Marina.
> A.K.

Buck shoves the note into his pocket and hops onto the motorcycle. He peels away, leaving a trail of black rubber and smoke. At the marina, Buck springs off the seat like a rodeo star and sprints onto the wooden dock. Apollina readies throw lines on her father's tugboat. She sees Buck, drops the lines, and dashes to meet him. They embrace and kiss. It's a mild winter day. The sun is out and the skies are clear, dotted by scattered pillows of white that float lazily against a sea of blue. The two stand there, teary-eyed, not wanting to break from each other. Ol' Barney is perched behind them, a beacon of hope and light to many, but a tall reminder of rocky barriers that lovers face.

* * *

"A gathering of oil tankers was headed to Port Newark that day," Buck explains to Yehuda, "and they needed extra tugs to guide them into the harbor. They asked her father at the last minute. Being an immigrant and all that, he was thrilled to help the war effort. Trouble was his mate slipped on some ice the week before. He was useless with a broken arm, so the old man needed Apollina's help."

* * *

A horn blast causes them both to jump deeper into each other's clutch. Engines come to life and the water behind the tug churns a frothy white.

Mr. Karras calls down to them. "Apollina, untie the rope and hand it to Buck."

She raises her eyes. They puddle. "I have to go."

"I'll be back before you know it," he says.

"I know."

"And when I do, we'll get married. Wait for me."

Her cheeks grow rosy. "Promise you'll love me forever."

He crosses his heart. "Forever and beyond. And I keep my promises."

They press against each other on last time, kissing through their tears. Apollina points to the motorcycle. "One more promise: next time we're together, I want you to sit in the sidecar and let me drive that thing."

"Nothing would make me happier." He pauses and grins. "Well, I could think of something else to do before we take it for a spin."

"Easy, soldier, I hardly know you."

The tug's horn blows; they kiss one last time. "You win," Buck says, loving the fire and excitement in her eyes, "the moment I get home, you get to drive the motorcycle, and afterwards . . ."

"Yes . . . afterwards will be the most special ride of all."

* * *

Buck points to the motorcycle through the window. "I never gave it back 'cause of her. She loved the wind in her face and her hair blowing all kinds of wild-like. We even talked about showing up to our wedding in that contraption! It's one of the only things I have that she ever touched, that, the note . . ." and he points to a glass vial on the shelf, "and a lock of her hair that she gave me."

Buck needs to take a moment. He stands up hands-on-hips. His lips tremble. He squeezes back tears, tries to control his breathing, and then says, "From where you're sittin' I'm probably a crazy old fool. But I gotta tell you that sometimes when I'm driving that cycle, I pretend that she's in the sidecar, just like the old times. And when I do, you know what? I actually feel that she's there with me."

Yehuda puts his hand on Buck's shoulder. "In a very special way, I bet she is there with you."

Buck sighs. "Wouldn't that be something?"

"What happened after that?"

Buck shakes his head. "Mail was spotty during the war. I didn't expect to hear from her for some time once I shipped out. I was being shipped out to the South Pacific. I wrote her a slew of letters. I loved writing her, picturing her smile when she read them. Thinking how happy we'd be together. When the fighting cooled down and they could deliver mail, there was a letter from my mother, telling me what happened." His voice sank into his chest. "Apollina and her father were both lost. She never got to read any of my letters."

Buck sniffles, and then flips the page to another article, different from the one posted at the police station. It's headline reads:

Local Tugboat Captain and Daughter Missing

Buck wipes his eyes.

"You've been hoping all this time that the *Searcher* would find their boat, haven't you?"

Buck takes a few steps and wheels around; his eyes are coals of fire. "She and her father just vanished that day. It was a clear day, perfect visibility. Engine blew. A fire. Explosion. Something caused her to go down. Maybe they were sunk. A casualty of war."

"Could she swim?"

"Must've been too far out. We don't talk about it much, but there are plenty of sharks in these waters. Folks 'round here still talk about the white shark attacks during the summer of 1916. Four people died back then."

"Sharks go to warm waters winter time. That's not what got your Apollina."

"You're right. Nothing's rational 'bout the way she disappeared."

Yehuda waits for Buck's emotions to simmer down.

Buck yanks open the refrigerator and snatches two beers. He hands one to Yehuda without asking if he wants one.

Yehuda is on automatic pilot, lost in a slew of thoughts and emotions of his own. He lifts the bottle to his mouth and takes a long draft without realizing what he's doing. As close as he has become to Buck, he has yet to tell him about Polly. After all, you make a new friend, the flesh and blood kind, and the last thing you want to discuss is that the other new friend you've made just happens to be a ghost.

It does not stop there. The names confound. Apollina. Polly. Coincidence?

Doesn't Carly always say that *nothing* is a coincidence?

While Yehuda is at Buck's house, Megan waltzes through her chores at the library daydreaming about hooking up later with Jürgen. After she shelves the last book, Megan parks the book trolley to the side of the front desk. She fusses a bit; like most days, library is empty. There's been talk about making the library a center for job postings. The idea of having a singles night, with wine, cheese, and book or poetry readings has also been tossed around. Anything to get people through the door.

She logs onto the computer, checks her emails, taps the keys for Facebook, catches up on her friends from Pine Brook and, after she can diddle no more, logs off.

She searches for something to occupy herself. She free associates from Pine Brook to Island Bluffs to the new house to the bones in the basement and to the discovery in the attic, and finally to Buck and Yehuda becoming friends. Next, her thoughts lead to the pages copied from articles she and Buck found on the microfiches. She opens a drawer to retrieve them. She scours the pages with a fresh eye. At the bottom of one page, missed before, a small article grabs her attention. She reads it. She turns wide-eyed and shocked. How did she miss this?

This changes everything.

CHAPTER 41

Saturday, 3:00 p.m.

There's a knock on the front door. Carly lets Jürgen in. "Megan's expected back from the library any minute now. How 'bout a cold drink?"

He stands awkwardly. "Orange juice, if it's not too much trouble."

Gabe enters the kitchen and exchanges greetings with Jürgen. "According to Cole, he's ready to get going on the house."

Jürgen smacks his lips and starts to use his sleeve when Carly hands him a napkin. "Now that everything's in place, we start Monday. I'm pumped."

"They expect rain," says Carly, noting the differences between teenage girls and boys, how he gulped all of it down without a breath and then was about to use his sleeve.

"Unless it's torrential, we work," says Jürgen flashing his whites. "Besides, it's not supposed to rain 'til late afternoon. That gives us plenty of time to start prepping the house, maybe even start on the roof."

Carly refills the empty glass without him asking. Jürgen drinks half, and then sets it on the table.

Buck is set to drive Yehuda home. The last few moments have been shared in a silence reserved for friends who have exposed their private thoughts and deepest fears to each other. In this case, Buck has not only told Yehuda everything about his and Apollina's dreams, he's confessed that he has never permitted himself to get involved with another woman because his love for her is undying. He promised to love her forever, and Buck Hopewell keeps his promises. And he has, for thousands of solitary nights and countless empty holidays, through decades of lonely dinners and over lonelier weekends.

"I can't explain it," he says as Yehuda slides into the sidecar, "but because I wasn't at the funeral—granted they never found her body—I have never been able to put her death to rest. I never will. In those first years, every time I walked into town and saw a woman from a distance, my heart leapt thinking some miracle had occurred and it would be Apollina."

"I understand those feelings. My parents, all my relatives, my brother, my sisters, almost anyone I had ever known growing up, were killed in the camps. Even so, I saw their faces everywhere I went. On the street. At the train station. On buses or in the subway. They were everywhere and yet never there. When you don't put a shovel in the ground and help bury a loved one, a piece of you never accepts that they've died."

"Sometimes, after all these years, I still think she's going to walk up the street, smile, and say 'Hello.' How crazy is that?"

Yehuda pictures Polly and says, "It's not so crazy at all. I've seen and heard of stranger things in this world."

Buck slaps Yehuda on the top of his helmet. "I know it's crazy, so don't humor me . . ." His voice trails, and then revives. "You and me? We may come from different places and have different stories, but we're so much alike. We understand each other, don't we, buddy?" And with that, they roar off toward the Berk house.

Megan sees Jürgen's truck in the driveway. She dances into the kitchen. "Hey," she says to Jürgen. He tightens his lips and lifts his head up. An imperceptible nod and twitch of his eyebrow acknowledges her. Mr. Cool in front of others.

After kissing her father and greeting Carly with a peck on the cheek that surprises, Megan pulls a sheet out of her backpack. "Look what I came across at the library." She thrusts the photocopy into Jürgen's hand, and then shoots furtive looks at Carly and her father.

Jürgen's lips move as he reads. He grows agitated.

A growling motorcycle splinters the stillness.

"That must be Buck and Grandpa," says Carly. "They will want to see this, too."

Jürgen's suntanned face turns slate gray. He lowers his eyes and bites his lip. He wants to say something, but nothing comes out. He rocks from side-to-side, the paper wagging in his hand.

The octogenarians enter the kitchen. Each senses electricity in the air, each feels drama unfolding, and yet have no clue as to what it could be.

Carly reaches for the photocopy. Her eyes make a silent plea. Jürgen nods that it's okay to read it out loud:

> ISLAND BLUFFS. Werner Hauptmann was reported missing today by his wife, Elsa, who returned from a two-week stay at Camp Nordland, located in Sussex County. Mrs. Hauptmann grew concerned when her husband was not at the train station to greet her.
>
> This was unusual, reported the agitated Mrs. Hauptmann, because "My husband is so reliable." Since all taxi service has been suspended due to the war, Mrs. Hauptmann, who is four months pregnant, carried her luggage three miles to their house, located at 24 High Tide Drive. Not discovering her husband home, and finding no note as to his whereabouts, Mrs. Hauptmann informed Sheriff Kreiser that Mr. Hauptmann was missing.
>
> Werner Hauptmann was born in Toms River, and lived in Brick Township before moving to Island Bluffs. He is employed by the American Fertilizer Company.
>
> Mrs. Hauptmann did remark that her husband's behavior was peculiar of late. He claimed their house was haunted. One recent morning, according to Mrs. Hauptmann, her husband awoke only to discover his dark hair had turned stark white overnight. Without her husband home, Mrs. Hauptmann was afraid to remain in their house alone and moved into the Hotel Baldwin.
>
> Anyone knowing the whereabouts, or with information that will help locate Werner Hauptmann, should contact Sheriff Kreiser of the Island Bluffs Police Department. All tips will be kept confidential.

At first, no one speaks. Megan clears her throat. "That's *our* address. The Hauptmanns lived in *this* house." She stares at Jürgen as she speaks.

"That Kreiser in the article must be our beloved sheriff's father," says Gabe.

Jürgen's voice cracks. "My father lived with the Kreisers growing up. He and the sheriff grew up like brothers."

"What about Werner Hauptmann?" asks Carly. "Is he your grandfather?"

Jürgen paces the room; he grows more agitated by the second. He doesn't answer.

"You told me you never knew your grandfather," says Megan.

Jürgen avoids their gaze; he slides onto a chair. He wraps his fingers around the half-filled glass of orange juice. "The story I heard was that my grandfather died while my grandmother was pregnant with my dad. Sort of like in the article, only that article says he went missing."

"Was Werner Hauptmann your grandfather?" Carly asks again.

Jürgen looks from Carly to Megan. "I'm not sure. I don't think I ever heard my grandfather's name mentioned. It was like he never existed. I'd have to ask my father to be sure."

"This article about Werner Hauptmann helps explain much of what's happened to us since we moved in here." Gabe refers to both the Nazi paraphernalia and to the bones in the basement.

"Hold on. Are you saying that all that stuff upstairs belonged to my grandfather?"

At the mention of "grandfather," a cold chill sweeps through the room. The orange juice glass shatters in Jürgen's hand. Blood flows from the wound and drips onto the table and floor. Jürgen studies it with a blank stare, as if he is observing an event occurring to someone else, not him. He feels no pain.

Carly grabs sheets of paper toweling and wraps Jürgen's hand. She points to the fleshy part of the palm by the middle and ring fingers. "Squeeze here with the thumb and index finger of your left hand while I get my first aid bag from the bathroom. It has everything I need for emergencies."

Yehuda looks at Buck. "Do you remember who used to live here?"

"For the longest time, no one."

"What about during the war?"

"Whoever lived here was gone when I came back after being discharged. There was talk of a squatter living in the house for a bit. Just after the war. But that didn't last long. It's been empty ever since."

At that moment, Buck's head jerks to the right. His hand darts to his ear, then to his cheek. He rubs his cheek as if he's been kissed. "Geez," he says, under his breath. "That's weird."

Yehuda does not question what he just saw. If Polly can go through walls and appear and disappear at will, then he prays she can receive this mental admonition: *Behave yourself.*

Carly bandages Jürgen's hand after washing it with an antiseptic; she makes certain no shards remain in the wound. "That should hold you."

"No stitches?" he asks, staring at white dressing.

"It was a lot of blood, but not very deep. This should hold you just fine."

"Thank you, Mrs. Berk. I mean, Dr. Berk." He looks up at her. "I swear the glass broke by itself."

"It must've had a crack in it that I missed."

Gabe puts the dustpan and broom away after sweeping up the broken glass, then says what's been eating at him for the last few minutes. "What if the skeleton in the basement was your grandfather?"

Carly speaks. "Surely Mrs. Hauptmann or the sheriff would have found him back then. They must've searched the house."

"The article said Mrs. Hauptmann moved to a hotel," said Gabe. "Remember, Hauptmann claimed the house was haunted and while she may have derided him for thinking that, she might have had her own suspicions that something was right here."

Carly rubs her belly. "Who could blame her for not walking down the basement stairs in her condition?"

Megan grows animated in stark contrast to Jürgen's gravity. "You're all missing a clue."

"Tune in next week for Island Bluffs, CSI," says Gabe.

"Don't pay him any mind," says Carly.

Megan rolls her eyes. "When Grandpa and I pushed that old chest aside . . ."

Yehuda finishes the sentence for her. "It was locked and the key was on the inside."

Carly picks up her thread. "A reasonable explanation is that the key we found was an extra one, and that someone locked the door, pushed the chest to block it, and stashed the key elsewhere."

Heads nod, all except Yehuda's.

Buck chimes in, diverting attention away from the lock and key. "Everybody 'round here knows that old Sheriff Kreiser and his son, Rudi, have always been in cahoots with the American Fertilizer Company. The old man and plenty of others had to know what was going on in this house during the war."

"Which means that Sheriff Kreiser's father and the town elders, back then, were most likely part of the German Bund," Yehuda adds.

"That's something I've always wondered about," adds Buck. "Ever since I can remember, the Sheriff and his cronies seem to share secret looks and talk double-talk, like they were hiding stuff. Now I know it wasn't my imagination."

"Dad," Gabe glances at Carly, "I wouldn't blame you if you wanted us to move out of here."

Yehuda waves his hand in a nonchalant, it-does-not-matter sort of way. "A house is a house. As long as it doesn't have any leaks and is warm in the winter, I could care less who lived here before or what he did or didn't do. It's wood and bricks and nails. People make the difference. Whoever lived here before is no longer here. We are."

Carly focuses on the unanswered. "That doesn't explain the unidentified body in the basement."

"You mean the bones," says Megan.

"There was once a face and a name attached to those bones," says Carly. "Add in the locked door and there's the chance he was trapped in the room and left to die."

"Or killed somewhere else and then dragged there so no one could find him," says Gabe. "Either way, it's a crime."

"How did they think they would get away with it? Bodies stink when they putrefy," says Megan. "I see that on every crime show."

"Consider how long ago we're talking about. Smells dissipate over time," Carly explains. Then adds, "Even horrific smells."

"The assumption was that the house would remain empty," Buck adds.

Gabe looks from one to the other. "I know what I just said, but what troubles me, is that if this was a crime, why hide the body in the basement? And why leave all the rain gear and supplies that would draw suspicion? They could've cleaned out the basement and buried the body anywhere but here." He collects his thoughts. "Something else occurred here."

Yehuda clears his throat. "You're forgetting about Nazi arrogance, the way they filmed everything from their parades to the atrocities in the camps. That's why we know so much about the horrors they inflicted—they recorded them."

"What does that have to do with this house, Grandpa?"

"The Bund members, when it was active, and their children who followed in their wake, purposely left this house untouched as some sort of shrine. What happened to the person in the basement, as terrible as it might be, was trivial to these people compared to preserving what was in the attic. This was the house that Bund members could point to as a symbol of patriotism for their Fatherland."

"I get it," says Buck, "they enclosed the room as an altar to their success."

Carly marveled. "That was quite a poetic way of describing it, Buck."

"And accurate, too," added Yehuda. "The reality is that no one knew what happened to Hauptmann, and it is quite possible they didn't care. By early '45, the Germans had their backs to the wall, they were going to lose the war and it was only a matter of when. The fertilizer company owned the house, so no one was going to bother with it. And they left it alone all these years so they could point to it when they drove by. Have a reminder how they did all they could to help Germany win the war."

"And then you folks ruined it for them," Buck says.

"Listening to you, it's a wonder this house ever came on the market," says Gabe.

"Blame the housing downturn. Made the banks look at all of their toxic properties," says Buck. "They had no choice but to foreclose and put it up for sale. And when they did, there was no one around who remembered much about this house."

Listening to this, Jürgen is drowning as if thrown overboard in the middle of the ocean with no one around to toss a life preserver. He struggles to speak. "You're saying that there's a chance my grandfather died in this house and that American Fertilizer kept it a secret, even from my father, for all these years? Even though my dad grew up in the sheriff's house as a young boy?"

Yehuda touches the boy's shoulder. "We can't be sure of all the facts, but there is more to this story. Gabe is right. Something else happened here."

How could you do this, Polly?

"Like what?" asks Jürgen.

"We may never know," says Yehuda, "but I think you need to consider that American Fertilizer didn't know what happened here, either."

Buck steps forward. "I do remember a time after the war, I can't say how long it lasted or exactly when, that some fellow did live in this house. Whoever it was, I know for a fact he never got any mail. Discussed it with Clem Rogers. He was the postman 'round here for years. He's gone now, but he always thought it was strange that the man living here never got one bill sent to the house."

"You're positive someone lived here back then?" asked Gabe. "When would you say that was?"

"I'm not as sharp as I used to be, but I do remember driving by here and seeing lights go on and off. Different ones at different times. Must've been right after the war for a couple of years. Maybe three or four. Then, whoever it was left, 'cause the house was always dark afterwards."

"But you can't see the house from the road," says Megan.

"Back then you could. The bushes were not so high and during the winter, when the leaves were down, you could see the house plain as day."

"Any suspicion whom that could have been?" Carly asks.

"I never thought much about it, and I wouldn't have known back then. But after hearing all of this now, I might have a clue."

"Care to speculate?" asks Gabe.

"Not 'til I do a bit of checking of my own."

"Now it makes sense why the sheriff was in such a hurry to get rid of those bones. He probably knew who they belonged to and wanted to keep the identity a secret. That's why he didn't make it a crime scene or do a proper forensic exam of the site," says Megan.

"You're sounding a lot like me, young lady." Carly looks at Megan with more than a gleam. She turns to the others. "Then there's the matter of the bone Megan found."

Jürgen's spirits run the gamut, by turns, from shock to denial to sadness to hope to acceptance. "Is there some sort of test to compare my DNA with that bone? Then we'd know for sure if it was my grandfather."

Carly takes a step toward him. "Are you sure you want to know?"

Jürgen nods. "How can we find out?"

"All we need is a test kit and a swab from the inside of your cheek, and then compare your DNA to what the lab can recover from that bone."

"How will they know if there's a match?" he asks.

"Because only males have a Y chromosome and this is passed from father to son. If we're able to extract the DNA from the bone and match it to your Y chromosome, then you would be a direct descendant."

"Is it that accurate?" Jürgen asks.

"As definitive as it gets. If there's a match, it will be your grandfather."

Buck's not happy about where this conversation's going. If the testing proves that the bone belongs to Hauptmann, then Jürgen's grandfather helped send Apollina to her death. And that doesn't sit well with Buck.

Not one bit.

CHAPTER 42

Saturday, 10:00 a.m.
"You wanted to see me, Rudi? Thought you were off Saturday mornings."

Otto Hauptmann knocks on the doorframe of Sheriff Kreiser's office. Kreiser points to the chair as he completes a call to meet one of their hunting lodge buddies. He covers the phone mouthpiece. "Got some odds and ends to clear up. Saw your kid over at the club the other day," the sheriff says to Otto. "He's quite the shot."

"Jürgen's a natural. Didn't need to teach him a thing. Steady as can be."

"Just like his father."

Otto smiles. "Remember the time your father gave us that BB gun?"

"Yeah, and you shot the lights out like no one else. Hit the damn oil-cans from a hundred yards away. Still can't get over it all these years later."

The boyhood friends reminisce about the days growing up in the same household, and then the sheriff grows serious. "I've got something for you."

"It's not my birthday."

He leans and hoists a bag that had been out of sight behind the desk. "In a way, consider this a major birthday present."

Otto makes a face. It's a black paper bag, glossy, imprinted with an image of a blue flaming skull. *Zazzle* is written across the bottom in large iridescent letters. He takes it from the sheriff. Feels the bottom. Notes lumps. "It's heavy. What's in it?"

"Your father."

Otto drops the bag as if it were aflame. The clunk resounds. "That's not funny."

The sheriff raises his hands. "I'm dead serious. I can't be sure it's him, but these were found in your old man's house. The one the Berks bought. They were hidden in a basement washroom. Didn't think much of them, at first. Truth be told, I used a rib as a lucky charm in a poker game the other night. Won big. Then it clicked after something Trevor Reichmann said."

"You know they never found him. My mother always thought he ran away with another woman."

"There's some truth to that."

Otto jumps to his feet. "How would you know? Did your father tell you that and you've been holding out on me all these years?"

The sheriff waves Otto to sit down. "Don't get so hot and bothered. It's not what you're thinking."

Otto slips down into the chair, looks at the bag and says, "After what I just heard and what's in that bag, I'm not thinking at all."

Kreiser explains. "You'd be interested to know that before your father went missing, he told my dad that there was a ghost in that house. A female ghost."

"You don't believe that for one minute, do you?" says Otto.

The sheriff shrugs. "There's been too many reports of ghosts around these parts to ignore them. You remember when we were kids, all those stories about The Jersey Devil haunting the Pine Barrens? Whether there's any truth to all them stories, I could give a rat's ass."

"We're not talking about some ancient legend or kids talking spooky things roasting marshmallows. Did my father actually tell your father that he saw it?"

"The way I remember it is that your father caused some young girl on a boat to die and that she haunted him until he hid in the basement bathroom to get away from her. Turned his hair white as the virgin snow, that's how scared he was. The Berks found these bones in the basement washroom, blocked by some big old chest." He points to the black bag.

"What does that prove? They could be anybody's," says Otto.

"Could be, but your father was the one living in that house and he's the one no one ever saw again. Stands to reason it could be him. Soon's they found them, the Berks called me. When I got there, there was a towel over his head—or more accurately—his skull. Trying to protect himself from the evil spirit that plagued him so much."

Otto clutches the bag to his chest. He starts to speak; he can't. He manages to stammer, "Are you sure?"

"Not exactly. But I think it's probable."

Otto turns to leave.

"Where you going?" asks the sheriff.

"I never knew my father. I'm going to take him home, pour two shots of twenty-one-year-old McCallum, light a couple of cigars, and then snuggle up real close to him when I go to sleep. I've waited a lifetime for this moment."

The sheriff nods in approval.

"Toss one down for me."

CHAPTER 43

Saturday, July 12, 4:45 p.m.

Jürgen storms into his house. He does not remember driving there after leaving the Berks. He finds his father, Otto, wearing magnifying loops.

The back door slams shut. Otto tilts his head enough to see Jürgen frozen in place, his fists clenched. Otto uses long-handled tweezers to maneuver a miniature boat into a clear bottle. He mutters that he will be with him in a moment, and then turns to prod the boat modeled after a four-masted Confederate cargo ship, into its final resting place. No detail is overlooked. The masts, the gunnery, the captain's deck, the round wooden steering wheel, the sails that are stained and tattered. The flag. Emblematic of a war that was lost. There was a time when it waved high and proud.

For some, it still does.

"Where's the fire?" asks Otto, his eyes riveted to the pull string that will raise the masts and forever seal the boat in the glass bottle.

"I'll wait 'til you're finished."

Jürgen stands there, rooted to the spot on the floor. He feels the pounding in his chest lessen, his pulse throttle down, his body unwind, his curled fingers loosen, and his breath grow less shallow. He looks at his palms, at the indentations caused by his nails from squeezing so hard, and rubs them. His right eye, however, continues to twitch. He does that whenever he's nervous. As a child, it betrayed him whenever he tried to get away with something. This time it heralds his excitement. His anger. His hurts.

He rocks from foot to foot.

What does his father know about the Burks' house? About the grandfather he never knew? About Werner Hauptmann. Did Otto know how his father died?

The wait dampens the fire raging inside him. His eyes roam the familiar room without seeing. He forces himself to focus. He notes a bag propped in Otto's favorite recliner. Two tumblers of amber liquid rest on the round wooden table next to it. Two stubs of smoked cigars top a mound of ashes in the green glass ashtray.

Otto eases back from the table and stands, cradling the bottle in his open palms the way one holds a newborn. He hefts the boat to the light. Twists it this way and that. Satisfied, he strides to the bookshelf. There is space for this new work next to replicas of Columbus's Niña, Pinta, and the Santa Maria.

Jürgen knows enough to wait until his father adjusts the bottle's position, steps back to admire his handiwork, leans to tweak its position, approves its precise place, and only when Otto turns his back on it and doesn't steal another glance can Jürgen interrupt.

Otto is ready to address his son.

He removes the bag from his favorite leather armchair with a surprising gentleness, and eases it onto the floor. The seat is worn and shaped to Otto's form. He picks up the closest glass and sips the McCallum. A reward for his latest *tour de force*? He offers Jürgen the other glass; Jürgen declines.

Otto caresses the bag on the floor, as if stroking a dog. He sees the bandage on Jürgen's hand. "What happened?"

Jürgen shifts his stance. His legs are now apart, his arms crossed.

He ignores the question. "Tell me about my grandfather."

Otto doesn't answer right away. He takes another sip of smoky scotch. Rolls it over his tongue. Savors it. Takes another.

"There's nothing to tell. I never knew him."

"Was his name Werner?"

"Why the questions all of a sudden?" He reaches out to touch the bag. "Does this have something to do with your new girlfriend? The one at the library?"

Jürgen's eyes widen.

Otto continues. "You think I don't know about the little Sabra?" Otto squeezes out a chuckle. It's more like a snort of disapproval. The message is clear. Unambiguous. Jürgen has crossed an unspoken line.

Any other time, he would have cowered. Cringed. Broken out in a sweat. Exuded a stink of fear. Not now. For the first time, Jürgen challenges his father and will not back down.

"What will members of your shooting club say when they find out your son's fraternizing with Jews? Think they'll keep you on as a member, Father?"

"You're the one who should be worried about seeing that Hebe, not me. It's not what I think; you know my feelings on that. But have you thought about what everyone else will say about you seeing someone who's not our kind? Who is one of *them*?"

Jürgen's eyes water. He expects remarks like these hurled at him. That's how it's always been. Like the time he befriended Jamal Johnson, when he asked if he could invite the only African-American on the football team to Thanksgiving dinner because his mother had to rush down south after her father had a stroke. "I don't care how good a player he is. Let him find somewhere else to eat turkey. I'm sure there's at least one bleeding heart in town who will take him in," Otto had said.

"He's my friend. I told him you'd be good with it. I know mom would."

"Your mother has no say in this. As for you, start picking better friends."

"But I promised," said Jürgen.

"Do I have to spell it out? A coon eating at my table? Over my dead body."

Jürgen refocuses.

"Megan found an article that described how Elsa Hauptmann reported her husband, Werner, missing in March of 1945. You were born six months later. You've got to tell me. Was Werner your father?"

"He's not missing anymore."

"What are you talking about?" asks Jürgen.

"In a minute. First, let me tell you a story about my father." Otto stands, slides past his son to the bookshelves, and opens a cabinet door beneath the volumes of books and ships in the bottles. He retrieves a thin album. He opens the once white cover, now yellowed and stained, to the first page. He hands the book to Jürgen. "These are your grandparents, right before your grandfather died." He studies it a beat before handing it to Jürgen.

Jürgen takes the book, studies the picture. "He looks strong and healthy in this picture. He died soon after? What happened?"

Otto downs the rest of the scotch before answering. "The one thing I do know is that something terrible happened to him in the days right before he died. And then he vanished."

"How could he vanish? Didn't anyone look for him?"

Otto paces the room.

Jürgen waits.

Something comes over Otto. He saunters this way and that, appears to read the plaque screwed into a team bowling trophy, and then touches the glass-framed Confederate money hanging on the wall. He spins around.

"Rumors had it that my mother would find him in a room, alone, talking to himself. Not exactly to himself. Like he was talking to someone else, but no one was there. The room was empty. When she asked whom he was talking to, he grew agitated. He told her to leave him alone, that he could handle it. But it only got worse."

Jürgen's anger melts into a puddle of understanding. "Did anyone else witness this behavior?"

"Sheriff Rudi's father. That's how I know."

Jürgen studies his bandaged hand and thinks about Polly. He hasn't seen her yet, not like Yehuda, but he believes she is real . . . especially after seeing the photo with her above him in the tree.

Otto continues. "Near the end, he'd lock himself in his room and wouldn't come out for days. Sometimes he screamed out. My mother heard him say, 'Get away from me. Get away from me.' He was going crazy. My mother said she couldn't take it anymore. She was pregnant with me and worried about her health. So she left for two weeks. Went to Camp Nordland. When she came home, he was gone without a trace. She couldn't find him anywhere. She didn't know what to think. It even struck her that he might have faked being crazy so he could run off with another woman."

"But that's not what happened, is it?" asks Jürgen.

Otto steals a glance at the bag on the floor. "No."

Jürgen turns to the last page of the photo album. There are two photos. In the first, Werner is smoking a pipe in front of a Christmas tree; his hair is black. In the second, labeled March 10, 1945, his hair is stark white.

"That's the last picture ever taken of him," says Otto. "When my mother couldn't find him after returning from Camp Nordland, she took a room in a local hotel. Lived there until her time was ready. She died hours after having me. That's when the Kreisers took me in."

"What did she die from?"

Otto shrugged. "Something about losing a lot of blood during the delivery. The medical care around here wasn't very good back then."

Jürgen wriggles the picture out of the pasted black triangle corners that hold it in place. He moves closer to a lamp and sees a reflection behind Werner's shoulder. He tilts the picture, brings it closer to his eyes.

It's Polly! He's sure of it. There's no doubt.

Jürgen looks up. "Before, you said something that grandfather wasn't missing anymore. What'd you mean?"

Otto pours himself another shot; he hands the glass to Jürgen. "You better take this." He's never offered Jürgen anything but beer before. Jürgen holds the glass.

"What's this for?"

Otto picks up the black bag with the iridescent lettering. "A little something I picked up at the sheriff's office this morning." He pulls open the handles so Jürgen can see what's inside.

"Meet your grandfather."

CHAPTER 44

Monday, July 14, 8:30 a.m.
The doctor does not need him so Buck drives his motorcycle to the Marina. Men lean over a rectangular screen mounted on four wooden legs. From a distance, dark objects clog the center. A crewmember grabs the hose used to wash down the daily catch after they are filleted. He sprays fresh water over the artifacts pulled from the sea.

Buck trots over, hoping to find a clue regarding Apollina Karras's boat.

Monday, 9:30 a.m.
"Dad," says Gabe, "could you bring yourself to give me a hand sorting through the stuff up there?" He jerks his thumb toward the attic with the cache of relics and Nazi paraphernalia. "Megan is going to record everything we do on her camera. She's already filming before we remove anything."

Gabe takes two steps at a time.

Yehuda strains to pull himself up by the handrail, and once at the top, pauses to catch his breath, and then hesitates before dodging passed the jagged edges into an inferno of memories.

To Gabe, the maritime charts, the picture book displaying the flags of every nation, the Nazi uniform, the picture of Hitler, the ship-to-shore shortwave, the ancient microphone and headset, the lantern that flickered blinking messages in Morse code to subs beyond Barnegat Bay, are all junk.

Yehuda sees these as icons of the Devil.

Badges of fear and terror.

Of an entire nation gone insane.

"I don't know where to begin," says Gabe.

Yehuda grabs a forty-two gallon black construction bag, four mils thick, and swipes everything from the desk into it. Dust flies. Yehuda sneezes. He wipes his nose on his white sleeve and continues to toss anything and everything into the bag.

"Dad, maybe Carly is right. Maybe we should keep some of this stuff."

Yehuda continues filling the black bag without looking up. "Everything here is trash. Trash of the worst kind."

Now Gabe has second thoughts. "Some of it could have historical importance."

"So?" Yehuda opens the desk drawers and tosses out pencils, paper, a brown wooden twelve-inch ruler, and a package of one-cent stamps. A postcard from the 1939 World's Fair.

"Carly suggested that we . . ."

Megan focuses the camera on Yehuda.

Yehuda slams an open palm on the desk.

Megan gasps; the recording continues.

Gabe jerks back a step.

"You don't get it. I buried all that these bastards did to me a long time ago. I swore they would never get to me again. Not in any way. Not even when we went to Israel a few years back and inched our way through Yad Vashem. Not even when they read the names of all the children who had perished in the Holocaust out loud. A million children. My brother and sisters among them. Not even when it caused me to remember hundreds and hundreds of faces. Faces of strangers. Faces of cousins. Some were my friends. Some were from the camps. I shared crusts of bread with them. When those names were read out loud, I went numb. I became numb to what those animals did to us. And now this," he sweeps his hand across the room, "it's more than a reminder of what the Germans did. It's proof that their culture of hate had believers living here, too. In America! Can you imagine? And from what I've seen, there are kernels still alive and real in Island Bluffs. We can't let them beat us. No, Gabe, everything must be thrown away. Nothing can be kept. There is no alternative."

Silence follows.

Megan continues to record every movement.

Bag after bag is filled.

Gabe struggles with objects too big to squeeze into a garbage bag.

Other than a wooden desk and a rectangular table, the room is soon emptied.

* * *

Outside Gabe wrestles with the last of the tainted junk; Megan follows and continues to record.

Yehuda remains behind. He stands in the middle of the room. Alone.
He reflects how this has been Polly's home all these years.
Her personal purgatory.
He wonders what she will do now that the Nazi shrine is dismembered. Will she leave the house?
Maybe it takes destroying this room to set her free.
He hopes it does.

Monday, 9:15 a.m.
"Where are you going?" Gabe asks Carly right before he and Yehuda are about to clear out the attic.

"It's better I'm not here when you destroy everything up there. Sure you still want to do this?" Carly asks.

"The Jewish Museum in Berlin has better artifacts, so do many others around the world," answers Yehuda.

"I understand why you need to get rid of everything, but I'm not sure why you can't save a few things," she says to Gabe.

"What's the point? The way I look at it, we are cutting a cancer out of this community. It has to be done so they can heal."

"Whether the stuff is destroyed or saved, won't change the way the diehards think in Island Bluffs. But regardless of what you do, I need to avoid sixty years of dust filtering through the house. Last thing I want to do is get sick from this stuff." She waves her hand. "I can see the headline now: pregnant forensic dentist made ill from Nazi soot sixty-three years after the war ended."

Carly drives away.
Gabe does not press the point as to where she is going, and she doesn't offer. Had he asked, she would have told him; he didn't. He rarely asks. He assumes she uses her time well. Always busy. Always doing something. Does that mean that he takes her for granted . . . or does he doubt that she is doing something responsible? Of course she is reliable and faithful,

but it would be nice to be asked where she is going once in a while. No one likes to be taken for granted.

Thirty minutes later, Carly is in front of Dr. Teplitsky's house.

She does not have an appointment.

The captain hands Buck a porcelain plate. The insignia is chilling: eagles on crossed swords surrounded by the black Nazi swastika. There are more spoons, forks, and knives. German names engraved on all. A belt buckle.

"Did you see any bones?" Buck asks.

The captain shakes his head, but it's clear that the partially exposed ship hull is not one of ours. It can only be a German submarine.

"And no traces of . . ."

"The tug? I'm sorry."

Carly parks next to the tree where she first met Olivia. Engine and radio off, she stares at the house. Why is she doing this? She knows why, but will not admit the answer to herself. The minutes roll by.

So much on the line. How will she feel when her son, the "other son," is living here, never knowing who she is, not knowing his brother or Megan, and maybe not even knowing Carly exists? How will she feel knowing that she can't see him? Speak with him? Carly imagines each scenario in her head. Then one occurs that she did not consider until that moment.

She opens the car door.

"May I help you?"

"You're Iario," she says.

"You're Mrs. Berk." He corrects himself. "Dr. Berk."

"You remember."

"Not all of father's patients, but you were here last week."

"I'm embarrassed to ask this, but I was running an errand and the babies started pushing hard on my bladder. Would it be all right if I use your restroom? I wouldn't normally do this, but it's an emergency."

He steps aside.

She stands in the entranceway.

She admires the fresh flowers.

She hears Chopin's Polonaise in A Flat being played somewhere in the house.

Feet scamper from the floor above.

"Thank you, Iario."

"Sure."

"May I ask you a question?"

"Of course."

"Are you happy?"

He frowns. "Of course I am. Why do you ask?"

Smells of fresh-baked bread fill the air.

She touches her swollen belly. "You know I'm going to give birth in a couple of weeks."

"Sure, it's in your chart."

"And do you also know that one of my twins will be your new brother?"

Iario turns confused. He starts to speak but stops.

One of Iario's brothers sprints toward the kitchen; this distracts. Carly turns but cannot catch sight of the boy's face. She continues. "Apparently, that's how all of you were born. Women, desperate to have a baby, sought your father's help. An arrangement was made. If we became pregnant with our baby, we would also carry a twin for him. Did you know about this?"

"Are you saying these mothers were surrogates for me and my brothers?" Her silence tells him he is correct. "I never knew for sure, but it makes sense."

"So you're okay with that?"

He shrugs. "I guess. How else would any of us been born?"

"Aren't you curious about your natural mother?"

"Not really."

This surprises. "You don't want to know who she is? Her name? What she looks like?"

Iario stiffens. "We have all the nurturing we need, and we want for nothing. In a sense, our father is our mother, too, and that is good enough for me. For all of us."

"What about other brothers and sisters? Wouldn't you want to know if you have any?"

Dimples appear. "Dr. Berk, I have nine other brothers now, and I just found out another is on its way. Do you think I need to know if I have more siblings?"

"You're right." Carly senses she has pushed this far enough. "I was curious about the house my other baby will be raised in. If it's a happy home. You can understand my concerns."

He mumbles that he does.

She turns to the door.

"I thought you needed to use the bathroom." He points. "It is right down that hall."

Carly does not move. "Thanks, but I don't need it now."

She is down the front steps when Iario calls out, "It's a really great home, Dr. Berk."

She waves without turning back, a bit guilty about unloading this shocker on Iario, but not guilty enough to regret it. She needed to know . . . and now she does.

Megan films Gabe as he tosses the last of the items into the green Dumpster. At the same time Gabe does this, Yehuda yanks on the pull chain, and the light in the hidden room is turned off for the last time. In short order, Cole's team will carve off the roof and destroy the room forever. Gabe and Yehuda had considered leaving all of Hauptmann's paraphernalia for the work crew to dispose of, but nixed the idea feeling obligated that it had to be sifted through their hands. Jewish hands.

Yehuda joins Megan and Gabe. They stand beside the Dumpster, each with their own thoughts, each numb. Yehuda steps forward and props himself up. He reaches into his pocket.

"Grandpa, what are you doing?"

Yehuda strikes a match. He tosses it onto the pile.

"Dad, that's not a good idea. It's too near the house."

Yehuda peers over the edge. The match flames out. He strikes another and the same thing happens.

Yehuda steps down. "I guess the good Lord wants this stuff to last a bit longer."

"It will all be destroyed," says Gabe.

"I wanted to see that for myself."

Tears cascade down Yehuda's cheeks. He lets them drip to the ground, consecrating it with years of remembrance. Years of forgiveness.

The moment is interrupted when Cole arrives with Jürgen and the other workers.

Gabe waves, Yehuda rocks in place, Megan turns gleeful.

The game plan is to raise the roof and add a second floor the full length of the house. It will have a playroom, three bedrooms, two bathrooms, and a study. There will be a balcony that faces the ocean, accessible from the study.

To enjoy sunrises.

Clear blue days. Celadon days. Whitecaps and churning waters.

The view of Barnegat Sound and Ol' Barney will be grand.

All in time for the new baby.

Now that the house's secrets have been discovered, the town will not bother them. The addition on the Berk house begins.

It is a new chapter for all.

CHAPTER 45

Monday, 11:00 a.m.
The ride from Dr. Teplitsky's house to the hamlet of Red Bank should take forty-five minutes. It takes longer. Today is surreal for Carly, like an out-of-body experience. How else to describe what happens when you visit the future home of a son not yet born—one you've agreed to give up—to see if the other boys living there are happy? Good environment and all that important stuff. It's the "stuff" that is getting to Carly. Meeting and speaking with Iario is shock enough, but for Carly, it is the first part of a most odd day.

Carly parks on Maple Street, which is a block from a dozen or so antique stores, some high end, some dust collectors. She sits in the car while the engine cools. It pings; she has pangs. Didn't she do the same thing an hour earlier? Park in front of a house and stare? There's a once familiar song on the radio, but now it's noise that irritates.

She finds herself outside the car, wind blowing, cars whizzing by. She locks the door.

Her anxiety increases with each step. She takes care to avoid the cement-sidewalk blocks that are atilt, willy-nilly like overlapping Scrabble tiles, caused by tree roots spreading that know no bounds. She stops and leans against a mighty oak. An oak on Maple Street. Someone has a sense of humor.

Is she really going to do this?

There's time to turn back. Gabe's still in the dark about this. He won't know if she bails.

Who would blame her?

She almost does . . . turn back, that is.

Carly enters Buono Sera, one of the better Italian restaurants in central Jersey. Gold, blue, and red Italian ceramic pots filled with ficus plants are scattered in strategic spots. The open kitchen is a study in entropy, the aromas mouthwatering. Yellow light bathes the room.

Carly wants to be anywhere else but where she is. She scans the tables; she hopes she has made a mistake. That it's the wrong day. It's not. The table to her left, set for eight, has one empty chair. They wait for her.

Olivia leaps out of her chair. "I wasn't certain you'd come. The others are anxious to meet you."

Three are missing; they live too far away to join. Carly surveys the other six. Those present are of different ages, all have decent figures, all are Caucasian except the one at the far end; she is dark-skinned.

Olivia takes Carly by the hand, sister-à-sister, and introduces her to each woman. The greetings are warm. Familiar. Two-handed shakes. A peck on the cheek. Kisses on both cheeks, à la European style. A hug. Three rub her swollen belly. One bends and plants an ear to it and listens.

Carly sits next to Olivia in the middle, on the side facing outward; a wall of folding doors, all bent open, exposes a sweeping view of the street. It's a cool summer morning. Low humidity. "Where do we begin?" Carly asks, scanning the eager faces.

They talk at once.

"Did you get a chance to see all the boys?"

"Are they being treated well?"

"What's the house like inside?"

"What are their names?"

"Is the doctor married?"

"Do they have a mother? More than one? He's not like those Mormons with all those wives, is he?"

"Can we visit our sons?"

Carly signals time out. "Ladies. Ladies. Ladies. I need you to slow down." She waits a throb until they all focus on her. "Let me start by saying I just came from Dr. Teplitsky's house."

Again, a storm of questions follows. Again, she signals a time out. "Ladies. Ladies. The only one I met is Iario. He's the oldest."

"He's mine." All eyes focus on a woman to Carly's right and across the table.

"You're Shelly," says Carly.

Shelly Granowitz is fifty-four. She has curly gray hair, and is wearing a sea-green dress cinched with a wide, white patent leather belt. Carly notes the small scar on her neck. Probably thyroid cancer. Shelly has hazel eyes and a friendly smile. "I'm impressed that you could recall my name after meeting so many. You get points for that."

"Everyone likes their name remembered. I make an effort to memorize as many as I can."

"Even so, I'm impressed." Shelly chats with the ease of kibitzing during a friendly game of bridge. "I was Dr. T's first. It was over sixteen years ago. My husband had already died. Colorectal cancer. He wasn't even forty. But before the chemo, we froze his sperm. My Arnie passed sooner than we expected or he would've been alive to see the babies."

"Why did you seek out Teplitsky in the first place?" Carly asks.

"I had four miscarriages. I was at my wits end. Not many good eggs left. If I was going to have *in vitro*, it had to work on the first or second try. We didn't have enough embryos for a third go 'round. I asked everyone I knew, even strangers, who was the best high-risk fertility OB/GYN around, and Dr. Teplitsky's name came up every time. Let me remind all of you that he was performing miracles on lots of women before us. None of us were any different than them, except we qualified as inductees into this special sorority."

"I'd do it again."

"So would I."

"But why us? Why not others?"

"I can answer that, to a point," Carly says. Eyes rivet on her. "If all of you are like me and Shelly, then the common denominator for Teplitsky was that we were all more desperate than most other women. For that reason, each of us was willing to accept his deal. That made each of us candidates for what my new friend, Olivia, refers to as *twofers*."

Olivia strokes Carly's arm. Kindred spirits.

"If you ask me," says another, "we were all human guinea pigs in some Bizarro, perverted way." When she sees quizzical faces, she explains, "In the comics, Bizarro was a mutant Superman that was everything Superman wasn't, sort of his opposite."

"If Iario is any indication, these kids are high functioning, polite, everything you'd want your child to be." Carly reassures.

Shelly continues. "Arnie passed before he had a chance to hold Ethan. My Ethan's tall and handsome, and the spitting image of his father. I don't know about you ladies, but I knew my husband when he was sixteen, so this part is a little weird. It's like having Arnie around all over again. Even though I am good with everything, it would make me happy to have a chance to meet Iario. Once would be enough. Just to say, 'Hello.' It would answer a lot of nagging questions."

Another pipes up. "Meet that boy once and you'll want to see him again. That's why Teplitsky keeps us away from them."

Seeing and listening to these women only serves to increase Carly's doubts about giving Teplitsky's son to him. What if she and Gabe decide to move to Florida or California? Have both babies there? What could Teplitsky do about that? Would he send the police after her?

Gabe would remind her that she did sign a contract. He would also remind her that they have no clue about the genetic history of this "other" baby. Who the biological parents are? Would Gabe and Carly elect to keep this baby knowing all the specifics?

"So can we?" asks another, clearing her throat to get Carly's attention.

"Can you what?" answers Carly.

"See the boys."

The woman with the deep, cocoa-colored skin speaks. "I've made my peace with that decision long ago. A deal is a deal."

"Then why are *you* here?"

"For starters, I *am* one of you. Like it or not, we're all bonded together by Teplitsky's master plan, whatever that is. The other reason is not about me, it's about my son, Rashad. Rashad wants to meet his brother."

"Why'd you tell him he's a twin?"

"I didn't."

"Then how does he know?"

"That's just it: he's a twin. Twins know."

"Identical twins know," added one, "I am not so sure about unrelated fetuses having any sort of special connection."

"But they shared our blood. That's how they're connected."

Carly takes a breath. "That's not how it works." All turn to her. "The one thing the mother and fetus do not share is their blood, and this holds true for multiple births. The mother delivers oxygen, nutrients, and antibodies to the fetus and removes its various waste products. The fetus's job is to produce the hormones necessary for the mother's body to maintain its pregnancy."

"Sounds like the baby and mother are totally linked."

"Linked, but their blood remains separate. Furthermore, developing fetuses are not connected except, of course, if they are Siamese twins."

Rashad's mother pierces their collective silence. "More to the point, how do I explain that he has a white brother? That I've lied to him all these years?"

"But you never told him directly."

"At this point, commission and omission are connected like twins. Somehow he knows. How can I explain their differences?"

"You are assuming that the other boy is white."

"Is there any reason to believe otherwise?"

Though none were ever bold enough to ask, each believes that their biological son knows about the other one.

"It is not Rashad's twin," says Carly.

Olivia has remained silent until now. "You're our only hope, Carly. You've heard what we have to say. Our reasons may vary but the goal is the same: to meet the child each of us gave up to Dr. Teplitsky. Will you help us?"

"What can I do?"

"You can ask for us. We can't; we've all received restraining orders. No phone calls. And we're not allowed within two hundred feet of the clinic or the house. Further for me."

"I used binoculars once, but I couldn't tell which was which," says a blond in her late forties.

An hour later, the Teplitsky *twofers* break up. Carly hadn't been sure what would happen when she would finally meet the others, but now that she has, she is glad she didn't turn her back on them. Driving away, she feels, by turns, lighter and heavier.

She faces a plethora of conundrums.

Carly bids each a good-bye.

"Will you help?" one asks again.

"I'll think about it," answers Carly. But Carly knows that she will ask Dr. Teplitsky to let the *twofers* meet their sons. She promises herself that she will.

And Carly Mason Berk always keeps her promises.

CHAPTER 46

Monday, 11:30 a.m.
While Carly is gone, Cole Brancusi's men outline the property perimeter by pounding pointed stakes every eight feet into the ground. They staple a continuous sheet of heavy-duty black plastic to the spikes to contain debris that tumbles as they work. To the right side of the house, a yellow backhoe gobbles mouthfuls of earth. Previous talks about building an addition, the frequent meetings with Verity Frizzell, the zoning board, Steve Freiberg, the sheriff's challenges, Reichmann, and Von Schroeter's blank check evaporate into irrelevance as the crew readies for phase one: carving out the extended foundation, digging out the new septic tank, and removing the roof.

Megan, Gabe, and Yehuda are at the far side of the house, out of harm's way. Two-and-a-half hours later, Carly picks her way toward them, still flummoxed from meeting the *twofers*. She glances at the beehive of activity.

"We need to talk," she says to Gabe.

At the marina, Buck stands with Captain Crenshaw. Crenshaw points to the lone swimmer paddling with methodical strokes toward the Barnegat Lighthouse.

"I almost hit that crazy fool the other day. Who is he, anyway? He's always out there."

Buck studies the plate retrieved from the ocean bottom. "His name's Larry Hanson. He's been living out by the Lighthouse as long as I can remember. Rarely comes to town anymore. Don't know much about him."

But others do.

Buck waggles the plate. "It's clear, now, from all the stuff you've been hauling up, that it's coming from a German sub out there. Do we know which one?"

"Couldn't find the part of the hull with the ID number. That part must've broken away. Could be anywhere along the ocean floor or buried so deep we'll never find it."

"So there's no way of knowing which sub?" Buck makes no effort to hide his disappointment. Every time a bit more information brings him closer to knowing what happened to Apollina and her father, it takes a blind turn.

Captain Crenshaw grins. "There was no way until we wormed our way into the Electric Motor room. It was a tangle of twisted pipes and rusted cables. Pretty dangerous for our divers. Took two tries. Almost didn't make it."

"Make what?"

"This." He hands Buck a brass plate. Buck turns it over. Brings it closer and squints. The engraving is clear: "U869."

Buck cycles into another dimension. "Boy, is that something! The 869 was a Type 9C-40 Deschimag-Bremen U-boat with a range of 11,000 miles. Carried fourteen half-ton torpedoes. What was it doing here?"

Crenshaw scratches his head. "We thought the same thing. Even went so far as to contact the U-boat Archive in Altenbruch, Germany. According to them, the *U-869* was lost on February 28, 1945. Trouble is they claim it was lost near Gibraltar on a mission patrolling the Mediterranean. No way it could be in these waters. At least that's their story."

Buck smacks it in his palm. "This brass plate says they're wrong."

Crenshaw holds out his hand. It takes an extra beat for Buck to give up the insignia. "Any way to double check?"

The captain nods. "I'm not taking any chances. I'm flying to Germany to show them this next week. Make certain it's the real McCoy."

Buck scrutinizes it one last time. "Oh, it's real all right. And so was the damage those bastards caused."

Poor Mr. Karras.

Poor Apollina.

While excavation progresses outside of the house, Jürgen works inside, preparing to remove the roof. He knocks down the remainder of the wall Yehuda and Buck busted through to find the hidden cache. Earlier, Cole explains to Jürgen why it wasn't a supporting wall. He teaches Jürgen the importance of collar ties and how they stabilize the sloping roofs from shearing winds and the heavy weight of snow. He points to the two vertical beams—six-by-six inches in diameter—that extend from the wooden floor to the center beam overhead for added support. "They're last. They need to stay in place until the roof comes off," Cole tells him. Then Cole reminds Jürgen to protect his eyes from flying wood chips and keep his yellow hard hat on, even though it was sweltering.

Cole pats Jürgen on the back. "It'll cool down as soon as the windows go and you start opening the roof."

"I am locked and loaded."

"This is every boy's dream. Knock yourself out."

Armed with a leaded sledgehammer, a crowbar, a claw hammer, and a gas-powered chain saw, Jürgen disassembles the wall that his grandfather built decades earlier. He smashes, cuts, pries, rips, saws, and hammers with a fierceness to cleanse.

Carly brings him bottled water. It's cold. Droplets condense on the plastic. He downs all sixteen ounces before speaking. "I was all set to ask my father about my grandfather, when he shows me this bag of bones."

"The ones the sheriff took out of here?"

"They're definitely my grandfather's. He's sure of it. We even toasted him with scotch."

"Whether he thinks so or not, that DNA swab will confirm if the bones are his. Until that happens, your grandfather is still considered a missing person. A cold case like that TV show. Let's not draw any conclusions until the report is back."

"When will that be?"

"Any day," she answers. "Assuming it's him, we still don't know the circumstances of how he came to be in that basement washroom." She wants to add more, but doesn't. *It's possible someone killed him, stuffed him in there, locked the door, and dragged the chest in front of it to prevent the body from being found. That would make it a murder scene.*

Jürgen is convinced that his grandfather died of fright, that Polly may have had a hand in his death, which is why he covered his head with a towel, when Cole calls up to him. "We need a hand down here for a minute."

Jürgen follows Carly down the steps. In the kitchen, before darting out, he unbuttons the pocket flap of his denim work shirt. He shows her photos of Werner. "These pictures were taken ten months apart."

Gabe and Megan join them. They had been outside watching the men at work.

Carly hands Gabe the pictures.

Gabe whistles. "He aged twenty years in a matter of months. Dark hair in this picture," he points to one, "and white in the other." He looks up. "Can that happen so fast?"

"Under the right circumstances, it's possible," answers Carly.

"You mean being scared to death," says Megan. She draws one picture closer. Moves it to catch a different light. She cocks her head. There's a mirror behind Werner in the picture with the white hair. "Oh my," she says to Carly, "do you see what I see?"

"I saw it right away," answers Jürgen.

"What?" asks Carly. "What did I miss?"

Jürgen points out the faint image of a young girl behind his grandfather.

"Well, I'll be," says Gabe, "my old man's been right all along."

"I told you," says Megan in triumph.

Earlier, Jürgen called Megan to tell her about the bones. She starts to console, he says he's okay. He says there will a brief ceremony.

She is about to ask him if he wants her to be there, to be by his side, but doesn't get a chance.

Cole calls Jürgen's name again. "Coming," he answers. He gathers the photographs, turns to leave, and trips over nothing anyone can see. He crashes to the kitchen floor, legs and arms akimbo.

Megan drops down to help; he's okay.

At that moment, the front door slams.

"Who's there?" calls Gabe.

There is no answer.

Gabe calls out again.

Silence greets them.

Gabe bounds out of the kitchen to make certain no one is lurking about. No one is. "Maybe it was the wind."

Maybe it wasn't

CHAPTER 47

Monday, July 14, 4:30 p.m.
For that second time that day, Iario answers the doorbell. A middle-aged woman stands there. She towers. She is every bit of six feet, turns out a couple of inches over, slender, with a long face blessed with striking features: delicate eyebrows, strong cheekbones, full lips, and a high forehead. Her skin is the color of cappuccino. When she speaks, shiny enamel pearls blossom into a dazzling, reassuring smile.

"Is Dr. Teplitsky home?"

"He's finishing with his last patient. Is there something I can do for you?"

He eyes the gold-plated badge pinned to the collar of her blue blazer. She is an official of some sort. She hands him a business card. Her name is raised in black lettering. A gold seal in the corner of the card matches the larger badge she displays with pride. It is standard issue for the Department of Social Services of Ocean County.

"I'm a county social worker. My name is Colleen Worthington. I need to discuss the fire in the tool shed with Dr. Teplitsky."

"The firemen put it out quickly, there was very little damage. And nothing happened to anyone else's property. There are no other issues, Ms. Worthington."

"How old are you, son?"

"Sixteen."

"My, my, you're quite a precocious young man. And well-spoken, too."

"My father taught us all to be direct and forthright."

"When I see him, I'll be sure to tell him he's doing a very good job."

There is an awkward silence. Iario does not know what to do. He waits for her to speak again. She does. "The trouble is, son, that this is between me and Dr. Teplitsky. It's something you don't need to understand, not just yet. Is it all right if I wait inside for him?"

Iario hesitates. He gawks inside, hoping his father will walk by at that moment. He prays for Gaston or Brigitte O'Leary to traipse passed. Any adult would do.

When he doesn't answer, she tries again. "It's pretty hot in the sun. Would it be all right?" Iario was told never to let strangers into the house. He was also taught to exercise his judgment when matters call for a decision. If the reasoning is sound, by all means do it, the doctor would encourage.

Iario steps aside. Long legs transport her into the foyer. She turns to him; she is ten inches taller than he is. "You called Dr. Teplitsky your father."

He nods his head.

"Then you are one of them."

"Them what?"

"Sons."

He nods again.

"Do you all share the same mother?"

Rather than answer, he points to the living room. "You can wait in there." He leaves before she can ask another question. She jars him into a memory, a memory drilled into him years back by his father.

* * *

"There may come a day when an official will ring the doorbell and ask a lot of questions about you and your brothers. Don't say anything to them. Just get me."

"But why?" asks Iario, never satisfied with a concept left unexplained.

"Because they will try to take all of you away from me."

It wounds. "How can they do that? You're our father."

"They won't win. I will stop them. But the process will be difficult and I would rather prevent it than let it happen."

"Even though there's no basis," reasons Iario, "you're saying it will happen anyway?"

Teplitsky sighs. "That day will come. All I ask is that when it does, be prepared. Promise me you'll do as I say. That you won't tell them anything."

Iario promises. Years pass.

Today is that day.

Today Iario keeps that promise.

* * *

During the fifteen minutes she waits for Dr. Teplitsky, Colleen Worthington moves about the living room with catlike ease. What interests her most are the framed pictures dotting the bookshelves, the family album resting on the coffee table, and the group picture taken by a professional that is mounted over the handmade, mahogany fireplace mantel that is stained a deep cherry color. All are of the Teplitsky children. The doctor is in most of the pictures. Some have more children in them than others, depending on who was born at the time. All smile. A photographic essay of entrance into the clan. The Teplitsky clan.

Even to the casual observer, no two children share similar features. None look alike. Different head shapes, noses, eye color, hair color and texture, smiles, teeth, dimples, no dimples, not a similar thing among them except gender and their last name.

She observes the furniture. It is out of her price range. Expensive. Custom fabrics on the sofa and chairs. High-end quality items from the D&D building in New York. Window treatments that cost more than her Honda Civic, and that's just in this room. Thick, patterned rug. Possibly Persian. Steuben bowl on the coffee table; Lalique statues on the bookshelves. The room is neither masculine nor feminine. Neutral at best. The heavy hand of an expensive decorator is apparent, the light touch of a woman is absent. No warmth. Nothing inviting. All technically correct, functional yet sterile.

Colleen is drawn to the lone painting in the room. It is an oil. The colors are brilliant. It is a man facing to his right. He has a cigar in his left hand. A tall blue, cone-shaped hat is perched on his head, topped with three red pompoms. She looks closer. The hat has a point; it is three-cornered. He is wearing a red uniform of sorts, with gold braid. Knickers lead to white stockings and pointy shoes. It is a clown. A harlequin. She eyes the brass plate on the bottom of the frame:

Torero. Study for *Le Tricorne*, 1919. Picasso.

Someone clears his throat. No footsteps or warning. She turns. Startled. A smidgen of guilt washes over her for studying the photographs and the painting without being invited to do so.

"I'm Dr. Teplitsky. My son, Iario, says that you want to see me. What is this in reference to?"

He does not move into the room. He stands in the doorway. Silhouetted. She can't make out his features. *Is this done on purpose*, she wonders?

"I'm sorry to intrude without notice, Dr. Teplitsky." Her long gait brings them face-to-face. More like crown to chin . . . his crown, her chin. She's at least fourteen inches taller. More. She extends her hand. He takes it; his grip is not strong. Just a few fingers. "My name is Colleen Worthington. I work for the Department of Child Services."

She hands him a card. He reads her title, sees the gold insignia. He pushes his glasses onto the bridge of his nose and stares up at her. "And you are here for what reason?"

"I'm here because one of the firemen who helped put out the fire the other day reported to our office that your youngest son . . ." she flips open her note pad to get the name right, ". . . Jovanni, was implicated in starting it."

"There was no damage of note. No one was injured. But that's not the issue here, is it? What business is it of his to report anything to Child Services? My children are exemplary students. Model citizens. They are dynamic young men blessed to have many gifts and talents, and I am fortunate enough to be in a position to help them. This is a special place, Ms. Worthington, where special children live and prosper. So again, I ask, why are you here?"

"Let me be frank, Dr. Teplitsky. You may have the best children in the world. And accidents like that fire do happen. But firemen, like the police, teachers and—I am sure you are also aware—physicians, are all officers of the court. Each has a moral obligation to report home situations that may not be best for the children. Once my office is notified, we scrutinize every report until we are satisfied that no child is in harm's way."

"And what did you find with my so-called *situation*?" he asks, motioning her to take a seat opposite him. He sits in a high-backed club chair, she, on the only sofa. Their heads at similar heights. Intentional, no doubt.

"I'll get right to the point, Dr. Teplitsky. There is no record of any of your sons' births in the county records. I'm told you have nine."

"Your investigators need to do a better job. I have ten sons."

"I'll make a note of that," she says without moving. "Can you tell me where they were born?"

"I could tell you some exotic place. It would explain why there are no records of their births in your system."

"But that's not the truth, is it?"

"They were born right here. In my clinic."

"Were others?" she asks.

"Others what?"

"Other babies born here that are not your children?"

"Too many to count over all these years," he answers. "All high-risk births. That's what I specialize in. That's why women come to me from all over the world. I am the fertility doctor of last resort. An article in the *Wall Street Journal* called me "The Baby Maker." I kind of fancied that."

She does not acknowledge his expertise, though she knows its extent and breadth. "Were *those* births registered with the proper authorities?"

"Every one of them."

"Except your sons?"

"Except my sons."

"Why? Surely you knew their births had to be recorded."

"I did not want any public record of them."

"There are laws."

"I have my reasons."

"Care to share those reasons?"

"Not really."

"Did it have to do with knowing that each one would be special?"

"That's part of it."

She uncrosses her legs and then crosses them the other way. Another man might have gazed as she moved, but not Teplitsky.

"C'mon, doctor. You're a scientist. There's no way you could've known anything about these boys ahead of time."

"But I did."

"How?"

"Let's just say that I knew *scientifically*."

His calm infuriates. Ms. Worthington is unsure if he mocks, if he is cynical, arrogant or merely being forthright. His answers are those of a verbal Mondrian.

"And what did their mothers have to say about this?"

"Nothing."

She lays her pen down. "How is that possible? What mother would agree to that? Everyone needs a birth certificate, a Social Security number. They are requisites for every U.S. citizen. How could you railroad this past the mothers?"

Dr. Teplitsky does not flinch.

"The mothers had no choice. These were my decisions and my decisions alone."

"What about immunizations? Checkups? What happens when they're sick?"

"Are you forgetting I'm a doctor? There's no need to take them elsewhere."

"Then there's the matter of their education. None of them are registered in the school system. Do you send them to private school?"

"Everything they need to learn, they learn right here." He wriggles to the edge of the chair and stands. "I believe I have answered all your questions. The only thing left for you to do, if you wish, is to check each child yourself. I will not object."

Colleen Worthington stands. "For the time being, I've learned what I need to know. After I file my report, you can rest assured these children will be checked. And checked thoroughly. Thank you for your time, Dr. Teplitsky."

There is no disdain layered on her last sentence. Nor is there a threat. Rather, Colleen Worthington thanks Dr. Teplitsky with the respect accorded any professional. She appeared unannounced, on purpose, with the main task of determining if the boys are safe. She leaves comfortable that they are. While she has little tolerance for citizens subverting the system, there is a subtle admiration for this doctor. She senses something unique occurring on these premises. Feels it in the air. She knows the doctor is no fool. He does not flaunt his apparent wealth or hide behind his panoply of accomplishments. He is current with taxes, does not use credit cards, has no mortgage on his house or clinic, and votes in every election, including primaries.

People like that do not break the law unless it is an elaborate cover-up.

Unless there is more than meets the eye.

Perfection can hide a myriad of sins.

She leaves wondering what his are.

And she will find out.

She stops at the door and turns. "What about passports? Driver licenses? They will want to travel when they get older."

"When the time comes that these things will be needed, they will be obtained through proper channels."

"You will need to prove they were born here."

"I can." He motions toward the door. "Now if there are no further questions . . ."

CHAPTER 48

Tuesday, July 15, 7 a.m.
Colleen Worthington rings the doorbell. It's morning. She's not alone.

Dr. Teplitsky answers the door himself. "Yes?" Though early, he is dressed in a blue-striped seersucker suit that covers a starched white shirt topped with a maroon paisley bow tie. Even before he opens the door, he knows it is Ms. Worthington. He expects her return after yesterday's visit; it is only a matter of when. He did not think it would be this day. A knot of anguish forms in his gut. He has not had this feeling in the longest time. Not since Germany. Not since the day the SS troopers knocked on the front door to take him, his brother and the rest of his family away.

Dr. Teplitsky stretches to see the officer behind her. Beyond them, is a yellow school bus that will take the boys away. He worries for them; they are ill equipped to meet strangers under these circumstances.

Ms. Worthington hands him a document with a raised state seal on the top corner.

"We're here for your sons."

The doctor tugs on his coat panel as if straightening out the jacket will smooth out the wrinkles of life. "By what authority?"

"The State of New Jersey. Every birth that occurs in this state needs to be properly recorded. A Social Security number has to be requested. Footprints should have been made when they were born that would help identify each child. These actions and documents are mandated to function in society. Without these rules and regulations, there is chaos."

"My dear, there was once a society that kept such good records that my entire family was taken from me. They, too, had rules and regulations. They, too, had mandates. Sadly, we are all witness to what was done with those policies and information."

"I know," she says in a softer voice, "but still, it *is* the law." She adds in the hopes that it will make a difference, "Our law."

"So I've heard. My sons are functioning well without those so-called formalities of state. Surely you know this. You saw it when you were here."

"Regardless, they must come with me."

"I can't let that happen. I won't."

Powerless words.

Her face remains lax; the officer hitches his belt and takes a step closer to intimidate. He does.

"Doctor," she continues, "you have no choice. These children are minors. None have a mother. There's no record of their births. We need to make certain they've not been abducted or bought from the slave trade market. For all we know, you could be making pornographic movies with them. They could be held captive against their wills."

These words are so far from the truth that the doctor opens his mouth but no sound squeaks out. He tries to process what she's just said, but it is alien.

He collects his thoughts.

He's been challenged before, by the worst in history: by Joseph Mengele. But this is America, not Germany. This is not Hitler's Reichland; this is the land of the free and home of the brave. This is New Jersey. The Garden State. Inhabited by the Lenni Lenape Indians. Home of more oil found (above ground, that is) than anywhere in the world other than the Middle East. Home of the most densely populous state. The chemical capital of the U.S. Where college football started and the first professional baseball game was played. Home of Sinatra and Bon Jovi, Nicholson and Streep. And Bruce.

From the doctor's retooled perspective? New Jersey is now a state that takes children from a loving parent, out from of a wonderful environment, and removes them from a safe home that, for no other significant reason, has a few papers out of order.

"I will not dignify those preposterous statements. There's no truth to any of them. I defy anyone to say otherwise." He grabs the brass doorknob; the officer leans past Colleen Worthington and plants his meaty hand on the door.

She hesitates. "In my heart I know there is not a shred of evidence that says these children are anything but living an enriched and wonderful life. And I know each will make a meaningful contribution to society when they get older. But there are rules."

"To Hell with your rules. You're wasting my time and the state's money. These are technicalities that I don't countenance. Now if you will excuse me, I must prepare for my patients." He takes a step back.

Iario hears all of it.

He quakes. This is the day his father warned would come. Should he run? Tell his brothers to hide? Call the police? That won't work; there *is* a policeman standing there. What should he do?

"The issue, Dr. Teplitsky, is that there is no one to vouch for the children except you," she says, her tone more severe. "The duty of the state is to provide a multitude of services, and to make certain its children are safe and not abused. That they are out of harm's way."

Dr. Teplitsky steps aside. He speaks directly to Iario. "Will you explain to this kind lady that you are safe and not abused? That you and your brothers *are* my sons. That you love living here and do not want to be taken from me or from this house."

Iario gulps. Before he answers, Miss Worthington speaks. "Regardless of what he or the others might say, without proper birth certificates I'm left with no other choice but to remove them from this house until this matter is resolved." She addresses Iario. "You don't want to break the law, do you? Rather than have me and the marshal march into your house and gather your brothers, would you be kind enough to ask them down here?"

"Do they need to pack clothes and their toothbrushes?" Iario manages to spit out.

"I hope this doesn't take more than a few hours," she says. When she glances to reassure Dr. Teplitsky that this should be cleared up soon, he's no longer there. He is on the phone speaking to his lawyer. She turns back to Iario. "Have them take toothbrushes and a change of underwear just in case."

The doctor lived through one madness; he will do all that he can to prevent it from happening again.

The boys huddle in the foyer.

There is a cacophony of protests.

Dr. Teplitsky raises his hands to quell their protests.

"For the time being, you all need to go with this nice lady and gentleman. It won't be for long."

"What if we refuse?" asks Leonzio, who is turning into a budding debater.

If it were another time and another place, Dr. Teplitsky would have answered differently. "That is not an option. We need to obey the law."

"But our projects?"

"Boys, I've already called my attorney. You will be back in time for dinner."

Dr. Teplitsky stands at the door, watching the boys file onto the bus. Each turns and waves, and he waves back. As the last one boards, Colleen Worthington rushes up the walkway.

"I almost forget to ask." She fishes for something in her purse. She pulls out a bag, which she opens and extracts a pair of latex gloves. Next, she opens a slender box and removes a tube with a cotton swab on a long wooden stem. "Would you mind letting me take a sample of your saliva?"

The doctor knows what this is for. "I've suffered worse indignities. Is it necessary? I am their father."

"I'm sure you are," she answers, "but the court is going to mandate this test and it would help get the boys home quicker if you cooperate now."

"Do I have a choice?"

She shook her head.

CHAPTER 49

Tuesday, 9:00 a.m.
After seeing his first patient and then cancelling the rest of those scheduled for the morning, Dr. Teplitsky replays every word, every emotion of saying good-bye to his sons as he drives to his lawyer's office. Could he have altered the outcome? Prevented them from taking the boys away—even for a few hours? The short answer? No. There was nothing he could do, and he knew it. Now it was a matter of damage control.

Jud Abrams is a crafty personal attorney who is a jack-of-all-trades legal beagle. When he practiced in New York with his father on East 50th Street, he provided a full-service legal shop that served the Norwegian, Swedish, and Danish consulates. He bought and sold houses for their representatives, dealt with divorces, traffic tickets, business deals, kids smoking weed, unwanted pregnancies, and more. If it had to do with people and negotiating, then Jud Abrams was their man. Jud was small of stature, tightly wound, with pockmarks sprinkled across his face and wiry gray hair. When he sold the apartment building that housed his law practice after his father died, he and his wife, Suzanne, moved to the Jersey Shore to lead a simpler life. Or so they thought. Jud's New York City smarts shined through and his skills soon became obvious to all who came to know him. In no time, Jud had a full-time law practice; taking what he planned to be an "easier life" was put on hold. That was more than ten years ago.

"Can they do that?" asks Dr. Teplitsky. "Take them away for no reason?"

"They have cause," Jud says in a gentle voice laced with vestiges of Brooklynese. "This is a different world. Nine-Eleven changed everything. It opened the door for Big Brother on the grounds that society needs more protecting, and that door will never close again. Middle initials and birthdays are now needed to travel on airplanes. The day is soon coming when scanning irises will be a way of life to buy a ticket, to get on a plane, or to enter a building. Probably be necessary to buy Scott's lawn fertilizer, too."

"So how do we fight them? How do I get my boys back?"

"First of all, tell me if what they say is true? Where are their birth certificates?"

Dr. Teplitsky lowers his face; his jaw grows slack. "I don't have them."

"That's an easy fix. We'll just order new ones."

He looks up to meet Jud's eyes. "There never were any."

Jud does not flinch. He has learned from years of experience and the widest array of clients: no matter how obscure or how different or how incredulous the story, Jud takes the answer in stride.

"Where were they born?"

"In my clinic."

"Did they all have the same mother?"

Teplitsky shakes his head.

"Different mothers?"

"They don't have mothers, in the classical sense."

"I'm not sure what that means."

"It means that each had a mother."

There is a subtext in the way the doctor answered; Jud isn't clear what it might be. "Are you their father?"

"In a manner of speaking."

Jud looks up. "Exactly what manner are we talking about?"

"In the manner that I created them. I'm their mother *and* their father."

"You fathered them?"

"You could say that."

Jud puts down the fountain pen, an implement he still employs—he likes the way the ink flows from the pen onto the paper—despite the advent of computers, notepads, tape recorders, and the like. Not a total Luddite, but close.

"If you want me to help you, you need to explain where these boys came from, Isadore. Otherwise, my hands are tied and I won't be able to get them back for you."

"I understand."

He resumes taking notes. "Is your DNA in them?"

"No."

"Did you buy them?"

"No."

"Abduct them?"

"No."

Jud puts down the pen again. He takes a long look out the window. His office is in Brick Township, overlooking a small inlet. White sailboats catch the wind, tacking left and right. This is one of those moments when he would prefer to be sailing than speaking with a client.

Where is this going?

He ticks off on his fingers. "Okay. So you are not their biological father. You didn't abduct them. You didn't buy them from an underground black market. You're not running a pornographic ring out of your house that caters to pedophiles."

Teplitsky interrupts. "Is that a question?"

"I didn't think it had to be."

"It doesn't."

"I guess I'm thankful for that." Jud continues. "They don't have mothers in the classical way, but I am not certain what that means." He looks at the doctor in earnest. "Where did these boys come from? Did you have that many relatives who died and gave you their sons? That's another thing: they are all boys. Or did you create them out of thin air?"

The moment these last few words come out of his mouth, Jud Abrams knows the answer.

Tuesday, 10:00 a.m.

Buck takes advantage of the unplanned day off and does what he tries to do every month since returning from the war: visit Gravelly Graveyard. It is a peaceful setting at the end of Fairview Avenue, just south of Princeton Avenue. Bucolic. The one-hundred-foot-long by one-hundred-foot-wide shaded plot overlooks the Metedeconk River. Gravelly Graveyard, also known as Old Wooley Cemetery, had its origins when a stranger washed ashore in the late 1700s. When found, his pockets were filled with gravel. It is unclear if the gravel weighed him down as to cause him to drown, or if it was collected as his body tumbled against the unforgiving surf. Regardless of how he died, the man was buried in this pastoral setting near where his body was found; it forms the oldest cemetery in Brick Township. There was a gap in burials here. The last person intended to be buried in Gravelly Cemetery was interred in 1901, that is until Apollina

Karras and her father joined the area's forbearers—the Johnsons, the Wolleys, the Osborns, the Lecomptes—and a few other families. It took an open mind to let foreigners in, but patriotism at the War's end erased years of bigotry that were masked by generations of snobbery . . . and a loyalty to Buck so that he could pay his respects to his love, even though her and her father's bodies were never recovered.

Buck places a dozen roses on Apollina's grave, the way he does each month. He notices a mound of dirt not ten feet away. It's fresh. He stands and inspects the grave. Clean lines, corners sharply defined. He wonders who received special permission since the Karrases were the last to be interred here.

Cars rumble to a stop.

There's a hearse with large Cadillac fins, a police car with red and blue lights flashing, a black limousine, and two open-backed trucks.

Buck watches the driver pop out of the vehicle to open the back door. Otto and Jürgen Hauptmann pour out, followed by Trevor Reichmann and Mr. Von Schroeter; Hank Gephardt gets out of one truck, along with the minister. Two others emerged from the second truck; Buck does not know them. The men lift the casket—it is easy to manage—and carry it to the freshly dug site.

Buck nods as they pass him, they nod back.

Without any words spoken, the casket is lowered into the grave. The minister opens his book of Psalms. He is about to speak.

Buck looks at the freshly dug grave. He looks from Apollina's tombstone to Mr. Karras's. Then it dawns on him with the impact of the gigantic asteroid that killed off the dinosaurs, that they are burying Werner Hauptmann—the man who directed the German sub that sent Apollina to her death—not ten feet from his beloved's grave.

Buck wants to shout, to yell at them, to scream for them to pick another spot. But he knows it will fall on deaf ears. Instead, he gathers himself, spins and stomps away.

To a one, the small assemblage turns to witness Buck hop onto his motorcycle and leave, but not before he revs the engine to its loudest decibels, leaving black skid marks in his wake.

That same morning, Megan scampers to the library, intent on opening it earlier than the posted time. She has a plan. She would have preferred joining Jürgen at the graveside burial of his grandfather's bones, but he never asked. Had she told him she wanted to attend the ceremony, it would've created a dilemma for Jürgen.

* * *

"Are you sure there are no hard feelings? I wanted to be there for you," says Megan when they finally had the opportunity to discuss it. "But, I know when I'm not wanted," she adds.

"It's not that," he stammers. "I can't help it."

"We both know my sort of people are not welcome here."

"That's not true."

"It's not your truth, but it is for your father. Let's drop it. Besides, if I was going to go to any cemetery, it would be to visit my mother." Hearing these words gives her a stab of guilt. Megan promises herself to drive to Pine Brook as soon as she's able.

CHAPTER 50

Wednesday, July 16, 8:00 a.m.
Megan does not have to be at the library until ten that morning; she is anxious to see how Jürgen is doing after yesterday's funeral. They will speak later.

Hearing noises, she and Carly wander outside the house. The yellow backhoe belches smoke and grinds away, filling a back loader with the excavated dirt. No sooner is one filled and pulls away then another takes its place. As the day progresses and the holes for the new septic and foundation take their final shape, countless loads are hauled away.

The footings for the extension off the master bedroom are about to be poured. Cole peers through a surveyor to double check that the rough-hewn wooden stakes, connected by kite cord, that demarcate the boundaries have not been accidently moved, that the measurements and placements are correct.

Droplets of sweat form on Carly's upper lip. "The heat's brutal for these guys."

"Don't forget the attic. Jürgen's probably sweated ten pounds off." The image of him with his shirt off and ripped abs sends charges through Megan. She grows still warmer.

Carly taps Megan's shoulder. "Help me make lemonade for everyone."

Gabe hikes over to Yehuda, who uses a stirrup hoe to weed his vegetable garden, careful not to disturb the young shoots. Gabe stands there for some moments, fixing the scene in his mind. How many times has his father wished he had his own garden? How many times has he said that he wants to live by the shore? To run his toes through the sand, to feel the ocean wind in his face?

Actually, garden yes, shore no. Yehuda never wanted to live at the shore; he doesn't like to swim and it's been decades since he basked in the sun. Yehuda is a shade worshipper. But that vegetable garden? That was the trump card Gabe used to get Yehuda to agree to move to Island Bluffs, rather than have him succumb to, "You're getting older and need someone to take care of you," or "What happens if you fall down and get injured?"

"None of those whatchamacallit pendants connected to EMS for me," said Yehuda when Gabe suggested he would get him one. "That's for old farts."

It's all about psychology, thinks Gabe, pleased how it works to the advantage of those who employ it.

And thank God for Buck.

Yehuda aerates the soil with slow, deliberate strokes of a hoe. Seeds sprinkled when they first moved in, send green shoots–radishes, beets, carrots–piercing through the brown soil. Greenhouse plants flowering, some bearing results. Green beans and pea pods, red and yellow peppers, Italian eggplant, and rhubarb. Yehuda stoops to pick weeds. He kneels to study the cherry tomato plants. He flicks dirt off the leaves so they will catch more of the sun's rays. He pinches off secondary branches that will not bear fruit but zap needed nutrients from the developing tomatoes. He stands when he hears gravel crunching under Gabe's weight.

"How's your garden doing?"

Yehuda surveys the green sprouts. "It's doing."

"I can see that. It's what you always wanted."

"All my life. After your mother passed away, I stayed in the Bronx out of respect and guilt for her. If I had moved away, I would've felt that I was betraying her. But things happen for a reason, and now I'm here. I admit that the shore had little appeal to me, but now that I'm here, like I was telling Sadie the other day, I like it."

"But are you still good with *this* house?"

"Whatever happened in this house had nothing to do with you, me, or that boy Jürgen."

Yehuda looks from Gabe to the house to the men at work and back to Gabe. He beckons Gabe closer. Gabe takes a step; Yehuda wraps his arms around him. "You're a good boy, Gabe. Your mother would be very proud of you. And so am I."

Gabe squeezes back, savoring words he wishes he had heard more often.

"I love you, Dad."

"I know."

Wednesday, 11:45 a.m.

Having left the house and construction, Megan enters the library on a mission. She first has to shelve the returned books, order books that have been requested since yesterday, and catalogue a shipment of new books. She speeds through these tasks.

Finished with her chores, Megan yanks open an oak drawer and snatches a small box of microfiche. She loads the machine and scrolls to the date Jürgen's grandfather was declared missing. Then she rolls the film backwards from that day, her lips moving as she reads each headline out loud. She processes each page the same way: top left to bottom, across to the right and up to the top, and then back down the middle. Not reading words, but seeing patterns of letters. Page after page. She does not know what she's looking for, or if there's anything to be discovered, but she persists.

Nothing jumps up at her.

She continues to scroll back in time. Days and weeks evaporate. Then she sees it.

"Holy shit!"

Megan copies the article, rewinds the film, returns it, and sprints from the library.

She calls Buck's house; there's no answer.

Buck doesn't have a cell phone.

She dials her house.

"Is Buck there?"

"Is who here?"

Between Jürgen destroying the attic and the bulldozer digging out the septic, Carly can barely hear the voice on the phone.

"Never mind." Megan ends the call and heads home. She assumes Buck is keeping Yehuda company. For a split second, she considers driving first to the marina to check if Buck his there, but thinks otherwise. Buck has to be at their house.

She starts toward the door and then wheels. "Ms. Merriweather, I am sorry to do this, but nothing much is going on and I have an emergency at home. Is it all right if I leave now? I'll make the time up."

Ms. Merriweather was engrossed reading an article on the monitor. Without so much as turning her head, she waved her hand for Megan to leave.

"I love you for this," she cried out over her shoulder.

Megan's heart starts to pound when she rolls up and sees Buck's motorcycle. She turns off the ignition, yanks out the key, jacks open the car door, and breezes past a load of dirt being dropped into a truck, and then arcs around men hacking and sawing on wooden beams. She pauses to gaze at what used to be the attic. The roof is off, and framing the new second floor is well on its way. She sees Jürgen but pays him little mind. She needs to find Buck.

CHAPTER 51

Wednesday 9:12 a.m.

The roar of Buck's motorcycle slices through the nostalgic mood Gabe has fostered speaking to Yehuda while they stand in his garden. He sees the antique contraption approach. "And don't forget Buck. He's been a godsend," Gabe says.

"And he's been a good friend," Yehuda adds with a twinkle.

As he says this, Buck scoots around a truck that is lumbering down the driveway, topped with a tarp to minimize the dirt from dripping over the sides like brown rain. Some escapes. Buck skids to a stop and rambles towards them.

"And don't forget Polly," Yehuda whispers in Gabe's ear, "she's become a friend, too."

"Do you know where she is, now?" Gabe asks before Buck reaches them.

Yehuda scans the area, and then brightens up. He points. "Over there. In the tree. On a branch about midway to the top." The tree, with its vast arms, extends in all directions, welcoming the sea, the sky, and its many avian visitors. It is on the side of the house furthest from the workmen.

Gabe shields his eyes. "You've been out in the sun too long, Dad. I don't see anything."

"When the time's right, if she wants you to see her, she'll let you. Right, Buck?"

Buck joins them. He has no clue what they're talking about, but answers, "Right, with Eversharp."

Polly sees Buck and bursts into the biggest smile.

Wednesday, 12:08 p.m.
Megan breaks hard on the driveway and her car skids to the right. She hops out of the car and sprints to where Buck is standing with Yehuda and Gabe. She thrusts a paper in front of Buck. "Read this."

Buck and Yehuda lean closer. The print is small. Blurred. Yehuda labors to extract glasses from their case. Buck squints. He snatches the paper and holds it so both can read. They mouth the words in unison:

Tug Sinks off Point.
Captain and 17-Yr Old Daughter Lost

Buck drops the paper; he doesn't speak. He stares off in the distance, out to the bay punctuated by the red lighthouse. Though he has seen this headline before, its shock remains filled with incredulity, as if he has just returned from war's end and is learning about Apollina's death for the first time.

Yehuda waits for Buck to collect his composure. Clouds darken the sky. There is a crack of thunder in the distance.

Buck faces them. "The war was almost over. At least in Germany. No one expected problems from the Krauts anymore. Certainly not off our coast. Not like back in '42 when they sank all them ships. This was three years later. A lifetime when it comes to war."

"Is that why you go to the marina all the time? Hoping they'll find something of hers?" asks Megan, her eyes filled with romance.

"I joined the Army when I was sixteen. Used a fake birth certificate. Toward the end, I got stationed in the South Pacific. Finally saw some action. But before I shoved off, it was February; I got a three-day leave to see my girl. Lucky for me, there was room on a mail carrier flying to the naval base down at Cape May."

As Buck speaks, the electric smell of a coming storm fills the air.

Cole's arthritic football knees ache. He turns to see dark clouds churning; charcoal gray rain spouts dot the horizon. Waves grow taller. Frothing whitecaps erupt from the black waters. Waves crash in a thunderous symphony.

He cups his hands to his mouth and yells to a hive of men, "Throw a tarpaulin over the exposed wood frame." He points to where the roof used to be. "Gotta seal it down to protect their stuff."

Gabe and Carly both wish they had put their things in storage and moved out during the construction: while each has regrets, neither stoops to proclaim the high moral ground of, "I told you so."

It's a little past noon. Buck fishes around in his breast pocket for a folded paper. "Do you have a beer?" Yehuda yanks open the refrigerator. Buck twists off the cap and takes a long draught. He uses his sleeve to wipe off the suds. They wait. Buck finishes the beer, and then sits at the table. He unfolds the paper; it's a list of the crew of the *U-869*.

One name is circled: Wilhelm Höernberg.

"Do you have a phone book?"

"What do you have there?" asks Yehuda pointing to the scribed letters that toe and imaginary line with military precision.

"Had time to do some research in the library the other day."

* * *

With the doctor closing the clinic the day before, Buck used the time to research everything he can find about the *U-869*. He hunted through the volumes cluttering his shelves. He piled tome after tome on the floor and until they soon became chimneys of books, stalagmites of information. He scoured over lists, charts, and data gleaned from footnotes and references.

He finds the one he's looking for.

He flips through the pages and stops at the heading: *U-869*.

* * *

"Be back in a flash." Megan dodges a bulldozer and dashes into the house. She jerks open the end cabinet under which a black, wall-mounted rotary phone—now useless—still hangs, a reminder of a long ago monopoly. A newer, silver-toned cordless phone sits on the countertop. She grabs the aged phone book.

Buck thumbs through the soiled pages, searching for the number that will challenge one of the last remaining secrets of Island Bluffs. He looks at Megan. "May I borrow your phone?"

Buck dials.

The skies rumble; the wind whistles.

The storm draws closer.

The call goes through.

Time to ask questions that should've been asked long ago.

Time to move forward.

Time to expose.

CHAPTER 52

Wednesday, 11:24 a.m.
"Wait in the car fifteen minutes and then find the County Clerk's office," Jud Abrams instructs Dr. Teplitsky.

Jud marches into the Ocean County Courthouse on Washington Street unannounced. The courthouse, built in 1850, reflects a mid-nineteenth century interest in classical architecture. In this instance, the county's interest was to copy the Greek Revival-style courthouse built a few years earlier in Hudson County, brick-for-brick, carried by schooners from Haverstraw, New York. The bricks were unloaded at Robbins Cove at the foot of Allen Street. The Ocean County version has the same number of white Doric columns and the same massive, pedimented portico. Nothing original appears in the Ocean County version; its strength is that it is identical to Hudson County's sister building in every facet and quoin.

Jud turns the weathered brass knob and swings the worn door open. Matilda Kornheiser, as much a local fixture as is the American flag in the corner, glances up from her desk. She scampers to the counter designed to block anyone from entering the inner sanctum of county records. She is the gatekeeper. Its goalie. She has a string of shutouts worthy of an NHL record.

Jud hands her a stack of papers. Without explaining, he says, "This will save the county a lot of embarrassment and a ton of money."

She doesn't react. No one comes through that door with a tale she hasn't heard before . . . whether true or otherwise. Without bothering to look down, she asks, "And you are?"

He flips her his business card. "A local shark trying be your angel fish . . . just for today."

She reads his name. "Well, Mr. Abrams," she nods to the wall behind her, "we have harpoons for fish such as you. The last lawyer who tried to bully me lived to regret it. The poor bloke has to pee sitting down. Can you imagine?" Not even a smirk from her. "Now what can I do for you?"

That image does give pause. Message delivered. "Seems we have a problem that needs resolving, and these papers are just the ticket."

"For the moment, I will presume that you have a problem and you need my help. Could you be more specific as to how you would like me to help you with *your* problem?"

Jud has met county employees like this before, men and women empowered by fiefdoms they've created, surrounded by walls of security and administrative support. Seemingly impenetrable walls. But all walls have a weak spot. Find it and their veneer will crack.

"The short version, Ms. Kornheiser . . ."

"You can call me Tillie . . . until I change my mind." Her lips curl from strength, and a desire to please, as long as she does not lose control. Control is her daily manna. Gluten-free, of course.

"All right, then, Tillie, the short version is that Social Services picked up my client's children yesterday based on a misunderstanding about missing birth certificates."

"Why didn't you say you represented Dr. Teplitsky, Mr. Abrams? Everyone around here knows about that case. Pretty unusual, wouldn't you say?"

"I wouldn't say, Tillie, but I am glad you're aware of the situation. It makes this much easier. You see the entire matter's an oversight. Dr. Teplitsky is a world-renowned geneticist, researcher, and fertility expert, not to mention the score of local charities he helps . . ."

She cuts him short. "Then he must know the law. The births of at-home babies and those born in private clinics, for whatever reason, must be registered with the state within five days of being born, in order to get birth certificates. Our records indicate that every baby born in the doctor's clinic was registered properly, all, that is, except the ten he calls his sons. How do you explain that, counselor?"

"A mere oversight."

"From the tone of your voice, I couldn't tell if that is a statement or a fishing expedition."

"Oh, definitely a statement. The paperwork must have slipped Dr. Teplitsky's mind."

"A passel of kids like that? That's two basketball teams worth of oversights. Come now, Mr. Abrams, we both know I wasn't born yesterday."

Jud hands her a stack of letters.

She eyes the wad of papers. "Mind giving me the elevator version? This lift has six stops, so don't hold back."

"Okay. These letters state that every one of the birth mothers gave up their rights as custodians to Dr. Teplitsky. It's straightforward. He's their father and I would like you to issue birth certificates as such. You already have proof of pregnancies. The good doctor will be here shortly; he not only witnessed each birth, he delivered each baby himself. The two together should satisfy the county so this doesn't have to get any uglier than it already is."

"Not so fast. Given the age of these children, I can't issue birth certificates on my own. Only the State Bureau of Vital Statistics and Registration can do that once I submit the purported information to them."

"Tillie, that's a bit inflammatory. There's nothing purported here. It's all perfectly legit. My client is being forthright and needs these matters corrected."

At that moment the door swings open and Dr. Teplitsky struts in—gimpy leg and all—with more drama than is necessary. Jud introduces the doctor.

"Is this what you require?" The doctor clicks open the brass clasp on his Ralph Lauren-weathered briefcase. He extracts ten thick manila folders, each belonging to one of the boys. The folders thicken with each older child.

Tillie opens the top chart. It's Iario's. She reads the entries of the first page written in the doctor's careful hand, pointing line-by-line with her right index finger. When she gets to the bottom, she writes down the name of the mother: Shelly Granowitz. The father: Dr. Isadore Teplitsky. She repeats the steps nine more times, each boy with a different mother but the same father.

When she finishes, she waves the paper, as much for their benefit as hers.

"Ten boys. Ten mothers. One father." She pushes her glasses down her nose, and takes a gander at Dr. Teplitsky. "Impressive."

Jud continues. "The father's attributes aside, Tillie, may we initiate the process to obtain their birth certificates? We'll be on our way as soon as we collect the boys. This entire thing has been a terrible mistake."

"That's the first statement of yours I will agree with," she says. "But there seems to be a sticking point."

"Ms. Kornheiser," says Dr. Teplitsky, "*Sprechen sie Deutsch?*"

"My parents didn't teach us. They spoke German at home when they didn't want my sister, brother, and me to understand what they were talking about. I wish I did."

"I've heard that story repeated many times before. It's a shame. What I was going to say is that these are special children. I admit I made a mistake, but it is one that has no consequence to the state or anyone else, for that matter. These papers prove I'm their father, and I would appreciate your cooperation in correcting this somewhat unfortunate affair."

She smiles at the doctor, but her lips deflate when she gazes at Jud. "You, I like. Let me see what I can do to help you." She lifts the phone and stabs at the buttons. She turns her back. Colleen Worthington answers, they speak in whispers. Tillie nods. Then louder, "I see. I understand. I will tell them." Tillie eases the receiver into the black cradle.

Matilda Kornheiser grips the countertop with both hands. "I've just been informed that I have taken this as far as I can. Miss Worthington will be here shortly."

Dr. Teplitsky turns to Jud. "She's the social worker I told you about."

"I don't think her presence is needed here. Everything is in order now. It's just a matter of filing the correct documents."

"There appears to be a new wrinkle."

Jud grows suspicious. "What did she tell you?"

"Do you really expect me to answer that?"

The doctor raises himself on his toes. Leans towards her. He glances at the brass nameplate on the counter. "Ms. Kornheiser, is it? I'm an old man. These boys are my life. I need to resolve this as soon as possible so all of us can get back to our normal lives. I have patients that need me."

"I appreciate all of that, and we are working as fast as we can to do just that. Ms. Worthington will be here in just a few. Until then, we all need to sit tight."

"I'd like to be prepared for her concerns," says Teplitsky. Then adds, "To expedite matters."

"Since you are going to hear it from her any minute, I'll tell you. Apparently, the boys' DNA needs some explaining."

"We told you, and the paperwork corroborates," says Jud, "that each boy had a different mother. Their DNA has to be different. That was to be expected."

"Different on the maternal side, yes," she says, "but you said nothing about the paternal side." She glares at the doctor. "You didn't father these children, did you?"

"It's a matter of interpretation."

"Well, that matter of interpretation is what Ms. Worthington wants to discuss with you."

Jud shoots a furtive glance at his client, and then starts to protest. "Did you give them a DNA sample?" He didn't wait for Teplitsky to answer. "They would've needed a court order. Did they have one?"

Teplitsky telegraphs resignation. Jud is about to protest that it was illegal and it will not stand up in court when the doctor says, "This has to end now." Teplitsky clasps Jud's arm in a powerful grip. The effect is clear: the doctor will take charge. "I will be honored to explain how these boys came to be my sons."

CHAPTER 53

Wednesday, 12:28 p.m.
Slashes of lightning slice the air. Bombastic thunder crashes above, sending billows of concern coursing through all. White-capped swells rise eight and ten, and then twelve feet high. Towering mountains of water slam into the sand, reclaiming more and more ancient silica with each angry wave. On land, trees bend to the point of snapping. Branches of the red oak near the Berk house churn like whirling dervishes.

Cole's men are unable to lash down the tarpaulin over the exposed second floor.

This is the calamity Verity Frizzell predicted could occur.

Cole promises himself this is the last time he gives in to a client. In the future, regardless of the inconvenience, if someone has to move out during an addition to a house, they move out. No more Mr. Nice Guy; no one benefits.

The rains haven't come. Not yet. There's still time to try and salvage the furnishings.

Buck puts the phone to his ear and waits.

Across the bay of violent waves, the phone rings in the Barnegat Lighthouse. It rings and rings. Buck is about to replace the receiver when someone asks who it is.

Buck answers. "Wilhelm Höernberg, please." He is greeted by silence. Stunned silence.

The rains begin. At first, drops splatter one at a time. Soon they will come with greater frequency, pounding with the same intensity of pellets belting a metal roof, of hail denting car roofs.

* * *

Cole's men reinvigorate their attempts to secure the tarpaulin before the deluge ruins the Berks' furniture and belongings. Jürgen and another man wrestle the last tie into place. They make it just in time; water streams from their faces. Jürgen licks his lips.

Droplets turn into pellets. The rain falls in sheets.

Large globules sting their skin and tap dance on everything hard.

The men gather around Cole. "Good job," he calls out above the shrieking wind. "The rest of the day's lost. Everybody take off."

With the call ending as droplets start to fall, Buck helps Yehuda gather his garden tools, sidetracked all the while by what he must do next. The two hustle, as only two eighty-plus-year-olds can, tossing the hoe and spade and rake into the small tool shed Gabe bought for Yehuda at Home Depot. The prefabricated box shimmies in the growing winds. They pray it won't collapse. Worse yet, they hope it won't blow away, taking the tools with it.

Megan observes Jürgen secure equipment in his pickup. She struggles to get to him and slips, mud soaking into her jeans. "Buck was supposed to get married right after the war," she shouts. "Before they could, his girl was killed by that German sub that the *Searcher* found off the point. A torpedo missed a tanker and hit Apollina's tug by mistake. A second torpedo missed completely, made a full circle, and hit the sub. That's how she sank in these waters."

"That explains why he stormed off and made a racket when we were burying my grandfather's bones."

"He was there? Buck, I mean?"

"We were walking from the limousine, behind the casket. I saw Buck puttin' flowers on some grave. I thought it was his mother's. Never imagined it could be anyone else."

"It was Apollina's grave. His girl that was torpedoed by the sub."

Jürgen whistles. "Explains a lot, doesn't it?"

A jagged bolt of lightning pierces the air. A deafening thunderclap follows on its heels. It cracks the air with a force that causes sphincters to tighten. More electric spears attack the skies, giving off a hollow, eerie halo. The ocean is a maelstrom of frenzied forces.

Nature has declared war.

* * *

Jürgen glances over Megan's shoulder to see a corner of the tarpaulin come loose. He points to it. She nods; he sprints to fix it.

Jürgen gets to the second story in a flash. The outer walls are up, replete with window frames. The wood is raw, green, cut from young trees. Rooms are delineated. No sheetrock. Good thing because it would've been ruined, turned moldy. The tarpaulin is thrown over Parallams, 14" x 5 1/4", that run the length of the framing strong enough to support the new roof. A scaffold dangles from the north side, the corner where the tarpaulin comes free. Close to the northern red oak.

Megan follows Jürgen's every move, and sees him hurry to the front corner and jump onto the window ledge to reach the rope flapping like a demonic kite tail poised to cause chaos. The rope is beyond his reach. It flips upward the way an elephant curls its trunk back over its head. Torrents of water start to seep into the house. Furniture will be ruined.

The wind dies down long enough for Jürgen to stab the loose end, tug on it, and angle it toward the corner. He's about to secure it when a gust of wind kicks up and rips it out of his hand.

Jürgen lunges for it and misses. He mounts the sill again and changes his grip on a two-by-four so that he can extend his range; the right toe of his construction boot is barely on the ledge. His back faces the crowd below. The errant corner lashes to and fro, close enough to grip and then in a flash, it whips away from him.

Megan shouts, "Jürgen, leave it alone. Come on down."

He can't hear her.

She moves closer. "Jürgen, it's too dangerous."

The wind ratchets up another notch.

Buck stands next to Yehuda and all but screams in his ear, "I figured out their secret."

"Whose?" Yehuda asks.

Gabe is to Yehuda's left. "Secret to what?"

"I know what they're trying to hide," says Buck, waving his arm in an arc.

Yehuda half-listens. He's more intent on what's happening to Jürgen than to what Buck is trying to say.

Try as he may, Jürgen can't grab the flapping rope that is now slippery. His arms grow leaden; his legs throb, his toe is charley horsed. The rain pummels. He curls back and jumps down from the window ledge, scans the exposed area and grabs a white plastic bucket that bounces across the wooden floor like a Ping-Pong ball. He slaps the bucket upside down, stands on it, and slips through the beams on the adjacent wall to shimmy onto the swaying scaffold. From there, he has a better chance of reaching up to grab the defiant cable. The scaffold is unstable. All but Jürgen see the danger in this.

Jürgen is now outside the structure, edging toward the elusive rope, determined to secure it in place. He lunges for an edge that flutters above his head.

A volley of hail assaults him.

Buck continues to shout to Yehuda and Gabe. "You know the guy who swims across the inlet all the time?"

Megan snuggles into them, her eyes locked on Jürgen. "The man from the lighthouse?" she asks without turning away.

The guy in the picture in the library.

"Yup. Larry Hanson. His real name is Wilhelm Höernberg. He was the radio operator on the *U-869*."

Gabe squares up to Buck, ignoring Jürgen for the moment. "That old man's been hiding here all these years? Since the war? He's a Nazi?"

"I don't know about him being no Nazi, but he sure enough was a German sailor. Something tells me that him still being around here is connected to everything that you folks have been experiencing. The town higher-ups were all in on it. First it was their fathers, and now it's the crew running the show today. Their sons. Larry Hanson must've been the one living in your house in those early years after the war."

"You did say you saw lights on back then."

"They knew they couldn't hide him in the house forever. So old Sheriff Kreiser, the father, put him in charge of the Ol' Barney before it became a state park. Got the guy grandfathered into the sweetheart job."

Gabe asks. "What did he know about running a lighthouse?"

"He was a seaman. They know about lighthouses and such. What he didn't know, he learned. The critical part was keeping him out there, away from everyone else, so there was less of a chance of him being discovered.

He managed to avoid being detected for over sixty years. No one's been the wiser."

Carly shivers. She hears the part about the man being the radio operator. "How could the man have survived his sub being torpedoed? Wouldn't the explosion kill everyone instantly? And if anyone did survive, wouldn't they have drowned?"

"If he's that good a swimmer, maybe he could've made it," Gabe says.

Buck answers. "That's not it. The lucky stiff wasn't on the sub when it was hit. He was already on shore. Maybe he was sick with strep throat or tonsillitis. My guess is that the lucky bastard got appendicitis. Höernberg was holed up here sick and they got some Kraut-loving doc to fix him."

"Grandpa, remember those rain slickers and boots we found in the basement? Crew members must've stayed in our house all the time. It was a perfect place to hide, especially when one of them was sick."

Yehuda edges a step closer to the red oak next to the house; its branches whip in the wind, close to the flapping tarp. He scours the limbs and finds Polly. When he does, he sees an ugly scowl on her face; her piercing glare trained on Jürgen turns to demonic glee.

A lightning bolt pierces the air; thunder follows a second later. It's nearby.

Yehuda mutters. "Damn you, Polly."

Colleen Worthington marches into the County Clerk's office. A puddle forms at her feet. She slips the wet umbrella into the metal stand next to the door. There are papers at the bottom, tossed by those thinking it a trashcan.

"It's vicious out there," she says by way of a greeting. The rain pounds its staccato rhythms, a thousand snare drums striking in unison. Winds whistle through the old building, sucking out the air, creating drafts in their wake.

"I heard a fire truck pass. How bad is it?" Tillie asks.

"Trees down all over. Lots of places without power." She looks about. "Lucky we still have ours."

Jud and the doctor plumb her face for a hint of how this will be resolved.

Dr. Teplitsky approaches, his right hand rests in his left palm. The image is deliberate. "I hope you've come to straighten this out. The boys must be terrified being taken from their home, and this storm doesn't help."

Jud steps forward.

"Ms. Worthington, I'm . . ."

"I know who you are, and am glad you're here." She eyes the plastic chairs against the wall. "Let's sit down. This will only take a minute, but what I have to say had to be said in person."

"That's never a good sign," Jud whispers to the doctor.

Colleen Worthington hears him. "Depends on who's speaking, counselor."

Tillie Kornheiser stands, watching the drama unfold. No . . . not unfold. She watches this act come to an end. The lingering question will be what's behind the curtain when the next act starts. Those in the Child Services' office at this moment know the drama will continue, perhaps in a different venue, on a different stage. But sure as it's pouring outside, the Teplitsky play and all of its actors will reprise on center stage.

"Let me be blunt," Ms. Worthington begins. "We did a buccal swab from each boy. They are not brothers."

There's a twinkle in Dr. Teplitsky's eyes. "That should not surprise you. They each have a different mother."

She stiffens; her tone turns more acerbic. "Do you think me a fool? Remember, we took your swab as well, doctor. Besides not being related to each other, none of those boys are related to you, either."

"Your science is off, Ms. Worthington, because one of the boys *is* related to me."

She shakes her head. "We were *very* careful."

"Not careful enough," he says with a calm that comes from knowing he's right. "Iario, the oldest, he's my flesh and blood."

"How can you be so sure?"

"Because I am."

She opens the file and rereads the report, finds Iario's name, studies his gene sequencing, compares it to the doctor's and says, "Fine. We were a bit hasty on that one. That still leaves nine out of ten who aren't. Where did you get them, Dr. Teplitsky?"

Jud puts his hand on Dr. Teplitsky's arm. "You don't have to answer."

"I want to. I have to. If I do, maybe we can get the boys released and they can be home for dinner."

Colleen Worthington is losing patience. "I'll ask you again, Dr. Teplitsky, where did you get them? The black market? Are they stolen? Kidnapped? What's going on here?"

"If I tell you, will you let them go?" he asks her.

"You cannot tell her what I think you are about to tell her," Jud says, "no matter what she promises."

Dr. Teplitsky throws up his hands. "What's the use? I've managed to keep them under wraps until now. The boys have prodigious talents; I can't hide them from the world much longer."

Now it's Jud's turn to squeeze the doctor's arm for him to stop talking. The implication is clear: Jud is about to take control of this discussion.

Jud engages Colleen Worthington, eye-to-eye. "If the good doctor explains what it is you want to know, will you issue birth certificates for these boys? That's the deal."

"You're in no position to bargain, Mr. Abrams, and I'm not in a position to offer you anything. If I was," she hesitates, "I still wouldn't negotiate with you."

She turns to Dr. Teplitsky. "It's time for you to tell the truth."

"I have told the truth, Ms. Worthington," the doctor says with a sheepish grin, "it's just that I've omitted part of their story."

"Which is?"

"I made them." Teplitsky avoids Jud's glare.

"As in the laboratory?"

He nods his head and raises his brow, as if to say, *I know that's a tough one to wrap your mind around, but believe me, it's true.*

She puzzles over this declaration. "Where did the sperm come from, if not you?"

"There was no sperm. That's why their DNA doesn't match me, or for that matter, anyone else you might care to check."

She stiffens. "I'm no scientist, Dr. Teplitsky, but I know that to fertilize an egg, you need sperm. It's been more than twenty-five years since the first test-tube baby was born. I get that. But still, a sperm and an egg are needed."

"Not always."

The lawyer stiffens. "Are you certain you want to do this?" Jud's tone is crisp and firm. He knows where this is going. Laws have been broken.

If they prosecute, he will not be able to keep his client out of jail. "Isadore, I must advise you not to continue."

Teplitsky nods. "It's over." He looks at Ms. Worthington, his eyes imploring the next question.

She stands. Takes two steps, engages Tillie to see if she gets it, too, and then wheels to face Jud and the doctor. She kneels down on one knee, her head level with the doctor's.

"You cloned them, didn't you?"

CHAPTER 54

Before anyone sees or can react to stop him, Yehuda stomps into the house. Jürgen's safety is in jeopardy, and it's not from the wind or pummeling rain. It's from a spirit no one else is able to see except Yehuda.

Yehuda doesn't trust Polly. She's been on a vendetta ever since the tug sank and she took up residence in Werner Hauptmann's house. Polly is the one Elsa overheard Hauptmann speaking to. Babbling to. She's the one who frightened the man so much that his hair turned white overnight. And she's the one Hauptmann tried to hide from in the basement bathroom one day. It will come out later that Larry Hanson, known as Wilhelm Hoernberg back then, moved the chest to block the door. It will never be explained how the key was found inside the bathroom, when it could only be locked from the outside.

Megan screams. She points to Jürgen who has lunged for the wagging rope, misses, and grabs onto the edge of the scaffold, as it breaks loose. Jürgen's feet dangle much the way Buster Keaton would cling to the ladder of a runaway fire truck, swinging this way and that. If he lets go, he'll plunge onto a jagged rock wall. His legs flail to reach something solid; there's only air between him and severe injury.

Yehuda reaches the attic, unaware of Jürgen's precarious state. Yehuda breathes hard. Pain claws at his chest. He reaches for an ever-present pill from his shirt pocket. He slips one under his tongue, and then charges forward, not waiting for it to take effect.

Jürgen calls out. The tarpaulin whips about like a mainsail in a hurricane, smacking Jürgen in the face. It dazes. At any moment, it could snap and fly away. Jürgen is seconds from severe injury.

Jürgen glimpses Yehuda near the window ledge that, under the present circumstances, is an unreachable chasm between them.

Megan steps closer; Buck holds her back.

Gabe sprints to the side of the house. He struggles to lift an aluminum ladder mired in mud. He tugs; it's stuck.

Lightning crackles above Jürgen's head. The acidic stink of electricity fills the air. Megan scampers to Gabe; the footing is slippery. "Dad, you need to put that down. It's metal. It's a lightning rod. You could be electrocuted."

"There's nothing else around. If Jürgen falls, no telling how badly he'll get hurt."

Gabe digs in; this time the ladder budges. He wiggles it free.

Hail, the size of grapes, zings Jürgen's face and hands.

He strains to hold on.

His fingers grow cold and numb. They burn at the same time.

His grip weakens.

Buck is drawn to the tree branch closest to Jürgen. He can see Polly. His heart skips a beat. Time stops for him. He continues to stare. What Buck stares at disturbs him: the apparition is gleeful that Jürgen is losing his grip and is about to be hurt.

"Apollina?" he mutters in disbelief. Then again, he says her name louder, trying to get her attention.

Megan shrieks.

Eyes rivet on Yehuda, who is now leaning through the open frame. He swings out, a train conductor grabbing a passenger sprinting to leap onboard.

Jürgen's hand is inches away.

Yehuda laser-locks on Jürgen's fingertips. If he can only touch them . . .

As he stretches, he shouts in a booming voice that carries over the storm, "Polly, leave the boy alone. He didn't do this to you."

The wind blows harder. Lightning sizzles over the house. The rain beats down in torrents.

Jürgen struggles to hold on, his grip slipping.

Yehuda leans closer. His right foot, toes only, rest on a spit of wood. His right hand clamps onto the frame. He stretches as far as possible, careful not to slip or fall himself. Their fingers touch, then the scaffold swings away. Yehuda summons his spine to open up, for his tendons and muscles to stretch. The next time Jürgen sways toward him, Yehuda can grab his hand and pull him in. At least he thinks he can.

Yehuda bellows again, nodding. "Polly. Over there. It's Buck. He can see you, Polly. Is this how you want him to remember you? Mean and cruel and vindictive?"

Yehuda's words register. Polly turns to see Buck. Her black veneer of anger shows signs of cracking.

"How many more have to die, Polly? It's time to forgive. It's time to let go."

* * *

February, 1945, 2:00 p.m.
The tug chugs out to sea. Apollina searches the receding shore for a glimpse of Buck, but they are too far out. Her father shouts, "Ready the towlines."

They near the oil tanker and cut the engine. Apollina goes into action. She lifts the sisal rope and tosses it to the sailor leaning from the tanker railing. It falls short. She gathers it back, grabs a few more coils and then, with all her might, hurls it upward. This time he catches it. She repeats this step four more times and soon the ships are tethered in umbilici of ropes. The tug, protected with black tires lashed to the side, kisses the ship, dancing hip-to-hip.

Secure, Apollina's father yanks the dangling cord with the red wooden knob above his head. Three horn blasts announce they are ready to proceed.

Beyond the tanker, deeper into the ocean, an attack periscope pokes through the surface. Its lens swivels this way and that, until it registers on its target. The German captain toggles the magnification from one power to six-times power. He barks out coordinates.

The tug is on the far side, unseen by the sub's captain.

Apollina catches her breath. She is not used to heavy lifting. She leans against the wheelhouse, scans the shoreline, and then notices a blinking light. It comes from Werner Hauptmann's house on the point . . . over on Island Bluffs. She recognizes the succession of short and long blasts as Morse Code.

Apollina knocks on the window behind her and shouts to her father. "Over there," she points. "The blinking lights. What do they say?"

Theodore Karras, born in Thessaloniki, was a merchant marine in Greece. He reads the message, scratches his mane of black hair, and then turns to her in panic. "They're going to sink this tanker. Hurry." He points to the towropes. "Start untying them."

He lunges for the cord above the steering wheel and yanks.

Three short blasts.

Three long ones.

Three short ones.

S.O.S.

Save Our Souls.

He runs to the side of the tug and screams to warn the tank crew.

The captain of *U-869* issues the order. "*Brand eins!*"

Fire one!

The torpedo swooshes from its bay and cuts through the water leaving a white trail in its wake. The captain's pulse quickens as he follows the streaming tail until it disappears out of the scope's view. Though certain it is on target for a direct strike on the tanker's hold filled with oil, he barks an order to seal the lumbering giant's fate. "*Brand zwei!*"

Fire two!

Towropes unlashed, Karras revs his engines, coaxing the tug to put distance between her and the tanker. Rotors grab the water and churn. At first no movement and then the tug creeps forward, inching past the bow of the ship. If this were the Kentucky Derby and Apollina's father a jockey, he would be whipping the living daylights out of the horse's flank. As it is, all this boat captain can do is push the throttle forward full speed ahead and pray.

Apollina stands by, helpless. Fear and determination are etched on her father's face. She follows the sightline between the blinking lights hammering its message to an unseen ship out at sea.

Engine straining, the tug chugs past the tanker, and that's when Polly sees the periscope.

The *U-869* captain's eyes are glued to the oculus as he follows the second torpedo out of its chute. It is dead-on, headed for the tanker's sweet spot.

The first torpedo should have hit by now; there is no explosion, no telltale plume of smoke followed by billowing fire. The captain's face becomes a mask of concern. How could it miss? He is glad the second torpedo is on its way.

The tug skirts ahead of the tanker only to smack into the path of the first torpedo.

The noise deafens.

Apollina is catapulted over the side.

In the next second, the tug explodes sending a spiral of smoke skyward and licks of flame everywhere. Captain Karras dies in a flash.

Apollina is tossed into the freezing water. She struggles to move her arms; it's like swimming in molasses. The water is dark. Black.

She wiggles and writhes but is disoriented. Is she going up or down? The pressure increases in her ears. Her lungs scream for air. She flaps her arms and legs but gets no closer to the surface. Pain increases. It grows dark. Apollina pictures Buck standing at the dock. Waving good-bye. The motorcycle. The sidecar. She relives the way he tilted his head, the way she stood on tiptoes and kissed him. Sweet image.

Fire fills her chest.

In the blackness of her mind, she sees the blinking lights coming from the Hauptmann house.

Her lungs fill.

She sees a last image of Buck. Sweet, sweet Buck. She sees his smile.

She smiles back.

She will never get to drive that motorcycle.

Then all goes black.

CHAPTER 55

February, 1945, 2:15 p.m.
The skipper of the oil tanker hears three short blasts, followed by three long ones and then three short ones again. The tug captain is warning them. Warning them of what? He snatches the binoculars hanging around his neck and jerks them up. The seas are calm, the skies clear. He scans beyond the bow into the distance, no ships nearby. Nothing to collide into for miles. Icebergs don't come this far south.

He trains his field glasses in a wider sweep. That's when he glimpses what can only be an imminent threat: the telltale oculus of a periscope, a sinister sea-cobra searching for prey.

Not a second to waste. He barks out orders.

The heavy ship comes to life. The powerful engines go into reverse.

A torpedo approaches.

"More power! Crank it up. Get this lady moving," orders the tanker skipper.

The ship glides back.

The German captain loses the white line of the first torpedo streaking toward its target. Sonar picks up the thud of impact; he feels the shock wave and lets his guard down as the corners of his lips turn up, savoring the moment. He swivels the periscope to view the damage.

What he sees confounds. He jerks the periscope first left and then right. This can't be! The tanker is unscathed.

Plumes of smoke and tongues of fire engulf a tugboat that lists, and then sinks.

He changes the magnification by a power of six times, searching for signs of the second torpedo; it is nowhere to be seen. Given that they were launched in rapid succession, the second should have found its target by now.

The captain flips to a lower power to scan a wider area. Through the sight he sees a white frothy line that should be streaming towards its target; instead it is looping back towards the sub.

It is a rogue torpedo.

"*Sheisse.*"

He slaps the paddles into their recesses and lowers the periscope. There is no time to think about his wife and two beautiful children, about his golden Labrador retriever, the hunting lodge in the Bavarian Alps. Or about his parents.

He growls orders.

"*Nach unten! Nach unten! Nach unten! Ankommende torpedo!*"

"Down! Down! Down! Incoming torpedo!"

It is too late.

The second torpedo slams into the *U-869*.

All on board are lost.

* * *

Dr. Teplitsky meets Colleen Worthington eye-to-eye. She kneels in front of him. He offers her a hand. "You had better take a seat. My story will take some time."

Jud starts to speak, but the doctor cuts him off. "You need to hear it, too. Then we will all do the right thing." This last statement is made never taking his eyes off Colleen Worthington.

Teplitsky speaks *sotto voce*. Jud leans forward to hear better; so does Colleen Worthington. The doctor motions for Tillie to come around the corner and join them. "Don't want to leave anybody out now, do we?"

Dr. Teplitsky starts slowly. At a crawl. He wants to make certain they grasp the magnitude of the atrocities that he and the others experienced. Uttering these next few words causes a lifetime of pressure to be lifted off his stooped shoulders.

"There were six thousand of us. Three thousand twins. Only a handful survived. I am one. Some might call me lucky, but I'm not so sure. They injected us with poisons. Removed organs. Cut off arms. They gave us diseases, and then studied how we died. They performed blood transfusions from one twin to the next. And when one died, they almost always dissected the other to compare internal organs. Who knows what Mengele was trying to accomplish. He was mad."

A clock ticks on the wall. Tillie has worked here for thirty years and never heard the timepiece pulse before this moment, its clipped staccato punctuating the doctor's every word.

Rain pummels the windows. Rat-a-tat. Rat-a-tat.

Thunder explodes above . . . and yet they hear the clock tick. Tick. Tock.

No one stirs.

For a moment, Dr. Teplitsky is distracted; he detects rhonchi coming from Tillie when she exhales. The sounds are low-pitched, similar to wheezes. Secretions clog her air passages. Probably congestive heart failure. Afterwards, he will talk to her about it.

He recalls much. It pains him.

"I remember one time when Gypsy twins, boys, came back from the experiments. Mengele cut away the skin on their backs and connected their arteries and veins, trying to make them Siamese twins." Tears stream down Dr. Teplitsky's face. "To what end, I ask you? Dogs are treated better."

He takes out a white handkerchief, honks into it, wipes his eyes and continues.

No one interrupts. They can't. They are barely breathing.

The doctor's eyes widen, his voice stronger. "The Angel of Death, that's what everyone called Mengele, had some sort of affinity for my brother, Issacher. I don't know why Izzy, and not me. We were identical. But he fancied Izzy." He remembers what Yehuda said about Izzy being older but chooses not to mention it. Teplitsky continues. "Mengele tortured Izzy worse than the others. One day he put him in ice water, he was all wired up. Mengele wanted to see how long it would take for his heart to stop. And when it did, he wanted to see if they could revive him. They were able to bring him back, but Izzy was never the same. Then they cut off his testicles. They compared us every which way they could. Our blood. Urine. Even our feces. They went so far as to count the hairs on our bodies to see who had more. They injected chemicals in our eyes to change the eye color. He went blind in one eye. They tortured my poor Issacher until he couldn't take it anymore. He begged me to kill him."

From nowhere, a screech erupts out of Dr. Teplitsky, then he grows silent.

Colleen Worthington jumps; Jud Abrams' heart skips a beat.

Tillie sobs.

The doctor speaks in a monotone. Trance-like. "He was in such pain and I loved him so. One night, he pleaded with me with his good eye. He didn't have to say a word. I knew. I put a pillow over Izzy's mouth. I held it with all my might, but I didn't have to. He didn't struggle." Then he looked at each of them: Colleen Worthington, Tillie and Jud. "I never told anyone this before. I killed my brother."

"You had to," whispers Jud.

"I know it was a mercy killing, but still," says Teplitsky. "Still," he repeats. Again, he reaches for his handkerchief and swipes away his tears. "That's when I promised myself that if I survived the camps, I would dedicate my life not only to understanding how the horror of the Nazis occurred, but that I would do something about it."

"How *did you* survive the camps?" asks Colleen Worthington.

"I wouldn't have made it except for the fact that the war ended soon after Issacher died. Mengele didn't have time to kill me. If the war had lasted another month, I wouldn't be here."

"Then what happened?" asks Tillie.

He stares at the floor most of the time while he speaks. "I was sent to a refugee camp. From there I could have gone to Israel but something compelled me to get to America one way or another. I don't know why, but that's where I asked them to send me. The route was a bit circuitous, but I did manage to get here. Distant relatives took me in. Cousins of cousins. They saw to it that I got a good education. I worked hard. I made it to medical school. Maybe Mengele affected me in a good way. I went into research and soon became an expert in manipulating cells. It led me to becoming a fertility expert. In those early years, I was also interested in diseases that affected Jews. As it turns out, Ashkenazi Jews, those Jews from Eastern Europe, the ones Hitler went after, have a ten-fold incidence of breast cancer if they have the BRCA1 and BRCA2 genes. Later, we realized Sephardic Jews suffered the same problem. I did much of the original research that helped develop the DNA test. The test is an indicator of susceptibility, it is not a predictor that any one person will get the disease, but most women with a history of breast and ovarian cancer in their families are encouraged to take the test. The royalties from that paid for my clinic and my real research. Recently, a judge overturned my patents, but I don't care. They served their purpose."

"To fund your research," says Colleen Worthington.

"To accomplish my ultimate goal: to insure that the Nazi terror never happens again."

"By cloning," she says.

"Yes, by cloning," he repeats.

"Why? You know it's against the law to clone humans," she says. "What did you hope to accomplish?"

"Please, dear lady, don't think for a minute that I'm the only one doing it. The moment Dolly was created, did you think man was going to stop at sheep? Not on your life. Cloning pets is a huge commercial business these days. But they didn't stop there either."

"Pets are one thing, but people?"

"Most human embryos are cloned for therapeutic reasons. Research must go in that direction. For me, I don't care what reasons other scientists give for what they do. My reasons are purely selfish, so who am I to judge?"

"We have an obligation to regulate cloning," Colleen says, then adds, "don't we?"

"I can't be bothered by what other people think, about what's moral and what's not. And I especially don't value anything politicians have to say about this matter," says the doctor. "If you didn't experience the concentration camps firsthand and live to tell about it, then you have no idea what happened there. *Schindler's List* and all the other Holocaust movies just scratch the surface. There's no way to transfer the German horror to film. Certainly not for entertainment."

"No matter the reason, why take these steps?" asks Colleen Worthington.

Dr. Teplitsky grows bolder. Stronger. Empowered by his experience and knowledge. He scans everyone's face. "I did what I had to do for a purpose."

"Which was?" She needs to understand.

"To bring dead Jews back to life."

Colleen Worthington whips up straighter. She looks at Jud, hoping he might speak. Prays that he might interject. Explain. Clarify. Elucidate.

Jud clears his throat. "Were you looking to create six million Jews? One-by-one?"

"No, no, no. That's not it at all." His lips crease upwards. The thought of creating six million people eases the tension. The air in the room expands a bit. "Though I admit the idea is intriguing."

"Then please explain it to us. I'm your attorney and I'm supposed to tell you to stop implicating yourself. But I gotta tell you, you've got my attention."

"All of ours."

The doctor continues. "With the money I received from the DNA testing, I was able to buy artifacts of great Jews in history. I concentrated on their personal items wherever and whenever I could find them. I bought things collectors tend to skip over."

"If they were an artist like, say Marc Chagall, did you try to buy his paintings?" Jud asks.

"I wasn't interested in finished pieces like paintings."

"I think I know," says Colleen Worthington. "You would buy things like hairbrushes or toothbrushes or anything else that you knew would yield their cells."

He nods. "It was easy. Other than a lock of hair of Louis XIV or maybe one from the Beatles, most people don't value everyday objects because they're nothing special. Not like paintings or manuscripts or original musical compositions."

"But they were to you," she says.

"Very much so. I bought their notebooks, their handwritten letters, their manuscripts, their diaries, and any tools they used in making their art. The more personal the better."

"Collectors want those things, too," says Tillie. "My grandfather kept a thank you note from FDR when he helped him run for governor of New York."

"That's where my patent royalties came in handy. Whenever I found what I wanted, I would make certain I made the best offer or the highest bid."

"So who are we talking about?" asks Jud. "*Are* we at the level of Marc Chagall?"

A smirk of pride crosses his face. "There are ten boys. Macario, Aurelio, Arsenio, Alberto, Felice, Savio, Jacopo, and Leonzio."

"That's eight."

"Plus Jovanni, who's the baby, and Iario, who is the eldest."

"Who are they?" chorused Jud, Colleen, and Tillie.

"You are correct about one. Macario is Marc Chagall."

Jud whistles. Colleen Worthington gulps.

"Aurelio is Alberto Giacometti. Arsenio is Arthur Miller. Alberto is . . ."

"Albert Einstein," says Tillie.

"Precisely. Felice is Felix Mendelssohn. Leonzio is the Chief Justice of the Supreme Court, Louis Brandeis. Savio is Sigmund Freud. Jacopo is Jonas Salk."

"What about the last two?" asks Jud.

"I don't understand," says Colleen Worthington, her brow becomes ridges of doubt. "Why go through all this trouble? To what end? These men have already made their contributions to society in the arts, science, literature, and the law. Do you think they can replicate those accomplishments or that they could do better a second time around?"

She doesn't wait for the doctor to respond.

"How could you even know if they would continue where they left off in their previous lives? I mean, they may have the same genes as before, but are they the same people?"

Pride replaced the chalky white appearance that bathed the doctor when Colleen Worthington first entered the county office.

"That wasn't my goal. The world is definitely a richer place because of what these men accomplished. If they do continue in their own footsteps, the world will benefit yet again. You would be interested to know that Alberto is on track to become a theoretical physicist. He's interested in space. He wants to develop modules that will teleport people from one place to another. Even from one planet to another."

"So in the future, if they say, 'Beam me up, Scotty,' it would be because of Alberto?" says Tillie.

"The original Albert Einstein already considered a universe that curves back on itself in three dimensions of space and a fourth, invisible dimension of time. These theories conjectured that teleportation could be possible," the doctor explains. "Alberto appears to be picking up the threads of this where he left off. But the others are quite special, too. You should hear the music Felice is composing. But that's not why I did this. I did it for Jovanni. To bring him up in a world of love and nurturing. To be surrounded by Jews in a traditional, Jewish home."

"And who is Jovanni?" Jud asks.

"You can't guess?"

Ms. Worthington glares at the lawyer, her voice somber. "He's Joseph Mengele."

Jud smacks his forehead. "You brought *that* madman back to life? How could you? Why? Of all people."

"To change him. To show him that Jews are not inferior beings to be tortured and mutilated or to be experimented on like lab animals."

"But you created him in an experiment, yourself," says Tillie. "What's the difference?"

He pauses. He didn't expect that question. "It's not the same. *I* did it out of love. Don't you all see? If I'm right, he will learn that Jews are good people, people to be respected and treated humanely. When that happens, something good will have come out of the war. Then there will be a better chance that history will not repeat itself."

"It already has, doctor: the Rwandans and the Tutus, the Serbs and the Croats, Hindus and Muslims," says Colleen.

"Shiites and Sunnis," adds Tillie. "Mankind is hell bent on destroying each other, especially when there are differences between them."

"All sad and horrific. Maybe I can help prevent that from happening again by showing the world that with love and understanding, we can breed hate and intolerance out of future generations."

Colleen Worthington clears her throat. "We need to focus on the situation at hand. You made these boys by implanting their embryos in the wombs of high-risk mothers?"

"You make it sound grotesque. Like something out of the horror movies. That's not the case at all. Each woman was able to have her own baby. Without me, they never would have conceived. One for them, one for me. No one ever questioned the idea. That's why there are ten different mothers and none of the genes are the same. That's why they are not biological brothers, but still my sons . . . and I want them back. I've been a good father to all of them."

"Even Jovanni?" asks Colleen Worthington.

"Especially him."

"What about Iario?" Jud asks.

"What about him?"

"Who is he?"

"He's my son."

"But who is he in history? The others are all so famous."

"He's my brother, Issacher. Remember, we were identical twins."

Tillie is quick to understand. "You mean you cloned yourself?"

"He's my brother, and he's my son."

"He's you!" says Colleen.

The last statement is punctuated by the loudest thunderclap yet. It's as if God, Himself, has something to say about Dr. Teplitsky and his accomplishments.

The question is, *"What is He saying?"*

CHAPTER 56

At that same moment, an earsplitting thunderclap explodes above the drama at the Berk house. Gabe holds the metal ladder without concern, transfixed watching Yehuda make a last-ditched effort to lunge for Jürgen.

Buck glides to the base of the tree. He angles for a better view of Apollina.

Megan and Carly clutch each other, terrified that Jürgen could topple down any second.

Jürgen hangs on by his fingertips.

After multiple stabs, Yehuda connects with Jürgen's right hand. He tugs Jürgen closer. The wooden plank below Jürgen slips a notch. Everyone gasps. The boy slips away from Yehuda.

"Jürgen's grandfather did this to you, Polly, not him. Let him be," shouts Yehuda, his eyes never wavering from Jürgen's fingertips, willing them to move closer. Polly answers with a high-pitched laugh that only can Yehuda hear. "Don't make the boy pay for a sin someone else committed. It's time to forgive."

Megan shouts at Gabe. "Daddy, you've got to help them." She grabs the ladder.

When he sees her holding onto the metal, it is his turn to warn. "What about the lightning?"

Across the yard, at the tree base, Buck takes a step forward and cups both hands to his mouth. He yells over the storm. "Apollina! No more."

Polly looks at Buck, then at Yehuda, and then at Jürgen.

The skies grow lighter. A tree branch sways toward Jürgen. Jürgen senses the branch under his foot and eases weight onto it. Not supportive but enough to steady himself.

Finger-by-finger, Yehuda guides Jürgen to a two-by-four. When the youth plants more than a toe on the wood, Yehuda yanks him into the house just as the dangling scaffold gives way and smashes to the ground below.

A collective relief spreads over everyone.

Megan drops the ladder and heads inside the house; Gabe sprints past her.

Carly takes baby steps, mindful of the slippery ground.

Buck swirls under the tree, searching for Polly. She's nowhere to be seen.

Gabe reaches the top floor first; Megan is right behind.

Yehuda lies on the floor. Jürgen cocks his head sideways, an inch away from Yehuda's mouth.

"Grandpa?"

"What happened? Is he breathing?"

Jürgen does not take time to answer. He feels for the carotid. No pulse. Jürgen does not waste time checking to see if something is blocking the airway; Yehuda was just shouting seconds earlier. Jürgen leans back, scoots down a few inches and starts to compress Yehuda's chest.

Tears stream down Jürgen's cheeks.

Though they only just met, Yehuda could be the grandfather he never had.

Grasping the gravity, Megan drops down, quaking in spasms. "Grandpa! Grandpa! Don't leave us. Grandpa! You promised." She sobs over his limp body.

Carly calls nine-one-one.

Gabe kneels down to help.

Thirty compressions, two breaths. This goes on for ten, fifteen, twenty minutes.

Carly calls nine-one-one a second time.

EMS is on their way. Due to the storm, there are emergencies all over town.

Carly feels for a pulse. She places her hand on Jürgen's shoulder. "You did your best."

Jürgen ignores her and continues to pump on Yehuda's chest. He is not ready to stop.

Sirens in the distance.

Gabe stands.

"It's enough, son. We tried."

Megan drops down and puts her arm around Jürgen, then grabs her grandfather's hand and brings it to her lips.

CHAPTER 57

Yehuda hears Megan call his name. He feels Jürgen pushing down on his chest, trying to make his failing heart come back to life. The boy presses hard. Ribs crack. He should feel pain, but doesn't.

Gabe blows air into his mouth; it's sweet. Warm.

Yehuda's eyes are open. Darkness descends. Then black. A thready beat, beat, beat. Before the last sine wave disappears, a crack of light appears from above. The aperture widens. Yehuda no longer hears Megan. No longer feels Jürgen trying to push blood to his brain. No longer feels his son trying to breathe life into him.

Storm clouds part.

Yehuda's spirit hovers above Gabe and Carly.

Megan drops down next to Jürgen and plucks Yehuda's hand, kisses his fingers. Holds them next to her cheek.

Yehuda watches from above.

Polly floats through the open rafters and reaches out; their fingers interlock. She and Yehuda rise in unison toward the shaft of light. As they wend their way to a new journey, Polly lets go. Yehuda floats above her. His eyes beseech her to come with him, that they should go together. Her mission is finished, the anger gone.

Her story is over.

But Polly is not ready to leave; Yehuda will have to go alone.

Yehuda floats away from Island Bluffs. He has no regrets as to what happened to him as a youth or how he lived his life after being liberated from the camps. He is keen to start yet one more journey, a journey that will reunite him with his beloved Sadie.

Could he have done a better job raising Gabe? Could he have left a greater legacy of forgiveness than he did? He did get Polly to let go of her anger. After all, she saved Jürgen. And he got Buck to make peace with losing Apollina and stop feeling that he wasted his life pining away for her.

And now? Now he can devote all his time to Sadie.

All in all, it was a good day.

It was a good life.

CHAPTER 58

Wednesday, 7:30 p.m.
The thick, fragrant smells of fresh baked bread fill the house. Gaston, Dr. Teplitsky's long-time chef, is in his glory. There will be pot roast drenched in gravy, homemade biscuits, creamed spinach, and hot apple pie topped with assorted Ben & Jerry's ice cream for dinner. Flowers—a luscious mixture of amaranths, asters, chrysanthemums from Israel, freesia, hydrangeas, and irises. Towering gladioli transform the bouquet into a majestic centerpiece that is perched on the center hall's antique marble table.

The crystal chandelier is ablaze. The boys are expected any minute; Dr. Teplitsky is ecstatic. The day before, Colleen Worthington had one last question. "Are there any more pregnant women with this deal of yours?"

"Just one."

"Will you register this baby's birth correctly?"

"He will," Jud answers for him.

"Will you?" she points at the doctor.

"Yes."

"Can I ask who it is?"

Dr. Teplitsky does not answer her right away.

She tries to reassure. "The boys are obviously well cared for, and Lord knows they are thriving. I can't imagine a better environment for them. But it has to stop after this one."

"It will."

"I'm fascinated by your choices. So who is it?"

"Dolph Schayes."

"He was a great basketball player," Jud explains.

"I know who he is," answers Colleen Worthington. "I played for the Rutgers women's team. Schayes is a Hall of Famer. Good choice. You don't have any athletes in your brew. I like the choice."

Jud turns to the doctor. "You could've picked Sandy Koufax or Hank Greenberg."

"I know they are all Jews, and I get what you're doing," says Colleen, "but Jesse Owens would've been a great choice."

"Given the '36 Olympics," says the doctor, "you've given me something to think about."

"You just said no more."

He holds up his hand. "Not to worry. It is a great suggestion, though."

"Given the irony that dominates this story, George Burns or Groucho Marx would have been good choices, too," she says.

"There's a reason for every choice," says the doctor, annunciating each word to emphasize his choice was scrutinized and well-thought out.

"No doubt."

"So when can I have my boys back?"

"I will personally rush the papers through the system. Sometime tomorrow."

"Thank you." He stands to leave.

"One last thing, doctor."

He turns without speaking. He waits for the question.

"Are there any more surprises we should expect?"

"None to concern you."

"What is that supposed to mean?"

"Mean?" he shrugs. "It means whatever else happens, it will not reflect on you or your office. No need for you to worry."

"I'm learning that everything about you causes me to worry."

He tilts his head and contorts his face.

"Good day, Ms. Worthington. Tillie. No more worries for you."

Just me.

CHAPTER 59

Wednesday, 7:40 p.m.

The boys march into the house by height order, shortest first . . . that pretty much correlates to age order, too. A receiving line forms. One by one, they wait their turn to be hugged and kissed by their father. Jovanni is the youngest and shortest and goes first; Iario, though the oldest, will be followed by Arsenio, the tallest.

"Who's hungry?"

Dinner is a success. The boys gobble everything in sight. They take turns describing where they left off on each of their projects.

"Jovanni, what about you? How is your science project coming along?"

"It's stupid. I'm going to do another one."

"He's already killed a cat," says Leonzio.

Jovanni shoots his brother a look that could kill. "It was a stray. I wanted to see what was inside of it."

Dr. Teplitsky is more than alarmed. "You know better than that, Jovanni."

The boy shrugs. "It didn't belong to anyone."

"Regardless, it's a living thing. We don't kill living things."

"We killed a cow for our dinner," he says with a grin.

"That's different. It was done humanely, with rules. It was done for food."

"I don't see the difference."

"You may not now, but you will when you get older."

Later, in his study, Dr. Teplitsky sits with Iario. "Did they treat you well?"

"The food was," he searches the ceiling to find the right word, "unpleasant."

"One of the joys of being a parent is to watch ravenous children devour their food."

"Then you must've had a lot of pleasure tonight."

"You should only know. What else happened?"

"For starters, Felice kept drumming on a table top, composing music in his head. Alberto argued for pen and paper. He had theorems he needed to write down."

Teplitsky smiled. "They are so true to character. And what about Jovanni? Did he behave?"

"You know Jovanni."

"Did he pick a fight with anyone?"

"Everyone. You have to do something about him. He's getting worse. Do you really believe he will become a doctor? I can see where Jacopo will. But Jovanni?"

"Jovanni will, too. It's in his destiny."

"How can you be so sure?"

"I just know."

"If he lives that long."

"Why do you say that?"

"One day, he will pick a fight with the wrong person, and he won't have one of us around to save him."

"I pray that will never happen."

"Pray hard, Father. I don't have the same faith in him that you do."

Dr. Teplitsky thinks about this, shakes his head, and then says to Iario, "Then I will have to pray harder for Jovanni."

"As hard as you can, father."

CHAPTER 60

Friday, July 18
In keeping with Jewish tradition of burying the dead as soon as possible, Yehuda is buried two days later. It is a graveside funeral. Gabe's rabbi from the Pine Brook temple, who remembers meeting Yehuda on any number of occasions, presides over the service. As he prepares to speak, the rabbi is reminded of another funeral in this same cemetery not that many years back: Emily Berk's.

Gabe has his arm around Megan; Megan holds Jürgen's hand. Buck is alongside him. Carly sits in a car with the door open wide, watching through the wrought iron gate.

Dr. Teplitsky plants himself behind the family. In all his years of medical practice, this is the first time he has attended a funeral related to a patient. Not even when Olivia's son died, did he elect to attend. He told himself it was not his place to be there, that he had no relationship to Robbie. But he knew that was not true: he brought the child into the world. More to the point, he was responsible for the boy's conception. He should have gone to the funeral.

While Carly's surrogacy was critical to finalizing his master plan, and while he felt no warm and fuzzy feeling to her family, he did feel a link between he and Yehuda. How could he not? They were both survivors. They both shared the horrors of the war and the depravity of the worst of the worst. Yet, Yehuda came through with few scars. Dr. Teplitsky felt he had much to learn from Yehuda Berkowitz and, for this, much to thank him for. The least he could do was to pay his respects.

The rabbi concludes the eulogy with these words:

> As each year passes, we lose more of the precious few who can be called "Survivors" of the worst holocaust perpetuated on a people.

Those still with us are old. Some sick. How much longer do any have? But each serves as a stark reminder that we can never forget what happened to them. What Hitler did to our people.

Out of this darkness, the one lesson Yehuda Berkowitz leaves us is a majestic legacy that, while we should never forget what happened to us, we must learn to forgive. This was Yehuda's greatness. There was not a bad bone in his body. Not an ill feeling. He taught Gabe and Megan, and then Carly, when she joined the family, that life is too short to be filled with anger and hate. He loved his family. He loved his neighbors. He loved his work. And he loved his new friend, Buck. And most of all, he loved his Sadie, whom he now joins.

May his memory be bound in eternal love, and his soul rest in everlasting peace. And let us say, "Amen."

One-by-one, they will take turns tossing dirt into the grave. Before they do, the rabbi places sacred books on top of and alongside the plain pine coffin, for them to be buried with Yehuda. He explains that books that mention the Lord's name cannot be discarded or destroyed. They can only be buried in sacred ground, only in a Jewish cemetery. Gabe knows Yehuda would approve of and want books to accompany him on his journey.

Gabe grabs the shovel. Rather than drive it into the fresh dirt and haul out a heaping load, he flips it over and cajoles a small amount on its backside to demonstrate—by tradition—the reluctance to bury a person. The particles tingle onto the wooden casket, their sounds resonating in Gabe's ears and in his heart: his father is really gone.

We are sealing you in forever, Dad. Good-bye.

After a beat, Gabe jabs the shovel into the mound and this time extracts a shovelful. He feels its weight, hesitates, looks down, and then tosses the dirt onto the casket. He does it one more time. Then a third time. Finished, he is ready to give Megan a turn. Rather than hand her the shovel, Gabe follows Jewish tradition and stabs the shovel deep into the dirt. He steps aside for Megan to pull out the shovel and perform this final act of farewell.

Megan cannot bear to drop dirt on her grandfather. Gabe touches her shoulder and nods for her to try. She turns the shovel to the reverse side and scoops only enough dirt to cover the tapered point. She holds the shovel out, tilts it, and watches the particles float downward, thumping onto the casket. She pauses, tears stream down her face. She flips the shovel over, scoops more dirt and tosses it down. She plants the shovel into the mound and steps aside. Jürgen follows her and then Buck takes a turn. A distant cousin and a business colleague of Gabe's step up and repeat the ritual. There are no others waiting to take the shovel, and then a voice from behind asks for a turn.

"May I?"

Gabe moves aside so Dr. Teplitsky can reach for the shovel. As the others did, he turns to shovel face down and edges a small amount of dirt on the tip, closes his eyes, mutters some words to himself, and then lets it drop onto the coffin. He turns the shovel over and stabs the mound numerous times, shoveling in more dirt than anyone else. He stops only when he tires. He takes Gabe's hand. "He was a good man. I wish I had known him better."

"At least you got to meet him."

"It was brief, but he taught me much."

As they exit the cemetery, Carly gets out of the car. "I'm sorry I couldn't be there with you."

Gabe gives her a peck on the cheek. "It's bad luck for a pregnant women to be inside a cemetery, but somehow Dad knows you are here. I'm okay but I have to tell you that I miss him already. At least he didn't feel any pain and he died doing something very meaningful." Gabe pats Jürgen on the shoulder and gives a nod of thanks for him being there. No need for words. Jürgen nods back.

"It's strange, but sitting here, watching the funeral, I kind of felt his presence," she says. "And it was nice that Dr. Teplitsky was here. I wanted to thank him, but he seemed to disappear the moment the service was over."

"When he put in all that dirt, I think he was burying some of his own memories while paying respects to dad," says Gabe.

"All I know is that I felt grandpa's spirit while I was standing at the grave," says Megan, who has been waiting for Polly to show up ever since Yehuda passed . . . but has not sensed her at any time.

Gabe turns to Buck. "Don't be a stranger. You weren't friends very long, but you were the best friend Dad ever had. He loved you."

"He was my best friend, too," answers Buck. "I'll keep in touch. Besides, I don't have any family . . ."

"We're your family," says Megan, and gives Buck a hug.

Buck kisses the top of her head. "You know, little girl, my Apollina was your age when she died. When I first met you, you reminded me a bit of her. Pretty and feisty. Full of spirit. Seeing you brought back some of the good memories; took the sting out of the others. So besides me caring a heap about your family, there will always be a special place in my heart for you. This isn't the last time you'll be seeing ol' Buck. You're stuck with me."

Megan smiles in delight, and squeezes him again.

"Any thought of retiring, Buck?" asks Carly.

"And do what? As long as Doc needs me, I'll putter around his place. Although there is one door I need to close in Island Bluffs."

"The swimmer?" says Gabe.

"It's time he and I had a talk."

CHAPTER 61

Monday, July 28, 8:30 a.m.
It is an all too typical Jersey Shore day. A three-H day: hot, hazy, and humid. The kind of day that plasters clothes to the skin. Buck's joints ache, and when they do, he knows the weather's gonna change. The sun is out now, but beware, rain is on its way.

Buck cruises over the bridge and turns left onto North Long Beach Boulevard. He heads north, to the tip of Long Beach Island. The street name changes to Central Avenue. He makes a left on West Third and pulls into the parking lot of Kelly's Old Barney Restaurant.

"I didn't think you'd come," says Buck, easing into the wooden chair. They're seated in an open area to the rear of the restaurant, which gets the overflow when the tables in front are filled. Regulars at Kelly's prefer facing the bay so they can watch the sailboats tack across the water. Ol' Barney looms above the tables out back, where Larry Hanson, a.k.a. Wilhelm Höernberg, waits. It's before noon, but the glass stein clutched in his right hand is half empty.

No longer a working beacon, the lighthouse is little more than a giant red needle piercing the sky. Seen by day, it gives comfort.

"That's all you've got to say?" says Höernberg. He is short and barrel-chested, with a few wisps of hair sprouting from his pate. His eyes are a remarkable blue. As blue as the water in a Caribbean lagoon. After more than sixty-three years living in New Jersey, he still speaks with an accent. His fingers are stubs. Strong. Powerful.

Buck shrugs. "I'm not finished."

Höernberg opens up a gold case, monogrammed with his initials, and takes out an unfiltered cigarette. "Do you mind?"

"They stopped that in restaurants a while ago."

"Only inside."

"Most restaurants choose to ban smoking for their outside tables, too."

"Kelly's does," says Hanson. He shakes out the wooden match's flame; there's a whiff of phosphorus. Hanson takes a long pull. His teeth are nicotine-stained and ground down to nubbins. There are spaces where some teeth have been removed and never replaced. Buck wonders if he pulled them out himself. When the menu comes, Höernberg reads without glasses. "They know me here. As long as there aren't any customers in the back, they indulge me."

Buck mutters something.

Höernberg continues. "Why now?"

"It wasn't until the *Searcher* found this." He hands Höernberg the spoon.

The man takes it and cracks a jack o' lantern smile. He shakes his head and the years gone by melt away. "It's been a long time. I wondered if anyone would ever look for us."

"You weren't supposed to be in these waters."

"They wanted us to remain around Gibraltar; they were fools. The war was lost. We all knew it. My captain wanted us to go down in a flame of glory for the Reich. 'We will go to the Atlantic,' he announces over the loud speaker. 'We will cause as much damage as possible. They will never forget the *U-869*.'"

"They almost did," says Buck. "Once you went down, you were lost forever."

"Until now."

"I guess."

Höernberg takes another drag. "I didn't care if we were never found. What did it matter? The war was over."

"How'd you survive?"

He laughs. "I was sick that week. At first it was my tonsils. They were always getting infected. I could barely swallow. I was dehydrated and running a high fever. The captain wanted me off the ship so I wouldn't infect anyone else. The whites of my eyes were a little yellow, too. Probably hepatitis. So I stayed in the house, quarantined. Otherwise, I would have been on the ship."

"The house on the point?"

"The one your new friends bought."

"You know about them?"

"I'm still in the loop."

"Why doesn't that surprise me?"

Höernberg smiles at the distant memories. "The crew stayed there lots of times. We used to come on shore in rubber dinghies. The Missus Elsa, she was a great cook. We'd go into the basement. Play cards. Drink. Sing songs. Locals visited us. They even had a room for us to . . . you know."

"Get it on with some of the girls?"

Höernberg nodded. "It was nice."

"And then you got stuck there. In the house."

"Not right away. I was treated as a celebrity in the beginning. There were so many Germans living here, or their children who still believed in the Fatherland. It was like being home. In the beginning, I moved from house to house. They fought over who would have me. But then I got tired moving around all the time, so they let me stay in Hauptmann's house for a while."

"Do you know what happened to him?"

"*Nein*. The man was crazy. Always talking to himself. That's why the missus left for a couple of weeks. After my boat was sunk, Hauptmann started acting weird. Talking to himself. I couldn't take it, so when she went off to Camp Nordland I went to Sheriff Kreiser's house for a few months. I never saw Hauptmann alive again."

"When did you say you moved back into the house?"

He looks up. "Let me think. It must have been two years from the time my sub went down. Hauptmann had disappeared. No one knew where he went. I lived in that house for a couple of years. Tried not to draw any attention to myself. Hank Gerhardt's father had some connections. Got me papers. A new ID. After a time, they brought me out here, to stay at the lighthouse. It was better that way, not hanging around town and all. It drew less attention."

"But your accent? A German here at the end of the war? No one grew suspicious?"

As if by magic, Wilhelm Höernberg morphs into Larry Hanson. His voice changes, the accent disappears. Höernberg speaks as if he has lived in Barnegat Light, the actual name of the town where the lighthouse is located, all his life.

Buck is speechless. "Where'd that come from?"

"Elvis. Ed Sullivan. *Leave It to Beaver*. Dick Clark's *Bandstand*. American television and music are wonderful teachers. I lived here alone. I practiced and practiced. Little Rudi and Otto were my best audience. The old man brought them here to play at the lighthouse. I would babysit for them, and practice my English. We made it a game; they were the ones who really helped me perfect my American accent . . . and we liked the same shows. When I was ready, I went to town and wouldn't you know it, I passed for a local. Same way terrorists do today."

He takes a last puff and grinds the butt into the dirt behind him. He flicks the shards into the bushes. "Fooled everyone all these years. What gave me away?"

"The picture in the library. Why'd you let them put it there?"

"The sheriff liked it. He said no one would catch on. No one did, except you."

"It doesn't matter now. You've paid your dues. Been out here all these years. Sort of like being in jail."

"A nice jail," adds Höernberg.

"Just wanted to meet you. Good luck," says Buck.

He watches Buck drive away in his motorcycle.

Höernberg shakes his head.

"Americans," he says under his breath. "Impossible to figure out."

CHAPTER 62

Saturday, August 2, 6:00 p.m.
"Where should we eat tonight?" *I told you so* couldn't begin to make up for the loss of privacy, let alone the feeling that everything they touch is filthy and disgusting due to the construction. Eating in the Berk house is out of the question.

"How about Rick's?"

"Works for me," Gabe says.

"Sure, Megan will have a fish burger and you'll have your cheese steak, but what will I eat?"

Rick's American Café sits on Fourth and Broadway on the northern part of Long Beach Island. It is one of the better eateries on the narrow strip of land.

"They always have fresh fish. Let's take the boat across so we don't have to sit in traffic over the bridge."

"Will you promise to go slow? I don't think the babies can handle you smacking into waves as if they aren't there."

"You mean the babies or the waves?"

"Do you really have to ask?" says Carly.

Gabe feigns a "who me" look. "When do I ever go too fast?"

"Daaaaad! When don't you go too fast?"

"Thrown under the bus by my own flesh and blood. Cross my heart and promise to go slow."

Saturday, August 2, 7:00 p.m.
Once they're seated at the restaurant and have ordered, Carly puts both hands on the table. It has been almost four weeks since she first told Gabe about meeting Olivia. "I need to ask your advice." She looks from Gabe to Megan. "Both of yours."

Megan cringes. "You two aren't getting divorced, are you?"

"Of course not," says Gabe. He turns to Carly. "Are we?"

Megan slaps his arm. "Not funny."

"You're right, I'm not. What's this about?" asks Gabe.

Their food is served. To Gabe, she says, "You know the story." She turns to Megan and fills her in about Olivia and the other *twofers*.

"I don't get why you are thinking of helping them," says Megan. "After all, the deal was the same for each of you."

"That's what I thought in the beginning, too," says Carly, "but now I am not so sure. I'm inclined to come right out and ask Dr. Teplitsky to let the other mothers meet their sons," says Carly. "Where is the harm in that?"

"It's not that simple," says Gabe, "they signed away their right to ever see those boys again."

"But they are their mothers. Kind of."

"Legally, they don't have a leg to stand on," Gabe says. "We won't either when ours is born."

"That's troubling me, too," says Carly.

"Are you thinking that you would want to visit Teplitsky's baby from time to time? We talked about this in the beginning. We agreed to do the deal with Teplitsky because it wasn't about him and what he wanted, it was about us and what we wanted. How could you let those other women get to you?"

"I'm way beyond that, now . . . and it is not because of these women. They helped crystalize nagging thoughts I've been having for a while."

"Such as?"

"What if I won't give it up? What if I go to a hospital where he won't be able to waltz in and take it out of the nursery? That would stop him in his tracks."

"If I were his lawyer, I'd say you don't have a proverbial leg to stand on. You're asking for a major lawsuit, one we can't win."

Megan sees both points and is conflicted. "Carly, would you actually volunteer to take care of someone else's baby forever?"

"Putting it that way, maybe not."

"*Maybe not* is an understatement. How could you?" Gabe says.

"I would consider it." She thinks for a second. "I *am* considering it."

He nods towards her belly that's half above and half below the table. "We're not getting anywhere with this. One of those babies belongs to someone else. That was the price we agreed to, end of discussion."

"What if something's wrong with our baby?"

"There's nothing wrong with him, and you know it. Even if there were, would you swap them? Give him the sick one and keep his? That's not you." He paused for effect, to let the words sink in. He lowered his voice. "Now, about the other mothers? What are you going to do?"

"I'm going to ask Teplitsky to let them see their sons."

"Will you at least wait until after our baby is born, so he's not upset with you while you're delivering?"

"That was my thought before, but it's not fair to make these women wait a moment longer than need be. My next visit is in a couple of days. I'm going to ask him then."

Carly's cell phone rings.

She answers, holds her hand out for them to quiet down so she can hear, and then gasps, her free hand covering her mouth.

She stares without speaking.

She pushes her plate away, too upset to think of food.

This changes everything.

Saturday, August 2, 6:45 p.m.

Dishes cleared at the Teplitsky abode, the boys disperse to their rooms. They work on projects. Jacopo is investigating the possible link between vaccines and autism. One concern is with the flu vaccine that's suspended in Thimerosal. The mercury-medium, while minimal, is essential for delivery of the medication. It is known to pass the placental barrier. If it accumulates, it can affect fetal brains. Throw in eating tuna and swordfish, and the frequency of multiple vaccines, and it is possible that delicate immunological systems do not have time to rebound and strengthen before the next mercury-based onslaught, regardless if it comes from food or vaccines.

Jacopo tests the frequency of vaccinations in albino mice. He injects one group daily with the MMR vaccine—mumps, measles and rubella—and another group every two weeks. He repeats the experiment with animals deficient in glutathione.

Jacopo knows that some children have genetically reduced amounts of glutathione. Are they more prone to develop autism? Are they more prone if vaccines are given in shorter intervals? Cells naturally produce glutathione. Its function is to neutralize free radicals and reactive oxygen compounds. It has a role in maintaining healthy levels of vitamins C and E. Jacopo feels he is onto something big. So does his father.

"What do you want?"

Jovanni stands in the doorway of his room. Jacopo wants him to leave.

"I can stand here if I want."

"I know you can. Stand there if you want."

"Did you count your mice?"

This gets Jacopo's attention. "What about them?" He walks over to the cages. He points to each and counts out loud. He whips around. "You little bastard. What did you do to them? Three are missing."

"I ate them."

"No you didn't. What did you do to them?"

"Can't you figure it out? Why do you think I killed the cat?"

"You fed my mice to a cat?"

Jovanni rocks on his heels, hands behind him. Jacopo charges him. "I hate you, you little shithead." When Jovanni gets near, he lunges to tackle Jacopo. When he does, Jovanni raises his right hand. There is a Ping-Pong paddle in it. He uses it as a club and crowns Jacopo. It drives his head into the hardwood floor. Jacopo cries out; blood pours from his scalp and his nose.

The fight spills into the hallway. Iario leaps up the stairs and struggles to separate the two.

Dr. Teplitsky is in his favorite chair. The most recent copy of the *New England Journal of Medicine* is in his lap. He hears scuffling, charging feet, screams. A herd of buffalo stampedes through the house.

Dr. Teplitsky tosses down the journal and strides to the stairs in his limited way. Shouting fills the house. He needs to stop it. He does his best to mount the stairs.

At the top, he sees blood pouring out of Jacopo's nose and dripping down the side of his face and over his ear.

Iario holds Jovanni, who is swinging his arms hoping to land a punch. He stops when he sees his father. A black face engulfs Jovanni. "They said you made us in a test tube. That we're all experiments. That you wanted us to be Jews. To act like they do. Is this true?" The boy rages. He does not wait for an answer. "You will never be my father." He glances at Iario, and then the others. "And these are not my brothers."

Dr. Teplitsky opens his mouth to speak. He is transported to Joseph Mengele's lab. To the experiments. To Issacher and all his suffering. Dr. Teplitsky takes one step toward Jovanni. He raises his hand, which is against every principle in his belief system, but he must, he must teach the boy a lesson before it is too late. He swings at Jovanni, the boy ducks and the doctor loses his balance, his knee caves, and he crashes to the floor, hitting his head with a thwack.

The boys are frozen.

Dr. Teplitsky's head dangles off the step.

Iario slides down a couple of steps so he can look at his father, who is motionless and does not respond.

Iario cries out. He screams at Jovanni. "Are you happy now, you bastard? You've killed our father."

CHAPTER 63

Wednesday, August 27

Gabe skids to a halt in front of the Emergency Room at Ocean Medical Center. It's nearly a month since they received the phone call in Rick's about Dr. Teplitsky's untimely passing.

Few in the community miss him, which is a product of the doctor keeping to himself. His sons miss him. So do Buck and Gaston, and the rest of the staff. So do his patients. But not many others. While he was always a courteous neighbor, those with an inkling of the comings and goings of chez Teplitsky were uncomfortable with a man raising ten boys without a wife. And when it came to comfort levels, few were at ease around the doctor because of his elfin size, his twisted body, his bad leg, and his foreign accent. He was not one of them and never would be. Then again, he had no desire to fit into any group other than the one of his own making. Except for the shed catching fire, no disturbances were ever reported from either the house or the clinic. No excess noise. No kids' parties. Nothing to complain about. Yet, for all the good he did, for all the right reasons that he was a model citizen, he caused discomfort.

"Did you call Dr. Zucker?" Carly asks.

"You asked me that fourteen times. He's in the hospital waiting for us."

"Will you have him paged the second we get there?"

"He'll be waiting outside when we drive up. He can even push you in the wheelchair. How's that for service?"

"You don't have to be sarcastic. It's not like I ever had a baby before. I don't know how fast it will happen."

Gabe kisses her on the forehead. "You are so adorable when you're stressed out. It's very sexy."

She rolls her eyes. "I don't feel sexy right now. There must be something wrong with you."

"Not a thing, honey. I'm just a man in love with his wife who is about to have my baby."

Dr. Zev Zucker, Zee Zee as many call him, is a fertility expert who did his OB/GYN residency at Yale. Though his office is in Tinton Falls and not as convenient as Lakewood, he admits to Ocean Medical, which is closer than Dr. Teplitsky's clinic. He is of average height, nondescript in stature and looks, and has a comforting manner about him. The moment Carly met him she liked his easygoing way. After he examined her—she appreciated his thorough yet gentle approach, she asked that he be her obstetrician.

Gabe edges close to the Emergency Entrance. By the time he hops out of the car and lopes to open Carly's door, an aide is there with a wheelchair. Dr. Zucker pokes his head out of the door, and tells them he will meet her inside.

"Is Megan on her way? I want her here."

"She and Jürgen will be here as soon as they can. You don't want Sheriff Kreiser to stop them for a mile faster than the speed limit, do you?"

"Ugh. Why'd you have to mention his name on such a happy day." She lets out a yelp. Her face contorts. She forms an "O" with her lips and sucks air in and blows it out rapidly, counting the seconds until the contraction passes. When it does, she dismisses any thought of the sheriff and the unpleasant events that occurred during the past months in Island Bluffs. Instead, she says, "I wish Dr. Teplitsky had lived to see this. Without him, we wouldn't be here."

"I wish my father could be here, too."

"Maybe they're both watching from above."

"Wouldn't that be something!" He trails the aide who pushes her through the automatic doors. Gabe fills out the paperwork as Carly is wheeled to the obstetrics floor.

"Hang tight, honey. Be there in a flash."

"Don't dawdle. The contractions are coming faster and stronger. It's going to be soon." Not a second passes after saying "soon" when another contraction rifles through Carly. A painful moan escapes from her lips. It hurts too much for her to be stoic.

"You're six centimeters dilated," says Dr. Zucker. "No matter what the urge, don't push. We've got to move fast."

Carly takes many short breaths. "You promised an epidural. I don't want general anesthesia."

"I know, Carly. But there's no time. If I don't get these babies out soon, there can be complications."

The doctor goes into high gear. Gabe watches through a plate glass window; the Lamaze training becomes irrelevant. The head nurse won't let him gown up and be in the delivery room. She says one patient is enough to worry about. Had Gabe been a doctor, he would have had a ringside seat. No matter. There's plenty of time to share the experience of twin boys without seeing them taken out of her belly firsthand.

Thirty minutes and a C-section later, both boys are delivered without a problem.

The blond boy comes out first; he registers a ten on the Apgar scale. The second has a mop of dark hair. He registers a nine. Minutes later, his Apgar is a ten just like his brother's.

Megan and Jürgen arrive; Gabe walks them to the nursery and points to the babies.

"What're their names?" asks Megan. "With all the excitement this summer, no one ever talked about that. I'm dying to know."

"We were so distracted that we never got around to it. The names are going to be easy, but for different reasons." He points to the baby on the right. "We're naming him after my father: Judah."

"Like Judah Maccabee. The 'Lion.' Grandpa would be so proud."

"Actually, he had the same name. Yehuda is the Hebrew version of it. Rest assured, wherever he is now, he knows about little Judah."

"And his middle name will be for your mother: Ezra."

"Judah Ezra Berk," says Megan. "I like it."

"What's his name?" Jürgen asks, pointing to other baby, who, at the moment, was screaming at the top of his lungs.

"That mystery will be answered as soon as Carly wakes up . . . which should be soon."

As they speak, a hall door opens to the nursery, and Iario, Jacopo, and Aurelio march in.

"Where are the others?" asks Gabe.

"We didn't think the hospital would like it if we all marched in at the same time, so we came first. The others will come later. Aren't there rules about how many people can visit in maternity?" asks Iario.

"Not for a private room. We could have a party if we wanted. I'm glad you guys are here. It will mean a lot to Carly. We still can't get used to having all of you around."

* * *

Monday, August 4, 11:a.m.
It happened after Dr. Teplitsky's funeral. Few locals attend, but if others had, they would have been stunned to see so many people at the service. There are the women he has helped over the years and their families, Holocaust survivors, Jewish leaders, heads of charities that received generous annual donations from the doctor, and medical colleagues. So many show up that the service is not held in a funeral parlor but in Temple Beth Am on Carey Street. Many are forced to stand. Respects paid, most do not attend the burial in the cemetery. Tears flow for the doctor who had suffered so much, but gave back more. All are concerned about the fate of his sons.

"May I have a word with you?"

After the last shovelful of dirt is placed on Dr. Teplitsky's grave, Jud Abrams catches up to Gabe. As at Yehuda's funeral, Carly sits in the car, though now she is unable to be on her feet for any stretch of time. She spots a stranger trot after Gabe.

"What about?" Gabe asks the man, who is a head shorter.

"I'd rather not talk about it here," says the lawyer. "Can you meet me in my office, say in ten minutes? It's nearby. That big professional building on River Road. Between Yale and Roosevelt Streets. And please bring Carly."

Gabe traipses past an empty reception area stocked with four seats and a receptionist's desk. There's a short hallway lined with mud-brown filing cabinets, Jud's office, and a small conference room. Not a big operation. A career winding down.

"What's this about?" asks Gabe seated in front of Jud.

"Let's wait for Carly," Jud answers.

"She needs to go to the bathroom every two minutes. If it's not one baby, then it's the other pressing on her bladder. It's amazing that she made it through the funeral without a crisis."

Carly returns and plops next to Gabe. The office is sparse. Diplomas on the wall. The office is towards the rear of the building. Small windows. Not much beyond. Some trees. Roofs of houses. A Jiffy Lube on the corner.

Jud begins. "Let me get right to the point. I am Dr. Teplitsky's attorney, and he made changes in his will that affect both of you."

Carly's eyebrows shoot up, yanked by the invisible cords of surprise. Gabe glances at her, then back at Jud. There is more than a modicum of suspicion as to where this will lead. Seems Teplitsky continues to be shrouded in mystery. Even in death, he cannot be taken at face value.

"The doctor knew he was not in good health. He had an inoperable aneurysm in addition to his heart condition. It was only a matter of time. He always said he was lucky to have made it this far."

"We're both sad for his passing," says Carly, "and I appreciate everything he's done for me. For us. Without him, I wouldn't be pregnant. But where's this going? What's this about his will? Didn't he leave everything to his sons? I am sure they'll need it."

Jud studied each and—try as he may—could not hide a smile. "He wants to give you his house . . ."

Gabe and Carly start jabbering at the same time.

Jud holds up his hand. "There's more. He also wants you to raise his sons."

Carly and Gabe are too stunned to speak.

"I know this comes as a complete shock."

"Yeah . . . like driving to Atlantic City, making a wrong turn, and ending up on the moon," says Carly. "I don't even know how to process this."

"You need to know that he did this with great thought. He assumed that if he was no longer with us at the time you gave birth, you would want to keep both boys."

"Our agreement was to carry a child for him. His death came so suddenly that we haven't had time to think of its ramifications," Gabe says.

"I think what little you knew of him, this sort of planning should not be a surprise. Besides," Jud focused on Carly, "he had the distinct impression you were having second thoughts about giving up his child."

"Was I that transparent?"

"Most of the others felt the same way. He always expected it, but in the end, it worked out."

Carly pictured the sisterhood of *twofers*. It did not *exactly* work out. Had he lived longer, Dr. T would have witnessed time fanning the flames of rebellion.

Gabe interjects. "Where are we going with this, Jud?"

"A few weeks ago, I executed a codicil to the will. The doctor didn't want you to have to pay for his son's upbringing, education, medical expenses, in short, everything it costs to raise a child."

"We would've managed."

"No doubt. But he also hoped that this boy would not be separated from his brothers."

"I did meet Iario. He is an impressive young man."

"They were quite the imposing group at the funeral, today," Gabe adds. "We won't have a problem with them visiting their brother living with us."

Jud presses his lips together into a straight line. "I am not talking about visitation rights."

"Then what exactly are you talking about?" Carly asks. "Do you expect us to raise all of the boys under one roof? Our place is too small for that."

"I was serious that he wanted to give you his house. That was the plan. Dr. Teplitsky hoped you would agree to it."

"Why would we do that? That's ten more children in addition to our new one," says Gabe.

"And Megan," adds Carly.

"We could have our own reality TV show."

"I don't think that was part of the doctor's vision."

"Let's get serious," says Gabe, "to raise all those children would be Herculean for anyone. We're not related to them in any way. Aren't there any relatives?"

"Sadly, not. All of Dr. Teplitsky's relatives were killed in the camps. And as for not being related to these boys, in a way, you are. In fact, so am I."

"I don't see how that's possible," says Carly. "That makes no sense."

Jud knew this moment would come. He then retells the events of the doctor's life leading up to, and after, he made his fortune. From the twin experiments to buying the artifacts of famous Jews in the arts and sciences.

"You're telling us," Carly begins, "that Macario is Marc Chagall, Alberto is Albert Einstein, and the others are Alberto Giacometti, Arthur Miller, Felix Mendelssohn. Sigmund Freud and Jonas Salk."

"And Leonzio is the Chief Justice of the Supreme Court, Louis Brandeis." Gabe expresses in awe.

"I couldn't believe it the first time I heard it. It's too stunning to comprehend."

Carly realizes Iario is not mentioned. "What about him?" Before Jud answers, she continues. "Given what we've just learned, and I understand how the first letter of each name matches, Iario is supposed to be Dr. Teplitsky's twin. Wasn't his name Issacher?"

"That's right."

"But he is more than that, isn't he?"

"I don't get it," says Gabe.

"Identical twins genetically are two of the same person," she explains, "so if Iario is Teplitsky's twin, he recreated himself."

"This is getting into *Twilight Zone* territory." No one speaks. "There's still one left. What about the little guy, Jovanni?" Gabe asks.

Jovanni requires no preamble. "Joseph Mengele," answers the lawyer.

Jud launches into Teplitsky's goals and more to the point, his dream of raising the Angel of Death in a loving home of Jews. The doctor believed that nurturing would be victorious when pitted against the predisposition so many attributed to genes, when it came to morality and values. Bad could be turned into good. If the doctor were right, his thesis—put into practice via his sons—would be the first step in engineering 'hate' out of our collective DNA.

"Teplitsky might have believed he was Sam Jaffe," Gabe says, "but this is not *Lost Horizon,* and I'm not Ronald Colman and Carly is not Jane Wyatt."

"Hold on. His goal was not to transform the world into a Shangri-La. He needed to renew his faith in man, to believe that the Nazi horrors were misguided, and to do what he could to ensure they would never be repeated. Is that so terrible?"

"Put in those terms, we all want that," says Carly, "but what you're asking us to do is monumental. Even heroic."

"And he felt you would be up to the task. What do you say?"

Gabe blurts out without thinking, "It would take some doing."

Carly shoots him a look of bewilderment. "Would you even consider this?"

"There would be challenges galore, but the day-to-day living details have been worked out so as not to stress. As I said, the doctor set up a trust for his house and property. The terms are for the two of you to move in and live there the rest of your lives, or at least until the last child leaves. Whenever the house is sold, its proceeds pass to the boys. Megan and your biological son would receive equal shares of everything that Dr. Teplitsky's sons would get. You will want for nothing."

Gabe grabs her hand. "You never liked this new place, anyway."

"But we just lived through that awful construction. Are you willing to walk away from that? Away from your dream house?"

"I don't know what I was thinking that day when I bought it."

She gives him a peck on the cheek. "You weren't thinking."

Gabe continues. "You know how my father said that some things are *meant to be*. Maybe we were meant to be in that house. To find Werner Hauptmann's bones and set Polly free."

"And now we're not meant to be there any longer?" asks Carly.

"Maybe not. Maybe that was a stepping stone to a greater plan."

Jud jumps in. "With the money the doctor left you, assuming you choose to accept it, you could finish whatever is left to do for that house and use it during the summers. It's on the beach. Think of it as a large cabana. It's minutes from here. The boys will love to hang out there."

Carly shakes her head. "Gabe, you didn't answer me: would you even consider doing this? No matter how much money, no matter how many in help, the responsibilities are . . . well, I can't even describe what they are."

His face displays wonderment. "Do you realize the genius we will be surrounded by? The challenges we'll face helping to guide these boys to realize their potentials?"

"Are we capable of that?"

"Who is? And think of our son. Our biological son. Look at who his brothers will be. Think of their influences on him."

"Have you stopped to consider Megan in a house full of boys?"

"She's older than all of them. In a year, she'll be in college."

"From the sound of it, so will some of the others. And real soon."

"I think we should do it."

"Gabe, I wasn't sure you wanted one more child when we got married."

"I told you I did."

"That's true, but we'll be raising a dozen children."

"Big families like this," says Gabe, "the children raise themselves."

"And don't forget the staff," says Jud. "You can have as many as you need."

Neither Carly nor Gabe dare speak. This opportunity could provide a life of enrichment, joy, and pleasure that few have ever experienced. Overwhelmed by the good of it all, they embrace the Dr. T's belief that a loving environment will prevail over evil, and that Jovanni will turn out okay.

"Well, not hearing anything to the contrary, I am assuming that you are both good with this. You won't have to pack a thing," says Jud, "that will be done for you, even down to finding new toothbrushes when you get there. I have some papers for you to sign. Arrangements will be made for you to move in this afternoon, if you so choose. Rooms have already been prepared for you and Megan."

"And the boys know about this?"

"They do."

"And they are for this?"

"They are."

"You were *that* sure of us?" says Gabe.

"I wasn't, but the doctor was."

CHAPTER 64

Tuesday, August 5, 11:15 a.m.
Carly, Gabe, and Megan move into the Teplitsky home the next day. Jud Abrams arranges for movers to do the packing. As promised, new toothbrushes await them.

The boys could not have been more welcoming or courteous. It will take time to learn the likes and dislikes of each boy, but they make it easy, especially for Carly, since none have ever had a mother and are hungry for the warmth and attention she showers on each. They do everything to make her comfortable. Felice even writes a sonata for her. Arsenio writes a poem.

Under any other circumstance the trauma of moving into someone else's house to help raise their children would have been overwhelming, but there is Gaston, the full-time cook, Brigitte O'Leary, the head housekeeper, her two helpers, and Buck, who stays on to keep tabs on anything and everything.

Jud Abrams stops by at the end of the first full day to see how Gabe and Carly are managing. Surviving. He and his wife, Suzanne, raised a lone son and cannot relate to what the Berks must be experiencing.

"Is Buck around? I've got something for him," Jud asks.

"He's out back," says Gabe. "He managed to get Jovanni interested in building things. Channeling his energy into something positive. It seems to be working. They're making an elaborate tree house."

"That's the first good news I've heard about that boy yet. The doc must be beaming from above."

Gabe and Jud round the corner of the back of the house to find Buck with his arm around Jovanni, guiding the boy as he cuts wood with a power saw. They both wear safety goggles. The boy is engaged. Joyous. Buck taps Jovanni on the shoulder, tips his head that someone's approaching, and flips off the switch.

Jud gives a slight twitch of his head; Buck gets the message. He turns to the boy. "Jovanni, can you get me a soda, please. This hard work is making me thirsty."

"Sure, Buck." And he dashes off waving, "Hi, Gabe. Hi, Mr. Abrams." Both raise their palms to slap the boy high fives. "Anyone else want a drink?"

They both thank him but decline.

When Jovanni is out of earshot, Jud says, "That's a good thing you're doing. He was such a worry to the doctor, challenging the basic tenets of his so-called master experiment. Looks like you're making a ton of progress."

"All the boy needed was some extra attention. No one ever had the time for him. The other boys are involved in their own projects. And the doc? Well, he ran out of gas. I've got all the time in the world to make Jovanni feel special. I don't think anyone has to worry about him. He's a good boy."

Jud steps closer and hands Buck an envelope. "Open it."

He stands and wipes his hands in the ever-present engineer's red handkerchief tucked in the back pocket of his overalls. "What's this?"

"Read it."

Buck unfolds the letter.

"Read it out loud."

Buck makes a quick survey of the first few lines. He looks up. Thinks. "Okay, then." He steps to the edge of the shade to capture more light. "Says here that a trust fund's been set up so I don't have to worry about anything for the rest of my life." He reads on silently, then says, "There's one condition where the trust would be forfeited and I'm supposed to ask you what that is." He lowers the paper. "How much we talking about here?"

"Enough to take care of anything you need or want."

"And what's this forfeit thing about?"

Jud smiles. He planned to play this straight-faced, but cannot; the secret is too great. "The doctor knew how you've been alone all these years."

"So?"

"And he knew that you were on to him with the cloning. We're able to talk about it now because it's out in the open. I mean, among us."

"Yeah, I knew about it from the get-go. Thought the doc was some sort of freaky Frankenstein. But I didn't see anything bad come out of his experiments, so I kept my nose out of his business and my mouth shut. No need to poke it into a place it didn't belong."

"The good doctor realized that you did know from the beginning, and he appreciated that you never challenged him about it or called in the authorities."

Buck turns shades of a ripening tomato. "Live and let live is my motto."

"Just the same, he left something for you."

"No need. I'm pretty set, 'specially the way I live."

"Be gracious and take it, Buck. He had plenty to spare."

"What's this condition he's referring to?"

"When he first started the experiments, he wasn't certain he could clone a baby. There were so many variables; he had to proceed with caution. He started to test his theories on extra eggs he had harvested from his patients for *in vitro* fertilization. When those experiments worked, he next gathered cells from the famous people he wanted to clone. You know all about that now. He tested the DNA in those cells, to make certain they came from the same famous person. When he knew the cells were pure, he extracted their DNA and inserted it into one of the donor eggs after he removed its nucleus. Technically, this is called Somatic Cell Nuclear Transfer. It's the basis of cloning."

"Why are you telling me this?"

"Because it affects you."

"Those boys do affect me, that's for sure."

"Indulge me a little longer. Each fertilized egg is then shocked into dividing. After a number of mitotic divisions—are you following this?"

Buck nods. "Keep going. I'm old but I'm not stupid."

"It forms an early stage embryo with almost identical DNA to the original specimen. But the doctor didn't stop there. He was concerned about how fast or slow the cells would age. Would he be creating individuals that had short or long life spans? That was a variable he needed to control."

With all that has taken place, with all the explanations, this is the first time Gabe hears any of this. "Are you saying he was able to control aging?"

"To an extent. He couldn't slow it down, but in a few instances, he could speed up how quickly the cells divided."

"Why'd he want to do a thing like that?" Buck asks.

"Keep in mind that in the beginning, he wasn't certain anything would work. Once he was convinced, he set about doing something special."

"Seems he did a lot of special stuff," says Buck. "Look how he made all those spectacular kids. Trying to change Jovanni and how that boy sees the world. What he's done for Gabe and Carly. That's all first rate in my book."

"There is one more extraordinary thing he did. It has to do with his will."

"Yeah, what's that?"

Jovanni kicks open the screen door with a Diet Coke in each hand and heads toward them.

"Buck," asks Jud, "where's your motorcycle?"

He points. "Behind the tool shed, where I always keep it."

"Show it to me, if you don't mind."

"Want a ride?"

Jud smiles. "Let's just say that, after what all of us have been through, I have a fascination for vintage motorcycles."

"This one's a honey," says Buck and leads the way.

Jud tugs on Gabe's arm, his look says, "*Not so fast. Let Buck get ahead of us.*"

Jovanni runs up behind them. The boy is about to blurt out that he has Buck's soda, but Jud puts his index finger to his lips, that Jovanni should remain quiet. Jovanni's eyes twinkle at the conspiracy. He thrusts his thumb skyward, spilling some of the soda in the process. He giggles.

The gray gravel parking area alongside the shed comes into view.

Buck points. "There she is."

Jud jabs Gabe on his side and then moves his hand in rapid motion, indicating that he should take smaller steps, to slow down.

Gabe drapes his arm around Jovanni, not knowing what is coming next.

Jovanni looks up at Gabe, smiles, and snuggles into him.

Then Gabe sees.

A stunning woman winds her way up the driveway. She approaches Buck. She is trim and clad in a colorful dress with swirls of white and turquoise. Her sandals sparkle. Her hair is a majestic gray that is rich and lustrous. It's pulled back in a bun, held in place with a tortoise shell comb, revealing smooth skin and eyes that are by turns, mysterious and luminous.

A flower is tucked in her hair behind her ear.

Buck is confused.

He glares at Jud.

What sort of prank is this?

Buck looks back at the woman with quizzical eyes. They register a flicker and a smile grows across Buck's wizened face wider than Barnegat Bay, wider than the largest rainbow. Now Jud's gibberish makes sense. He recalls the day Dr. Teplitsky visited his little shack and poked around. He asked Buck about the jar with a lock of hair that was tucked behind the picture of a beautiful girl.

Could he have a few strands?

Sure, but why?

For an experiment.

Now Buck understands.

The woman exudes elegance and grace.

She nods towards the motorcycle.

"I believe you owe me a ride in that contraption."

CHAPTER 65

Soon after moving into the Teplitsky house, Carly experiences bloating. Her blood pressure rises above normal. At present, it's a mild case of toxemia. With the end of the pregnancy nearing, Dr. Zucker prescribes complete bed rest. "This is common in first pregnancies," he tells her. "For now, there's little risk to you or the babies. I want to make sure it stays that way."

"What could happen?"

"To you? Anything from a stroke to kidney problems to a case of diabetes. For the babies? Nothing much if you manage to keep everything at their present levels. You're not spilling any proteins, so your plumbing's working okay. If your blood pressure goes up, delivering the babies fixes everything. Try not to let that happen early. These little ones need to cook in that oven of yours a bit longer. The best recipe is total bed rest except for bathroom breaks. Got it?"

Sunday, August 17, 1:00 p.m.
Carly complies with the obstetrician's orders with one exception.

"Can't you wait until after the babies are born?" Gabe asks. "You know the doctor will have a conniption if he finds out that you're out of bed for a whole day."

"If it were for anything else, I wouldn't take the chance, but this is special." She rubs her belly. "These little fellas will have to understand. If they get rambunctious and decide to greet the world early, it will be Zee Zee's problem."

"Are you sure you want to go ahead with this? You can still bail."

The doorbell rings.

"Too late," she says in a singsong voice.

One-by-one, the *twofers* arrive; all have accepted Carly's invitation to meet their "other" sons. Vena Labriola flies in from Toronto; Shelby Andrews flies in from Beverly Hills; Breanna Macfarlane drives down from Boston. All bring their biological sons except Olivia. It was Jud Abrams's idea to invite Colleen Worthington. Tillie comes, too. Buck brings his special girl, whose name is Ipolani. It's Hawaiian and means "heavenly sweetheart."

How appropriate!

* * *

The week before, Carly and Gabe gathered the boys together in the spacious living room. Though there was enough seating for all, some chose to sit cross-legged on the floor. Jovanni fidgeted. Iario was inches from him, though it is no longer necessary to keep a tight watch. He is reacting well to Buck's personal touch and to the Ritalin their new pediatrician prescribes for his attention deficit hyperactivity disorder (ADHD). Jovanni is a different child.

"First of all, Gabe and I—and Megan—want to tell you how wonderful it has been for us living here with you. You've made what could have been a difficult transition for us, quite easy."

"We took a vote last night, Carly," says Iario, a grin plastered across his face. "We love having you." He flashes Megan a thumbs-up. "And it is great to finally have a sister."

Megan giggles.

Gabe clears his throat with as much drama as he can muster.

The boys chorus, "You, too, Gabe."

"It's mutual all the way around," Gabe says.

"Can we call you 'Mom' if we want?" asks Savio.

"I would be honored. But let's make that a personal decision for each of you. Carly or Mom, whichever is more comfortable." A couple of the boys clap, a couple whistle, and a couple more start chanting, "Carly. Carly."

Cheeks flushed, Carly raises both hands for them to settle down. "The 'mom' issue is the reason we wanted to speak with you tonight. About two months back, I met a woman standing across the street from this house. Her name was Olivia. We got to talking. You see she was one of the *twofers*. That's the name she gave to your birth mothers, herself, and me. *Twofers*. Your father made a deal with a select group of women that he would help each one have a baby if they would carry a second baby that he implanted in them. The arrangement was clear: each mother had to give up one baby to your father."

"How did they know which one?" Alberto asked.

"Because one was genetically related to the mother and one wasn't. That was the one they handed over at the time they gave birth. These women were surrogates for each of you."

Carly didn't know how they would understand, but she decided to spell it out without holding back.

"So," she continued, "each of you sort of has a twin born at the same time, but he doesn't share your genes. I want to make it clear that these are not blood relations."

"But according to Ms. Worthington," says Jacopo, "none of us are related by blood and yet we're all brothers. I don't see any difference between all of us and all of them."

Carly does not expect this logic. Then, again, these are not your average children. "You're right. If you want, you may all consider these other children your twins."

"Can we meet them?"

"What are their names?"

"Do we look anything alike?"

Carly claps for their attention. "First of all, I've not met any, but that's the reason for this talk. I want to invite them here, along with their mothers, so you can meet them. I'm thinking next Sunday. We'll have a barbecue. You can swim, play basketball, show them your projects, and do pretty much whatever you want. It will give you a chance to get to know them. But we're only going to do this if there's unanimous agreement to meet these brothers . . . along with their mothers. So what do you say?"

At first, no one speaks.

"Aren't you our mother now?" asks Leonzio. "I don't want to go anywhere else."

"No one is asking you to go anywhere. This is your home. And I'm your mother or your guardian or whatever you want me to be. The important thing here is that I need to know if you all agree to meet these people."

"What if they don't want to meet us?"

Carly glances at Gabe. She turns more animated. "I had lunch with most of these women a few weeks back. They invited me for the sole purpose of helping to arrange to meet you. If you agree, everyone will be here."

There are in accord.

"Now that that's settled, I need to speak to Felice alone." She tells him about Olivia and her loss.

How? What was his name? Does she have any other children?

* * *

By one in the afternoon, the *twofers* arrive with their sons in tow. Olivia comes alone. Awkward handshakes. Fist punches. High fives. Names repeated. Mothers meet "sons." Brothers meet brothers.

Carly promises Gabe that she will remain on a chaise lounge in the backyard where she can watch how everyone interacts.

Groups form. Some swim. Some mothers watch, others change into bathing suits and jump into the pool. The tennis net was taken down and some play three-on-three basketball at the far end of the court. Gabe makes certain that teams are intermixed with Teplitsky boys and their counterparts. There is a horseshoe pit. Beach volleyball with imported sand. Badminton. Gabe, Jürgen, Megan, and Ms. O'Leary oversee the activities.

Gaston flips hamburgers, turkey burgers, ribs, and Nathan's hotdogs. There are vegetable crudités, layers of fresh mozzarella and Jersey beefsteak tomatoes drizzled with aged balsamic vinegar stacked high like Napoleons, miniature potato knishes, tiny pizzas, and so much more. Jonathan Schwartz is heard over the backyard speakers, describing in detail, as only he can do, each piece played over Sirius FM satellite radio from the American songbook. Sinatra. Tierney Sutton. Jessica Molaskey. John Pizzarelli.

"Felice, I would like to introduce you to Olivia. She is the woman I told you about."

Felice wears khaki pants and a blue, buttoned down Polo shirt. He looks right at Olivia. "My mother told me about your loss. I'm so sorry."

Olivia is speechless. She steps toward him. Touches both shoulders with a feather stroke.

Felice and Carly wait for Olivia to speak. When she does, she says, "You don't know how many years I've waited for this moment. To see you. To be able to say, 'Hello.'"

"I'm pleased to meet you." He does not try to wriggle from her grasp. Olivia steals a furtive look at Carly; Carly nods in approval.

"Felice, would you like to get something to eat?" asks Olivia.

"You are quite remarkable." Ipolani leans close to Carly. "Most people in your situation would have left well enough alone. You and Gabe have done the right thing organizing this so they finally get to meet."

"It evolved from its own energy; it's nothing I deliberately planned to do." Carly shrugs. "It's true, the deeper I got into the pregnancy, the more doubts I had about this Faustian deal we all made. But meeting the other mothers put me over the edge, and I knew that this day had to come. Once it was fixed in my brain, I needed to do it. The sooner the better. I'm glad that day is finally here." She rubs her belly knowing she has few free days left.

"Regardless, you've taken quite the chance that some of these children—from either side—will become confused. One of yours may want to leave here and try living with the other family. Maybe more. Who knows what's going through their minds?"

"I realize I can't control what happens after today. But I don't want to. The boys should know who carried them. They should know there are other people in the world who care about them. Who love them."

"As I've said before, you're a brave woman," says Ipolani.

As the afternoon wears on, Carly gathers that Ipolani is an apt student. Dr. Teplitsky has given her a history. She is animated, charming, and becomes a wonderful friend to Carly. They chat away, stopping only to speak to one of the *twofers* that stroll by to thank Carly for arranging this opportunity. In time, as they get to know each other better, Ipolani becomes Carly's substitute mother. Buck, well, no one can take Yehuda's place, but true to his word, he looks after all the Berks and the Teplitsky gang.

The sky is a wondrous blue, speckled with small white puffs that float out to sea. Gabe runs helter skelter making certain there are enough drinks, towels, and whatever else might be needed as the afternoon progresses. Gaston wipes the sweat and smoke from his face. Feeding forty-plus hungry people, mostly teenage boys, challenges.

Around five, Gabe announces that all activities should wind down so that everyone can move into the conservatory. Buck has rigged a series of hoses for quick outdoor showers; mothers shower in the house.

When all find a place to sit either on the chairs, sofas or on the floor, Gabe introduces Colleen Worthington and Tillie, and Jud and Suzanne Abrams, as the professionals who helped make this gathering possible. Applause erupts.

"I am going to pass this pad around. If everyone will put your email, home addresses and cell phone numbers down, I will copy it and send it to all of you."

"Don't forget yours," a *twofer* calls out.

Carly, still sitting, claps. "It now gives me pleasure to introduce Felice, who will play a piece of music he has composed for this event."

They clap.

"In appreciation for all of you coming, I will play *Yesterday's Fantasy, Today's Reality.*" He steals a peek at Olivia. "I wish to dedicate this piece to Robbie."

Few know who Robbie is, but when they see Olivia, who is sitting next to Carly, squeeze Carly's hand and tears stream down both their eyes, they know.

The piece is breathtaking. It reflects the traumas and stresses, and the hopes and dreams of all present. The notes are, at times, lyrical and sonorous, they float and arc into ethereal spirals, they tease and turn playful only to swirl into a dramatic crescendo that climaxes in a delicate, yet urgent arpeggio.

They beg for an encore, but not before Jovanni presents Felice with a dozen roses, courtesy of Gabe's planning.

Nice touch.

The *twofers* and their biological sons thank Carly and Gabe for the wonderful afternoon, their generous hospitality, and for making their dreams come true.

Promises are made and promises will be broken.

Some will keep in touch; others will not.

No matter, it was a good day for all.

CHAPTER 66

Thursday, August 28, 5:00 p.m.
Back in the hospital, days after the party with the *twofers* and *their* sons, Megan, Jürgen, Iario, Jacopo, and Arsenio are in Carly's room after viewing the babies in the nursery. Carly's lids flutter.

Gabe whispers. "C'mon, guys, Carly is still dozing. It'll be feeding time soon; let her get a few more winks."

They traipse out of the room after each plants a kiss on her forehead.

In the cafeteria, they snack and talk about this past summer's happenings. So much has occurred. They take turns telling stories about the doctor and Jürgen fills them in about Buck's glory days as a star athlete. Megan enlists Gabe to share tales about Yehuda and Sadie. Periodically, the table erupts in bouts of joyous laughter.

"She's so beautiful," says Megan. "Do you really think she is Apollina?"

"Buck does," answers Gabe, "and that's all that matters."

"She has a cool name," adds Megan. She says it out loud, "Ipolani."

"Ipolani is Apollina," says Iario. All heads turn to him. "Father told me so. She was the first . . . before any of us."

Gabe has a hard time understanding who or what Iario is. Yes, he's the doctor's son. And, he is the reincarnation of his twin brother. But he's also Dr. Teplitsky, himself. It's bizarre to talk to him knowing that he's dead yet still alive in a different form. Does science know no boundaries?

"But what about Polly? I saw her spirit. She was there when Grandpa died."

"She tried to kill me," Jürgen mentions as a statement. By now, this is old news. He harbors no anger.

"Ipolani may be Apollina's clone, but did Polly's spirit enter her? How can we ever know?" asks Gabe.

"I don't know how much of this I buy into," Megan says. "It's such a stretch for me."

"I get it," says Jacopo. "The spirit knew to inhabit that house. It knew that Jürgen was the grandson of the man who killed her. Why not inhabit the body Father created so she could reconnect with Buck? You told us that Polly saw Buck at your house. It all fits."

"Regardless of what's real and what to believe," says Gabe, "Buck is happy. It's a shame he had to wait until the end of his years to find joy, but at least he found it. That's one more miracle your father created." Gabe looks at his watch. "Why don't you guys go home now? They should be bringing the babies in for feeding any minute, and Carly will need some help."

"Can't I stay?" asks Megan. "I want to hold the babies."

"There will be plenty of time when you come back tonight. Besides, Carly and I have something we need to do, and we need to do it alone."

"The letter?" asks Iario.

"Yes, the letter."

When Gabe enters the room, he notes that Judah has been fed and is sound asleep in his basinet. A nurse, who is from the Philippines with an ever-present smile, is taking Carly's vitals before she feeds the other baby. The nurse wraps the stethoscope around her neck like a scarf, puts the sphygmomanometer back in the silver basket hanging on the wall, and proclaims, "All normal." Next, she leans down, and snatches the dark-haired baby, who is wailing at the top of his lungs, and hands him to Carly, saying, "I can tell already, this one is going to be a handful."

"How do you know?"

She touches her head. "See these streaks of gray? I've been doing this for many years. The ones that hold tight onto my finger and don't let go, for the love of Jesus, until they get what they want, they are the tough ones."

"Should I be worried?"

Gabe discredits the statement; how could anyone know how a child is going to turn out?

"You've got an angel and toughie." She shrugs. "In the end, it balances out." The nurse opens the door to leave. "Push the button if you need me."

How long will it take for Carly to get into her maternal rhythms and be able to manage her twins' yin-yang needs?

The soon-to-be-named baby takes her left nipple and sucks hard.

Gabe leans over and kisses Carly on the forehead. "How do you feel?"

She winces.

"Does the incision hurt?" he asks.

"No, this one's a tiger. You heard what the nurse just said. Glad he doesn't have any teeth." She strokes the boy's head. "They're both so beautiful. I don't know how I could've ever given him up."

"That is no longer an issue," says Gabe.

"In the end, I know a deal is a deal, and I would've honored it. I steeled myself for just one baby." She kisses the boy again. "I will always be grateful to Dr. Teplitsky. But, two?" She beams. "This is more than I could ever have hoped for."

"Don't forget the other ten. They count now, too."

"I'm not, but I didn't give birth to them."

"Just the same, they've all embraced you, especially Jovanni."

"What was that movie? *Cheaper By the Dozen*?"

"Jeanne Crain and Clifton Webb," he says, pleased that he knows the story of the twelve children raised by a husband-and-wife-team of efficiency experts in Montclair, NJ.

"We can't forget Megan."

"The best and the sweetest."

"Spoken like a proud father." She eyes the envelope in his hand. "Is that the letter? Open it. We've waited long enough."

She strokes the baby's head.

The newborn continues to guzzle; she feels pleasure.

Carly could not be happier.

Gabe edges open the flap.

He unfolds the paper.

There's only one sentence.

Carly watches Gabe's eyes dart across the paper.

He reads it again; she wants to know.

His hand drops to his side, still holding the paper between his thumb and index finger.

"What does it say? What's the baby's name?"

He looks at her with hollow eyes, starts to speak, and then stops.

He whips his hand up and rereads the words.

"C'mon, how bad could it be? It's only a name. Is it that Jewish basketball player the doctor mentioned to Jud and Colleen Worthington? Dolph what's his name?"

"Could be," he says in a deflated breath. Carly misses the fact that the blood has drained from his face.

She snaps the fingers of her free hand. "Dolph Schayes, that's it. I was hoping for Sandy Koufax. That would have been so cool."

Without a word, he hands her the paper.

She reads the name out loud.

"Adolpho." She frowns. "Why'd he pick another name starting with the letter 'A'? We already have Aurelio, Arsenio, and Alberto."

Gabe doesn't respond.

Carly looks at the paper again. "I guess it makes sense. Dolph Schayes's real name has to be Adolph, and making it Adolpho is in keeping with the others."

Gabe still doesn't say anything.

At that moment, the door to the room swings open. A fair-skinned woman in her fifties, with salt-and-pepper hair, dressed in a powder-blue pantsuit with a cream, silk blouse, and a bit too much makeup, enters.

"How'd you do?" she says to them, her singsong voice a bit on the shrill side.

"And you are?" Gabe tilts his head toward her.

"I'm Siobhan Durning. The name lady." She waves a clipboard; it is apparent she is not a nurse. "Your doctor has cleared you to go home, but we can't release you until son number two is named."

"We were just discussing that as you walked in," Gabe says.

"So what'll it be?"

Carly is about to answer; Gabe squeezes her shoulder and says, "We need more time. Can we do it in a day or do and submit the paperwork ourselves?"

"Maybe in a parallel universe, but not here. This hospital is straightforward and non-negotiable about this: no unnamed babies leave this place. You should know that if you do need more time, the insurance company won't pay for another day, so you really do need to make up your minds. Once I have the name, we'll send in the paperwork and you'll receive his birth certificate in the mail in a couple of weeks. Then everyone's happy:

both of you, the little one who needs a name, me and my administrator." She steps closer and leans in toward the baby. "May I?"

Without waiting for Carly to reply, Siobhan scrutinizes the baby's face. She glances back at Gabe before studying Carly.

Carly fidgets with her hair.

"It's too early to tell who he looks like," says Siobhan.

Neither Carly nor Gabe answer.

Then Siobhan looks at Judah. "This one looks like you."

"Seems that way," Carly mumbles.

She steps back and looks from Carly to Gabe and back to Carly and, in her right hand, hoists a pen ready to record the name. "For the last time, what's it going to be?"

Gabe clears his throat. "Look Ms. . . ."

"Durning."

"Ms. Durning. You really did come in the middle of our discussion. If you don't mind, we'd appreciate it if you would step out of the room and let us discuss this further. After all, once we pick a name, the child is saddled with it forever. We just want to be sure."

Dimples appear. She waves her clipboard and the papers make a rustling noise. "You're not the only ones stuck on a name. I've got two other rooms paralyzed by the same dilemma. I'm going to goose them to choose and then I'll be back for yours. Work for you?"

Carly and Gabe nod.

When the door eases shut behind her, Gabe drags a chair closer to the bed; the baby, in need of a name, continues to feed.

"Why didn't you let me tell her?" Carly asks. "If Dr. Teplitsky wants Adolpho for Dolph Schayes, we have to honor that request."

He takes her free hand. "Carly, nothing would please me more than to name this boy after that great basketball player. Granted I'm tall and I played for Princeton, but I was never that good. To have a super athlete in the family would be a dream come true."

"So what's the problem other than by the time little Adolpho here becomes a star basketball player, you'll be in your early sixties and too old to play with him?"

"That's the least of my concerns."

"Then what is the problem?"

"When Dr. Teplitsky told Colleen Worthington and Jud Abrams this baby's name, he was telling a half-truth."

"Sure, he was. He told them the Americanized version of Adolpho: Dolph."

"Not exactly."

Her chest heaves. "Gabe, I'm too tired to figure out the innuendo and subtlety of what all this means. Could you drill it down for me?"

Gabe continues to hold Carly's hand. The baby is no longer feeding; he is sleeping peacefully.

"Think of Teplitsky's grand plan: fill the house up with famous Jews and then raise Mengele among them, showing the Angel of Death that Jews are kind, warm, generous, and cultured, and worthy of admiration. It would teach Mengele to be humane, and if he did become a physician, it would be to help people, not to torture or experiment on them."

"And it's working. Look how terrific Jovanni's been now that we're one large family and Buck is giving him the extra attention he needs."

"Don't forget his medication. I admit that all is good with him now, but the race isn't over."

"What's that supposed to mean?"

"It means, Jovanni is only nine-and-a-half years old; he has a lifetime ahead of him. You and I really don't know how he will turn out, do we?"

"But he's on a better track."

"Sure he is. No one will argue that. But tracks have a way of warping, and trains run the risk of derailing."

She pulls away from his hand, and strokes the baby. "I believe in Jovanni." She frowns. "You still haven't explained why you didn't want to tell that woman about Adolpho's name."

Gabe draws in a deep breath. "Because this baby is not the basketball player."

"That's the name the doctor gave him."

"*Dolph* was a diversion, so as not to alarm Colleen or Jud."

"Then who *is* this Adolpho supposed to be, if not Dolph Schayes?"

Gabe points to the baby. His eyes puddle. His lips quiver. "For Teplitsky his penultimate experiment was not really about Jovanni and coming to grips with what was done to him, to his brother, or to the other twins."

"I'm still not following you."

"Everything he did led up to his grand experiment."

"He told us that."

Gabe continued. "And for Teplitsky, there was only one Adolpho."

"That's what he named him."

"Carly, think about this. Who was behind the greatest tragedy in the history of the world?"

Adolpho equals Adolph.

Carly's eyes widen in horror. She eases the sleeping baby off of her and holds him out to Gabe. "Take him. What are we going to do?"

CHAPTER 67

Labor Day: Monday, September 1, 2008
The story of Island Bluffs is almost over . . . or is it?

Let's start with the town officials of Island Bluffs. No one directly associated with Werner Hauptmann remains alive: not Hauptmann or his wife, Elsa, not the original bosses at the American Fertilizer Company, not the elder Sheriff Kreiser, nor anyone else, save Buck, who may have had an inkling as to what was going on at that house off High Tide Drive in Island Bluffs during and after the war, but was unclear about it.

Then there are the offspring: Rudi Kreiser and Otto Hauptmann, and toss the son of the original owner of the local soda fountain–Hank Gerhardt–into that mix. Did any of them know what happened in the Hauptmann house during the war? It turns out, they knew plenty. But does possessing a sliver of knowledge make them guilty of anything? Should the blame of their fathers be extended to them?

The one who needs greater scrutiny is William Höernberg, a.k.a. Larry Hanson. He was a German sailor who had the good fortune not to be on his sub when it was hit by its own torpedo, sending his mates to meet their Maker. For whatever reason, the town felt responsible to hide him from the rest of the world, and therein lays the spinning of an elaborate web of lies and deceits by elders of Island Bluffs exposed when the Berks bought a certain house in foreclosure.

Should the powers that be in Island Bluffs be accused of harboring a war criminal?

Maybe. Maybe not.

Where does guilt by association fit into this tale?

While it is now common knowledge that the unraveling of the secrets of Island Bluffs began the day Gabe tied his boat onto that rickety dock, a public resolution of the assorted injustices foisted on the Berks by the town's elders did not occur right away. Rather, it began to take on a life of its own the day Megan captured Sheriff Kreiser slapping handcuffs on Gabe. She sent that video to the *Asbury Park Press*.

The responses and reactions to this tipping point were not immediate.

What took so long? Had Megan posted the video on a fledgling website known as YouTube, action may have been swifter. But Megan didn't do that.

Here's what happened.

The email containing the video finds its way to the managing editor's address of the *Asbury Park Press*, except she does not see it right away because she needs to deal with the issues linked to the new academic year. Asbestos in the school, mold in the kindergarten, hazing freshman as an initiation to the varsity football team, the upcoming presidential election, debates, Iraq, Afghanistan, nuclear enrichment programs, hole in the ozone layer, and more. No time to investigate a sheriff cuffing a citizen violating the building code.

Breathing room unfolds like an emerging crocus as local and national news slows to a trickle during Christmas week. Having little to do one day, the managing editor trolls through her spam file and that's when she stumbles across Megan's email.

"I want you to take a look at this," she says to the Monmouth County reporter, Pete Gerber. "The charges against this Berk guy look as phony as a three-dollar bill. Find these folks and see how it was resolved."

"It was nearly four months ago. How can there be a story now?"

"That's what I want you to find out."

"Can't it wait a little longer? My kids are home for Christmas week."

"Neither of us expects this to go anywhere. Take a few hours to check it out, and then put it to rest. Go enjoy your family."

Humoring his boss, Pete first attempts to call the Berk house in Island Bluffs. He discovers that the phone service has been disconnected while Cole completes the revised renovation that will expand the original plans to turn it into a beach house large enough to accommodate a dozen children, adults, and staff.

Pete next calls Sheriff Kreiser's office. When the reporter reminds the sheriff of Gabe's arrest, Kreiser says, "Oh, that? It was dismissed. No story there," and hangs up.

Pete renews his efforts to locate the Berks, but their new contact information has not been updated by the many landline and mobile systems that need to make these changes. The phone number for the Teplitsky house does not yet list the Berks as the new residents.

Pete Gerber calls his editor. "Boss, coming up with goose eggs on that video arrest. I thought it would be easy to locate them, but it's turning out to be harder than I expected. Can you forward the sender's email address to me? Let me see if that is still active."

That's all Pete needed. The reporter finds Megan, who leads him to her parents, and the secrets of Island Bluffs are revealed.

Carly is busy with the babies. The boys are now four months old and she needs to remain upstairs with them when Pete rings the doorbell.

Gabe ushers Peter Gerber into the study and shuts the door behind them, amused that the story has finally caught someone's attention, albeit time has rendered it irrelevant now.

"What do you want to know?"

"Everything about that day you were arrested for making an addition to your house. What got the town in such a tizzy? What was the real reason they came after you?"

"It's history now. Everything's been resolved."

"That's what Sheriff Kreiser said, too, but my editor smells a story. Can you review the key points?"

Gabe sighs. "There's so more much to tell than what was on the video."

"That's why I am here. We sensed there was more to the story"

"Where should I start?"

"At the beginning."

And Gabe does. He starts on the day he docked his boat and first walked around that dilapidated house. He fabricates a reason why he moves the family to Island Bluffs. No need to reveal anything about Carly's fertility issues or Teplitsky's grand experiment. Gabe grows animated discussing Reichmann and Von Schroeter, and how they try to first prevent them from making an addition to the house and then how they make multiple attempts to buy the house back at any cost.

"She really wrote five million dollars on the check?"

"Can you imagine? I thought he was going to stroke out right there."

Finally, Gabe tells the reporter bits of Yehuda's history, how Yehuda figured out that there was a false wall in the attic and how he, and then with Buck's help, discover the ship-to-shore radio and the forest of antennae and the ledgers used by Werner Hauptmann to help guide ships to their doom.

"So what happened to all of that stuff from the attic," Pete asks Gabe.

Gabe runs his fingers through his hair. "That's the darndest thing. We tossed it into a Dumpster and my father tried to burn it, but it wouldn't catch fire. We assumed the contractor got rid of it all."

"But he didn't, did he," said Pete, the story shaping up in his head.

Gabe explains. "Turns out he was a member of the local historical society and couldn't bear destroying any of it until some professionals could cull through it to see if there was anything important to save."

"Are you telling me that it's all been preserved?"

"Almost everything."

Gerber flips through his pages of notes, asks about a few points for clarification, and then follows, "Anything that I'm missing?"

"There's a matter of some bones in the basement."

"Whoa! Bones? Can't skip by that. Spill it."

Gabe fills Pete in on how the bones were confirmed to be those of Werner Hauptmann, but the mystery still remains as to how Hauptmann died.

"No foul play?"

"Not in the usual sense," says Gabe, "at least that's what my wife thinks. She's a forensic dentist." He does not want to share their notion that Werner Hauptmann was scared to death by a ghost named Polly.

"So how did he die?"

"Probably went crazy when he realized the Germans were going to lose the war and everything he had done and lived for was for naught. He just died."

Pete closes his book.

"Once I review my notes, I'm sure that I will need to call you to clarify some facts."

"Not a problem. There is one more thing."

"Oh?"

"We call him the swimmer."

Gerber's face gets contorted. "This gets stranger by the second. Who, pray tell, is the swimmer."

"This may take some time. Can I get you some coffee?"

Gabe starts with the first time any of them see a swimmer in the sound off the rocks near Ol' Barney. He describes the *Searcher* finding the fork and spoon, the plates with the Nazi insignia, and how they eventually identify William Höernberg. Gabe then relates how Buck drives to LBI and meets the swimmer.

"You're confirming that this man is still alive?"

Gabe nods.

"And his whereabouts have been covered up all these years by the folks in charge of Island Bluffs?"

Gabe nods, again.

Pete Gerber jumps to his feet and pumps Gabe's hand. "Mr. Berk, I can't thank you enough. For a little paper like ours, this is a story of a lifetime."

And it was.

Pete Gerber validated the manner in which this story began.

Many of the important characters in this story are already dead, yet it remains for the living to find the truths in the secrets buried in Island Bluffs.

In the end, Pete Gerber and the *Asbury Park Press* will collect the detritus dredged up by the storm of deceit that surfaced when a certain house on a certain bluff was purchased by Carly and Gabe Berk.

As a result of Pete Gerber's dogged determination and the many articles that resulted from it—for which he won the prestigious Best News Writing Portfolio Award from the N.J. Press Association—Megan's video is brought to the attention of New Jersey's rather rotund new U.S. Attorney General who will soon declare his candidacy for governor. After he is elected, the new governor will play a role, albeit a minor one, in this story.

A meeting is held in the Hughes Justice Complex on Market Street in Trenton. There, the fates of Sheriff Kreiser, the Island Bluffs' officials, and William Höernberg—a.k.a. Larry Hanson—are discussed.

Gabe's arrest is not at issue.

How Steve Freiberg finagled the rules and regulations and code violations is also not at stake.

Could the mayor of Island Bluffs and the other officials who helped harbor Höernberg through the decades be accused of a crime? Could it be considered an act of treason? In today's environment, have they committed an act of terrorism that transcends national boundaries or can it be construed as aiding and abetting a foreign agency, one that was once our enemy?

The Attorney General decides that this would have been a conspiracy had it been brought to the attention of the authorities when it happened in 1945, and during those first few years afterwards. More to the point, they would have been acts of treason punishable by prison and, in some cases, death for aiding and abetting the enemy. But that is no longer the case because the perpetrators are all deceased. While the secret of Larry Hanson was preserved over the course of two generations, one cannot accuse their sons for this dark chapter in Island Bluffs' history. Was living a lie all these years punishment enough? Perhaps it was . . . for all of them, Larry included.

While the authorities gave Sheriff Kreiser, the mayor, and the others an indirect pass, the townsfolk of Island Bluffs do no such thing. Those that did not resign from their positions were turned out of office at the next election.

Business at Hank's soda shop fell off dramatically and he needed to shutter its door.

Where does Larry Hanson come into this? He was, after all, a German sailor. But was he a Nazi? No. It turns out he was never a card-carrying member. Like all other German and Japanese soldiers at war's end, other than the worst of the worst who were hunted down, captured, and tried for their crimes, the everyday grunts who did the actual fighting were free to return to their countries, to their homes, and to their families.

So in the end, there was no need for the folks of Island Bluffs to harbor William Höernberg. Had he made it known to the authorities that he was trapped here, the consensus is that he would have been released and free to return to Germany. In a way, he was the longest-serving German kept in confinement since the end of the war.

When given the choice to return to Germany, he elected to remain on Long Beach Island.

Epilogue

October 28, 2012

A little less than four years after Pete Gerber broke his story about the secrets of Island Bluffs, a unique series of weather events combined to what would be forever known as Super Storm Sandy. It is a Sunday. The governor, a former United States Attorney who has now had lap band surgery to control his burgeoning weight as he considers a run for the presidency, orders a mandatory evacuation of Long Beach Island and the surrounding communities. Having made a few friends while living a shadow life on the island over the many decades, and with the veil of secrecy lifted off him when the Island Bluffs scandal was exposed, Larry Hanson chooses to ignore the evacuation order. He lives alone in a tiny cottage, takes long strolls on the beach now that he has stopped swimming in the sound, and engages every opportunity he has to fish.

On this particular morning, there is a striped-bass tournament after which the beachfront bar, the Sea Shell, will host an elaborate banquet for the contestants. In spite of the order to evacuate, most contest participants—one hundred fifty strong—attend. With the governor's edict set to go into effect at 4 PM, most will leave the island with two hours to spare. Not Larry Hanson. He catches a ride part of the way with an evacuee who drops him off at the Dorland J. Henderson Memorial Bridge, which is more often referred to as the Manahawkin Bay Bridge.

"You sure you don't want to come with us?" the man asks Larry.

Larry dismisses him with a wave of his hand. "This one will blow over like all the rest. Seen it a hundred times."

"This one is sounding beaucoups different," says the man. No matter, Larry will not be persuaded. He hoofs it back to his bungalow where he intends to ride out the storm.

Sleep is fleeting. Winds rip through the island that night, rattling the walls, ripping off roof tiles, and pelting windows with the rat-a-tat of a Gatling gun. Larry dozes on and off, and when he awakes that morning, he finds the ocean has breached the dunes north and south of his cottage. Power is lost; phone service is dead. Seawater pounds his front door; water fills his rooms. Outside, fires rage. Wires are down. Danger is everywhere. Landmarks vanish as waves roll across the island, submerging the island one foot of water at a time. Without power or news, he cannot know that this Monday morning, what is now described as an extra-tropical cyclone, has thrashed the island to a pulp.

The waves increase and smash Larry's house with the fury of a runaway bulldozer; the bayside front wall collapses inward, the roof snaps off and dangles in a severe slope. He snags a bottle of single-malt twenty-one-year-old scotch floating by and steps outside. The water is now up to his chest. Larry faces Ol' Barney, puts the bottle to his lips, and sucks down a long swig. It burns, the good kind of burn that makes you shake your head and think you can spit out fire.

He lifts his arm for another mouthful; Larry never sees the boat, ripped from its moorings, hurtling straight at him. It blasts into him like a Mack truck steamrolling over a doll, sending Larry spiraling into the dark abyss of the waters that, years back, had swallowed Apollina Karras.

Soon after Carly had the babies, Ipolani moved into Buck's house. She accompanied Buck each day as he continued to care for the former chez Teplitsky until rheumatoid arthritis limited her ability to help Carly. At first she could manage a walker but then grew too weak and was confined to a wheelchair. Ipolani deteriorated rapidly. The end came one night as she snuggled into Buck's arms. He held her without stirring for fear of waking her. He stroked her hair through the night. At daybreak, he snaked his arm out from under her head—it tingled with pins and needles—and kissed her forehead. Her skin was cold, but Ipolani sported the most angelic, peaceful appearance he had ever seen. He hugged her a bit longer, thankful for the time they had together, and made arrangements to bury her in the empty coffin in the grave in Gravelly Cemetery that he had visited each month since returning from the war.

* * *

Megan and Jürgen did not last past that first summer. He attended Lehigh, made the wrestling team, and joined the Theta Chi fraternity. He majored in mechanical engineering and had little time for a girlfriend. Their emails became less frequent, and he was not one to use Twitter.

No matter. Megan had little problem getting past her puppy love for Jürgen when she met Lucas Rothstein on her first day at Monmouth Academy in nearby Howell, NJ. Both seniors, they dated throughout the year and went to the prom together. Megan attended American University in Washington, D.C., and Lucas attended the University of Maryland. Megan played field hockey, joined the Alpha Epsilon Phi sorority and majored in international studies. In time, she outgrew Lucas and started dating others.

Carly and Gabe rose to the occasion, fulfilling Dr. Teplitsky's wishes to give his sons the greatest opportunities to advance their skills and interests. In short order, though younger than the majority of their future classmates, most of the boys soon left for college. Only Iario was age-appropriate. He enrolled in Harvard, majoring in philosophy. He would not follow his father's footsteps into medicine, but would become a leading scholar in humanism, studying and lecturing about the ethical theories of reason and scientific inquiry that lead to the practice of human fulfillment.

Macario (Marc Chagall) and Aurelio (Alberto Giacometti) displayed such prodigious artistic talents that local teachers could only help them so much. Though fifteen, Macario was mature enough to attend Yale's art program, after which he will attend École des Beaux-Arts in Paris. Aurelio needed more time at home, so he commuted to Princeton three times each week to take private lessons from the chairman of the art department. When the time comes, he will attend Columbia, and then join Macario in Paris.

Felice (Felix Mendelssohn) attends Juilliard and wins the Van Cliburn Competition at seventeen.

Unbeknownst to Carly and Gabe, Arsenio (Arthur Miller) submits the manuscript of his first novel to Ethan Ellenberg of the Ethan Ellenberg Literary Agency. It is built around the lives of Issacher and Isadore

Teplitsky—of course their names have been changed—and how the human spirit will triumph over evil. It is an instant bestseller and helps launch what will be a giant literary career.

Alberto (Albert Einstein), Savio (Sigmund Freud) and Jacopo (Jonas Salk) all go into the sciences. Alberto attends M.I.T. and Savio will trail Iario at Harvard and study neuroscience. Jacopo will continue Dr. T's interests in genetic engineering and attend U.C.L.A.

Leonzio (Louis Brandeis) will opt to attend the University of Chicago and major in economics, after which, he will apply to law school. Not surprising, he becomes a jurist.

Jovanni, now thirteen, has blossomed into an outstanding athlete and student. While he is no longer as rambunctious as he was as a child, he is stubborn in his own ways. Science appeals to him.

During these years that Carly and Gabe continue to nurture them, each boy starts to develop blood values that are higher than normal. Good lipids a bit too low, bad ones too high, glucose trending higher, glomerular flow through the kidney diminished, higher than normal blood pressure, mitral valve prolapse, and so on. None are life-threatening; most are controlled by stricter diets and more exercise. In each case, medications are avoided. But this will not always be possible in the future.

Jovanni is the first to come down with a major condition: Type I diabetes. He is stabilized with insulin but is stimulated to learn more about this disease. He spends more time in his father's lab, which has been maintained and used by his older brothers for their research. He leans toward a career in medicine, and wants to learn more about stem cells and how they may help cure his problem.

* * *

Monday evening, October 29, 2012

The generator in the Berk house kicks in as most of New Jersey loses electricity. Monster winds jangle the house, shake the windows, cause the aged lumber to cry and wail at the stresses they are forced to endure.

Electrical transformers explode in the distance. Pop. Pop. Pop. Fires erupt. Sirens blare. Flames lick the black skies in spite of the continuous downpour.

"Can we watch the storm from the porch?" asks Felice, who managed to leave New York on the last train out of the city before the MTA slammed the breaks on rail travel. A musical theme forms in his head and he wants to get closer in order to capture the sounds of the storm.

"This is not a time for any of us to be outside," says Carly. She grows concerned. "Gabe, where are the boys?" As everyone has come to call them, the boys are Judah and Adolpho. They are inseparable. Adolpho is the dominant one who chooses most of their activities. If Adolpho doesn't like what Gaston prepares, Judah won't eat it either. Adolpho appears wiser than his years and his droopy eyes give him that "old soul" appearance.

Gabe and Carly do everything possible to nurture Adolpho and make every conscious effort to give him the love he needs, that all children need. The boy soaks it up like a sponge. Adolpho shows an artistic flare, and his older brothers, when they are home, work with him on his drawing techniques.

"I thought they were playing in their room."

"I'll check." Buck has remained in the house since Sunday morning, not because he didn't want to be in his smaller home during the storm, but he knew Sandy was building up to an historic weather system and wanted to be available if anything happened to the Berk/Teplitsky house.

Moments later, he returns. "They're not in their room. I didn't see them anywhere."

Panic sets in. "What if they're outside?" says Carly.

Gabe darts toward the front of the house.

"I'll check out back," says Buck.

As soon as Buck lopes down the back stairs, he sees Judah and Adolpho on the merry-go-round that had been installed just the other week. Judah holds on for dear life as Adolpho makes it whirl faster and faster. They throw their heads back, laughing great big belly laughs.

Buck grabs Adolpho. "Stand here until I get your brother. Then I'm taking the two of you inside where you'll be safe, and before you catch colds."

Buck grabs the metal bar and rotates Judah back to him. In those couple of seconds, Adolpho traipses off toward the swings. Buck tells Judah to return to the house and watches to make certain he does.

Buck starts after Adolpho. Lightning crackles overhead and hits the tree ten feet from the swings. Buck looks on in horror. If the lightning goes down the tree or jumps to the swing, that's the end of Adolpho. Buck calls out to the boy, but he doesn't stop. Buck dashes toward him but slips on the wet grass, and falls face down. Buck struggles to get up. A large limb snaps off the tree and crashes down on him with a ton of blunt force. He dies instantly.

Adolpho hears the snap of the branch and turns. He sees Buck slip and fall and then the tree limb crash down on him. This amuses him.

One week post Super Storm Sandy

The aftermath of Hurricane Sandy devastates millions and millions. Fortunate for those in Lakewood, it is far enough away from the ocean that a tidal surge was never the issue; wind and tree damage created enormous problems and loss of life.

All mourn Buck.

As day-to-activities resume, Jovanni, who has bonded with Adolpho in a way different than he has with his other brothers, and who is more protective of Adolpho than of Judah, performs experiments on stem cells. He hopes to find a better treatment for his diabetes than having a glucometer sticking into his sides to help regulate his insulin pump.

Jovanni has always been aware of a freezer in the lab, but has never explored it.

On this day he does.

Deep in a corner, he approaches a brightly polished silver cylinder tucked behind a large storage cabinet filled with beakers and supplies. This specialized freezer is vacuum-sealed. Locked. He notes a liquid nitrogen sign. There is also a yellow, Biohazard label.

He glances about for the key, finds it, and opens the container. A plume of white vapor erupts into the air. Adolpho peers inside: racks of test tubes. He grabs tongs and, with a feather touch, lifts the first one: his father's name is on the label. There are a dozen more like this one. He studies the next batch. Albert Einstein's name is on each. Adjacent to these, are a dozen Arthur Millers. Twelve Jonas Salks. One-by-one, he discovers the cells that formed his brothers. That formed him.

He views the last groupings: He picks up a tube and grins.

Joseph Mengele.

Here is the answer to his diabetes. He will use his own stem cells to make a new, functioning pancreas. Then it dawns on him: why bother?

Let me take the stupid insulin a few more years, get the necessary schooling and continue Father's work. "When I'm ready, I will create a new and improved Jovanni."

Jovanni revels in this idea. A perfect solution to his vexing problem.

He stands straight and gazes at all the racks that are now lined up on a counter. He plucks a "Mengele" and then snatches one "Einstein." He clinks the tubes together, as if they were drinks.

Cheers! What if I combined Joseph Mengele with Albert Einstein?

The idea grabs him.

What about Mengele and Louis Brandeis?

With the greatest delicacy, he lifts a tube from the last rack. He caresses it. He kisses the bottom of the tube and holds the label up: Herr Führer.

Jovanni clicks his heels.

The epiphany is swift and complete.

It will fall to Jovanni Teplitsky to combine the DNA of *Joseph Mengele* with that of *Adolph Hitler's* . . . and create the perfect leader to guide the world for the next one thousand years.

Author's Notes

Readers often ask authors where they get ideas for stories. They also want to know if any part of a story is true. Where the story of *Island Bluffs* came from will now be explained and, for the record, a good part of this story *is* true. Let me also be clear about the following: there is no such community as Island Bluffs in New Jersey; it is a fictitious town as are all of the characters in this book except Verity Frizzell.

Island Bluffs would never have been written if it were not for a passing comment by a renowned international labor lawyer, Burton Abrams. When asked how he felt one day, Burt answered that he was fine but tired, that the ghost in his house had kept him up all night. Intrigued, I asked Burt to explain and he reluctantly told me the story of how he and his wife had bought their "dream" house in Brick Township, New Jersey. He went on to say that the house was in foreclosure, and that he knew from the moment he saw this house he wanted to buy it . . . so much so that he yanked the "For Sale" sign out of the ground to make certain no one else would grab it before he got the chance. Sound familiar? As soon as they moved in, someone knocked on the door and offered to buy it back. Burton politely declined and went about the business of hiring an architect to design an addition, which included breaking through the attic, removing the roof, and adding a new floor to the house.

From the moment they moved into the house, strange things started to occur. Tools went missing. A worker once laid down a screwdriver and then could not find it; it was later found in the dishwasher. Another time, a worker lost a tool only to find it inside a locked car. Music would spontaneous play when there was no radio in the house or any other device that could make music.

Not too long after they moved in, an apparition of a young girl appeared, whom Burt named Polly. In time, he would see Polly in the mirror, looking at him. Polly was gentle and playful and non-threatening. Knowing Burt as I did, a man who could be dramatic and embellish a story, I asked his wife, Marguerite, when I had the chance to speak to her alone, to verify that Polly existed. "Oh Burt's ghost? Yes, she's real. I don't pay her any mind. She's harmless."

As the Abrams's building plans went before the town zoning board, the stranger who offered to buy the house returned, this time with a blank check. Again, Burt turned him down. As soon as construction started on the house, a false room was discovered in the attic that was described in this book exactly as told me by Burt. The items—the raincoats, the boots, the cans of food—found in the basement, by Yehuda and Megan, again, were as described by Burt and Marguerite.

Burt put his lawyerly research skills to work. He accepted the notion that ghosts could exist, and he felt—like many others have been known to believe—that they are spirits of people who died before their time was due. Often, they are young people. In Polly's case, Burt was certain she had experienced some sort of accident and was determined to find out what it was. He spent hours in the local library, reading newspapers dating back to World War II. He pieced together that in late January or early February of 1945, a small fishing charter was inadvertently sunk by a German sub–U869 off the Jersey coast, within site of the Ol' Barney Lighthouse. The boat's captain and his daughter, who was seventeen, were both killed.

Burt conjectured that Polly saw the blinking lights coming from his house and vowed to seek revenge on the owner who sent her to her death. She inhabited the house and literally drove its resident crazy.

Burt's research uncovered that a German-American had lived in the house during the war, that this spy had even entertained sailors from the sub who came ashore on a dingy. It had been rumored that toward the end of the war, that the spy had gone crazy, that his black hair turned white seemingly overnight, and that he had suddenly died.

Corroborating evidence for Burt's story took shape when, in 1991, a sunken German ship was located by a team of divers in 230 feet of dark, frigid water off Point Pleasant, N.J. It took six years and untold heartache, pain, and danger, for the crew of the *Seeker* to finally identify the ship as U-869. Three divers—Steve Feldman, Chris Rouse, and Chris Rouse, Jr.—lost their lives trying to solve the mystery of this ship but John Chatterton and Richie Kohler would not cease operations. Eventually, the team recovered a knife inscribed with "Horenburg," a crew member's name. They searched the U-boat archives and discovered that *U-869* was supposedly sent to Africa, so this piece of evidence was initially disregarded as not being connected to the *U-869*. A few years later, they found part of the UZO torpedo-aiming device, and spare parts from the motor room engraved with serial and other identifying numbers. On August 31, 1997 they concluded that they had found the *U-869*.

Torpedoes manufactured later in the war had acoustical seeking capability. It was theorized that a torpedo was initially fired in a turning pattern, When it missed its target, the torpedo—known as a circle "runner"—picked up the sound of the submarine's propeller—the *U-869*—thus sinking the very ship that had launched it.

Chatterton's and Kohler's story, and the story of how they persevered to discover the truths about the *U-869* was turned into a best seller written by Robert Kurson, *Shadow Divers*. I deliberately did not read this book while researching and writing *Island Bluffs*, and to this day, have not read it. But I urge interested readers who want to learn more about this fascinating story to seek it out.

Was someone left behind that survived the torpedo explosion into the U-869? Yes, a crew member was onshore when the *U-869* became and underwater tomb, but he wasn't in the U.S. when it happened, he was left behind in Germany. So Larry Hanson and his exploits were a complete fabrication, invented to give the town elders of Island Bluffs another secret to hide over the years.

The lucky sailor who survived was Herbert Guschewski. A few days before U-869 departed from the Vulcal Shipyard in Stettin, Germany, where it was docked for repairs, Guschewski suffered from a double-sided pneumonia and pleurisy and was hospitalized. He never returned to the ship and was unaware of its fate until he watched a show that eventually became a *NOVA* episode, "Hitler's Lost Sub." He contacted the producers and they were quick to interview him. Guschewski died in 2007.

Recently, another German submarine was discovered—the U-576, off the North Carolina coast on October 21, 2014. http://www.cnn.com/2014/10/21/us/north-carolina-u-boat-wreck/index.html "This is not just the discovery of a single shipwreck," said Joe Hoyt, chief scientist of NOAA's Office of Marine Sanctuaries expedition, which found the vessels. "We have discovered an important battle site that is part of the Battle of the Atlantic."

That brings us to Dr. T and his master plan to clone great Jews from the last two centuries in order to bring Joseph Mengele and then a certain child named Adolpho into a loving, Jewish home. Can human beings be cloned? It is conceptually possible, but extremely difficult to accomplish, not the least of which it is unethical to do so. It has been left for the reader to dissect and discuss the morality of the cloning issue along with the themes of forgiveness, and if children and grandchildren should be responsible for the sins of their parents.

Alan A. Winter
Bernardsville, NJ March, 2015
www.alanwinter.com
alanwinternovels@gmail.com

P.S. When I visited the Abrams' house, Polly was no longer there.
P.P.S. Dr. Teplitsky is a fictitious character and out of convenience, I attributed the discovery of the BRCA 1 gene to him. The real discoverer is the amazing scientist—Mary-Claire King—who demonstrated, in 1990, that a single gene on chromosome 17, later known as BRCA 1, was responsible for many types of breast and ovarian cancers, and make it possible to identify that as many as 5-10% of all cases of breast cancer may be hereditary. Dr. King's discovery revolutionized the study of numerous other common diseases, as well.

Read other novels

by Alan A. Winter

"Best Book of 2013" selection by Kirkus Reviews

Kirkus Review SAVIOR'S DAY

An ancient text contains a shattering truth in this apocalyptic thriller. Winter's (*Someone Else's Son*, 2013) tense, tightly plotted novel opens with an exceptionally effective dramatic hook: Two men—one Christian, one Muslim—perch in hidden spots on rooftops above Jerusalem's Western Wall, patiently waiting for an elaborate ceremony to start. It's a ceremony that has the attention of the entire world, as the pope, the U.S.

President, and the leaders of Israel and Palestine plan to handle an ancient biblical text, the Codex of Aleppo, in a symbolic gesture of peace. Jerusalem will then formally become an international protectorate under the jurisdiction of the United Nations, thus resolving territorial controversies that have plagued the region for centuries. Both gunmen, spurred by fanatical visions, are prepared to stop it from happening—even at the cost of their own lives. As Winter ratchets up the tension leading to the climactic moment, he switches abruptly to the story of Cardinal Arnold Ford, who witnesses a man getting shot on the steps of New York's St. Patrick's Cathedral; the man hands him a strange slip of paper before he dies. Ford, a craggy, magnetic, middle-aged black man, later meets the intriguing LeShana Thompkins, a New York police detective investigating the shooting. They both have hidden depths: The cardinal sees visions (one early scene in a confessional is particularly chilling), and the detective knows both the Hebrew language and the complicated history and significance of the Codex of Aleppo. As she relates this history to Ford, Winter interweaves chapters that richly evoke the various main characters' pasts. The complicated plot resembles a pair of interlocking spirals, with Detective Thompkins' revelations taking readers steadily further back in time and the gunmen's parallel back stories bringing readers forward to the moment of the shooting. Winter's command of his historical material is impressive, as is his skill at shaping his characters—particularly Ford and Thompkins, whose unfolding relationship is the best thing in the book.

The textual mystery of the codex will please Dan Brown fans, and its execution is a significant step above that in *The Da Vinci Code* (2003). A thrilling, satisfying and multilayered adventure story.

Snowflakes in the Sahara

Set in the backdrop of the ever-worsening global warming, *Snowflakes in the Sahara* is the story of a Svengali-like mind-manipulator (Lute Aurum) who teams up with an American Business icon (Jeremy Steel) to take over the White House. When their puppet is installed as president, Aurum and Steel are poised to pull off the greatest heist in history: Canada. And they almost pull it off, if it weren't for Carly Mason, the Big Apple's tooth sleuth : . . A Kay Scarpetta-like forensic dentist who joins the pantheon of investigators that readers hang on every clue. A dental CSI.

One terrible day, two disasters strike America at the same time: the president's helicopter carrying him to Camp David crashes, and a bomb explodes in Rockefeller Center leaving three bodies unidentified. Carly is by turns tough and inquisitive, clever and cunning. She will need all her skills to discover the victims' names. As she gets closer to the truth, a killer is dispatched to silence her. What follows is a gripping tale of heroism against all odds. What's frightening is that *Snowflakes in the Sahara* is a tale that is only a presidential election and an ecological disaster away.

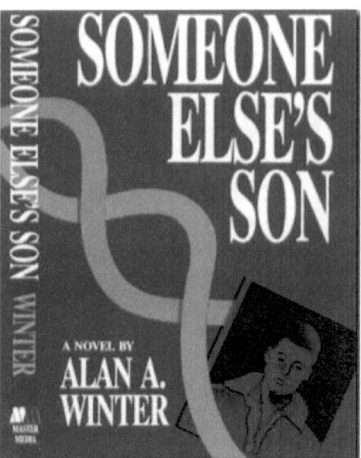

Someone Else's Son

"*Someone Else's Son* should speak to a lot of people because it probes universal emotions. The situation of an ordinary couple, at an unrecognized crisis point in their marriage, discovering that their oldest son is not 'theirs,' at least biologically, stirs up a host of issues about the nature of parenthood. . . . The novel has much to say about the way we live today, and I hope it finds the wide audience it deserves."

    Richard Lingeman, Reviewer for the New York Times, editor of the *Nation*, and author of *Theodore Dreiser: An American Journey*.

"Emotionally charged and moving . . . *Someone Else's Son* goes beyond family melodrama to explore an issue that may touch all too close to home Readers will be moved and beguiled."

    Judith Gould, Best selling author of *Sins and Forever*

"Thank you for letting me see the new book. You really are working it. Good subject too-something you can sink your teeth into. Keep at it."

    Jack Geasland, Co-author, with Barry Woods, of *Twins*, which was made into the movie **"Dead Ringer,"** starring Jeremy Irons.

"*Someone Else's Son* is a contemporary novel that deals with ageless questions. It's a mystery whose secret we do not learn until the end. Winter is by turns serious and funny, but always on the mark. He'll keep you turning the pages."

John Bowers, Best selling novelist.
Including *In the Land of Nyx* and *Helene*.

"Someone Else's Son"

Trish and Brad Hunter are in limbo. Eighteen years after bringing their first son, Phillip, home from the hospital, they discover that they are not his natural parents. Who are Phillip Hunter's real parents? And who is Trish and Brad's biological son?

Someone Else's Son explores the host of questions, curiosities, family secrets, and changed relationships that have come with the discovery that Phillip was switched at birth. As doubts abound and relationships go awry, the once solid family structure begins to shake.

Brad Hunter feels it's his fatherly duty to assist Phillip in searching for his biological parents, while Trish wants no part of it—insisting that Phillip is their son no matter what. The escalating conflict between husband and wife, and the unfolding of Phillip's first love affair, both add emotional stress to Phillip's search for his biological parents.

Phillip's questions could be anyone's—adopted children's, children from alternative forms of insemination or surrogate pregnancies, or those real-life children whose identities may have been mistaken in hospital nurseries.

At one time or another, most of us have stared into a mirror, touched our lips, our noses, or checked our smiles to see if they were similar to a parent's or sibling's. It is human nature to wonder about our origin. And when we do, what is most important? The years spent to together with our parents, those shared experiences and moral values, or is our upbringing trumped by our genetic make-up? Though written when DNA testing was in its infancy, *Someone Else's Son* is as poignant today was when it was first published.

www.ingramcontent.com/pod-product-compliance
Lightning Source LLC
LaVergne TN
LVHW040035080526
838202LV00045B/3345